VISITING HOURS
and other stories

For Diane
For Sher,
among our treasures
6/09

VISITING HOURS

and other stories

edited by

Daniel E Wickett

with an introduction by

Kyle Minor

All rights reserved. Except for brief quotations in critical articles or reviews, no part of this book may be reproduced in any manner without prior written permission from the publisher: **Press 53 PO Box 30314, Winston-Salem, NC 27130-0314**

Copyright © 2008 by Press 53

"Waiting" © 2008 by Kyle Minor; "Where to Begin" © 2007 by Benjamin Percy. First published in *Minnesota Monthly*; "Open My Heart" © 2001 by T.M. McNally. First published in *The Yale Review*, and subsequently in *The Gateway* (Southern Methodist University Press, 2007); "Not a Leaf Stirring" © 2006 by Quinn Dalton; "Picnic" © 2003 by Max Ruback. First published in *Edgar Literary Magazine*; "Wash, Rinse, Spin" © 2003 by Beth Ann Bauman. First published in *Beautiful Girls* (MacAdam/Cage, 2003); "The Garden Plot" © 2008 by Philip F. Deaver; "Vanishing Act" © 2006 by Steven Gillis. First published in *Opium* and subsequently in *Giraffes* (Atomic Quill Press, 2007); "Regrets" © 2004 by James R. Cooley; "The Rain Barrel" © 1990 by Jim Nichols. First published in *Esquire*; "Gaarg. Gaarrgh. Gak" © 2001 by Pamela Erens. First published in *The Literary Review*; "A Face in Shadow" © 2008 by Joseph Freda; "Survival Traits" © 2004 by Nancy Ginzer; "My Father's Heart" © 2007 by David Abrams; "The Kiss-Me-Quick" © 1999 by Rochelle Distelheim. First published in *North American Review*; "The Well-Head" © 2004 by Gabriel Welsch. First published in *Ascent*; "One Moment: 1330 South McLeod" © 2008 by Kaytie M. Lee; "The Dead Woman from the Newspaper" © 2002 by Patry Francis. First published in *The Ontario Review*; "If I Die Before I Wake (excerpt)" © 2008 by Lauren Baratz-Logsted; "Not Waving But Drowning" © 2004 by Ron Rash. First published in *Nantahala: Fiction in Appalachia*, and subsequently in *Chemistry and Other Stories* (Picador, 2007); "Taughannock Falls" © 2001 by Bill Roorbach. First published in *Witness*, and subsequently published in *Big Bend* (University of Georgia Press, 2001); "Wanderlust" © 2007 by Michael Milliken; "Visiting Hours" © 2008 by Roberta Israeloff

In all cases, this initial printing, or reprinting of material is by permission of the author.

The characters and events in this book are fictitious. Any similarity to real persons, living or dead, is coincidental and not intended by the author.

Book design by Steven Seighman

First Edition November 2008
ISBN: 978-0-9816280-4-2

Printed in the United States of America

CONTENTS

WAITING vii
Kyle Minor

PREFACE xvi
Daniel E Wickett

WHERE TO BEGIN 1
Benjamin Percy

OPEN MY HEART 18
T. M. McNally

NOT A LEAF STIRRING 42
Quinn Dalton

PICNIC 59
Max Ruback

WASH, RINSE, SPIN 69
Beth Ann Bauman

THE GARDEN PLOT 88
Philip F. Deaver

VANISHING ACT 116
Steven Gillis

REGRETS 120
James R. Cooley

THE RAIN BARREL 126
Jim Nichols

GAARG. GAARRGH. GAK 134
Pamela Erens

A FACE IN SHADOW 155
Joseph Freda

SURVIVAL TRAITS 167
Nancy Ginzer

MY FATHER'S HEART 184
David Abrams

THE WELL-HEAD 193
Gabriel Welsch

THE KISS-ME-QUICK 217
Rochelle Distelheim

ONE MOMENT: 1330 SOUTH McLEOD 220
Kaytie M. Lee

THE DEAD WOMAN FROM THE NEWSPAPER 235
Patry Francis

IF I DIE BEFORE I WAKE (EXCERPT) 254
Lauren Baratz-Logsted

NOT WAVING BUT DROWNING 261
Ron Rash

TAUGHANNOCK FALLS 270
Bill Roorbach

WANDERLUST 284
Michael Milliken

VISITING HOURS 292
Roberta Israeloff

CONTRIBUTORS' NOTES 314

For Mom and Dad, whose wall of books and visits to the library got me started, and for Chase, Stassie, and Dalton, who make every day exciting and worthwhile.

"Waiting for visiting hours to start is different from waiting for visiting hours to end."

—Jami Attenberg, *The Kept Man*

Introduction: Waiting

Kyle Minor

The math is not precise, but I'm gonna try anyway. Here's a good estimate: I spent an average of five hours a week in church my first eighteen years. (That's Sunday School, Sunday morning service, Sunday evening classes, Sunday evening service, Wednesday night service.)

5 x 52 = 260

260 x 18 = 4680

Plus another two hours a week in chapel, at the Christian school I attended from pre-kindergarten through the twelfth grade—fourteen years—and school met maybe 40 weeks a year.

2 x 40 = 80

80 x 14 = 1120

1120 + 4680 = 5800.

5800 hours, not including all the potluck dinners, and church softball and bowling leagues, and Tuesday night visitations, and Royal Ambassadors camping trips, and out-of-state trips to youth conventions, and so on.

Nor does it include—and this, to me, is staggering—the eighty and one hundred hour work weeks I sometimes put in during the two or so years, post-college, in which I worked in churches as an associate pastor. To play those numbers conservatively:

80 x 50 = 4000

4000 x 2 = 8000

8000 + 5800 = 13800

13800 hours. And, still, this leaves out huge swaths of time spent in college internships, at church leadership conferences, at weddings and funerals.

I no longer go to church, and I have lately been mourning all that time unredeemed.

My first week of graduate school at the Ohio State University, a man stood in front of all us fresh-faced recruits, and said, "Mastery of a new field requires three years of engaged, full-time study." Let's call that a forty-hour work week, fifty weeks a year.

40 x 50 = 2000

2000 x 3 = 6000

So, in roughly six thousand hours, one can become a master of this or that. You can fit two sets of six thousand hours into 13800, and still have 1800 hours left over.

And I have secret avocations. Musical avocations: the guitar and the piano. Choose one or the other, and I could be supporting my writing by playing Manhattan jazz clubs at night, or scoring films on some Hollywood backlot, or chiming the choro or sertanejo in São Paulo.

Or I could have been indulging a newish love for languages and linguistics, for Italian, and Breton, and, hell, the whole Finnic-Ugric family of languages, and using all of it as social currency in Bologna, Budapest, Brittany . . .

But this talk is unfair, and maybe in some ways unwise, because it doesn't account for the ways in which we—unknowingly, often—turn time, as E. M. Forster prescribed, in the direction of beauty.

I'm thinking now of those hardwood cherry pews—surely they weren't cherry, but as a child it appealed to me to think of them as cherry—at our Baptist church on Cherry Road, right across the street from the Palm Beach Kennel Club, with the airport just beyond. It hurt, after awhile, to sit on those pews. The bum would numb, and the mind, too, intoxicated by the cadences of a preaching style passed down from the circuit riders of old—the anapestic rhythm and the repetition of *Beloved, Beloved, Beloved*—and the waxing and the waning and the waxing and waning again of what I now know to be the iambs and the iambs and the iambs of the King James Bible's sixteenth century prosody.

I'd crawl under the cherry pew—Bible in hand, since my mother would have, by then, taken away my copy of the Hardy Boys' *The Twisted Claw*, its lurid scarlet cover redolent, anyway, of the demonic affliction the traveling preachers said had lit our world invisibly aflame—and, six, seven years old, mind you, I'd begin following along with the Bible reading, let's say Genesis.

What they did in those days was called proof-texting. They'd read a verse in isolation and use it to make a larger point about morality. But those preachers weren't accounting for the boy beneath the cherry pew. Nor were they accounting for the power of the book itself. Because there was nothing in the Hardy Boys that could near compare to what happened after God saved six hundred year old Noah and his family and a hand-built ark full of animals from the Flood that destroyed the rest of the world. What happened next was that Noah planted a vineyard, and made wine, and got drunk, and passed out naked in his tent, where his son Ham found him and raped him, then bragged about it to his brothers Shem and Japheth.

The preacher, for his part, would be talking about the rainbow God sent in promise that he would never again destroy the world by water, but the reader below the pew would be thinking about the qualifier—*by water*—knowing full well, because of last Sunday night's sermon, that God, in the Bible's last book, the Revelation of John, had promised to destroy the world next time, irrevocably, by fire.

Around this time a certain heat would come over my own body, and, guilty and a little inflamed by the titillation of all the human strife I'd been living vicariously by way of the Book, I'd crawl from under the pew, and sit again next to my mother and father on the cherry or not-cherry pew, and wait for the altar call. While we all of us sang "Oh, Lamb of God, I come," the preacher would be standing at the altar, hands clasped in front of him and shaking, and extemporizing over the music—"If you were to die this very evening, if you were to walk out those front doors and be hit by a speeding truck, if a man were to put a bullet through the back of your head while you sleep this very night, do you know where you would go? To heaven, to the very bosom of Christ, or to the dark place, the eternal fire?"—and the thing you must understand is that the fire in those moments, amidst the swirl of the organ and the hundreds of voices in their four- and five-part harmonies, and the stories and the stories and the stories . . . all of these things that we, in our waiting, had allowed to build and build, the borders between them blurring away until they were nothing . . . if you had known that fire in the way that the child had known it in those moments, you would know that there was nothing in the world that could burn more purely, and here a stray Scripture would become one with the fire—*Rightly dividing the word of truth*—and you would think, then, of a sword, and remember the story of Solomon, who once threatened to cut a baby in two and give half to each of the mothers who claimed him theirs. If these things seem somehow disassociated one from the other, then you have not dipped fully enough into the mind of that child, have not wanted for a taste of the living water that the preacher was even that moment offering, so that when the child—and, make no mistake about it, the child was, and in many ways still is, me—went forward for perhaps the fifth or sixth time that preaching season, it was to get some assurance that his eternal soul wasn't in danger of that fire, or, more pressing, that Jesus was, in fact, living inside his heart, by which he certainly meant inside his very body as a means of protection, and this because a very grave man in a white three-piece suit had just the week before given a sermon about the movie *Gremlins* that included secondhand accounts of children who watched the film waking to find their bodies bloodied by claws and teeth of demons given license to behave as gremlins by the child's act of watching.

The thing to remember, here, is that the scene I am painting is a scene in which nothing happened, or almost nothing. A child sits beneath a church pew, reads, half-listens to a sermon, performs a religious ritual, goes home. Mostly, the child waits. Waits for the singing to begin, waits for the singing to end, waits through the prayer, waits through the sermon, waits at the altar for the preacher's blessing, waits after the service, for his parents and the other people of the church to make the rounds of pleasantry exchanges and hand-shakings, and many of these people—it is already apparent to the child, on account of all his time listening to people speak candidly one to another, while waiting—do not care very much for one another.

I have now written you 1454 words, and I am thirty years old, and it has taken me those thirty years and, now, 1471 words, to realize that the very 13800 estimated unredeemed hours I have been lamenting are, of course, the very substance of the life I am beginning to make for myself and my family by way of words, the source of my obsessions, my peculiarities and peccadilloes, the very language that is mine to mine and mimic.

What has all this to do with *Visiting Hours*, this book you right now hold in your hands? Our great Western myth is that we are a people predisposed to progress, to forward motion, to action, and it's true that when we tell our stories, if we're good at telling our stories, we learn to give our listeners what they're listening for, what Aristotle called What Happens Next. *Action is eloquence,* Shakespeare said.

And yet so much happens between the action, in the quiet, between our ears, among the Hows and Whys and What Ifs we can articulate, and the Huhs we can't.

"But when night came," Benjamin Percy writes, "when there was no more racket, no sunshine, no neighbors ringing the doorbell to hand him peach pies and hamburger casseroles—crying came with it."

Here we must consult our great philosopher from Alabama, one Charles Barkley: *If ifs were gifts, every day would be Christmas.*

Indeed. And don't the writers in this volume know it. Here, instead of Christmas, we get an empty house, the dry cleaners, a burn unit, a garden plot, an emergency animal hospital. The Kansas Department of Corrections and Osawatomie State Hospital. The rehabilitation center at Muskego and the Indian Arm fjord. All the places—often somber, often solitary, often static—in which we must wait the other 364 days a year.

I leave you with one Visiting Hours story of my own, this one from Good Samaritan Hospital in downtown West Palm Beach, where I was born. My grandfather, my father's father, was dying in Room 211. I was thirteen. I walked into the room with my father, and we looked at him. His eyes were closed, and he was laboring at his breathing. My grandmother said how nice we were all dressed. She said other things, too, but we weren't listening to her. We didn't say anything. We stood and looked at him for a long time and waiting for something to happen, but nothing happened.

Then we went down the hall to the visitor's room, and we waited some more. I suppose we were waiting for my grandmother to leave. I thought my father might have something he wanted to say to his father before he died.

After awhile, my grandmother passed the visitor's room, not knowing we were still there, waiting. Then my father and I went back into Room 211. We waited and waited some more, but still nothing happened. I didn't say anything. My father didn't say anything. His father didn't do anything but keep his eyes closed and try to breathe. I don't know whether he was awake or not.

The next morning, news came that my grandfather had died. After the funeral, while we were waiting for the graveside service to begin, I asked my father why he didn't say anything to his father that last day at the hospital. I waited for him to answer, but he did not answer, and then I realized that whatever he was waiting for had so captured him that he was not able to hear what I was asking, and I thought, too, that the question I was asking might be a question that did not have an answer.

I thought about these things for a long time, all the things we did not say and did not do, and the questions we could not ask, and the questions we could not answer, and the more I thought about them, the less I seemed to understand them, and what all of it brought to me was the opposite of comfort.

A few years later, my senior year of high school, I fell silently in love with a cheerleader who nearly every day was kind to me, who would bring me hand-drawn cards sometimes, or ride with me from the school to her house to decorate our homecoming float, and all of this meant a great deal to me, because it had been a long time since anyone at my school had treated me kindly.

One Saturday, someone called my house to say that this girl was suffering some kind of surprise organ failure—the liver, maybe, or the pancreas, the caller wasn't sure—and that she had the day earlier undergone emergency surgery at Good Samaritan Hospital.

That afternoon I went to the floral shop and spent my grocery-bagging money on a basket of flowers and a stuffed teddy bear and an oversized card, and when I arrived at the hospital, I was given her room number, and it wasn't until I went through the door of Room 211 that I realized she was recovering in the same room where I had last seen my grandfather alive, and it wasn't until I saw her in the bed that I realized she was reclining in the same bed where my grandfather had died.

These all were things I immediately wanted to tell her, and they are things I certainly should not have told her, and they are, anyway, things I did not tell her, because in the hours preceding my arrival in Room 211—all the hours she had been awake and lucid after her surgery—she had been waiting for a phone call from another man, a college boy a year ahead of us in school, and one who had nearly every day slapped my ears with his open palm when we had been in junior high together. Before I could hand her the basket of flowers or the teddy bear or the oversized card, the phone rang, and it was this other man, and it did not take long, standing at the foot of her bed, waiting for her to end the conversation, for me to put the pieces together.

The phone conversation went on for a long time. Whatever he was saying on the other line meant enough to her that her cheeks flushed and her eyes lit up the way I hoped they would when I gave her the gifts I brought. But I never gave them to her. Her mother, sitting in a bedside chair, tried to make small talk, and, after awhile, tried to discreetly signal that she should end her phone conversation. But she did not, and I didn't chalk it up to any sort of malice, but rather as an affirmation that the things I had long suspected to be true about my place in the world were true in the ways that hurt the most.

I left the flowers and the bear and the card with her mother, who promised the girl would call later. I went home, and I waited by the phone for the rest of the evening, but she never called. I thought I might dream that night about Room 211, and that girl, and my grandfather, and the fate I feared they would share, both of them dying in that bed, but that night I did not dream, and the girl did not die, and last I heard she had married a man who treated her badly, and he had divorced her, and then she was living again with her parents, and waiting for a better man to come along. If this news had arrived at another time in my life, I might have paid her a visit—this time without bringing flowers—but by then I was myself married, and waiting for someone to give me some money so I could make a movie about an illicit tobacco smuggling operation in Appalachian Kentucky, and I waited, and, she waited, too, and neither of us, so far as I can tell, ever got what we were waiting for.

All that time we were waiting, we thought we were waiting to live, but we weren't. We were living.

Preface

February 7, 2007. That is when I received an email from Sheryl Monks asking if I was still interested in having Press 53 publish what at the time was to be called *Precious Moments*. That email was the culmination of close to four years of work.

> "I don't know what it is, but I can't stop thinking about the dynamic of visiting. How one person is going to leave and the other will stay. How there is a time limit on it. I don't know what it is yet that plagues me about this situation. Is it the conflict, the unfairness? Hopefully, through doing this anthology I'll figure it out."

This quote came to me in an email from Amy Koppelman, author of *A Mouthful of Air* (MacAdam/Cage, 2003) and *I Smile Back* (Two Dollar Radio, 2008), in early 2003. As I became involved with the project, first by sending out a call for submissions to authors I knew, then by helping Amy go through those submissions, and eventually, as Amy got deeper into her second novel, taking over the project as Editor, this dynamic became one of great interest to me as well.

The thing with visiting hours is this - if a place, be it a hospital, a prison, a retirement home, etc., has visiting hours, then it has the potential for conflict. Visiting hours are constrictive - one person has to stay, one will eventually have to leave. There's always a story behind the person (or animal) that can't leave, and another behind the visitor. These being visited cannot just up and go - they're trapped into being visited, like it or not.

I don't know if reading this collection has helped Amy figure out what was plaguing her. It hasn't stopped me from hoping to continue to find more stories that I'd love to have included—I am still of the belief that situations that can cause visiting hours create a great dynamic for a story. As to the pieces included here, while I began putting this collection together, many people had great suggestions about stories in this vein published by the likes of Richard Yates, TC Boyle, Amy Hempel, Lorrie Moore and the list goes on and on. However, as the guy that formed and runs the Emerging Writers Network, my thoughts always returned to finding newer, or perhaps lesser known writers that I've always believed were deserving of wider recognition.

What excited me most as I began seeing the shape of the collection was exactly what I had hoped for from the beginning—a wide variance of story types, of conflicts, of resolutions and various emotions. There was James R. Cooley's "Regrets," set on death row, Kaytie M. Lee's "One Moment: 1330 South McLeod," which takes place in a veterinary hospital, and Max Ruback's "Picnic" which involves an orphan on visitor's day to the orphanage, hoping to finally find a couple to go home with. There was Steven Gillis's "Vanishing Acts" which takes place in the narrator's home, and Gabriel Welsch's "The Well-Head" which takes place at an elderly woman's home—she's confined to a wheelchair.

Michael Milliken's "Wanderlust" finds a son and grandson placing a visit to a VA hospital. Rochelle Distelheim's "The Kiss-Me-Quick" has a friend visiting a dying friend, but I'm not really sure where—but the knowledge of her impending death creates a visiting hours atmosphere for the piece.

There are also stories that take place in nursing homes like Patry Francis's "The Dead Woman from the Newspaper," Jim Nichols's "The Rain Barrel," Quinn Dalton's "Not a Leaf Stirring," and Nancy Ginzer's "Survival Traits." Ron Rash's "Not Waving, but Drowning" is set in an emergency room, and Roberta Israeloff's "Visiting Hours" involve an operating room. T.M. McNally's "Open My Heart" is placed in a burn unit.

Then there are the stories set where one picking this collection up might expect—in your everyday hospital rooms: Benjamin Percy's "Where to Begin," Beth Ann Bauman's "Wash, Rinse, Spin," Philip F. Deaver's "The Garden Plot," Pamela Erens's "Gaarg. Gaarrgh. Gak," Bill Roorbach's "Taughannock Falls," Joseph Freda's "A Face in Shadow," David Abrams's "My Father's Heart," and Lauren Baratz-Logsted's "If I Die Before I Wake."

The thing is, even this last group, with all of the stories taking places in hospital rooms, the authors take the reader many different places and for many different reasons. They do not always actually set the majority of their individual story in the above listed locations—but that's where the visiting hour aspect of these stories takes place. In each story though, the writer captures something essential from the main idea of visiting hours—one person visiting, another visited. One allowed to leave, but can only visit at certain times, the other there for the duration. The conflicts and situations each of the stories within this anthology present will bring hours of enjoyment and thought to those that read them. They'll bring to mind situations we've all gone though, and will probably go through again, and maybe, just maybe, these stories will resonate back to our minds when we do go through the situations again, helping us learn how to deal with them.

So, it is with great thanks to Amy Koppelman, for having the idea, and Kevin Watson and Sheryl Monks, for agreeing to publish it, Steven Seighman for the great cover design and immense patience in laying the book out, and the authors you'll find within for their work, that I now urge you to read Kyle Minor's fantastic introduction, and the 22 great stories that follow.

Enjoy,
Daniel E Wickett

VISITING HOURS
and other stories

Where to Begin

Benjamin Percy

Louise died, things changed.

The dying part started with a stroke and ended a month later at the Muskego Rehabilitation Center. All this time her husband, Harry, told the neighbors she would be home in no time. He would nod when he said this and continue nodding, as if he never wanted to stop saying *yes.*

Then he would show them the earmarked article from *Modern Maturity*, the one about Kirk Douglas and his extraordinary recovery. "Get this," he would say, "Kirk wasn't doing so hot at first, but now he's good as new. A little bit of slurring, of course, but otherwise, as I said, as good as new." At this point he would clear his throat and read out loud: "Stroke victims generally heal in one-month, three-month, and six-month increments." He would adjust his glasses and study his audience down the length of his nose. "I figure by the end of the year Louise will be as good as new."

Optimism came easy, particularly during the day when there were distractions, his meals and his newspaper and his TV, which he hated as much as he loved, constantly yelling at the screen, criticizing the tennis players and the politicians, the music that wasn't music at all but *racket.*

But when night came—when there was no more racket, no sunshine, no neighbors ringing the doorbell to hand him peach pies and hamburger casseroles—crying came with it. He called this blubbering. Crying was for pantywaists. Blubbering he could deal with, somehow.

In the month before her death—after his breakfast of tea and Cream-of-Wheat, after he paged through the *Journal-Sentinel*—he would change from his slippers to his loafers, get in his Lincoln and turn the key, waiting five minutes as the engine warmed up. He warmed up the engine for the same reason he put on driving gloves for the same reason he always ate Cream-of-Wheat for breakfast—because he did things in a particular way and didn't like change.

The drive was long and winding and he never thought about anything except avoiding the black ice and how he had to take a right at the dairy even though the receptionist originally told him left. He didn't know why she told him left but she told him left and when he made that right turn he felt irritated. Maybe she had done it on purpose, he thought. Maybe she was one of those young people who got a kick out of mistreating old people.

His irritation grew as he considered her, a young Latino girl who popped her bubblegum. She was probably an illegal—he thought—her and her whole family, breeding their way into this country, hooked on drugs and welfare. By the time he arrived at Muskego he felt so angry that when he stormed past her desk and down the long buttermilk-color halls and into room 193, he hardly recognized his wife lying there, slack-faced, with tubes running into her body.

It was easier that way. It was easier to pretend she was permanently in the bathroom or the kitchen, tending to things. That was why, when somebody rang the doorbell and handed him a hot dish, he would think, *why in the world?* And then, *oh.*

But when he was forced to acknowledge her condition, to see her small chest rising and falling under a white sheet, something would crack open inside him and all at once a great bunch of sadness would bubble up from his chest so he couldn't breathe. He would cross his arms and study her from a distance, his lips trembling with the want to scream I-love-yous in her ear. But instead he brought her up to speed on the news, the kids, the neighborhood.

All this in an ammoniac room, where everything was white, especially her skin, and the fluorescent lights buzzed like a thousand flies he wanted to swat with a rolled-up newspaper. When he was done talking, he would kiss her on the forehead, and on the lips—and then he would shut off the lights and leave her in darkness.

No visit lasted more than ten minutes. Partly this was because of the way she looked, limp and doughy, with a bit of drool sliding down her cheek, her lazy eyes not recognizing him. But mostly he couldn't stand the way it made him feel.

Like his wife of sixty-three years was already dead.

When his daughter and son-in-law—Susan and Peter—when they drove an hour from Madison to visit, they would bring Harry homemade cinnamon rolls and crab quiche and pasta salad, magazines and videos, too many hugs.

"Things to keep your mind off stuff," Peter said.

"Yeah," Harry said and turned up the volume on the TV.

They would watch a few programs and maybe Harry would complain about Bush and those crooks in the District of Corruption, that colored general—what's his face—how they bombed the heck out of Sadman Insane only because Dagbad was full of Texas tea, not that he cared a whole heap about the towelheads, mind you, but this country had already gone to hell in a hand-basket and war was just the icing on the cake.

He talked like that.

When he talked like that, Susan would say, "Don't talk like that." And then, "Did you talk to the nurse about bringing Mom in a TV to watch? Would that be okay? I think she'd like to watch her soaps, don't you?"

He studied her a moment with his mouth hanging open. Then he closed his mouth and said, "Like I said, I don't know anything about it. If you're so curious, *you* ask."

In a little while they piled into the Lincoln and waited for the engine to warm up. While they waited, Peter said in a resigned tone, "I read an article that said January has the most deaths of any month."

Harry said, "What's that supposed to mean?" He said it quickly, as if the words tasted bad on his tongue and he wanted to get rid of them. Then he checked his watch and saw that February wasn't for another two weeks.

Susan changed the subject to a joke she heard. The joke was about an atheist in heaven and how he kept tugging on God's beard to see if it was real. Everybody got a kick out of the joke. But once Harry started laughing, he couldn't stop. The laughter went on and on.

Later that day, at the rehabilitation center, Harry and Peter stood off a short distance, their arms crossed, watching Susan comb Louise's hair and rub her hands with cream. Susan said—more to herself than to the men—how Louise looked healthier than ever, how the right side of her face wasn't so limp and maybe her eyes seemed a bit more focused.

"Don't make so much noise," Harry said. "You're disturbing her. She needs her rest."

"All she does is rest," Susan said. "What she needs is for us to make some noise and touch her and stuff. You know, stimulation." She blew on Louise's face and it twitched a little.

Harry said, "Says you," and gave his eyes a theatrical roll and said to Peter, "Who gave her a medical degree anyway?"

All of a sudden Susan jumped up and screamed a happy scream and did a dance.

Harry hurried over and grabbed her by the hand and said, "What? What's wrong?"

"She winked at me," Susan said and clapped her hands. "Did you see that?"

But he hadn't seen a thing.

January ended and Harry took this as a sign. "She beat the odds," he said to Peter on the phone. He imagined her hopping out of bed, maybe tomorrow, with a yawn and a stretch, yanking the tubes from her arm and stomach, complaining about how hungry she was, and so he would take her to the London Grille, their restaurant, and order a bottle of cabernet—an expensive one—plus Caesar salads, New York strips, bananas foster, the works.

But the next day, Louise contracted pneumonia and the doctor listened to her heart and to her lungs and scribbled something on a piece of paper and said there was nothing he could do. She was going to die. It was only a matter of time, maybe minutes, hours.

"I don't pay you to say things like that," Harry said.

Everybody came to see it happen, Peter and Susan, some cousins, a sister, and Harry—that was everybody—besides a nurse, who watched them with bored eyes, as you would a film seen a dozen times already, and touched Harry on the elbow and said, "If there's anything I can do."

"Don't bother," he said.

"No bother," she said and smiled in a way that made him hate her. "Anything?"

"No," he said. "Nothing," and wished she was the one about to die.

She took her hand off his elbow and said, "Doctor is on his way." She said *doctor* like it was his name. His name was Paulo and Harry had had enough of him. He couldn't tell if Paulo was Mexican or Indian or what. But he was definitely something. He worked for Aurora Health Care and a year ago put her on Warfarin, which Harry blamed for her deterioration over the past few months: the thinness and dizzy spells, high blood pressure, and finally the stroke.

When Paulo walked in wearing a stethoscope and a concerned expression, Harry called him a border-hopping witchdoctor who ought to be put in the can for monkeying around with people's lives like he did, and if he knew more than a crap about medicine he would have realized that Warfarin was originally used as a rat poison. "That's right, I've been doing my research. Now you dirty chiselers repackage it as Coumadin. Call it a blood thinner. Anything for a profit. The thing of it is, my wife isn't a rat and she sure as hell doesn't need to be poisoned." This went on for another minute and Paulo nodded the whole time and this made Harry even angrier, so he told Paulo to take a hike and Paulo said, "Of course," and took a hike.

Louise's breathing had gone ragged. It sounded like a straw seeking out the last bit of milk in a glass. Harry stood off to the side with his hand over his mouth while everyone else hovered around her, combing her hair, touching her cheek, saying, "It's okay. It is okay." They smiled to show her it was okay, even as her face twisted up in pain. Eventually she stopped breathing and the room filled up with quiet.

Right there they decided to have a memorial service. She hadn't wanted a funeral—said they were tacky—had only wanted to be cremated and forgotten, so this was their best shot at closure. They made a circle and held hands and cried in a gulping way and after awhile they gathered the strength to say something, a memory or a prayer.

When it was Harry's turn, he could of nothing to say—he could only think how a stroke *sounded* like such a safe and good thing.

A strange time began.

Harry couldn't sleep, nor could he stay awake, so he shuffled around in a half-dream, Louise's face emerging from shadows to smile and then to snap her teeth, retreating back into shadow as quickly as she had appeared. Muddled voices babbled in his head and he more than once mistook the sound of his own heart as a threat—as one of those hungry old widows knocking at the door, as horse hooves stampeding toward him—and was seized by a terrible panic where the air felt too warm and thick to breathe, like a sick green fog that filled up his lungs and then his skull.

He missed meals, hardly noticed or cared. Milk and crab quiche and everything else in his fridge and freezer, it went bad and stayed that way until Susan threw it in the garbage. The washer broke and he didn't bother calling a repairman. He didn't feel like it. He didn't feel like doing anything, so he wore the same dirty clothes and began to stink as bad as the fridge. When Susan and Peter told him as much, he dismissed them with a wave of his hand and said he'd been cooped up too long, is all. He didn't want to tell them what was wrong with the washer or anything else. He wanted them to think everything was fine. Otherwise, they'd likely ship him off to one of those retirement farms, he thought. For this same reason he kept his grief bottled up whenever they came to visit, smiling too much, talking too loud, hating how his voice sounded like it had a bad back.

When the latest issue of *Modern Maturity* arrived, he tore it up, along with the endless parade of Hallmark cards that marched through his mailbox and said things like, "We're here for you."

Sometimes he walked into a room or drove to the store and couldn't remember why. He was like a ghost: someone who could travel through walls and find himself someplace else in the middle of a sentence or thought, and not know what doors had brought him there. One cold night he woke up to discover he was walking down the driveway in his pajamas, bare feet blue in the moonlight. He was carrying a shovel.

And sometimes—when Peter and Susan came to visit, for instance—he wanted to be alone more than anything in the world. But once alone, he felt he couldn't have stayed that way another second. Everything was mixed up.

All at once, he got angry. He blamed the Warfarin and he blamed Paulo the witchdoctor and he blamed himself: if I had only called the ambulance sooner, Louise would be alive right this minute—he thought—up to snuff and probably yelling at me to take a bath. And then his anger faded as he was overwhelmed by a crushing indifference, and then a dark sadness, touching a finger to his wrist and willing his pulse to stop thumping—for it all to end, quietly.

And then he woke up one morning and felt a little better. Just like that.

That morning he began to clean. He started with himself, shaving off the gray beard that crept across his cheeks, standing for close to half an hour under a shower so hot it left his skin red and ticklish. Then he washed a few shirts and boxer shorts in the kitchen sink and in a little while was rummaging through the fridge and the cupboards. Some things had gone rotten. Others he would never eat since they were Louise's treats. The sweet pickles and freezer-burned strawberry ice cream, for instance. He filled up a garbage bag and got out another and dusted and vacuumed and by mid-afternoon everything sparkled like you wouldn't believe.

When he had finished, he walked from room to room with his hands behind his back, enjoying the freshly vacuumed carpet, how he could follow his footprints right back to where he began. He felt like celebrating, so he poured himself a drink—Christian Brothers brandy mixed with 7-Up—but when he tasted it and smacked his lips, he felt guilty:

Louise would have never let him drink before dinner.

He slowly brought the glass to his mouth and took another sip. Nothing happened. A second later he took another drink, and another, and before long the glass was empty. He filled it up again. He looked at the telephone as if he expected it to ring. He went over to the coffee table and deliberately set the glass down without a coaster. Then he took off his slippers and his socks and put his feet up on the table right next to the glass.

How good it felt.

He noticed in the sliding-glass door that led to the patio his reflection. He looked like an old man. But he soon discovered that if he squinted his eyes just so, the wrinkles and the gray hair faded, and it appeared he was sliding backward, into his seventies, his sixties, all the way to fifty.

Fifty years old, just a kid with plenty of life ahead of him, Harry picked up his brandy and toasted his reflection, grinning, his jowls gathered up like curtains.

He remembered hearing a girlfriend of Louise's say, "How does Harry tolerate such feminine surroundings?" The question had given him some pause, but he soon forgot about it and for a long time had lived in a pink house, so long that he forgot about its color, until now.

He lived here, he had lived here for years—in a house of many shades of pink and lavender. Porcelain cherubs stared at him from every corner. Lamps, clocks, chairs they had owned for thirty-odd years suddenly looked ridiculous to him, with their floral designs and gold trim.

Louise had referred to the figurines and tassels and antique perfume bottles as her foo-foo. Well—Harry decided—starting right this minute, he refused to be surrounded by foo-foo.

He parked his Lincoln in the driveway and swept out the garage and began to fill it up with furniture and clothes and vases, everything he no longer found any use for—until the house was no longer hers but his alone.

When Susan saw what had happened, all she could say was, "What on earth?"

Peter told her to be quiet but she put up a finger and he went quiet instead. She fixed a sharp look on Harry, who shrugged and played dumb, fiddling with the change in his pocket. "What's that you say?" he said.

There were dimples and squares in the carpet where the ottoman had been, the Victorian end table, the pump organ. She walked over to the bare china cabinet and ran a finger through its dust. "I just can't believe it." Her mouth pursed around her disgust like a word between words that told him he had done something wrong.

His eyes did a shifty thing. "Thought it was time for little spring cleaning, is all."

She squeezed the bridge of her nose as if she had a headache behind her eyes. "What was wrong with the way things were?" she said.

Plenty, was what he wanted to tell her. Instead he said, "A man gets used to things and maybe he shouldn't." He nodded at Peter. "You know how it is."

Peter smiled as if he knew how it was.

Susan said, "Oh, is that how it is?" She pinched her husband's belly, hard enough to make him jump. "Are you just going to throw all my stuff in the incinerator once I croak?" She flinched at the word. "*Pass*. Once I pass?"

"Of course not," Peter said. They looked at each other a minute and then Peter sighed to show he was tired of her game and went over to the window. Outside a skeletal tree shook against the force of the wind.

Harry aimed his thumb at the garage and said whatever they wanted, they could take. The rest he was going to sell. And that, he said, was that.

Susan made a sound like some little bird. Then she drew in a sigh and said how unhealthy it was to push things away. "You're pushing Mom away. You're trying to forget about her." Didn't he realize that by doing so, he was letting poisons build up, like the pus inside a boil? And we all know that a boil can't heal unless you lance it open every once and awhile and let the pus drain.

Harry made an irritated gesture and said, "I don't appreciate people who talk in abstractions."

"Okay," she said. "Then get this. You need to sit down." She pointed to his chair. "So sit down. Let's discuss things." She had a determined way of talking that reminded him of Louise.

For this reason he stepped close to her and made a big production out of how he was a good foot taller and said, "You seem to think you're the boss of me."

She didn't say anything.

He said, "Crapo," and refused to sit down right away. He didn't want her to think she had that power. So he went in the kitchen and emptied the dishwasher and then studied the *TV Guide* a second, though he knew it inside out, before finally sitting down. When he sat down she began to ask him questions—about Louise and the life they had shared, about what he missed most, and did he remember that killer potato salad Mom used to make? "I made some last night," Susan said, and it was out in the car, along with some pictures they wanted him to have. Oh, and what about last Thanksgiving? When the cat got into the turkey, did he remember how she screamed and raised such a fuss? What about the ornaments she made for Christmas? The gold shoes she wore to restaurants? Those shoes made her shiny all over. And how about her feet, how they were always cold?

He listened and laughed a little and answered as best he could and tried not to cry but that didn't do any good.

Harry got on a sentimental kick. He decided to hang on to a few things after all, and designated the living room as a memorial. Here he put a great deal of foo-foo, but not all of it. The porcelain cherubs, for instance. On the couch he laid some of her dresses and blouses, some photographs, such as the one where she leaned against their old Plymouth roadster with her lips parted, her hand shading her eyes. And then he walked through the room and examined everything, carefully, quietly, like you would in a museum.

This made him feel like holding hands made him feel. Like a kind of conversation was taking place.

And then he dug through his desk until he found that gold pocket-watch Louise had given him so many years ago. It had a picture of her and Susan in it, framed by the inside cover. For a long time he had worn the watch with his avocado-green vest, which frayed and faded and went out-of-style, and so Louise snuck it off to the Good Will because she knew he'd throw a fit.

When he learned about this, he threw a fit, and tossed the watch in a desk drawer, as a small sort of revenge and also because he felt—the same as his need for tea and Cream-of-Wheat at breakfast—that only this particular vest could do his watch justice. It had stayed in the drawer until now. Now he took it with him to Sears and told the clerk his story and when the clerk said, "I'm sorry, sir, we don't carry that vest, but perhaps you'd like to take a look at some of our more contemporary designs," he grew angry and said, "Listen, kiddo. There's nothing contemporary I'd touch with a ten-foot pole. And if you don't have that vest, then I'll go to the next joint and give them my dime." So he went to the next joint, and the next, and was told the same thing.

Finally, on a whim, he decided to check out the Good Will, and hanging right there, among the tweed pants and corduroy jackets, was an avocado-green vest—four pockets, just like the one he had worn back in the day. For all he knew, it was the same vest, only now it was three sizes too small and he could only fasten the top two buttons, his respectable belly hanging out its front.

The next day he wore the vest to the grocery store, where he told the cashier all about it. "Five bucks was how much this cost," he said and made a show out of checking the time on his pocket-watch. "Once in a blue moon you'll actually run into an honest price and here it is." The cashier—*Hello My Name is Brian*, his name tag read—listened to Harry talk and when Harry finally stopped talking, Brian said he was sorry to hear about his wife and that the vest was great, real cool.

Harry was tickled. He had planned on complaining about how they were robbing him blind for a carton of milk and a lousy flower bouquet, but he didn't complain. He paid in exact change and when Brian told him thanks, Harry hesitated a second, before dropping a quarter—two bits, he called it—on the counter. "Some Coca-Cola money for you," he said and turned to leave.

He wasn't sure, but he thought he had made up for something.

When he got in the car he examined himself in the rearview mirror. *Cool.* He tried on the word and liked the way it sounded. His vest was *cool. He* was cool. He wondered what kind of music Brian listened to and hoped it wasn't the racket kind.

Without really thinking about it, he drove to Aurora Health Care, ignoring how people honked their horns when he switched lanes without looking, when he ran a stop sign and zipped up an exit ramp and nearly collided with some knothead in a Jaguar.

Another five minutes and Paulo the witchdoctor was walking toward him in a white lab coat, looking tired and depressed, dark around the eyes, and not all that excited to see that Harry was the one who had paged him.

Harry thought: someone died today, one of his patients, a beautiful young girl who dreamed of being a movie star. When he told the parents, "I'm sorry, but—" the mother slapped him, the father began to cry.

"Here," Harry said and shoved the lousy bouquet in Paulo's face.

Rain fell, carrying with it a headed-for-summer smell, and the world slowly turned warm and green. Buds broke, pollen dirtied up the windows, and Harry spent a lot of time in the garden, which had always been Louise's thing. It felt good to do something with his hands, even if they were crooked and clumsy and ached with arthritis. He watched Louise's daffodils sprout and bloom, and after that her tulips. He trimmed hedges and mowed the grass and turned over dirt with a shovel to discover earthworms, bright as bubblegum, twisting under the sun. A long time ago someone had told him that one earthworm was like a million other earthworms, all packaged into one slick container. If you tore one in half, it wouldn't die, but go on living as two earthworms—and so on.

He thought what the heck, he'd give it a try. So he tossed one on the pavement and used the shovel to split it down the middle. The worm that was now two worms twisted and knotted into hieroglyphic designs. One part found the other part and for a time they looked to be wrestling, or else violently hugging. Eventually one of them slowed down and then stopped moving altogether. The other soon followed.

Right then Bert—this forty-something divorced guy from across the street—he came outside whistling, carrying some rags and a bucket. He wore a white T-shirt that hung outside his denim shorts. The shirt clung to his big sagging belly and Harry thought, that's why I don't wear T-shirts. Bert backed his car out of the garage. It was a brand-new car, one of those maroon PT Cruisers that look like 1950 all over again. Then he uncurled the garden hose and attached a spray nozzle and turned the spigot. The water hissed, splattering across the driveway to strike the hubcaps, where it made a shrill metal noise. A second later the metal noise faded into a gentle pounding as water ran across the hood and windshield. The air got misty and when the sun hit the mist it made a little rainbow around Bert.

Harry didn't realize he was staring until Bert laughed and waved and said, "Come on over here, will ya?"

When Harry was halfway across the street he said, "That's some jalopy."

Bert stopped spraying the car. "Say again?"

"Like I said, that's some jalopy you've got there." By this time Harry was standing next to Bert and could smell the soap in the bucket. Smelling it was like remembering something—a lot of things—he couldn't put a finger on. "Slick as a whistle."

"Isn't she?" Bert said and aimed the spray nozzle at Harry. "Hey!" Stick 'em up."

Harry's put up his hands like a good sport, but his voice was serious when he said, "Don't monkey around with that thing. I'm wearing my good vest."

Bert said, "Oh, I was only fooling." The nozzle made a *tick* when he set it down on the pavement. He wiped his hands on his shorts and gave Harry a thoughtful look.

Harry knew what was coming. He didn't want it to come, but then it came.

Bert drew in a long sigh and said, "Heard the news."

There was nothing to say to this, so Harry cleared his throat.

"You know how it is," Bert said, "neighborhoods." He laughed in a sarcastic way. "Anyway, I heard the score and I've been meaning to come over, but you know how it is." He cocked his head. "Don't really know what to say, Harry."

Harry studied the neighborhood, as if remembering. "Yeah."

Bert said, "You holding up okay? Because if you ever need anything, you know."

Harry took off his glasses and wiped at an imaginary spot. Then he walked over to the car, which was dappled with a thousand drops of water—one for every dozen things he missed about Louise—all shrinking under the sun, soon to vanish. He pointed at the door handle. "May I?"

Bert did a butler thing with his hand and said, "You bet."

Harry opened up the car and looked inside and whistled. "All the trimmins," he said. "Seat warmers even. You weren't kidding around."

Bert said, "Hey, you only live once," and Harry turned around in time to see him flinch.

They did some more talking, but mostly they looked at the car.

Bert said "Hey, how about we take her for a spin?"

Right then Harry made believe he was Bert. He made believe he could put on a T-shirt and drive away in a brand-new car, windows down, warm wind in his face, not a concern in the world except the cheapest gas, the next hotel, and would he throw a piston as he rocketed across the cornfields of Wisconsin, Iowa, Nebraska, up and over the Rockies, and maybe he would make a pit stop in Vegas and play the slots, but soon enough and he'd be on his way, all the while staring into the rearview mirror, watching the world slip away at a hundred miles per hour, nothing to lose.

For a second he wanted this so bad he could taste it, but only for a second.

Bert punched him lightly on the shoulder. "Harry?" he said. "Hey, what's the matter?"

Harry started to say something, but decided against it. He wouldn't have known where to begin.

Open My Heart

T.M. McNally

The boy in the burn unit had been weeping silently, which is why nobody on the nightshift had noticed. His pillow was damp and smelled like seawater. She had seen before the tears running from the corners of his eyes. Mornings, while she bathed the boy, he tried to be cheerful. It was important, she understood, always to be gentle. He had the body of a seventeen-year-old—capable, certainly, but not yet the solid mass of a grown man. She drew the cool, cotton cloth across the nipples on his chest, the tender rib cage, and on toward his navel. From there a thin ribbon of blonde hair, occasionally blotted out by fresh scar tissue, led to his loins—a road to heaven. But once there his genitals and pubic region were simply scarred beyond all recognition. Red, angry, the scar tissue raising itself insistently as it healed. *Proud flesh.* The boy had been here now for several months. She adjusted his catheter, which was constantly slipping from the knob of flesh which constituted the remains of his penis.

As she made the adjustment, the surgical plastic digging into his urethra, the boy cried out.

"There," she said, patting his elbow, one of the few places on his body not seared by the fire. "There."

"Thank you," said the boy. "I'm sorry."

"Nonsense," she said. "We are going to make you better. How many glasses of water?"

"Two," said the boy.

"I'll bring you another. Your sister is here. She brought flowers. Dr. Nick says you're well enough for flowers. They're lovely."

"Susie?"

"Yes?"

"I won't get an infection? I mean, any more?"

"No," she said. "You're healing fine," and she drew the sheet up to his waist. She waved aside a lock of her own hair and leaned down to kiss him on the forehead. "Don't be sad," she said, kissing him, and then she left the room.

Later that morning she had a conversation with the plastic surgeon who would be reconstructing the boy's penis. The testicles had been consumed by the fire, gone to smoke and ash, but the doctor seemed hopeful he might be able to lend a degree of normalcy to the boy through a series of reconstructive surgeries. These were miraculous times. In Louisville an amputee had just recently been given a new hand with which to touch his wife. Fingers had become easy to reattach so long as one located them quickly. Despite the thinness of the boy, his relative small size, there appeared to be a viable amount of material to harvest from his buttocks and thighs.

"How is he," said the doctor.

"His spirits are low," she said. "But his sister came to visit. I thought I'd try another book."

"The Jesus freak?"

"Yes," she said. She watched the doctor struggle to keep his eyes from gazing at her breasts. It was a routine they passed each time they spoke. He was handsome and prosperous and good at what he did—a beautiful wife, two happy children; he was also at risk of falling in love with her. Were she a cruel woman, she would have permitted him to trip.

His eyes met her own, and he averted his eyes to her ears, then her hair, and then the fire-extinguisher located in the wall behind her. To meet a woman's gaze was dangerous for a man—it left him naked, unprepared for the suddenness of possible invitation. Now his eyes fell again toward her cleavage, then rose immediately, embarrassed by the possibility of having been caught looking. It was the sign of a good man, she knew. He would look, because he simply could not help himself, but he would never linger, and he would always, always apologize afterward by stepping back, turning his head, this way, then that—anywhere but here, the center of her chest.

A plastic surgeon, a man who bi-weekly performed two dozen silicon implants, even he could not be made not to look. Like it or not, her husband would say, it was a law of geometry. A man leads with his chin; a woman, the tip of her breast. A good man, she knew, would steal a glance at a woman and save it up for later.

When you were left alone, only then would it be safe to look at what you'd seen—a passerby who'd caught your eye, or a particular vision of another's life. Granted, too, she knew she could have dressed more quietly, but she did not like to wear a lot of clothes, especially in the heat of Phoenix, and she *did* like to feel the sun on her chest. She liked fine cotton and silk sundresses. She liked the fact of her skin, and the air and water which moved against it. At work, she conceded to the uniform and wore her lab coat; but once into the world, she liked to feel as undressed to the elements as the world might actually permit. Her husband, who understood the elements of fashion far better than she, would underscore at times like this the fundamental premise of all fabric—that which conceals, also reveals. There was no fabric known to man more essential than the skin upon his body.

Or hers, she would say, reminding him. Her husband, who was a good man, a man who generally preferred Cerruti to Zegna, said she wore her heart upon her sleeve. At home, she walked through the house, briefly checking the mail on the drysink; she stepped out to the backyard, where she removed her sandals and then her dress, which she hung upon a lamp. The sky was brilliantly white, the desert sun at its peak. The heat around her wrapped her up. She slid off her underwear and slipped her body into the pool, the water defining the very heat around her, and then she slid her head beneath the water. She returned to take a breath. A deep breath, and she thought about her husband, seventeen years her senior, who would be in Rome now. She fell in love with him when she was just a girl. Seventeen, the age of the boy on her ward. The boy had a road to heaven, same as she. Eight years ago, she began electrolysis treatments, thinking to please her husband. Then he surprised her, the first time in several months, and asked her to desist. He loved the stripe of fur, he explained, as well as the few vagrant strands of hair upon her nipples—and he made her promise never, never to have reconstructive surgery, which was then becoming popular even in the West outside of California. He said, placing his hand upon her breast, "Let them drift, let them curve. Let them be."

Of course she hadn't had any children, and she'd been twenty-four at the time, a set of particular circumstances which would make it far easier for a man to insist on his beloved following nature's course. This, too, during a time when they made love regularly. She still didn't have any children, and this lack was beginning to annoy her. While she wasn't certain, she believed he was increasingly made nervous by, among other things, his lack of stamina. Not that he wasn't in fine shape, but fine shape at fifty wasn't thirty-four. She was seventeen when she fell in love with him, seventeen years ago, when he was thirty-four—they'd been together the same amount of time the world had taken to make the boy with the mutilated genitalia. She'd married her husband in Cambridge after she'd finished college. He brought flowers—a lei, orchids and plumerias, shipped overnight from Oahu—to her graduation and draped them around her neck.

To remind themselves of the possibility of the ocean, they had insisted on the pool being treated with a salt chlorination system, which in turn caused the water to feel like silk. Saltwater, they reasoned, was good for the skin—cuts healed more swiftly—which is why the body shed saltwater to begin with—through the pores, through the very eyes. The garden needed watering, she thought. And she loved the heat, the sun on the back of her neck, and knees. She lifted herself from the pool, the water dripping from her body. She would need to water the bougainvillea and the oleanders in the garden. She loved the fact of water, and she missed her husband, who most likely had a new lover in Italy.

She wanted him to hurry home. She wanted him to hurry home to her and take her in the pool.

What makes marriage possible? A willingness to be perfectly honest—tastes, habits, fantasies, mistakes. Also a willingness not to punish your partner for those very same tastes, habits, fantasies, mistakes that you insist on knowing. She loved her husband to the quick: that he should have a mistress in a foreign country caused her distress, to be certain, but she would never punish him unnecessarily for it, if only because to do so would destroy the very fabric of the marriage, and that was sacred. The marriage—the union of each—was inviolable, built upon, to use her husband's language, a commitment guided by reason and law. The heart was a sacred object, necessary to protect—by the ribs, by the fabric of our public lives—if only because the heart insisted on following the paradoxical rules of its own making. The heart's desire was not necessarily the mind's. Her husband, who in the initial stages of their courtship would often masturbate beside her, sometimes coming between her breasts, or against the small of her back ... at first she had been surprised. But she had also been seventeen, and then everything had been brand-new. Eventually, she had begun instructing his hand, just so, here and there, often in the spirit of efficiency. A quick fifteen minute trip, just before rising to leave for work. A car ride home from a tedious business dinner. They had learned she understood to work together. They had learned to work together because a deep marriage is an efficient one guided by trust, and lust, and mercy. Because a deep marriage is one that understood its depths.

Made in heaven, you hoped. It was the woman in Italy who threw things off balance, and before that, the one in Paris. He explained. He explained that these women required nothing from him—except for gifts, and sometimes cash. He explained he might be tired, and lonely, and he explained he was too old a rooster to change his ways. He explained they helped him to sleep.

"But why won't you make love to me?"

"Because with you I have to please, and sometimes I just can't. I just can't, Susie. A wannabe model in Paris," he said, "I don't make love to that. It is not the same. She fucks me, thinking I'll introduce her to Lagerfeld, and I fuck her, thinking I'll never, never do this again." He said, "Either way, it is not about you."

"It is if it hurts me," she said. "I see it, you know. Sometimes. I can actually *see* you in bed with another woman. The way she bites your lip? You can't imagine."

"Then stop looking," he said. "Because that will make you angry, and anger will destroy us."

"Poison," she said. "The pus beneath the blister?"

And so she had agreed not to raise a fuss, so long as the terms were clear. First, she must always know. Second, nobody else must ever know. Third, he must promise to leave her—Susie—the moment he understood he wanted to.

She, too, would do likewise. She'd had a brief affair with a surgeon from the third floor—a cardiologist, named Bigg, but he was looking for a wife. Too, he was insufferably correct. He was a short, fit man, with the name of Bigg, a name he wore upon his breast as if it were equivalent to Guggenheim or Givenchy. He was, after all, recognized across the world for his surgical skill. Among other things, he thought she should be a doctor. He wanted to send her to medical school.

"No," she said.

They were sitting on the eighth floor of the Hyatt. The air-conditioning was blasting through the duct work. They were sitting naked on the bed picking at a plate of fruit. It was afternoon, and he would have to return soon to the hospital for his rounds.

"You could go anywhere," he said. "With your experience."

"No," she said. "I like to make people feel better; that's my job. To comfort. Sometimes, I hold a woman's hand, or arm—she's been blown up in a car wreck, or set her house on fire, drunk, smoking in bed—doesn't matter. People burn themselves up every day. But if you can find a healthy patch of flesh, and just touch her. Just that—it's a gift, one I'm good at. I make people feel better," she said.

"People who will be disfigured beyond their own mothers' recognition—"

"You'd make more money," her doctor said. "More responsibility. People would respect you."

On the way to the hotel, she had stopped at the Shell station, and her hands still smelled like gasoline. She said, looking him in the eye, "Respect is more than a half-dozen terrified interns kissing your ass. I've seen doctors. I've seen the way you treat anybody you deign beneath you. Even veterinarians, it's shameful. A doctor steps into the examining room and says, never extending a hand, I'm Dr. So and So, you know you're dealing with an asshole, pure and simple. As for money," she said, reaching for a strawberry, "after how much is it okay to stop worrying about it? What, I'm going to drive a Jaguar? My husband's rich. My father was rich. A very nice thing about being rich is not having to buy a Jaguar, if you know what I mean."

He said, "You should be a doctor. The profession needs you."

And she said, getting off the bed, "You're not listening, are you?"

"Your husband might divorce you—"

"Well, he might. Or I might him. It's always a given choice which makes any decision possible. Enough," she said, stepping into the bathroom, "is enough, don't you think?"

And then she peed. She had left the door open so he could listen. After rinsing her face, she dressed, and then she left for the elevator. At the concierge she stopped and left a note addressed to her Dr. Bigg.

Sorry to be so bitchy, she wrote. *I was lonely.*

A woman who wears Natori lingerie, she knows what she wants, or so her husband would have the world believe. What you see is what you get. He was in Rome now consulting the board of Gucci about positioning itself against Louis Vuitton's hostile takeover bid. Months ago, he'd seen this coming.

That night, after her run, after her dinner of salad and soup, she went to their bed. There she called her husband's hotel. He wasn't in, of course—time changed the way one felt all across the world. She thought of that line from the poet Robert Hass, *Longing, we say, because desire is full of endless distances.* She said into her husband's voice mail, "I was really hoping you'd be there. I was hoping you could help me out."

She said, "I love you. And I want you to love me back."

In the morning, she woke, and took her morning dip. She chose a navy dress with spaghetti straps, and then a cashmere cardigan to fight the hospital air-conditioning, which always caused the early part of a day to feel as if she were inside a refrigerator. At 10:00, the cooling system would finally kick off.

The boy's sister was waiting for her. She wore a silver bracelet in honor of the unborn. She was reading the bible, from the looks of her bookmarked place, something from the new testament, post-gospel. The girl smiled the drug-induced smile of those persistently enthralled by the Holy Spirit. Her T-shirt said, *Young Life!*

Susie said good morning to the girl.

"He's better," the girl said. "In spirits." The girl said, crossing her arms against the cold refrigeration, "I prayed for him again all last night."

"Yes," Susie said, nodding. "That was very thoughtful."

"It's the sin," the girl said. "He was filled with sin, and shame. Jesus takes our shame away from our bodies. He's better now. No more lusting."

"Excuse me?"

"On account of, you know. His. His—"

"Testicles," Susie said, gently. "It's not a dirty word."

"Yes," said the girl. Susie now understood that the girl was embarrassed by her erect nipples, which were poking through the lettering of her T-shirt. "I told him," the girl said, as if hoping to change the subject, "he can always adopt. Later on, after he gets married. Personally I think he should go to Bible College and become a pastor."

"You do?"

"Jesus saved him," the girl said. "For a *reason.*"

Susie sat beside the girl and shivered, crossing her own arms, and then her legs. She said, "You are here on vacation?"

"Uh huh. Then back for my semester internship. I am being called to North Carolina."

"It's beautiful there," Susie said. "The mountains."

The girl began to cry. Her open bible fell from her lap to the floor, and Susie picked it up for her. She saw that the place was marked, and closed it. The bible was stuffed with notes and small pieces of paper indicating essential passages. The girl wiped her face on the sleeve of her T-shirt, and then Susie, after setting aside the bible, put her arm around the girl. She wished she could at least remember the girl's name.

"There," Susie said.

The girl began to recover. "He likes you, and Dr. Sanders. He says everybody is always nice. But he says you're his favorite."

"He is everybody's favorite," Susie said. "So sweet. He gets the very best care. The very best."

"Our dad—he won't visit him. And now Mom lives in Florida. And the insurance is all run out. The plastic surgery ... how can he afford that?"

"It's been worked out," Susie said. "The surgeon is volunteering. It's called *pro bono.* Like I said, everybody likes him—"

"He thought he had lice," the girl said. "Crabs?"

"Yes."

"They made him itch. He thought he'd have to go to the doctor. He was scared of the doctors." She began to cry again. She said, wiping her eyes, "Before. Before I gave my life to Jesus, I used to sin. I mean a lot. But Christ's blood gave me back my virginity. I mean, I am a virgin in Christ's eyes—because He, you know. He took the pain of the cross."

"You believe this in your heart?"

"I do," said the girl, nodding. "I know you're not a Christian. I can tell. But lots of sophisticated people are saved later on. Even Paul. Just like Paul."

"St. Paul," Susie said, thinking, *Crystal. Her name is Crystal.* She said, "Crystal, I think God will forgive your brother long before your brother forgives himself. I don't think God was ever angry to begin with. I think it's very important your brother not dwell on guilt, and sin. Mostly he needs to feel loved."

"But God's love—"

"And yours," Susie said. "Which is directed by God. Bring him flowers—freesias, especially. The way they smell."

"He tried to kill himself. That's what people say."

"He tried to cure himself, and he was scared, and lonely, and now he's in the burn unit. This is not about you, Crystal."

"But I told him. I told him it was a sin. I told him, sexual lice is the vermin of Satan!"

"No," Susie said. "You told him how you felt. And he told us how he felt. But nobody, nobody ever makes us speak."

She rose and, after making sure Crystal knew her way to the cafeteria, excused herself. At the nursing station, she learned that the married man in 605 had died last night. His wife was expected later, as well as his three children, because they drove in each weekend from Amarillo. They were still on the road. By now they would be near Flagstaff.

There was also a message for her from David, wanting to have lunch. He was an Anglican priest, with whom she had dallied, off and on, after leaving Dr. Bigg on the eighth floor of the Hyatt. David was easier, if only because he too was married, as well as literate. Often they had read together in bed.

Sharon, the new nurse, asked her when her husband would be back.

After Thanksgiving, she said. Three more weeks. Then Bangkok in December.

The nurse was perplexed, of course. Certainly the nurse would never permit *her* husband to travel abroad like that. And why work, while on the subject, anyway? And why here? Her husband was a school teacher in Tempe. They were going to buy a semi-custom house with loads of upgrades and amenities in Auwatookee. And have kids, properly.

Perhaps if her husband were not sterile, things might be different. Susie could never be certain. She considered sometimes having a baby. David, for example, would make for a fine genetic line, but in general she was uncertain of her need to bring another life into an already over-populated world. It seemed faintly self-indulgent, insisting that any child she raise must belong to her by blood. Her husband, despite his protestations that he would not be hurt, that he would welcome the new life into his home, regardless of paternity—she knew, too, he *would* be hurt, and she knew he would resent the upheaval in their life: diapers, nannies, diapers—lots of crying late at night. And whenever she arrived this far in her thinking, she knew she wanted to be pregnant, and swollen: sick in the mornings, starving by night. She knew she wanted to feed a baby from her breast. And she knew, likewise, she was running out of time, and that she must be absolutely certain this particular baby was not being invented for the purposes of assuaging her loneliness, or for ratcheting up the territorial boundaries of their marriage. If she was lucky, maybe she could have both, her husband and her child. But if it came down to either, she would pick her husband.

The risk, of course, was that her husband would leave her anyway. And it struck her, just then, that she was afraid this might be happening at this very moment.

Shock is caused by surprise, which is caused by not knowing. It's why the eyes dilate—to see more. She felt her heart palpitate. David, she knew, would be on the floor later, making his rounds—the woman in 611 was from his parish: during a monsoon, last August, a microburst had caused a power line to brush against the lap of her thighs. The neighbors found her skirt hanging from a mesquite tree.

A bolt of lightning, a bolt of cloth ... each heightened equally the body's essential nakedness. She went to the boy's room. He was attempting to defecate, and she waited outside, listening to the clenched, tangled violence of his bowels. She entered first the bathroom and ran the tap, and before the boy knew it she had stepped outside of the bathroom and scooped away the bedpan, out of sight.

Later, after washing him, she sat by his bed.

"I had a nice talk with your sister," she said. "She loves you very much."

He nodded shyly. "Dr. Nick saw me last night. He brought me that," he said, pointing to a Diamondback cap. "When I get better he said we can go to a game. He's going to do the first operation day after tomorrow."

"He's sweet," she said. "He sure does love the Diamondbacks."

"It's 'cause my dad never visits," he said. "It's okay. I mean, Dr. Nick doesn't have to take me to a game or anything."

She said, "Have you ever heard of Patrick O'Brian?"

"No. Is he an actor?"

"He writes these books about the sea. Lots of battle and gunpowder. My husband loves them."

"My English teacher brings me books, too. I'm all caught up now. I mean, I won't be held back or anything. Next year I am going to graduate on time, even."

"That's wonderful," she said.

"Uh huh. I've read *All Quiet on the Western Front* and *The Red Badge of Courage* and *The Scarlet Letter*."

"*The Scarlet Letter*?"

"It was a movie, last year. I mean the book came first."

Susie said, carefully, "It was written a long time ago. People sure did think a lot differently then."

"I guess," he said. He said, looking out the window, "I can't have any children. It's cool, I guess. I mean, that could never happen to me now."

Pearl, she thinks. Hester's little girl was named *Pearl*.

The day to day, the lives she intersects with her very own—the stories here will break your heart. Loneliness, she thinks, is what endangers a marriage most. It is the root of all distractions. Of course, it is also what makes possible your ability to join—if not with one, then with another. Mouth to mouth, to the hip, by the balls of your feet. Truth is, she likes to be alone, and then she loves to reunite. She wants to be hungry before she eats a meal. She thinks, I am getting lonely.

She thinks, *He's leaving me.*

On the way out of the hospital with David, they passed Crystal, who was bringing in more flowers.

"I got the freesias," she said. "They *do* smell pretty." Then Crystal turned to David, who was wearing his collar. "Hi," Crystal said to him, beaming.

"Will I see you again?" Susie asked.

"I don't know, ma'am. I have to catch my bus later this afternoon."

"Well then," Susie said, stepping forward. She removed the flowers from Crystal's arms, passed them to David, and embraced her. She hugged the girl to her bones. She kissed her cheek, and said, stepping back, "Look at me."

"Okay," Crystal said, nodding.

"It is not your fault. What happened to your brother. You did not cause it."

Then Susie took the flowers from David and returned them to the girl. "If you hurry, you can get lunch. Macaroni and cheese. Strawberry ice cream."

"Thank you," said the girl, and as she scampered away, Susie understood that someday the girl would know a little bit more. She would have a husband, and a family. Someday she might become a nurse, assuming her bus didn't crash, or she wasn't seduced by her pastor. Assuming there were no surprises, which there would be. Still, looking at the girl, she understood the girl was presently out of danger. It was something she just knew.

At lunch, she ordered a green chili quesadilla, which would cause her agony, later on. She loved green chilies, but she would nonetheless be miserable through the next digestive cycle. She also ordered a Vodka martini.

After ordering the very same, David said, "I thought you didn't drink."

"Only when I'm lonely."

The martini tasted flammable, which David explained was on account of the vermouth. He talked for a while about his sons, his wife's endless struggles with the parish wives. He said, after a while, his eyes falling to her chest, "I'm boring you?"

"No," she said, smiling gently. She said, "You know, I spend all day, touching people. I like that. I do. But sometimes I want to be touched back."

He took her hand, reaching across the table.

"No," she said, laughing. "That's not what I mean. And I don't mean I want to be laid, either. I mean I'm afraid someday nobody will want to. When I'm old. You go to a nursing home—who ever, ever hugs these people? And on the ward—that woman with the thighs. She's lucky, but she won't think so when her husband sees the damage. A power line!"

"He was pretty shook up," David said. "Apparently her heart stopped. He had to punch her half a dozen times in the chest. Kept breaking her ribs. It tore him up."

"Pre cardial thump," she said. "It's designed to start the heart back up." She said, pushing away her drink, "If you and I went and got a room and got it on, right now, that would be nice. But you still couldn't tell your wife. She'd be hurt, crushed, she'd be betrayed et cetera. And your kids would find out. And all the time we are making love, you are thinking about your wife, and how you'll have to remove the smell of my perfume from your hair. Your collar."

"Well, yeah. But we've been there before."

"And then there's the possibility you bump into my husband. In a parking lot. At the symphony?"

"So," David said. "So?"

"He's going to leave me. I think. He's going to leave me because he feels guilty about his women and because he knows I want a baby."

"He doesn't have to treat you like this, you know. You do not have to accept it."

"Accept what? I love him. I could love you, or another, and I do love you, but not the way I love him. And right now I love *him*. You know, sometimes, before, I used to go to your services. I wanted to hear you give a sermon. And your wife, she's absolutely beautiful. That hair, and her eyes. She has incredible legs. Once you gave a sermon on forgiveness. That's why, you know. Because I knew you were speaking to your wife. And I had seen your wife. She poured me a cup of coffee during the social hour. I mean, I wanted her to be my friend—"

"Fidelity and monogamy are not the same. The body has a mission. God knows that. Hell, a man will fuck a goat."

"Fine," she said, teasing him. "So I'm a goat?"

"That's not what I mean. You shouldn't cheat like that in conversation."

"Last week, on the nature channel, I swear to God I saw two Rhinos humping the same cow. On the Serengeti or some place. These Rhino studs, there they go, back to back. It's not the erection which bothers me, or what one even does with it. It's just not knowing."

"How do you know he's leaving you?"

"Oh God, David. The guilt! If he loves me, and I know he does, he can not want to hurt me."

"Maybe—"

"No. He's going to leave me. Did you know the penis of a rhinoceros weighs fifty seven pounds? He's going to leave me because he does not want to have a child. Because he doesn't want to have to worry about anybody but himself. He's going to leave me because were the sexes reversed, it's exactly what I would do right now to him."

The next day she was off and did not go in to the hospital, and that night she ate dinner with a friend, Jacqueline, who lived down the street. They met at a restaurant in Tempe. To get there, Susie had to drive past the university. She drove past A Mountain—the small hill tucked behind the stadium branded with the university's crimson initial, *A*. Sometimes she would hike the mountain with her friend, Jacqueline, who was married fairly recently. Jacqueline had broken off a six year love affair with a woman before falling in love with her new husband. Susie thought about that, driving past the mountain, loving another woman. Certainly she'd had her various opportunities. At the same time, she loved the man whom she'd seduced at the age of seventeen.

He was recently divorced, a friend of her father's. He spent two weeks in their home in Paradise Valley. At night, after taking a shower, she would walk by the guest room wearing a T-shirt. Her hair was always wet; she remembered that. She would stop by his bedroom, just to say hello, and then one morning her father scolded her, and she went off to school. That afternoon she cut her classes and, while her father was still at work, returned home early.

The man, her father's guest, was in the den, reading the *Wall Street Journal*.

She said, "I am going to make you fall in love with me, whether you like it or not. My father will be angry."

She turned on her heel, which she had seen Ann-Margret do in a movie, and went out to the pool. There she removed her Catholic school clothes—white blouse, plaid skirt, knee socks—and leapt into the pool. After a while, he stepped out onto the Kool-deck. He said, "I'm thirty-four. Which is handsome now. But it won't be in ten years. A man my age only disintegrates."

"Beauty," she called from the pool, treading water, "is skin deep."

"You're going to Harvard? Next year?"

"Yes."

"I will be living in Boston. Maybe we can have dinner sometime."

And that is how she knew she had not been mistaken, because despite the nervousness in his voice, the obvious and self-asserted erection beneath his trousers, he instead turned and went into the house, where he called her father to explain he would be dropping by his office in a very short while.

In college she dated boys, and a professor, and almost a Caribbean woman who lived across the hall her sophomore year until the girl was suddenly deported for drug smuggling. Eventually Susie began seeing regularly the man who would become her husband, and they married. For the ceremony, she wore a dress by Vera Wang, and her father, not knowing what to give the couple, bought them a Chagall he thought particularly cheerful and optimistic. They spent their first two years together in Vienna, another three in Manhattan. Then they came to Phoenix, city of the flaming bird, rising from the ashes of modernity and a couple hundred thousand parking lots. They made their friends. They passed their lives.

A road to heaven took you to a place, preferably home. She called her answering machine from the restaurant. There was a message from her husband. By the sound of it, he was sorry to have missed her previous call. He explained he would be taking the London flight to Phoenix. He explained enough was enough. She could return to Italy with him, and then on to Paris, or he could cancel the trip. He had already canceled Bangkok, he said. He'd been doing a lot of thinking, he said. He wanted to build a nursery.

She was crying. She replayed the message, just to hear his voice. All around her, well-dressed married men from the bar kept their eyes peeled. She thought about adultery, and the men in the bar, checking out the women, as if the act of it had actually become a fashion symbol among the up and coming. She thought about her husband, who would arrive dehydrated from the flight. He would be jet-lagged for days and sleep like the dead. Happy endings, she thought. Happy endings weren't supposed to be permitted, and she understood this was not an ending, but rather just another beginning—a rocket, entering another stage, adjusting to its new orbit around the center of their lives.

The heart of the matter, her husband would say, falling into their bed.

She returned to her table, and Jacqueline looked surprised and happy at the same time. Later they parted company and Susie drove to a bookstore. Inside there were people reading magazines. She wandered to the back and found the fiction and plucked from the shelf a hardcover copy of *Master and Commander*. She stood in line behind a half-dozen people purchasing compact discs and calendars. One woman was buying several copies of *Vogue*. The cover featured a dress by Versace, the Kingpin of Slut.

"I love him," said the bookseller, ringing up her purchase. "Did you find everything all right?"

She wanted to say, Why do you ask?

She thought, Why does anybody ask anything of anybody?

She thought about her husband reading a novel on an airplane while crossing the Atlantic. The heart, she thought, is an open book; it wants only to be read. Her husband would be arriving in Phoenix at nearly the same time of his departure from London. So where did the time go? In the parking lot, where it had begun to rain, she located her car while the air filled deliciously with mesquite. Twenty minutes later, she arrived at the hospital.

The lights to the room were off, the room lit up by the city lights. The boy was gazing at the ceiling, his face riven in agony. A dish of melted strawberry ice cream sat beside his nightstand.

She knocked gently. At first he didn't recognize her without her lab coat. Her dress was damp from the rain, like her hair. He wiped the back of his hand across his eyes.

"Hi," he said.

"Tomorrow's the big day."

"They gave me something," he said. "To help me sleep. But I can't sleep. Just dopey."

She thought about her husband, who for many years simply could not fall asleep without first ejaculating. She said, stepping closer, "I brought you a book, for after. If you like it we can get the rest. There are a dozen more. Lots of sea air."

He said, brightening, "Thank you."

It was then she realized his sheet was twisted at his ankles. He was naked, had obviously been inspecting the damage. She said, reaching for the sheet, "Aren't you cold?"

"It itches," he said. "I can't scratch."

She thought, How quickly shame escapes. She said, "That means you're healing."

"It itches," he said. "Like before."

"Soon," she said, which is what she always said. "Soon. Life is long."

She drew the sheet up toward his thighs. He was crying again—exhaling, inhaling.

"It was my dad," he said. "Not me."

"Your dad?"

"I was in the garage. And he came home early. They'd sent him home for drinking. And he came into the garage, and I had all this gas over me. I was scrubbing it, you know, to kill the crabs. I read that if you don't get rid of them you can give them to your family."

"It's okay," she said. "And it's easy to catch. Really."

"I never did it, you know. Not properly. I went to this strip joint, just to *look*. And this lady kept touching me. She, you know, she kept doing that, and I knew it was wrong to have them. And my dad, he sees me with no clothes on in the garage by his tools and blows his top. He starts calling me faggot and candy ass and then he pulls out a cigarette. And then he says, *Here, I'll kill the critters.*"

She gazed out the window overlooking the Valley of the Sun.

"He used a match," the boy said. "Everybody thinks I did it."

She felt his hand, first on her arm. She turned, and smiled. He was gazing at her body. He could see the nipples of her breasts, she knew that, taut from the rain and now chill air. He brought his hand to her waist.

"You're so beautiful," he said.

She took his hand and held it close. She could feel her heart beating wildly. He was struggling now to lift his face to kiss her.

So why, she thought, does she love her husband? *Because I can.* She said, more sharply than she'd intended, "No."

The boy fell back as if slapped.

"It's a body," she said, stepping back. "This is my body. And that is your body. You must not fall in love with me, because my heart belongs to my husband, whom I love." She said, stepping closer to him, "You don't believe this, but someday you are going to fall in love properly. And she will love you more than you can bear. She will love you to the grave."

"I can't, you know—"

"You have your eyes. You have your mind and a good, strong heart. The body is not the essence. It's what protects that essence, so you can keep it safe. So you can nourish it and give it back to others."

He said, "I love you, Susie."

"And you will love another," she said. "And then another, perhaps at the same time, which will make your life complicated and rich."

"I want—"

"Shhh," she said, letting go. She said, receding further from his view, and making him a promise, "Sleep, and tomorrow you will wake."

So why do you ask?

That night, before she went to sleep, she kicked off her shoes and opened up a bottle of wine. It was red wine—a burgundy, her husband would say, with body. She put music on the stereo and raised all the blinds to her house. She drank a glass of wine, and then another. At times, when the music was particularly moving, she danced by herself in the living room. By the third glass, she had begun a conversation with her husband, who was flying somewhere overhead, and then she started a conversation with David, who was lying in bed beside his sleeping wife. You don't understand, she explained to David. *She's sound asleep!* Then she had another glass of wine. The wine, if one tried hard enough, could taste like blood, like the iron which informs the bloodstream, and which at certain times became the Son of God. Frankly she was used to the smell of blood; it caused her to feel at home and grateful for the dirt below it. She stepped out into the yard, the dust beneath her toes, the music pumping into the night, and admonished the half-moon sailing across the sky to travel safely. In the morning she would greet her husband at a place called Sky Harbor International. Without even knowing it her husband had become a ward of the sky. She said, setting down her wine, preparing to make a point, that a boy should not have to burn in hell. A boy should burn instead inside the body of his beloved.

In the reflection of the windows to her house, the house she had made together with her husband, she saw herself clearly in the half-light of the moon. The flood lights streaming across the desert landscaping—everywhere the plants had been selected to grow and prosper in the desert sunlight, each according to its means. An ocotillo here: there, across the light of the pool, a thriving ironwood. The plants had been given root by the seeds from which they sprang. Last spring the boy's father had lit a match in order to set his son on fire. She watched him now, the boy, rolling on the ground, putting out the flames. She watched him reach for cover. And just where did one keep a blanket inside a man's garage? Maybe a pup-tent or a drop cloth. Had she been there, she knew what she would do. Had she been there she would have used her dress, and she removed it now, beneath the sky, before the image of herself removing her dress beneath the sky.

She kicked off her underwear. She removed the comb from her hair.

It's a body, she had said to the boy.

She stood before the windows to her house, holding the fabric of her dress before her, trying it on for size.

Now you see it, she could have said. Now you don't.

Not a Leaf Stirring

Quinn Dalton

I used photographs when I ran out of words. I handed them to Hannah one at a time; she clutched them as if bearing down on a pain. Her hands shivered in her lap, but her fingers, pressed together so that the flesh whitened, were surprisingly strong.

I visited Hannah when I came home on holidays to stay with my parents, her son and daughter-in-law. We met within the eggshell-white, cinderblock-walled television room at Spring Haven Nursing Facility, situated in a former cornfield near Toledo, Ohio. Several times as a college student, and later a graduate student, I made the two-hour drive from my parent's house west across the rutted turnpike alone. When my parents and brother and I came together, we stood around Hannah's bed and spoke as if we were on a stage: this is how a family acts when one of their own has lost what we recognize in them as human—language, memory, traceable emotion. My mother did not say much, but held Hannah's hand and stroked it. My father paced the room as he talked, his voice booming, his laugh too high in his throat. And my brother, tapping a marching band rhythm on his thigh, stared ahead as if his trance could pull us all out of that room to another place.

As for me: I could say, "Hannah," and she might look at me, but not because she knew her name. Her hands remembered me: they clasped my fingers and squeezed my palms the same way they'd reassured me as a child, and when she touched me that way I *was* a child, and we knew each other again. She might at that moment teach me a card game or how to bake bread—I could feel that and at the same time look at her and know better. Time had stopped for us, or actually, ground to a barely perceptible crawl, the way Hannah had once approached stop signs in the green Buick, taking me to the grocery, fallen blue jay feathers stuck in my headband. With her I was a little Indian, the woman I was trying to become denied recognition or greeting.

The nurses held whole conversations with her as if they could hear her responding. Or more likely it was the way they said, "You're looking well today, Hannah," (a prayer, really) instead of "How are you?" My endurance for one-sided conversation was short. So I brought pictures for the few afternoons I spent with my grandmother at the end of her life.

Where I live now reminds me of my grandparents' home, although the landscape is quite different from the flat farmland of western Ohio, where you can see a road threaded straight for miles. Here, broad-backed mountains twist the graveled roads; low houses lean into the curve of the land. But like the farm where my grandmother was born, the water here is sweet and cold. I buy unpasteurized milk from a local farmer and drink it just to taste its thick sweetness. I think of Hannah when I buy produce from the backs of trucks built when she was my age. This was one of the stiff photographs I always showed her: she's standing in front of just such a truck, maybe fourteen or fifteen years old, barefoot, wavy hair backlit and face mostly in shadow, but blurred with movement as if she's turning to glance at something outside the frame. There is her straight nose and even-toothed smile, smooth as the crescent of sky behind her. That truck, I learned, was the first vehicle she'd ever driven, and the story was that she'd somehow landed it in the flood ditch bordering her father's farm. It took four horses and six men to pull it out. The road, unspooling a line, gives no clue—what could she have been looking at across those fields that so distracted her? And could she remember what she had seen, decades later, her life contained in those cinderblock walls, the photograph trembling on her lap, the words locked behind her lips?

Today I will drive down the mountain from my home to visit a doctor in the next town, an hour away. On some of the road's turns I will almost be able to see the back of my car from the corner of my eye.

Another photograph I showed every time I visited: Hannah and my grandfather Reynold's house, on its small rise of land, with the twin pine trees in front. The garage, halfway in the picture on the left, its heavy oak and window-paned doors gleaming, later burned to the ground. The highly contrasted snapshot, probably from the late forties or fifties, records the brick as black. The white second-floor balcony off my grandparents' bedroom glows, ghostlike.

Laying the picture on Hannah's lap, I'd talk her through the two main floors, the attic and the earthen basement that ran the length of the foundation. The baseboards, mouldings, and mantle of hand-carved mahogany; the twelve-foot ceilings. The windows, fitted with blown glass, stretching from knee-height to a foot below the ceiling and trimmed in a mahogany that shone from deep below the glossy varnish.

I'd tell her the back door led into the kitchen, where linoleum was tacked over the wood floor sometime in the forties, my father told me, to accommodate the spills and footsteps of three growing children. There were two ways to go upstairs—the wide, high-banistered stairway that curved above the piano in the front room, or the narrow, sharply angled passage that led from the kitchen to the bedrooms. The darker, secretive staircase was my preference, another way to go to the same place.

I'd recount how her husband, a traveling salesman, bought the house for sixteen thousand dollars in 1927. In 1929 he sold his stocks four days before the crash and so they kept the house. Hannah fed drifters sandwiches and coffee from the back door in the coming years. Then came her children and twenty relatives for Sunday dinners and then grandchildren and their children, and she fed all of us.

But of course I didn't talk about Reynold's death in 1981 at the age of 78. Sometimes he was still alive for her, even then, and I saw no reason to deny her that. But I remember, as his diabetes and multiple sclerosis advanced, he and Hannah cared for each other in this way: she was his legs and he was her mind. More and more, in his final years, he directed her on how to care for them both. In 1991, when it became clear Hannah could no longer stay in the house, I helped my family and relatives to clean it out, starting with the attic, with its lining of carefully folded Christmas gift wrap and magazine stacks. One of us found a letter addressed to Reynold from a woman in Toronto who wanted to know how he'd lived four decades past diagnosis in a time when multiple sclerosis killed quickly. She'd heard about it through her doctor. *I'm desperate; I have four children*, she'd written. Now I wonder—as I start my car, as my child, newly discovered, grows within me—what had he told her?

When Reynold died, there was no way to ignore that Hannah's memory had begun peeling back, layer by layer, year by year. On the day of the funeral, she began to talk of going home, even as she stood in the parlor of the house she had lived in for fifty-five years. My parents and brother and aunts and uncles and cousins and I stayed at the house, where my grandfather's canes leaned against corners and doorways and were never moved in hopes they would serve as markers until she too had gone, and we gathered again to disperse what was left.

The canes were narrow, thick, black, tortoise shell, aluminum, ivory with silver filigree, wooden with inlaid turquoise, silkily turned, cool to the touch. They matched buckles and cufflinks and hats and suits. Taking them from the shadowed corners was like pulling my grandmother's flowers from the roots—poppies, irises, and tulips—after all the years they had bordered the deep backyard where we played badminton, where I watched squirrels gnaw on the Indian corn my grandfather dried in the shed, where three generations of my family's babies had stumbled through the grass.

In the summer of 1984, a few years after Reynold died, but before Hannah moved to Spring Haven, my father transferred jobs, and we moved closer to Hannah. The first year, we rented a house in a newly built development on the edge of a small town in northeastern Ohio. The owners had advertised a spacious four-bedroom house with all appliances included. When we arrived in the truck that we had packed ourselves because my parents would not entrust our furniture to movers, we found that it had what could barely be counted as three cramped bedrooms. No refrigerator. The trees in the yard were stunted; the water smelled like sulfur. My mother cried as we moved in. The first winter was a prolonged twilight; In January the sun remained behind thick clouds, backlighting them to a gray in the daytime that faded to pale orange from the lights of Akron and Cleveland at night.

The following spring, my family and I drove to western Ohio to pick up Hannah to spend a week with us while her day nurse went on vacation. Hannah sat in the back seat across from me for the drive home. My brother, eight years old, slept between us. My father locked her car door so she wouldn't forget and open it.

It was getting dark when we left. I'm not sure what in the truck headlights streaking past us made her think of my grandfather, but then she said, "Reynold?" Her voice was clear and certain above the motor hum. At that time, what was happening to her was still happening. So each new disorientation was another part of her taken from us. I had not heard her ask for her dead husband before and I felt the skin heating on my cheeks and neck, as if I had been the one to forget he was gone.

There was a long pause before anyone said anything; finally my father answered in his characteristic gentleness, "Reynold isn't with us anymore." Of course she asked where he was.

A green service center sign flashed in the headlights. My mother asked, "Do you need to go to the bathroom, Hannah?"

My grandmother said, "Sure," as if we had asked her if she would like a cup of coffee.

The rest room was empty. Red stall doors stretched ahead of us like a mirror trick. My grandmother stopped, confused. My mother guided her into a stall. "Can I help?" she asked.

"Oh, no, no," my grandmother said.

"I'll hold the door for you," my mother said, and we both listened to the rustle of my grandmother's dress and hose. I looked in the mirror and fluffed my permed hair, pretending I was someone famous or perhaps a spy, traveling by myself, avoiding recognition. The sound that came out of the stall so startled me that I flinched and saw in the mirror that my mother had done the same. My mother looked in the stall door and then at me. "Go get your father and tell him to get a new outfit for Grandma," she said. "And call an attendant."

I stared at her, daydream clinging to me.

"Now, now, now, now!" she said, her voice rising. I heard my grandmother murmur something and then I saw her in an instant as I reached for the rest room door—legs covered in excrement, her dress and the floor streaked with it.

I wanted to cry because I believed I should cry as I went to find my father. But in truth I felt calm. I simply wanted this moment erased, fading in the taillights.

I found my father in line for coffee, whispered in his ear. He handed me the car keys wordlessly. It felt unnatural to take the keys from him—I was thirteen and already begging for parking lot test drives without success—but as his eyes moved from my face to the floor, I realized that he could do nothing but rely on me and my mother, the way men often do in the face of a woman's sickness.

The car keys clicked in my hand and I pretended I was going to drive away to someplace I had to be for a meeting, a photo shoot. I checked through everything I had taken from my grandmother's brown, hard-sided suitcase—hose, underpants, slip, bra, dress, shoes. I carried them in and asked a woman sweeping the floor if she was the rest room attendant. She pointed. "She's already in there," she said, not looking at me. As she turned I thought I saw her eyes narrow, the corners of her mouth pull down in disgust. And what I wanted then was never to be looked at that way. I remember thinking, *Better to kill yourself.*

In 1991, the year we moved Hannah into a nursing home, we cleaned out her house and sold it. It was August, a few weeks before I was to go back to college. The attic air was so hot it dried my mouth and made my scalp tingle. I carried box after box down the stairs and daydreamed about a boy I was dating.

My mother and father, my brother, my aunt and uncle and their spouses, and two of my cousins and their husbands were also there. We carried out chairs and tables and sofas and dressers and headboards of heavy oak, cherry, walnut. These, along with the crystal, china, silver, jewelry and some knick knacks a great aunt had collected on her travels around the world, were distributed among the three children. Pictures of ourselves at various awkward ages were divided and boxed, to be buried in garages around the country.

My father told me then that he and his brother and sister had made a pact in their childhood never to squabble about their inheritance—the result of witnessing in their youth a nasty estate battle between their grandfather's second wife, who survived him, and his children—and yet there were some lengthy discussions over the crystal and the two Tiffany lamps and the diamond brooch. As for me, I found in a shoebox a pair of porcelain daisy snap-on earrings (my grandmother never pierced her ears) that I remembered her wearing. These I slipped in my pocket, undeclared. Many things were sold at auction.

Many other items in the house could not be sold but had been preserved with equal care and then forgotten: my grandfather's suits and hats, his canes, monogrammed handkerchiefs, his favorite chair. Also there were drawers and cabinets full of aluminum pie plates, folded foil, rubber bands and twist ties, plastic bags, mason jars. Old toys down in the earthen canning basement. The fender from a long gone car. Coats, tiny mittens, fishing lures and nets, faded comic books. Peaches, squash, and beans canned in the seventies. Bread frozen for at least that long. The sugarless candies my grandfather never really liked, gone to syrup. All piled in the sunlight in the front yard.

We did it because Hannah had begun to wander at all hours; a full-time day nurse was no longer enough. Hannah wanted to walk to her family farm, she wrote checks to children and salesmen who came to her door, she continued on her secret way past slow moving cars with pounding bass, past boarded houses and closed shops, her navy blue purse swaying under her elbow.

There were no more alternatives to the nursing home. The family assembled, and the process of decision-making and property division began, faster than we had expected. It made us all edgy, easily tired. A year after entering the nursing home, Hannah would fall in the tile bathroom and break her hip, and the problem would change all in a moment: the problem would no longer be her wanderings, her continuing ability to slip out of side doors in search of the farm in Rising Sun, but the fact that she could now no longer take herself anywhere.

Our aim had been to contain her, to keep her safe. And to do what we had to do as quickly as possible, not just because it was hard work, and not just because the three children lived in three different states where jobs and schools awaited them and their children, but because it felt as if we were clearing out our own homes, throwing ourselves away. At the end of that first night I took a cold bath and washed my fevered skin with soap slivers my grandmother had pressed together to save for people she no longer knew.

But the memory is uneven. In the early spring of the next year, a few months before my grandmother's fall, my father, brother, and I drove to the house, which had not yet sold, to trim the bushes and clean the gutters. In the afternoon we finished and took baths. Then we picked up Hannah at the nursing home to take her to dinner at Frische's, where in years past my father and grandfather and argued, smiling, over who would get to pay the bill. This time, Hannah held her menu like something fragile, polishing the plastic with the cuff of her dress sleeve.

After we ate we took her to the house. We walked with her by the flowers she had planted, from which my parents had taken cuttings to grow in his own garden. My brother tinkered with a scooter we had all played on as kids. I held Hannah's arm just under the elbow, steadying her. My father told stories and my grandmother responded with a sort of mimicked speech, much the way a baby does, linked syllables that copy the lilt of adult speech. But then she pointed and said, "Tulip." My father and I began talking at once—oh do you remember planting these? You used to get so mad when I ran through your garden—but then she was gone, her blue eyes pleasant but unseeing at the same time, wherever she was now a mystery to us.

What would she think of me? I have never loved someone so much and yet shared so few confidences. Now that she is gone, I pretend she can see me, that she knows who I am. I wonder how she would forgive my quick temper, my experimentation with drugs, the number of lovers I've had, these meager indiscretions. What will my children and grandchildren have to keep from me?

I visited Hannah several times after she broke her hip. I drove the hundred miles or so to the Toledo exit off the Ohio turnpike, paid the toll. I arrived at the nursing home by early afternoon and stayed with Hannah until it was time to help the nurses feed her at dinner. She was not often in her room, but that was where I looked first. On the way I passed other women and men—mostly women—their chests sunken, their voices weak as they responded to my greetings, if they responded at all. I could feel their eyes following me as I passed, their disappointment a scent in the air.

My grandmother's roommate cried out constantly to her daughter to save her. Her voice grated, metallic, against the pastel cinder block walls. Hannah moved by pulling herself along the hallway railings in her wheelchair and pushing with the toes of her shoes. When I found her I would put my hands on her shoulders to stop her. Sometimes her hair was in a bun, sometimes in a long braid down her back. But never the figure eight twist that she had worn every day before then, the one I had never seen another woman wear.

By this time the most common expression her face registered was pain. She ground her teeth and picked at her skirt and blouse. Whereas before she had returned smiles or hugs, even when she had stopped speaking, her mouth now seemed permanently drawn in a grimace of effort and discomfort. One day—probably during Thanksgiving or Christmas vacation because I remember it was cold—I noticed a bird's nest tucked into the rafters of the gazebo outside.

"Look," I said, pointing out the window, and amazingly, Hannah's eyes followed the direction of my finger. Just then a brown bird fluttered into the hive-like nest and then back out again. "I can't believe that bird hasn't flown south," I said. And Hannah shook her head, her blue eyes crinkled as she smiled, perhaps at the wonder of it.

Later that year, in summer, I decided to take Hannah for a drive. It was muggy and hot, but a nurse gave me one of Hannah's sweaters and a cap for her to wear, and she called an orderly to lift her into my car. The orderly was a boy of about sixteen. He had limp black hair and pale skin, as if he, too, rarely got outside. I stood behind him as he lifted

Hannah from her chair into the passenger seat. Placing her inside, he bumped her head against the rubber door seal.

"Shit," he said, almost in my grandmother's ear. When he straightened up and turned, I was in his way, and he looked at me, waiting for me to move. I was about three or four years older than he was and a few inches shorter. I opened my mouth to say something, but then I looked into his flat dark eyes and knew I would say nothing, because he would see her every day and her comfort depended on him, on his thin arms and the benevolence of his smoky, sour words.

There is a picture of Hannah taken the day of her graduation from Reserve Normal School in 1927. She's probably twenty-three. She stands outside at the top of three curved steps, wearing a black linen dress that gathers at the hips and falls to her calves. It has three-quarter sleeves, a jewel neckline and unusual detailing, at least to me. Thin strips of black linen fall from her hips to hemline, and they bow slightly out from the material. Her face, porcelain-like in the fine-grained print, is in tighter focus than her body because she's leaning forward, but it's a subtle inclination and serves to reinforce her expression, which is determined, or perhaps anticipatory. She's squinting because she's maybe been told to face the sun. She's not smiling, but her mouth is relaxed. Her face is smooth, glass-like, the perfect focus on it making it seem to float closer to the eye than the blurred edges of her hair.

Hannah was the only one of her five brothers and sisters to earn a degree; until she married, she walked from her father's house down a road lined with sighing corn to teach.

The photographs I brought to her changed with the seasons and years. But there were some I brought again and again, hoping the images might draw her back to me. I showed her the earliest ones first, because they marked where her memory was stronger; for as long as she still talked, she mentioned her hometown of Rising Sun and sometimes her parents' names. So I started with the one of her with the old truck she wrecked. Then the graduation photo. Then one of Reynold with two of Hannah's brothers, one now dead and the other in a nursing home, afflicted with the same memory-stealing disease. In the photo, the three men are ready for a hunting trip; they wear heavy flannel and trousers, rifles in their hands. My grandfather poses with his foot on the fender of the truck, hair slicked back, broad face shining in the sun. Skip forward about fifty years: there is one of me seated beside him in the wicker swing on the back porch. My brother sits on his lap, horrified at the set of false teeth my grandfather holds in one hand; I am clutching my fists to my chest in delight. Now, here's one of my parents and Hannah at the lake in South Carolina where we once lived; my grandfather's shadow extends from where he stands behind the camera to our ankles—you can tell it's him from the line of his fedora on the pine needles. It was the last long trip they made together. And—we're a little out of order here, but who's going to notice?—one of her and Reynold, newly married, their faces touching in a photo taken on their honeymoon.

On their wedding night, Reynold unpacked the pistol he always carried and it went off. The bullet tore through my grandmother's thigh and lodged in the floor. When I came to this picture I could not resist asking her, Do you remember that night? How Reynold carried you downstairs from your hotel room overlooking Niagara Falls, and you both had to beg the local doctor (who'd maybe seen his share of misguided marriages in that honeymoon town) to believe it had been an accident? And were you glad, later, that love had pierced you in this way, so that even after death, or the forgetting of a life—prospects you never would've considered then—you would always be marked by it?

On the last visit I had with her, several months before she died, my grandmother's teeth were worn nearly to the gums from her constant grinding. Her head nodded forward and backward as if she could not bear its weight. She did not look at the photographs anymore; it was not possible to direct her attention. I could not let her hold them because I was afraid she might crumple them, so strong was her grip on my free hand. I showed her one I had found in a box of things I was packing in preparation for moving to join my husband-to-be: me, age ten, hugging a snowman I'd built in front of their house in Fostoria. My grandfather stands on the porch in shadow, hands in his pockets, smiling at me. This was before he began avoiding slick surfaces like a porch step in wintertime, before my grandmother, the retired teacher, forgot the words she used to ask me to spell.

Hannah stared out the window, the bones of her teeth slowly eroding each other. I sat with my knees against hers, as close as I could pull my chair to her wheelchair, and yet it seemed she couldn't feel me. She had drawn within herself; the loss was complete. She reflexively squeezed and released my hand. I decided to read this as that old gesture of comfort, because I was crying by then, no longer seeing the point in trying to hide it. I was crying, hunched over, spit thick in my mouth, my words thickened too: Please don't forget me, I said. I was asking her not to forget me because that is what death is, erasure.

But then this happened: She lifted her free hand from the arm of her wheelchair and touched me, fingertips brushing my forehead, my hair, and I want to believe this was to bless me, to say, *I won't.*

When Reynold died, it was late summer, and mosquitoes clouded the streetlights and swarmed through the screen door whenever it was opened. People came and went all day—relatives, frail neighbors who had grown old with my grandparents, and my brother and I, running in and out, stirred by the activity and the tension of the adults. We slapped at ourselves all through the night, not wanting to cover our damp skins and miss a breeze through the window screens.

At Hannah's graveside, the earth was as hard and slick as metal, and my feet ached from cold in my thin dress shoes. The minister, a round-faced man who seemed ready at any moment to burst into tears, kept his prayers short. I cannot remember anything he said during the eulogy only a few short months ago; I remember instead the squeaking of the funeral home's wooden folding chairs as people shifted their weight, my cousins' children sniffling and tired, whining quietly into their parents' shoulders. And then, as we pressed together for warmth at the graveyard, I recall thinking that we were the ones who were trapped now; Hannah, who had lost everything that most people want—her husband, her home, her memory and connection to this world—was finally free.

On my car radio, the announcer is talking about worm holes, *related to black holes, they are the crushed corpses of stars and could be the key to space travel, scientists believe.* What would my grandmother think of worm holes? When I was a child she told me she saw her first plane land in a farmer's field. She was twenty. Already a veteran jet traveler myself, I could scarcely believe her. When I was ten, I saw my first desktop computer. The elementary school of our small town had purchased it great cost for the older students to use. That is my worm hole, the thing that will link me to an irretrievable past in my grandchildren's eyes.

The fog lies thicker in the hollows. I drive slower than I want to, trying to adjust my habits to a level of caution appropriate for a pregnant woman. I am more conscious of the waistline of my jeans, of the seat belt across my hips. To my right, hills appear and recede behind shifting layers of gray; the road and trees look familiar but changed, their lines frozen, statue-like. I used a home pregnancy test twice to make sure, and the results, certain and silent, make my fears seem deafening. I can't even decide to take a walk, so strange is my own body to me. But of course my husband and I have planned this, tried for this, and when I told him last night he kneeled to press his head against my belly even though we knew there was nothing moving yet. If it is a girl I will call her Hannah.

It was the spring of the first year after my father's transfer to Ohio, and we drove to Fostoria to take Hannah back with us for a week while her day nurse went on vacation. By then my family and I had started to become familiar with our new home, but Hannah's wonderings through our cramped, low-ceilinged house reminded us of everything that was strange to us. She got lost in the hallway; she palmed dust from our crowded furniture, her blue pocket book swaying from the crook of her left arm. She picked invisible lint from the carpet and tucked it into her dress pocket.

My mother would guide Hannah to a chair near the window and my brother and I would watch her watching the new leaves turn their pale undersides against the breeze. Soon we knew she would say it, and we waited, not daring to look at each other. She would look out the window and say *Not a leaf stirring*, and I would feel my brother's gaze slide to my face, and we bit back our laughter. But it wasn't meanness. It was child's coping. Our grandmother was not the woman we had known. She had become the narrator of one-line poems, endlessly repeated. She paced through our home, a friendly but worried expression on her face, and soon we knew she would call out a goodbye in her sweet reedy voice and say it was time for her to go home to Rising Sun, to the farm of her girlhood. *Not a leaf stirring.* We didn't want her to leave us. For my brother and me, the only recourse we had was to predict it, and to feel gratified when our predictions came true.

I said goodbye to her again and again, every time I saw her, every time I thought of her. On Sunday evening of the weekend my family and relatives gathered to clean out her home, I tried to feel an ending in the plastic bags I filled with folded foil, balls of twine, soap slivers. The day gone, I stepped onto the front porch by the open door, looking for my father, the youngest, the one who, I'm told, always wandered off. My aunts and uncles and cousins and their children were standing in the yard, their voices muffled in the heat.

My mother, forehead pinched from exhaustion after that final afternoon of packing and cleaning, leaned against our car, waiting; my brother sat in the back seat. The last light came green through the thick tiers of leaves above. I peered in the open front door and opened my mouth to call my father, but then I saw him in the dark living room with his back to me, facing the stairs. He bent over the banister, as if to study something he hadn't seen, as if to talk to a child. He leaned forward, his hands light on the banister, and kissed it where the wood swelled into roundness and ended.

Picnic
Max Ruback

The night before, staff goes around and makes sure that everybody's ready for the picnic where all the future parents will be waiting for us. Staff makes sure all of our fingernails are trimmed and that we got nothing gross growing in our ears. They lay out the new clothes they want you to wear even though there's no tags sticking out, so I don't think they're so new. The newest little white kids are the most excited, because they haven't been through this before and because they believe they'll find parents who will love them and make them a part of their family. They'll believe almost anything you tell them anyways. They have the best shot out of all of us, actually, and a few of them probably won't be here for too long, once tomorrow happens. The newest little black kids are just as excited, but they'll learn sooner or later about the way it really is. That they ain't exactly like the white kids. Plus, there's always way more white folks looking for white kids than black folks looking for black kids. Sometimes, white folks adopt a black kid. But it's very rare. It's never the other way around though, for some reason. You never see black folks who want a white kid. That's just the way the real world works.

I'm checking myself out in the mirror when I see Arnie walk up behind me.

"Why don't you shave that mustache off? he says. "Clean yourself up a little."

"Why should I?"

"I thought you just might want to have a clean shaven face. Make yourself look presentable."

"You mean younger, don't you?"

"I prefer presentable," Arnie says. He's looking at my reflection and I'm looking at his reflection.

"I'd rather leave the mustache," I say. "I like the way I look."

"Whatever you like," he says, moving on to the next kid.

Arnie's white. He doesn't want to tell me what he really thinks, that nobody's going to want to adopt a fourteen year old black kid with a mustache. He's afraid to tell me the truth, even though he knows that I know how things work. He tries to help though, so I give him that, even though I'd just rather he was honest from the get go.

Nobody sleeps. The newest little kids are too excited, talking about what their future parents are going to look like, describing the homes and their rooms they see in their imaginations. I want to tell them the truth, but I remember how it was for me. Sometimes, just looking forward to the possibility of having future parents is a good thing. I close my eyes but they just jibber jaw away.

"I bet you I'm going to get a mother and father before you do," Roger says to the others.

"You're never going to get a mother and a father," Lenny says back. "You piss the bed at night. Nobody wants a kid who pisses the bed."

Some of the kids start laughing. And that makes me feel sad for Roger. Roger will end up being like me in the future, not because he pisses the bed, or anything like that, but because he has emotional problems and no future parents want a kid who has emotional problems that make him talk to himself and takes legal drugs to calm him down.

"I can't help it," Roger says. "It's not my fault."

The kids are still laughing at him.

"Shut up," I say. "Or I'm going to get up and do something about it. You hear me?"

"Yes," a few of them say.

I hear Roger crying.

"Don't worry about them, Roger," I say. "It's not your fault."

Most of the kids look up to me because I've been here so long. I've been here ever since I can remember. I never knew my real parents, and don't know anything about them. They could be dead and buried for all I know. When I think about it, I think I was one of those front stoop babies, where my mother couldn't take care of me and so she just left me on the front stoop of this church and ran away. It used to bother me, when I was a kid, but I don't think too much about it anymore. There's nothing I can do about it, so there's no reason to let it bother me. That's the way I figure it, anyway.

Once, I was a Thursday's child. Back when I was a kid. A Thursday's child is a foster kid that the local news station tries to find a family for. Every Thursday there's a new Thursday child. That's how they get the name. What happens is that there's a fishbowl with all the foster kids names on scraps of paper in one of the government offices. Once a week, they pick a name. If they pick yours, you're the Thursday child. Then your caseworker picks you up from the group home and takes you to the park, and introduces you to a news reporter. And the reporter introduces you to the cameraman. Then you sit next to the reporter and they ask you what your favorite subject in school is, if you like sports, and what kind of things you like to do for fun. Then they go ask you to play on the monkey bars or something, and the cameraman films you hanging upside down or something, and keeps telling you to smile. Even if you get sand in your eye or something. Then the reporter and the cameraman shake your hand goodbye. And your caseworker maybe buys you a soda and takes you back to the group home and tells you how wonderfully behaved you are and maybe gives you a hug goodbye. Then you see yourself on the evening news like a day later. You watch yourself hanging upside down on the monkey bars and answering all those questions. Then the reporter asks people who watch the news if they'd like to become your big brother or something, or adopt you into their family. They make it seem very sad that you've got no family. The reporter then talks to the caseworker and they say all these good things about you, but people aren't stupid. They know they're being sold damaged goods. And the next day at school, everybody knows you've got no real parents and you have to go on the news to find some. And so you get into fights with kids who make fun of you for not having real parents. And you get a bloody lip and have to go to the principal's office. And the principal asks you what exactly happened and the whole time you sit in the chair talking to him you see the pictures of his kids on his desk. And it makes you want to cry, but you don't. And the next time you see your caseworker, you ask her if anybody called about you, and your caseworker tells you to be patient, that patience is a virtue or something like that, and all that means is nobody wants you. So you stop asking whenever your caseworker comes around. And when she asks you what's wrong, why you don't talk to her anymore, you say, Nothing's wrong. Nothing at all.

I hear the little kids whispering, carrying on about the picnic. What I want to tell them is not to get their hopes up. I want to tell them how it really is. I want to tell them the real truth. I want to tell the kids with histories of sexual abuse that it's unlikely that they're going to get future parents. I want to tell them that no matter how cute they are, once the future parents get their histories, they'll just choose some other kid without the histories they have. That's just the way it is. It's like choosing fruit at the grocery market. They'll examine you so they can get the best piece of fruit. The future parents know we're all damaged in some way, but they just want the one kid that's less damaged than the rest of us. But I keep my mouth shut. They'll learn just like everybody else. Just like I did. And they will learn that this is their home and that we are their family.

Even some of the older kids that still have some hope of getting future parents are praying.

Shut up, I tell them.

And they get quiet too, although I can hear them whispering deep into the night.

After breakfast, staff warns us about our bad habits. They tell us not to pick our noses, and to cover our mouths when we cough. They tell us not to get too angry if things don't go the way we want them. They tell us that if some future parents start talking to us, then we should look them in the eyes at all times because eye contact works in our favor. "Speak clearly," Arnie says. Talk english, not like you were raised in the street. "And smile," Arnie says. "Make sure you smile and don't look sad."

"Because nobody want sad little boys around," I say, and some of the older and wiser kids laugh, because I know Arnie's speech by heart.

"Thanks, Jojo," Arnie says.

"No prob."

Has everybody brushed their teeth? staff asks before we leave.

Yes, all the little kids answer back.

Right before we leave, a fight breaks out between Iggy and Carter, but I get in between them before anything bad happens.

"What's the problem?" I say.

"Carter told me that no future parents would ever take me home with them because he said I was ugly."

I look Carter right in the eyes, mean like. "Did you say that Carter?

Carter looks up at me, almost crying. "I didn't mean it."

"Then apologize," I say. "Don't be saying shit like that."

Carter apologizes to Iggy and they shake hands.

These picnics always bring out the worst in the little kids. They get all competitive with each other and forget who they are in all the anticipation.

We take the little yellow bus. Staff smile at us as we board. "Remember to smile," they say. All the little kids take the front and all the older kids take the back. That's how it always is. I make my way to the back of the bus.

"Comb your hair," I say to Iggy.

Staff tells me to get a move on, that I'm holding everybody up.

"Fuck off," I say, under my breath.

I sit in the very back, alone.

"I'm warning you now," Arnie says to me. "Don't you even touch that emergency exit. You hear me?"

He's looking at me in the reflection of the mirror.

"What did you say?"

"You heard me," he says.

I ignore him, but I stare at his reflection until he starts the bus up and we head out.

I stare out the window and watch the people in the cars. I stare at them until they look back. I keep staring until they turn away. Nobody likes to look at anybody in the eyes for too long. I've learned that much.

Everybody gets quieter and quieter the closer we get. Then one of the new kids, Porter, says he doesn't feel well. Staff tells him he's just nervous and to try and calm down. He says he thinks he's going to be sick. And then he gets sick, pukes on himself. Everybody pulls their windows down so we don't catch a whiff, but it's too late, and a few kids start gagging. Arnie just looks in the rearview mirror and shakes his head. Staff tend to Porter, trying to clean him up best they can. I stick my head out the window, even though Arnie tells me to get my head back inside the bus before I get it torn off.

"Spray some cologne on the puke, or something," I say. "I'm going to yak."

I used to be just like the little kids, all excited and hoping I would get parents someday. I used to think about it all the time. I would be all nice and respectful to everybody, always on my best behavior, and doing whatever I was told to do. I thought that if I was good then good things would happen to me. I thought that if I did the right thing, all the time, then God would make sure I would get future parents someday. Whenever I went to one of these picnics, I always looked good and had a nice clean shirt on and made sure my shoelaces were tied. I came close a few times, but nothing ever amounted to anything. I would talk to these future parents and they would ask me all sorts of questions about what I liked to do and what my favorite school subject was, and that sort of thing. They never got personal. They always asked the same questions, like the social workers gave them a list of standard questions to ask. You get tired of saying the same thing over and over again. But that was the way it was. And the worst part was that you had to always act happy, even if you weren't. The staff would say things like, always smile, because nobody wants a sad child. So I would smile, do everything I was told to do. Then these future parents would tell me that they hoped to see me again, real soon. Which just got your hopes up. And that's all you would think about for the next couple of weeks until you realized that the future parents were just lying, and you would never hear from them again. Once, I liked these future parents so much, I came out and asked them if they would please take me home with them. You're not supposed to do that. But I really wanted them to be my parents. I was getting a little older and I knew my time was running out. I told them that if they made me their son I would do whatever they asked and they would be real proud of me and that I would never do anything to upset them. I started crying. And they didn't know what to do, so I leaned into the future mother so I could give her a hug. I put my arms around her and everything. And she put her arms around me and ran her hand through my hair. Then a social worker separated us, and apologized to the future parents and sent me away with a staff. They ended up taking some other kid anyway, so I just started to give up after awhile. You get tired of being good all the time. You get tired of being good and nothing good ever happens to you and you get nothing in return. Now I don't even think about getting parents anymore. It's not a big deal to me anymore.

We make it to the park. There are a whole bunch of cars already in the parking lot. The future parents are sitting at picnic tables and they look our way and we look their way. I stare until I make contact with one of them, and stare until they look away.

Arnie reminds us what to do. He tells us not to walk up to any of the adults, that we are just supposed to play in the park and act natural. He says not to get dirty if we can help it. He tells us to smile for the hundredth time.

"Hurry up," I say, "This bus reeks of puke."

"Calm down, Jojo," Arnie says.

"You calm down," I say, getting all worked up. "What's the point?"

Arnie ignores me this time.

I glance over the future parents and see them checking us out. All the little kids are staring at me.

"Just look them in the eyes," I say. "It makes them feel guilty. It helps."

"That's enough, Jojo" Arnie says to me.

I watch everybody make their way off the bus. I stay in the backseat, watching.

"You're not coming?" Arnie says.

"Nope."

"You're just going to sit in here and mope?"

"Yep."

"What's your problem Jojo? Why can't you just learn to deal with the situations? Why do you have to act this way? It doesn't do anybody any good. At least look at me when I m talking to you Jojo."

I look up at Arnie. I'm quiet at first, thinking of what I want to say. "What's the point? Nobodies going to want me for their son, I say. You know that and I know that. So what's the point? How old am I? I'm fourteen and how many of those future parents out there want some fourteen year old kid for a son? They want cute little white kids, Arnie. They don't want me. They'll never want me. So, what's the point? I'm sick of it."

Arnie sits in the seat in front of me. "You're absolutely right," Arnie says, "I'm not going to bullshit you anymore. You know the game. And you know how it's played. There's no fooling you. You just never know. That's all I'm saying. I mean you can go out there and at least help out with the other kids. But I understand if you don't want to. Hell, if I were you, I'd be pissed. So I don't blame you if you want to stay in here. Its cool with me," Arnie says, sticking his hand out.

We shake.

Then Arnie leaves.

I take out a cigarette, light it. I watch from the window as the future parents talk to the social workers about us. All the future parents have smiles on their faces, smiling at the kids and smiling at each other because now everything they've been waiting for is actually happening. They look nervous, too. I can tell.

I watch the kids keep looking at them as they pretend to play. Arnie claps his hands, trying to get them in a group, but they're not paying any attention to him. He claps louder and louder, but they pay him no attention. It's pretty funny.

Then Roger starts walking towards the picnic tables where the future parents are. Arnie tries to redirect him, but Roger starts running away from Arnie, heading straight to the picnic tables. Then a few other kids start running towards the picnic tables. The rest follow. A few of them trip or get pushed and fall to the ground. All of them running like hell to get there first, like it's a race and the first one to get there, gets future parents. Problem is, there's way too many kids and not enough future parents. The social workers and the staff try and control the situation, but they can't really do anything about it. All the kids surround the future parents. I know exactly what they're thinking. They're already picking out the ones they want to go home with someday.

Wash, Rinse, Spin

Beth Ann Bauman

Her father is spelling with his finger. M-O-N and then the rest is gibberish. "Slow down," Libby tells him. He slaps the bed sheets and mimics choking her. Without language he's been reduced to bad acting: smirks, eye rolling, mugging. There's no subtlety; even his eyes are luminous and bald. Some days, like today, he's just too tired to move a pen across paper. He blinks up at her and tries again, slicing his angry finger through the air. "Okay, M-O-N." Her mind is as dull and heavy as a butter knife. "Monkey, monsoon, money."

For a second he looks truly helpless and closes his eyes on her, on everything. From the pillow he offers up a bored, calm face; is this the face he'll wear when he's dead? "Do it again. I'm sorry, Dad." Libby tries a laugh. "Pretty please with sugar on top." She's become a moron.

He continues to ignore her, and in their silence the room is kept alive with sound – the bleep of the heart monitor and the earnest, steady wheeze of the ventilator, poking out of his neck and pushing air into his lungs. Her dad then snaps open his eyes and slowly, as if she is brain-damaged, spells M-O-N-T-H.

"Month, for godsakes," Libby says. He rolls his eyes to the ceiling in exaggerated, delicious contempt. Bad moods now swoop down on him in an instant and leave him puzzled and disheveled, hair poking out, gown slipping off a thin shoulder. But as quick as they come, they leave.

He looks at the slice of sky through the narrow window and patiently starts to tell her something, gesturing with his good hand, the one that isn't large and soft as an inflatable paddle.

"October," Libby says. "It's the middle of October." He raises his eyebrows, surprised. They both stare at the little slice of blue sky—they could be looking into a chlorinated pool. Where has the time gone? Libby wonders. Where has her life gone?

Libby's dad has been in the hospital for weeks. Before then, he had a terrible cough that sounded as if he'd hack up a lung, and even though he spent hours in his garden the sun wouldn't tan him. She remembers visiting one Saturday and watching him move unsteadily across the yard, his fingers reaching for the side of the house as the late-day sun cast his long and crooked shadow. After Labor Day he reluctantly went to the doctor and wound up here in the CCU. Each afternoon Libby takes the train from Manhattan, where she lives, to this small tree-lined town in New Jersey, the same town where she grew up, although it's no longer familiar.

While her dad sleeps, Libby rests her head against the chair back and instantly she dreams—dreams that are filled with unpleasant smells and involve public transportation. The infectious disease doctor, who runs, doesn't walk, now flies into the room, waking her. He makes some preliminary pokes and prods before pressing his ear to her dad's chest, as if using the stethoscope would take too long. Before a question forms in her mind, and she has many questions, he's gone, out the door.

Milling in the hall is the useless-though-energetic-and-good-looking oncologist, who won't be treating the tumor clinging to her dad's lung. This tumor, which isn't the worst kind, she's been informed, probably has some relatives that have taken up residence in his spine or liver. No one knows for sure since there's nothing to be done. His heart, sorry to say, simply isn't tough enough. Standing with the oncologist is her dad's primary physician, a squat, morose man who delivers all news in the same monotone. Dumpy Downer—Libby's name for him—is looking to wean her father from the ventilator, maybe send him home for a short while, bring in hospice.

Libby eyes a small bag on the nightstand marked "Libby" and realizes it is from one of her dad's girlfriends. Inside is a jelly doughnut, and as she takes a big bite jelly oozes out the side and a glob lands on her suit. She wipes it off, but a dark, glossy stain remains. Something smells funky and she sniffs the air, wondering if it could be her; she can't remember when she last cleaned her five suits.

Libby stands on the platform waiting for the 8:18 to take her back to the city. Tonight her dad asked her to tell his girlfriends, who are actually ex-girlfriends, not to visit anymore. They talk too much was how he put it. She told him no. The girlfriends arrive in the mornings, often carpooling together, and stay for hours. They are excellent lip readers, excellent mind readers and excellent at charades. They've acquired the good grace that comes with age. They are a flurry of laughter and perfume. There must be people around him, she reasons to herself. She can't imagine he'll up and die in the face of all this activity. She boards the train and it moves swiftly through suburbia, cutting past trees and highways and people walking their dogs under a pale shine of moon. Libby's head lolls against the dirty window as she fights sleep.

Back in her apartment, she sniffs every suit she owns and dumps them into a pile by the door. Four are food-stained and a fifth has a jagged tear from a barb that pierced through the plastic couch in the CCU waiting room and stabbed her in the thigh. "Dry cleaners," she says aloud. She walks around her apartment in a bra and underwear, watering the brown plants, eating a ham sandwich, and holding counsel with herself. "I want the morphine given every two hours, regardless of whether he asks for it. He's not going to ask until it's too late." She nearly trips over a body bag of laundry in the middle of the floor. "Laundry," she shouts. She's almost out of clean clothes, but there's no time to do it. How can she be so weary and buzzed at the same time? "How am I coping?" she asks, cupping her face. She tosses herself onto the bed, finishes eating her sandwich and then curls up under the covers, blowing crumbs toward the wall.

In the morning, she's forced to put on the least sour and wrinkled of the suits, and unfortunately it's the one with the tear in the butt. She stumbles down the stairs with the bag of dirty laundry, the suits piled on top, and lurches up Eighth Avenue toward the laundromat. The suit on the top of the heap is the color of lime juice. Libby heads for the nearest trash can and dumps it, and she also dumps the purple one with the gold buttons because it too, she realizes for the first time, is butt ugly. Without thinking, she stuffs the remaining suits in with her dirty clothes. At the laudromat Hugh the laundry attendant tosses the bag into a giant bin and tells her it will be ready "pronto tonto."

Libby works at the end of a long wing in the semi-vacant legal department of a large corporation, where the air smells of whiskey and cigars and she has very little to do. Gautreaux, Bilox and Sodder, senior attorneys, arrive late each morning, take three-hour alcoholic lunches and return midafternoon, crocked. Each man weaves toward his office, shuts his door and falls asleep on his respective couch. Gautreaux, the most long-winded of the three, sometimes tells her boring stories after these lunches, always ending with a parable or lesson. "You see, girlie," he says, "you see where this is going?" Often he forgets Libby, too, is a lawyer and asks her to water his plants, as he lies helpless and drunken and gurgling on his couch. Once he asked her to call his tailor in Hong Kong and order him another pair of "those natty herringbone trousers."

There are two actual workers, who tirelessly seem to do the work of the whole department: Mr. Muskon and his trusted assistant Miss Perry. Apparently, there once was a departmental secretary, known as Imelda because she was always sneaking off to buy shoes, who disappeared and can't be accounted for.

Acquisition forms arrive midmorning each day in a wire cart pushed by Marianne Switzer. First Bilox, the one with the bowtie, initials the stack, then Libby, Gautreaux, and Sodder. Afterwards, Libby rings Marianne Switzer, who arrives twelve minutes later with her wire cart to whisk the forms to the third floor for further processing. In a nutshell, this is Libby's job. When she asked Gautreaux about more work, he'd said, "All in good time, Pearl." Who was Pearl? She'd started to look for something else, but then her dad got sick, and now she's stuck in her no-job job.

Growing up, Libby's dad had been a good father from a distance. His attention never landed directly on her, but good energy radiated off him in all directions and she felt it as a kind of love.

When Libby was small, her mother's cousin's kid Wilhelmina from New York City spent several summers with them. Wilhelmina was a sour girl, tough as a spike, whose favorite game was Choir Girl, a sadistic version of church in which Wilhelmina would play the plastic organ, and Libby, draped in a sheet and Amish bonnet, would solemnly descend the staircase and make her way behind her father's recliner, which was the pew. When Libby got the speed of her descent right, which wasn't often, there would be communion of the watery scotch left in the bottom of her father's glass. Or if Wilhelmina was feeling chipper, the host might be a gumball, although chewing wasn't allowed. Most times they didn't get to communion because Libby didn't descend the staircase slowly enough, and Wilhelmina would pinch Libby hard, hissing, "*You're not doing it right.*"

Once during these church services, Libby's dad reclined in his chair with a copy of the *Tribune* held out in front of him as his bonneted and glum daughter worked her way to and from the pew. Perhaps because Wilhelmina was no relation of his, he caught Libby's eye, pointed to the organ-playing girl, and twirled his finger next to his ear. At this, Libby dove onto his lap while he continued, serenely, humming a happy tune, to read the paper. Wilhelmina, sensing a conspiracy, lifted her bony fingers off the keys and glared at them.

Libby's parents divorced when she was twelve, and she divided her time between them, travelling from one end of town to the other with her ratty blue suitcase. Her mother sighed a lot during Libby's teenage years while her dad threw himself into goodwill and charity. Each year he planted an enormous garden and went door-to-door distributing his eggplants and zucchinis, and it was in this way that he met his three girlfriends.

All the equipment in the hospital room gives off a smothering heat that leaves Libby and her dad sticky and soft-brained. A portable fan, precariously balanced atop a garbage can, makes a low, jumbly noise while Libby feeds him ice chips. She's not doling them out fast enough and he snatches the cup, shoveling in three or four chips with his good hand before she grabs it back. "It's gonna go right into your lung and you'll turn blue," she tells him.

"Kiss my ass," he mouths.

"Dad, you can kiss mine."

"Go," he writes. "I'll sleep."

Libby is suddenly so tired, so very tired. She stiffly lowers herself into a chair. Does he really think she can just leave? Each time this happens, she is frightened to think that he might believe she really will leave, that her leaving would be all right with him. She wonders what kind of a life he imagines she has in the city while he is here. "Won't you be lonely without me?" she asks.

"Boring?" he writes. "Hanging out with the old man?"

It's true, dying is boring and tedious among all the other terrible things ascribed to it.

"Boyfriends?" he writes.

"Not at the moment," she says.

"None in this joint," he writes. She frowns. He shrugs with a small smile.

"Pain in the ass," he scribbles on his pad, pointing to himself. She nods. He points to the same words, and then points to Libby. She half-smiles. He writes the word "Talking," circles it, and then draws a diagonal line through it. In solidarity, she zippers her lip.

On TV, Fred Astaire dances across the screen. "Fred again," he mouths. Every time they turn on the TV Fred seems to be swinging around a pole or dipping Ginger. Such poise, such dexterity, such sheer joy. Fred exhausts them. Her dad reaches for her hand and closes his eyes. As he falls asleep, he slides down the pillows and rests lump-like in the middle of the bed. The ventilator keeps a steady, dull rhythm. Something livelier, like a salsa, would better encourage health and healing, she thinks. As he sleeps, his fingers fly up to the ventilator and he wakes. It's been weeks, but he still hasn't gotten used to the tube protruding from his neck. Often he makes like Frankenstein's monster, jutting his arms out in front of him, widening his eyes and letting his mouth go slack. "Your kind of poison," he once scribbled on a pad.

"Not anymore," she'd snapped.

Before her no-job job, and before law school, Libby worked on the production crew of low-budget horror/sci-fi movies that went straight to video. The actors were snarly and unprofessional, the pay was crap and the hours spilled into each other, leaving her with no time for a life. They often shot several movies at once, and in holding at any given time there might have been a group of corpses playing poker, assorted fanged creatures complaining about the air-conditioning, and gross-out, flesh-eating lumps chowing down on meatball heroes. Libby raced from set to set, where several times a day she'd get chewed out for not doing something she hadn't known she was supposed to do in the first place. There were some compensations: Libby, who was never good with clothes, had Jane, her best friend in wardrobe, help her dress when she was dating the cute though underachieving cyclops, Peter. Jane would flip through racks and come up with something chic yet understated, maybe slutty footwear; there was always plenty of this stuff on hand for the hapless heroine whose job was to traipse unwittingly through the cool, serene world before meeting early doom.

One day when none of the bloody corpses was cooperating—one even had the nerve to snap gum while lying on a stone slab under a fake moon—and the director futzed endlessly with the lighting, Libby parked herself behind a tombstone and filled out law school applications.

"But you like the ghoulies," her dad had said.

"I don't."

"Well, all right."

"I'm going to be a lawyer. It's *great* news, dad."

"I'll say. You can write my will. You get everything. Make sure none of my girlfriends get anything." Ironically, he is generous to a fault. He bought Geri a barbecue, Sue an aquarium, and Mary a front-end loader, even when she had moved to ex-girlfriend status. He didn't expect much in return and rarely phoned the girlfriends. He claimed to hate the phone, referring to it as the "squawk box," and yet he called Libby every Saturday without fail.

Early the next morning, Libby puts on a coat over her bra and underwear and heads to the laundromat, but Hugh can't find her laundry bag. "It's *huge*," Libby says, cornering him by the fabric softener. "Where could it have gone?" She tries to remember what was in there—shirts, jeans, fuzzy slippers.

"Man," Hugh says, dejectedly. "I don't know what to say."

"Find it!" she says, giving him her address. "Apartment 2G. Two." She holds up two fingers. "G as in goddamn it."

At home, she pulls out her horror clothes, a speckled mess of paint- and fake-blood-splattered T-shirts and holey jeans. So comfy, she'd forgotten.

A handsome young kid who reminds Libby of Neil Lubin, who was supposed to ask her to the prom but never did, pushes a wire cart down the east wing as she sits at Imelda's desk.

"Filing?" he asks. Libby gives him her letter to Gautreaux's tailor, requesting another pair of the size 42 herringbone trousers with a little more room in the seat, please. The handsome kid puts it in his empty cart and winks at her before speeding the single sheet down the hall to the filing room.

The women's bathroom in the east wing is always empty, with Imelda gone and Miss Perry not seeming to have the need, but today someone pees in unison with Libby. They exit the stalls at the same time, and Libby stands face-to-face with Miss Perry, who eyes Libby's outfit with concern. As Libby washes her hands, staring into her raw and crusty eyes in the mirror, she suddenly confides to Miss Perry about her dad.

"Dear, you must go to him now. Give me your work," Miss Perry says, kindness and duty shining in her eyes.

"But I don't have any."

Miss Perry looks at her incredulously. "Well, then you must go now." She ushers Libby to the east wing coat closet, and by this time Libby is crying, crying because why hadn't she gone to the prom? So when Miss Perry accidentally grabs Bilox's coat—long and black, woven with a touch of cashmere—Libby is mildly aware it isn't hers, but what difference does it make at a time like this? Little Bilox, tidy and delicate as an egg in a nest, is just her size, and she grabs her token and flees to the subway.

When Bilox comes in the next day wearing her coat, at first Libby thinks he's just being polite by not mentioning the mix-up. But when he leaves for an early appointment, he slips into her velvet-collared wool coat and waves at the room before departing.

It's not that surprising when the sepsis comes. Her dad's body has been invaded at too many points and the armies of antibodies wave a white flag. A ridiculous fever shakes his entire body, a smoldering heat rises from his limbs, and the back of his head, which has been pressed against a pillow for weeks, reveals a strange and snarled hairdo.

Sepsis isn't a bad way to go, the Dumpy Downer tells her. The toxic shock brings on delirium and then coma, after which her dad would float away to a better place, leaving behind his soggy body. Her dad wears a finger cap to monitor his oxygenation, which isn't good, and in his furor he pulls it off and the machine begins a steady ding. Libby places the cap on her own finger and the room is quiet again. Why didn't she fight with that Gestapo nurse yesterday — let him have the damned milkshake! Really, what are they doing here? She doesn't know if she's done right by her father, and she's not sure he's done right by her. He's abandoning ship, and she blames him a little.

Libby walks the twenty blocks from Penn Station to her apartment just to feel the cold breath of air on her face. On the way, she stops in a Korean market and buys a beer and drinks it out of a paper bag. It's late, but when she gets to her door she finds Hugh sitting on the stoop, holding a bag of laundry as if it is a small child. "Maybe you'd like this," he says.

"You can't give me someone else's laundry," she says, peering into the bag.

"It's been in the lost and found for a year, man." He looks at her kindly. "You could probably use some underwear, right?"

"Well, you're sure this is nobody's?" Maybe there are some towels inside. She needs a clean towel. Bingo. Inside are four towels, several aprons, knee socks, a large shapeless sweatshirt with many zippered pockets, and a daisy-printed muumuu.

And so this becomes her routine: in the mornings, Libby pulls on her soft and comfy horror clothes and puts

Bilox's coat over the colorful, shabby mess. Then she dashes to the office, sits at Imelda's desk chewing a nail, waits for Marianne Switzer and her wire cart, runs the forms in to Bilox, then Gautreaux, then Sodder, adds her own initials in four minutes flat, phones Marianne Switzer for a pick-up, dashes down the hall at the sound of the breakfast cart, shovels a doughnut into her mouth, tosses Miss Perry a sesame buttered bagel, snatches Bilox's coat from the east wing coat closet, runs for the elevators, thinks bad thoughts all the way to the lobby, flies through the double doors, takes the shuttle across town, hops on the 2 or 3 to Penn Station, scrambles for a ticket, steps onto the Jersey-bound train and falls into a wicked hot sleep.

Libby's mother calls late one night from Chicago, where she's married to a placid radiologist. "Tell me how I can help," she says.

"Do you want to see Dad?"

"Well, no, not that," she says. "I'll come visit you!"

"But I'm never here."

Today Libby's cab sits in a traffic jam en route to the hospital. She pays the driver and gets out and walks, her feet crunching over autumn leaves. Directly across from the hospital is a mini-mall with a deli, a clothes shop and a laundromat. Above the stores are apartments with tiny curtained windows. I should move here, she thinks, digging her hands in Bilox's pockets, which are filled with crumbled bills, sticks of gum, train tickets, ATM receipts.

Her dad's pulled through the sepsis, and he's looking good. In fact, as he becomes sicker he's more alert and the color has returned to his cheeks. Maybe this is some kind of crazy antibiotic flush, a crazy antibiotic buzz.

A boisterous nurse with a smock that pulls across her stomach announces it's time for cognitive tests. "Cyril, who's the president of the United States?" she asks, checking his intravenous bags. As his body grows waterlogged and inert, they need to check and see that he's still home.

Her dad makes little effort to hide his irritation, but he is more of a charmer than a crab, even in sickness, and finally he smiles wearily. "George Washington," he mouths.

"All right, wise guy," she says. "Let's try movies and entertainment for $500."

He scribbles on his pad, "Frankly my dear I don't give a flying," and then for modesty's sake he's drawn a line.

"Oh!" she hollers. "Cyril's getting fresh." He offers a half-smile and a silent laugh. He's always been handsome and easy in a reluctant way. Sometimes while he sleeps, the nurses will confide to Libby, "I like your father."

Now as they joke, Libby sees he's already folding in on himself. "Are you in pain?" she whispers. For a moment he's quiet, then shakes his head. He can't name it. They don't have a language for any of this. Libby pats his hand, and his fingers wriggle against the sheet as if movement might carry him somewhere else.

As Libby walks down Eighth Avenue, shivering and drinking a beer out of a paper bag, she bumps into Hugh from the laundromat, who tells her he will personally do her laundry this time. Funny, she asks, but isn't it his personal job to do all the incoming laundry? He tells her he will protect her garments as if her jeans and underwear are the Ten Commandments delivered by God to Moses. She considers letting him wash her horror clothes, but she doesn't trust him. Instead she asks him if he wants to sleep with her. He arrives a bit later, shyly slurping on a chocolate drink, and she greets him at the door wearing the daisy-printed muumuu.

Her law school friends start taking her out for dinners when she arrives back at Penn Station late in the evenings. They eye her speckled clothes, the same mess of a wardrobe she wore through law school, and her headbanded friend Marcy suddenly offers to take her shopping at Loehmann's. "Maybe it's time we found your softer side," she whispers. Libby, tired and drunk, says, "Maybe it's time for one of my friends to do my frigging laundry." But the laundromat can do it for her, Marcy insists. Libby just smiles. They have better jobs than hers, and they insist on tiramisu and picking up the checks. Hang in there, they say nicely.

Her horror friends bring over Chinese food late at night when she's already under the covers in a bathing suit and knee socks, and they spread out all over the floor, eating lo mein with their fingers and discussing tracheotomies, incontinence and hemorrhaging. Sleep, they tell her, we'll lock up when we leave.

Late one evening, Peter the cyclops calls. He's heard about her dad and wants to know if there's anything he can do.

Libby, though wound up and hungry, feels touched. "Come over and do my laundry for me one day."

"No, really?"

"Really."

He hedges and then suggests she take it to the laundromat, where they'll wash, dry and even fold it. Imagine that. "One, two, three," he says.

"I did that and they lost my freaking laundry," she tells him. "It's gone. Vanished!"

"Really?"

"What do you want, Peter?" He's quiet, and it's clear he has nothing to offer. But never mind him; what can she expect from a cyclops? Libby discovers deep in the recesses of her dresser drawer many wearable things—old tank tops and lacy bras still with the tags. She's running out of clothes again, but there's still something for the morning.

She stuffs her laundry into a backpack, all of it, including the bathing suits and the muumuu, and she takes it to the office, where she packs it up in one of Gautreaux's Seagram's boxes. She addresses the overnight packing slip to the hospital, calls the mailroom for a pick-up, and ten minutes later a young man with a wire cart carries the box away.

There is some problem with the elevators. Flashing lights, a bleating noise. Misbuttoning Bilox's coat, Libby weakly considers the stairs, but then she spots the handsome kid who looks like Neil Lubin, who didn't take her to the prom, as he rolls his empty wire cart down the hall. "Is there another way out?" she asks.

"There's always a way out," he says slyly. "Freight elevator."

"Show me," Libby says, hanging onto his sleeve. She's bone-tired and wants a helping hand. Without thinking, she hoists herself onto Imelda's desk and lowers herself into his wire cart. "I have a freaking headache," she explains. He is as kind as he is good-looking. He finds her an aspirin and gives her a paper towel to blow her nose and deposits her outside the service entrance at 44th and Lexington, where a light rain mists their heads.

The next day, the doctors make another attempt to wean her dad from the ventilator, but he struggles for breaths and his eyes dart wildly around the room. Both he and Libby stare anxiously at the monitor, which measures his vital signs, as if this will make his lungs work better. He starts mouthing words, and she stands there dumbly, trying to understand until finally she runs into the hall yelling, "He can't do it! He can't!"

Now, exhausted, he sleeps. Libby sits beside him, patting his hand. She wears a cocktail dress, argyle knee socks and the large, shapeless sweatshirt with many zippered pockets. On her dad's nightstand she notices a trick-or-treat bag decorated with goblins and witches. There's a note attached that reads, "Libby, provisions for the long haul. How you doing?" Inside are a combination of sweets and health foods and multivitamins. Libby's eyes tear up, and she is overwhelmed with love for the girlfriends and finds herself wishing they were her friends, wishing her dad could have another chance with one of them if he wanted it.

A friendly nurse brings in the Seagram's box and says, "Do you know what this is?" Before Libby can get out of the chair, the nurse tears off the cover of the box, and together they stare down at the dirty, faintly smelly laundry.

"Mine," Libby says.

Libby grabs quarters from her purse and then shifts through the trick-or-treat bag, stuffing one of her zippered pockets with a V-8 juice, another with homemade chocolate chip cookies and another with a bottle of multivitamins. The Seagram's box is large and cumbersome, and she weaves unsteadily down the hall until she finds an abandoned wheelchair to place it on. Outside, she rolls the wheelchair across the street to the mini-mall and into the laundromat, past the long line of washers, all of which are in use. The attendant, an elderly man who jingles with coins, looks at her strangely and tells her to come back later. She leaves the Seagram's box and wheels the chair back to the hospital.

Later, when she returns, the air has changed. The darkening sky is a swirl of winter grays, like an old bruise. The same attendant pushes a mop and tells her he's closing in five minutes. She sits on the folding table, as if her unmovable presence will make him soften. The cocktail dress rides up her thighs, exposing the bare skin above her argyle socks. She touches the stubbly hairs.

The attendant sweeps lint into a pile and eyeballs her sitting on the folding table. "I can lock you in, if that's what you want. Do you want me to lock you in?"

"All right." You can never be locked in, only locked out, she reasons. "I'll be very neat," she tells him.

The man finishes sweeping and ties up several garbage bags, turning to her every so often to see if she is still there. Libby tries to smile, but can't quite pull one off. Her body feels leaden and she's struck with the terrible feeling that maybe she, too, is dying. She pats her ears and then feels her neck for enlarged lymph nodes. Reaching into one of the zippered pockets, she pulls out the vitamins and dumps a couple on her tongue. She unzips another pocket and washes them down with a V-8, then unzips another pocket and nibbles on a cookie. She slides her hand under the sweatshirt and does a discreet mini breast exam.

As soon as the man leaves, she separates the whites and darks, gathers her quarters and gets three loads going. She stretches out on the folding table, looks over at the sloshing, soapy water and feels a kind of hope. Please God, she thinks. She doesn't wish for anything in particular, just that things remain as they are a while longer; she simply needs to be suspended in the moment. Time, she believes, is a kind of hope.

The police escort her back to the nurses' station, where the nurses gather around her. There's whispering. The elderly laundry attendant confides, not quietly, that "she looked like a crazy to me." Dumpy Downer impatiently eyes the small crowd and moves toward Libby, touching her elbow.

"I need to speak with you and your father," he says.

"What about my laundry?" Libby asks, looking at the cops, then the nurses and then the mean-spirited laundry attendant. Everyone talks at once, and the cop's radio sputters at noisy intervals. "We know her. It's fine," the friendly nurse says. "There's no need to make a fuss," the boisterous nurse says. Dumpy Downer is now yanking on her arm. Finally, the cops and nurses wind up flirting with each other as Libby is pulled into her dad's room, and the door is closed behind them.

The bottom line, begins Dumpy Downer, is that her dad can't live without a ventilator. His lungs can't do it. They've made every effort. Sad to say, but there's no justification for keeping him in CCU. He'll have to go upstairs to the ventilator wing. The doctor frowns. He's been through so much. There is another option. They can put him on a morphine drip, make him as comfortable as possible, turn off the ventilator and leave it in God's hands. Libby reels, feeling static travel up her neck and gather in her head. She slumps into a chair. God, she thinks; what does He have to do with it, the slacker. Staring at Dumpy Downer's round, freckled head, she can tell he's not a believer. He believes in medicine, and medicine's failed here. Well, off to the ventilator wing.

"Let's turn off this goddamn thing," her dad writes on his pad. He's sitting up, a picture of health. You flip the switch on invalids; her dad looks as if he could be going to the grocery store. Really, if anyone were to ask, she would have thought that a dying person would be half-gone, unrecognizable, yet her dad is here, terribly present, cocking his head to the side when he hears something dumb. When a vein quivers beneath his eye, he reaches up to touch it.

"Think good and hard," the doctor says, with a finger raised for emphasis. "Good luck, sir."

The doctor shuts the door behind him, and Libby and her dad are left staring at each other. "What an asshole," her dad mouths. She sobs, lowering her head to the bed, and she feels his fingers dance across her hair, light and graceful as Fred Astaire. They are quiet for some time. Finally, she closes her eyes and almost reaches sleep, but at the last second she rushes back from it and lifts her head.

He's laughing without sound. On his pad he's written, "Would you want to go to ventilator wing??? What kind of characters are up there?" He's drawn a picture of a skinny little figure covered in a cobweb. She shakes her head. Why make decisions? She wants to hang out. She's got this crazy routine down.

But then he does the unthinkable. He reaches for her hand, tells her how much he loves her, how everything will be okay. He's reaching for movement, to move beyond this moment; his decision's been made. How dare this hospital rush them, how dare they. She simply isn't ready. She heads for the door, throws it open and yells into the quiet, pale hallway, "DO NOT RUSH US!"

The nurses' station is unoccupied, but on a wheelchair by the door is the Seagram's box filled with clean, folded laundry. She touches it, and it's still warm.

The Garden Plot

Philip F. Deaver

In the middle of the block, behind Dave and April's house, isolated on all sides from street access, was a triangle of land which the neighbors had informally subdivided into garden spots. The city had once planned to put a park there, but never got around to it. Rocky had had a garden out there for several summers, maybe three, and he knew the history of things in the garden area. He was the kind of guy who was always on top of things around the home, whether it be putting out a garden or putting on his own addition, or artfully introducing a woodburning stove to his den.

Dave, on the other hand, was always a little behind the game around the house, and, despite the symbolic unmanning of it, even had Rocky over once to help him when a gutter fell off. But this spring Dave and April had ambitiously decided (very late) to have a garden, and by that time the Kimballs, a frail, tottering, great-grandparentish couple who didn't even live adjacent to the land but resided across the street and down a ways, had staked off an enormous garden exactly where Dave and April would have put theirs if they had one, just over their back fence.

April was mildly irritated at the Kimballs for being out there at all, and for taking nearly all the area available to her for her garden. Off to the side, she had tentatively placed several tomato plants, plants she'd sprouted from seed in the kitchen beginning back in February. She placed them the best she could, trying to secure a sunny spot out of the Kimball's way but where the hose would reach from the house for watering. The spot was quite modest in comparison to the truck farm-sized operation the Kimballs had going.

The first Dave heard there was a problem had been in early May. It was on a Friday, and April and Dave met at McDonald's for lunch.

"Virginia Kimball shouted at me in the garden area today," April told him as they slid into one of the plastic booths. "She said I was on 'her land.'"

When April said garden area, Dave's mind went blank. She may have mentioned it before, that there was a problem with the Kimball's, and he'd never heard—he wasn't sure. In March it seemed like a good idea, this garden. In May, Dave was on to other things. He looked down at the seat in the space next to him, where a previous patron had left the morning paper. He tried to speed-read the sports page while April talked. The Cardinals were in an early-season slump, and Whitey Herzog had just announced to the *St. Louis Globe-Democrat* that he had never seen such a terrible hitting team.

"I know," April said. "You're thinking 'here we go.'"

One columnist wrote some pointed criticism of Herzog for speaking out like that against his own guys, especially so early in the season. Managers aren't supposed to do that.

"I know you think we shouldn't be out there anyway," she said. "Because we never have a garden, we aren't gardeners, we don't have the touch. No green thumb. Right? You're not really crazy about having a garden anyway. Right? Anymore?"

Clearly, if the Cards were going to stay in the race they were going to have to count on the Mets sustaining some injuries.

"Don't look at me like that," April said, and it was only then that Dave realized he was looking at her at all. "Nevermind then," she said.

Dave could see that she was hurt by his look, and he was unaware of what look it was. He tried to cover even though he hadn't heard her.

"Did Rocky like the Kimball's?"

"I don't know. See, Virginia is just plain tough—I mean really. She's made of granite. I can't talk to her."

Dave had seen the old woman out there a few times. Virginia Kimball wore old flowered dresses, a black Amish bonnet, gloves and actual galoshes when she worked in the garden area. Rocky, a perennial gardener of course, knew the Kimball's from the summer before and continually warned April about them. Evidently they'd begun with a modest garden that previous year, and during the course of the season had encroached on other garden space and gotten sideways with most of the other neighbors out there. It made Dave positively weary to hear about all of this from April, knowing how it was so completely occupying her time and her mind.

"Did you hear that Jimmy Buffet's going to be here in concert?" There was an ad in the paper—he'd heard about it a couple days ago and kept forgetting to see if April might want to go.

"Rocky agrees. He says those people—and particularly Virginia—are tough, and they know exactly what they're doing. Last year they swiped other people's space and were cranky all the time like they were the victims. Rocky said he knows he shouldn't, but he hates them."

Dave had heard about disputes in the garden area the previous year, and that was one of the excuses Dave would use in explaining why he and April had decided not to have a garden then (not that they'd ever really had a garden in their lives April would clarify).

"I just don't think I have time to spend the summer bickering," Dave said.

"People manage to work it out. C'mon. We've never had a garden."

"Bickering, bickering. Maybe people like it, I don't know."

"Are you saying I thrive on this?"

"One family stopped speaking to anyone and eventually moved—what was their name?"

"Parmenters, and he was transferred. C'mon. It isn't that bad. We just. . . we have to . . . "

"Communicate. One guy put up rope to separate his stuff from everybody else's. The Bookers simply petitioned the city to buy the whole works. Rocky himself—he's got marriage problems because of all this tension. Bickering, bickering."

"That's not it," she said, in Rocky's defense. "It's not marriage problems—just normal stuff."

"Doesn't anybody out there have anything else to do but fight and argue and bicker?" Dave said. "By midsummer you got flowers and potatoes and beans and sweetcorn and the whole area's a wonderland of gardenly delights, the wives out there tending the plants and while the husbands stand guard, for God sake—it sounds like Jamestown in 1750." Dave laughed to himself about it, the human comedy played out in the garden area behind his house.

Mostly he wrote it all off. Just what you'd expect. People get a little free land, they start fighting over it. He stayed clear. He laughed to himself about the follies of human nature, how predictable behavior could be. In his mind, he saw Austria and Hungary and France and Germany and Czechoslovakia facing off in the garden area, or Texas and Mexico, the cattlemen and the sheep herders, or all the old battles between villages in feudal times. Secretly, he had a little trouble believing Virginia Kimball was as cranky as people said. He was pretty sure the fault was shared equally among the combatants in the garden area. Human nature.

One day, a week after the McDonald's conversation, April phoned him at the office (he worked on staff at the university where day in and day out he heard all the bitching he needed to hear) and told him Virginia had put out stakes and string and had actually staked April away from some of her own plants. Virginia's case was that she had a right to that footage, that she had been fertilizing and preparing that ground since last fall for this garden.

That sounded reasonable to Dave.

"We *were* a little late getting out there," he said.

"Dave! She cut my tomatoes!"

"Well, now, honey," he said, "do we have any plants left?"

"A little more than half of them, I guess."

"She cut half of them? Jesus. She must be pretty mad." He heard April sigh on the other end. "Look," he said. "Let's just leave it at that and not get in a big thing. This is kind of a squatter's rights deal, sounds like. Sounds like Mrs. Kimball's got you, squatter's rights. We'll have half as many tomatoes to give away because we have too many for us." He chuckled, trying to get April to lighten up.

"Well, it's the principle of the thing, David!" She was upset. "I was standing right there," April muttered after a moment.

"If she prepared the ground since last fall, principle may be on her side. Squatters' rights with a grandmother clause." He chuckled. "Great grandmother, in fact, probably—look, I don't know what to tell you. Want me to come home? Call the police? What do you want?"

"Grandmother clause. Cute," April said. "The whole idea was that the people who lived adjacent to this space would have gardens, not that everybody in town would. But I'm not disputing her garden. I just want . . . "

"C'mon. You don't want the Kimball's out there at all, c'mon—"

"Dave!—a small slice . . . "

"April, it's me, your spouse. Tell me. You don't want them out there at all, because they aren't very likable and they took the space logic would have reserved for us. Say it."

"Look," she said, all pumped up. "I want a piece of space for myself, right there close to the house, that's it, that's all I want. Rocky and some of the other people out there, they say Kimball's garden is way too big for Virginia Kimball to handle and she's just being a pig. That's the first thing.

"Secondly, my plants weren't anywhere near any of hers. Rocky broke the ground for me with his tiller clear back in March, and she never complained. Six foot square. Nothing. This is a little area I'm pushing for. I'm not in this woman's way out there." Now there were tears coming. "Then the bitch—I put plants out, and she cuts them down. Marigolds, tomatoes. Chopped." Now April was away from the phone getting Kleenex.

Dave could imagine how this atmosphere would stir up an old couple, too. They came through life in rural times. People put up barns for one another, had dances and festivals, shared food and company in order to weather the hard years—wartimes and depression. Community as a concept had done a lot of deteriorating since then. Most of the neighbors working in the garden area, they were from somewhere else—they weren't local, didn't know the area back in simpler, more real times, didn't go to these schools as children, and so on—strangers, hooked to the privacy, mobility and achievement cycle and never putting down roots or subjecting themselves to the accountability of generations, or so it must have seemed to the Kimballs.

Dave didn't mean to be unsupportive of his wife, but it just wasn't a clear case of us right, them wrong. These poor people had outlived the neighborly rural times, and now were trying to get along in a dog-eat-dog world where everybody was 35 except them and they were 90. He felt for them. This was the kind of deal people always talked about, how the older people just aren't getting a fair shake in this world. It's what drove these proud elderly citizens into the squalor of nursing homes. Frankly, Dave hated being a part of it, and he hated April being a part of it.

Virginia's husband, D. Y., was a decorated WWI veteran, positively picturesque, ancient and gray haired, a kind, soft, white face like an old parson. On Memorial Day, he was usually photographed by the town paper, heading up the VFW parade or standing at attention in his chrome Army helmet at the grave of the town's unknown soldier. The old man still insisted upon driving everywhere, and Dave would see the large blue aging Ford Galaxy go by, notice a new dent in the front, a new rip in the bumper, or once the car passed dragging what looked like thirty pounds of sod from someone's yard hooked to the bottom, pulled out of the ground by its roots when D. Y., somewhere in an ostensibly simple three block trip to the grocery, had missed the street. Always wearing a suit and tie, intense about his business, his hat down, his body bent forward over the wheel, D. Y. would drive by Dave's house at half the speed of progress, behind him a line of cranky taxiing moms bumper to bumper, late for dance lessons and little league practice. Whenever D. Y. backed out of his driveway on Tuesdays, the rear end of the car came all the way across the street and into the yard of Abe

Minever, routinely flattening his garbage cans. D. Y. would shift gears and drive away, never noticing. Minever called the police on him a couple of times for that, but the police allowed that it was an accident and that Mr. Kimball was aging and perhaps declining in his ability to navigate a car and they sent over some guys and a truck and got the mess cleaned up, which usually calmed Minever down.

One afternoon in late May, April called Dave at the office with an update. She was getting hesitant with him about this subject, because he showed so little patience about it and seemed in many ways to blame her.

"She hoed my tomatoes."

"All of them?"

"There are a few left, five or six. Why do you keep asking that? How many does she have to get? We require a complete massacre before there's a concern."

"Don't use that word. I hate the new way people are saying 'concern.' Nobody can say 'terrible, ghastly, perplexing problem' anymore. They say there's a 'concern.'"

"She's moved over the stakes and string. She's cut my little plants. Goddamn it, it's a terrible, ghastly, perplexing problem of a growing nature. What am I going to do, David?"

"Five or six is enough, really. Tomato plants. How many did Rocky have last year—he gave us so many bushels I tried to make V-8 juice with the blender, remember? We don't need many plants, April. We can get plenty of tomatoes from five or six if Virginia prepared the ground well in the fall."

"You are hopeless," April said. "Rocky said he'd cut down a few of her beans to square accounts."

"Great. Let's get in a big . . . "

"Hopeless!"

"Okay. Let's get in big, major thing with a ninety two year old woman who just wants to have a garden before she dies. Wonderful. Let's have a great summer turning the neighborhood into an armed camp over some tomatoes. April, do me a favor," Dave said. "Go out in the garden area and communicate with Virginia Kimball. You have a specialty in 18th century literature—you should be able to speak her language."

"Oh, that's so cute, David—you show these people less respect than I do, with that kind of talk. I swear . . . "

Dave laughed but April didn't. "Ah, geez. Look, Hon," he said. "What you do is, you ask her what she wants, negotiate, come up with an agreement. And let's get the hell on with life." He was conscious of his voice carrying in his office, out the door to the area where his secretary was sitting. April was silent. "Ask her what she wants, April. Get it clear, get it out on the table. Give a little, get a little. What do you say to that? Babe? April?"

April was off the line.

That evening when Dave got home, April wasn't there. The kids were gone, too. He looked through the house for them. The toys were scattered, dishes were on the table from breakfast, the TV wasn't warm. It was as though they'd left suddenly. Around ten she came home, the kids asleep in the back seat. The two of them silently worked to get the kids out of the car and carried them to their respective beds, worked their playclothes off of them and worked them into their pajamas, tucked them in. Dave made a couple of tries at conversation, but it wasn't going to happen. She was still mad about the phone call. He finally went to bed.

The next day she didn't call at all, and, while he wondered, he didn't call her either. That evening when he got home April's car was parked askew in the carport, the left turn signal still blinking and the driver-side door open. The key was still in place, and the battery was still trying to let the world know with a high, sad and wavering whine. The kids were playing out in front and hadn't had supper. The hamper was upside down in the hall, and the dishwasher was open and leaking. April was crying in the bedroom. Things appeared to be coming apart.

"She staked off the whole area. I tried to stake off my remaining plants, and she hit my string with her hoe."

"Are your tomatoes all gone?"

"There it is again—your only earthly question on this topic."

"Are they?"

"No. But they're behind her string."

"They're on 'her land' now? How about I go out and move the string."

"You sure you want to get in a big thing with this nice old lady?" She was face down on the bed, talking into her damp pillow.

Dave sat down on the edge of the bed, put his hand on her back. "I'll move the string."

"She'll cut your goddamned string."

"How about I go out and do it while she's there, tomorrow. And if she trespasses, I'll talk with her about it. I'm telling you something, honey—we got a failure here . . . "

"Okay, Cool Hand Luke," she muttered into the pillow. "You get out there and communicate." Dave could tell she was glad he was entering the fray. Clearly, somebody needed to take charge and settle it.

So, that was the plan. And sure enough, on Saturday morning, Virginia was out at the crack of dawn. From the bedroom window Dave could hear her out there working in her garden. Sometimes she'd catch her breath in her old steel lawn chair which she'd taken back there and placed in the embracing shade of Dave and April's mountain maple. This must be how life looked everywhere in 1919, Dave thought, lying on his stomach on the bed, looking out the window through the narrow crack beneath the pulled shade. He watched her for a while. So solitary and peaceful out there in the morning air. He thought for a moment he caught a glimpse of the mood and essence of gardening, what it was that everybody liked about it. The quiet, primal labor of it, the nurturing. He got up, put on his old basketball jersey, a pair of shorts, and some sandals, and went out in his back yard. He pretended to be doing things out there, until the old woman's movements took her near the postage stamp-sized area April was contesting for. Dave recognized April's spot because it looked like a tomato's version of Custer's Battlefield.

Dave took April's little hand-hoe and went out the back gate and into the garden area.

"Good morning, Mrs. Kimball," he said, conscious of the generous, communicative smile he was offering her, and she said nothing back. Possibly hadn't heard him, since her back was turned. He hadn't said it loudly, but he had meant to convey pleasure, happiness, like the song-birds when the sun is just up.

Dave saw her new stakes and April's old ones. The stakes were in place and the cut string just dangled across weeds at the side. Dave decided it would be as easy as reconnecting the string. He dug a little around the decapitated sprouts, and then reached over and took both ends of the string and in a moment had masterfully rendered a square knot and that was that. If he had to connect the string to a stake, he might try the bowline hitch, which he hadn't thought of for fifteen years. The string was re-established. The woman worked nearby, head down, bent over, and paid no mind. Things were quite peaceable, so Dave weeded a bit around the beleaguered remaining tomato plants on his re-established turf. He could hear Mrs. Kimball working. From time to time he'd look her way. A relic from rural times, she was so natural, bending into her garden toil, her flowered dress disappearing behind a denim apron, her old but freshly sharpened hoe glistening in the morning sun. This was a good life, a fresh air kind of life, the way things were meant to be.

That's something you forget, Dave thought to himself—you forget the realities of sex in disputes like this. Women might tend to get in squabbles, and a couple of men might square off out there and settle it straightaway, but a man and a woman, no matter what their relative ages—well, some different dynamic is operating. They might not squabble. They might actually mesh.

"You know, this is really a fine morning," he said toward her, and he really meant it. He thought she might even have acknowledged his statement. Some movement she made seemed to acknowledge him and what he was saying. Anyway, after a while Dave realized there wouldn't be a conversation, and he began to sort of get into gardening, hoeing a precious little ditch so that water could travel to the plants from the length of garden hose April had stretched out that way from the tap on the side of the house. One optimistic and somewhat naive tomato sproutling had actually been so presumptuous as to pick itself back up and apparently start to sprout a second layer of leaves, which Dave dutifully pinched off so it would grow from the bottom. He didn't even know if that was the right thing to do, but it worked with coleus. Then he remembered that plants and man have a symbiotic relationship and that he could safely go with his instincts on this. He hoed some more rows and was happy that April had decided to have a garden this year.

When suddenly he heard a twang, and his repaired string was down again.

"Ah. Mrs. Kimball. My wife mentioned that, that you and she didn't agree on the garden boundaries." The woman didn't really acknowledge him, and again he was certain she hadn't heard him. Her head was down and she was hoeing, and now she was past the line and onto April's ground. He recalled that sometimes people who are hard of hearing seem cranky when really they don't fully understand. What was the guarantee that she could even see well? Maybe she hit the string totally by accident, and here everybody was getting all excited.

"Where would you like us to put the string, Mrs. Kimball? We can put it about anywhere. This is a very big garden space, and all April was doing—April's my wife—all she was trying to do is get a spot so the hose would reach. See through here?" He pointed through a crack in the fence so Mrs. Kimball could see where the hose had to reach from. She didn't look up from her work.

"We can buy more hose, shoot. We don't need much space for these tomatoes. There aren't but a few anyway." He smiled.

Suddenly Mrs. Kimball hacked one of April's plants. It fell over and died.

"Now wait. Don't do that! Just tell me where we can put the stakes so we aren't in your. . . " Zick, another tomato plant went down.

"Golly, Mrs. Kimball, I wish you wouldn't . . . "

"You just get out of here," the old woman muttered. "This is my land." She hacked another one. By this time, there were a few other people in the area, some distance off but watching out of the corners of their curious, neighborly, pea-sized little eyes.

Dave went over and obstinately retied the string she'd cut. One thing he had over Mrs. Kimball was a cool head and plenty of energy to just keep re-establishing the line. Youth has a distinct advantage in these confrontations, Dave was realizing. Not only that, Dave knew his experience in the business world had made him a communicator, yes, and also, this was important, a cool and calculating negotiator—how could he have expected his wife to negotiate out here? Housewives—they're capable of learning these skills but there just isn't the opportunity.

"I think you're past your line, aren't you?" he said sternly. Rule one of negotiation. Establish your position. He had no intention of strong-arming the woman, only showing in his voice that he was absolutely in control.

"My line," Virginia said. "There's no line. This is my land here. Go away."

"Those are my wife's tomato plants, and surely you wouldn't just cut them off."

"She planted them in the wrong place," the woman muttered. She kept working, head down.

"Well, I. . . "

She looked up at Dave. She was a very pretty old woman, but cranky like an old, old cat. Dave could tell he had the upper hand with the audience, that the other neighbors working out there, and watching from a distance, didn't like her much. He knew they knew Mrs. Kimball was out of her depth now, going toe-to-toe with Dave. Like April, they too were probably glad to see a professional communicator step in.

She wore black-rimmed glasses, the rims round after the style in perhaps 1910. The glasses formed perfect circles around her eyes—really added to the old woman's glare when she was getting ready to pounce. "Your ugly wife planted her tomatoes in the wrong place."

Dave stood there. She went back to hoeing. In a set of amazingly efficient moves, she changed the direction of April's rows, from north-south to east-west, conforming to the rest of her garden. Then she changed the direction of Dave's new rows. Then she hacked the nozzle off the hose.

"Tell your ugly wife to go away, too. She's got no respect for old people." Virginia kept hoeing.

"Oh, you're wrong. She loves old people, honestly," Dave said. "I'm not saying you're old, " he said, shifting directions, then immediately regretting it. "I mean, I know you are kind of old but . . . "

He was off track there. He shifted again: "This thing could be worked out in a snap if we sat down and talked. Is that your chair?"

"Your wife. She's been pushing me around out here all spring. This is my land. I'll get a lawyer and fight you. I'll fight you." She looked up at him. She was standing pretty close, and was only about five feet tall. She stepped even closer to him. "This is my land," she said straight up into Dave's face. "Mine." He felt the ancient breath on his chin.

Dave saw some laughter among the gardeners watching from a distance. He felt sorry for her, the underdog.

"Now listen," he said, taking up the cut string again, and pulling up April's stakes. "You tell me where to put these. They will be here, and you and I have to decide where." He smiled. "You get first choice." He liked this tack. It felt refreshing. Aggressive but not rude. He was prepared to wait for her to help him solve this problem. Reminded himself of a pastoral Adlai Stevenson, prepared to wait. They would have a discussion, agree on a strategy. That way, as they would say at work, he'd have her "buy-in."

"Get out of here!" she yelled at him. "You get out of here! Leave me alone." She raised her hoe—it glinted in the sun. Dave flinched, and in the blink of his eye the hoe went down on another of April's tomatoes. This woman was very good with a hoe.

Now everyone—the morning gardeners scattered throughout the garden area—straightened up and looked. This was the moment they were waiting for, the moment when Dave took charge. He looked across the garden area at them, straightened himself. He'd been up against tougher people than ninety-two year old Virginia Kimball, five feet tall. He'd sat in budget meetings with the governor, for God sake.

"Okay then. I'll decide," he said. His heart was pounding in his chest but no one could tell. He calmly hammered in the stakes in a line re-establishing April's border, and strung the string, isolating a modest zone a couple of yards square and encircling the dead and wounded tomato sprouts. April was going to be proud when she heard how Dave handled this.

In the corner of his eye Dave saw the woman raise the hoe high above her head again—this time it was certain she would slice him. Quick, he raised an arm to block the blow, fell back, but she got the string instead, twang, and hacked the final plant with a second short chop.

"That did it," Dave said.

Setting on the ground near him was Virginia's shovel. Rule two of negotiation. Grab a shovel and take her out with it. Dave got up off the ground, dusted himself off—then stepped over to the shovel, picked it up, calmly felt the weight of it, and then, like a discus thrower, whirled once, yelling loud, and let it go straight into her sweetcorn. Boldly, he grabbed the old woman's hoe right out of her hand, and, yelling again, and threw it over a tree—the handle making a whipping sound like a helicopter blade. It stuck in the back yard of Ben Hall, the retired registrar out at the college. He threw it so hard that in the follow-through he fell down in the dirt. He scrambled back to his feet so fast she probably didn't notice, though, and stood there staring at her. His heart was about to come out of his chest, but to the ordinary onlooker he might well have appeared completely collected, a man about his wits, taking care of business.

"What do you think of that," he said, rhetorical question. He stared at her, wide-eyed, sweat dripping down, catching his breath.

"Ah. The great Mr. Nichols overpowers the old woman," she cackled. "The great Mr. Nichols. Bullies an old woman. He and his ugly wife, just alike. Now you listen to me, great Mr. Nichols. This is my land. You get out of here. I'll fight you."

Dave was bent over, reestablishing the stakes and string so that Poland was completely separated from Germany. But one stake was destroyed and the string was no longer repairable. He had to go back to the house for string. Without a word, he went through the gate. In the house, he couldn't find any string, so he sat in the living room staring out the front window.

"I was watching," Rocky would say when he ribbed Dave about it. "I was out there. She ate you up. She had you for breakfast, Big Dave." Rocky laughed hard.

"I did fine."

"You were eaten alive."

"I said all along that it was a big thing and you couldn't get into a big thing with old people and win."

"Well, you did and you didn't," Rocky would say with a big laugh. He got a good laugh out of it, remembering back.

The day after the scene in the garden area, a gleaming Sunday morning, D. Y. Kimball phoned.

"Mr. Nichols?"

"Right." Dave had never spoken with him, didn't know his voice.

"This is Mr. D. Y. Kimball."

"Mr. Kimball?"

"Right, sir."

"And?" Even the name Kimball, pronounced in that kind of archaic way, like an old parson might say it, didn't ring a bell.

"I imagine you thought you'd hear from my lawyer, didn't you?"

"Well, I . . . " Dave was placing the name now.

"He died. Of an infection. 1956, it was. But I can get another one. I don't appreciate your assaulting my wife while she was in her garden yesterday."

"Sorry."

"Yes, of course you are, but the damage is done. I wonder if we might talk. Could you come by?"

"Right. I'll do that. I'd like to talk. Straighten this thing out."

"Yessir. Let's do that, us men. Straighten it out with a good talk."

"Good."

"Right. Good," Mr. Kimball said. "Would you come over then?"

"Sure will," Dave said, and in saying it communicated that attitude of certainty upon which negotiation is built if it is to tip one's own way in its outcome.

Dave took the shortcut to Kimball's across the neighbors' yards. There was a tree in the front yard, a willow, split evidently by a recent storm, a big limb down in the yard, the rip in the tree deep and long, a deep gouge in the ground where the limb tore in as it landed.

Dave knocked. No one answered. He knocked again. No answer. There was no car in the driveway, which relieved

Dave. It probably meant Mrs. Kimball was gone somewhere. Yet he couldn't remember ever seeing her drive the car. He knocked at the back door, in the car port. Still no answer. It was sad, he thought. Mr. Kimball was probably hard of hearing.

Finally, there being no answer at all, Dave wandered home. He stirred around an hour or so, and finally it became afternoon. He flipped on the ballgame and watched the Mets catcher, Carter—playing first base for the first and last time this year—fall and hurt his thumb. Dave laughed and got a beer and started to get into the game. The innings passed, Dave sitting there motionless in his chair. The Mets were losing. It was a relief to get into the game.

The phone rang.

"Mr. Nichols?"

"Mr. Kimball?"

"Yessir."

"How are you?"

"I thought you were coming by. I've been waiting."

"Mr. Kimball, I . . . "

"Maybe you decided not to have a talk with me. Maybe you'd rather see me in court."

"You didn't come to the door."

"I can't come to the door."

"Well, then I . . . "

"You have to come on in. I'm on the third floor." These were tract houses, no basements and damn sure no third floors. Mr. Kimball had clearly drifted into some kind of elderly gray fog.

"Well, could you . . . "

"They've got me hooked up to machines. I'm hooked up here. Maybe you don't want to talk about this, man to man, and you're avoiding it. That's okay with me."

"What machines?"

"Just come by, Mr. Nichols. I want to discuss this matter with you face-to-face."

Dave was feeling exasperated. "Which door should I come in, the back door or the front door?" he said. "Is it unlocked? Where's your wife?" Time was being eaten up by this. The Mets game was in the eighth inning, and he didn't even know the score. The weekend, the precious hours of recuperating from work, they were evaporating into the afternoon clouds. He could hear Monday coming, bearing down on him like the Panama Limited, and he wanted peace. He didn't want a big thing.

"Maybe you don't want to talk me about this," Mr. Kimball said. "I understand. It's okay with me."

"I'll be by, Mr. Kimball. I'm coming in the back door. I'm coming in without knocking, and I'm coming up to the third floor even though you don't have a goddamned third floor, even though there isn't a house with three floors between here and Olive Street. I'm coming over there. I'm coming up. I'll be there in three minutes."

"I'm not at home, sir. I'm at the hospital."

Dave drove over, parked, got out, walked in, rode up, followed the numbers on the doors, and found Mr. Kimball's room. Mr. Kimball had a bandaid over one eye and was hooked up to a catheter. They shook hands.

"How come you're here?" Dave asked.

"Doc said. They checked me over. I'll get out. Thought you'd never come."

"How was I supposed to know you're in the hospital?" Dave was conscious of raising his voice.

"You don't listen, maybe." Now Dave wanted to get a hold of the old man's wrinkled little chicken neck. "I said it. Said I was here. People don't listen to old folks—you'll find out soon enough. They don't listen, and when they talk to us, they shout."

D. Y. looked for all the world like a parson in the movie "Friendly Persuasion." White, white skin, gleaming gold-rimmed glasses, a kind look ever on his face.

"My wife, Mr. Nichols—she don't ask for much. A garden, some quiet and peace to work there. Used to be, we lived in the country. Down on the Tennessee line. And the people were nice. That was a long time ago. 19-and-22."

Dave stared at the old man.

The old man stared back. Finally he cleared his throat.

"I've drawn a diagram, sir. There is a tree back there, very shady under it. Actually two trees. A soft maple of some kind, mountain maple I think, and a Chinese elm."

He referred to his drawing, on a sheet of schoolboy paper on the blanket on his lap. "You know where I mean?" He pointed with a shaky white hand. He indicated the area beneath the Chinese elm. When he said "elm", he pronounced it "ellum."

"Mrs. Kimball won't want that place to garden."

"Why's that?"

"Because nothing worth a person's time will grow there."

"I see," Dave said.

"So your wife can put her plants there, flowers or whatever she wants. *Nolo contendere,* as we say." The old man smiled, gray teeth, pink plastic gums.

"And?"

"And then you can cut down the tree. It's one of those shabby old Chinese elms. Weed. Imported by heathens before the revolution. Cut it down. And you've got your garden. And the world is better all around."

"And?"

"And while you've got the saw out, maybe you could get over there to my place and cut down my corkscrew willow. I ran into it full-bore two nights ago, totalled the Ford; Virgie says I totalled the tree, too—you didn't hear about it? Abie Minever, you know him? Lives across the street? He stood there laughing. There I was with the tree on the car and he didn't know but what I was killed in there somewhere, and he was laughing. I could hear him. I knew his pap, Boomer they called him—trash. And his granddaddy—one of these moonshiners with no principles, you know what I mean. You got moonshiners, and then you got moonshiners. What was his name—married that dark girl, I forget, from over by Tri City." Mr. Kimball rubbed his soft, stubbled chin, trying to think, then waved it off, nevermind. "But anyway, my neighbor was laughing at me. You wouldn't believe how old people get treated in this world." He sighed. "You'll know, soon enough. Soon enough. Do you know where my office is?"

"Office?" Dave said.

"It's downtown. I sleep down there mostly. Mrs. Kimball don't want men around much. I've slept there in recent years, since '68. May seem like a long time ago to you. But to me it's yesterday. I got a saw—real good one, if you need it—keep it at the office to remember the old days. You'll need another guy on the far handle, back and forth, down she goes. It'll do the job, and then some."

He handed Dave his diagram of the tree and the area around it where he and his wife would allow April to have a garden.

He said, "Yup. I think I can sell this arrangement to Virgie, the tree idea. She don't like that little elm. Her pap had a bad time with a Chinese elm once. Fell on his mule and after that he cussed them like the devil. Them and the French." The old man smiled, having a private recollection.

Dave ignored this. "Well. My wife is very bothered," Dave said. "Her plants got cut down, Mr. Kimball. I imagine if we'd cut Mrs. Kimball's plants down, she'd have been concerned about it."

"Mrs. Kimball's got a temper on her all right," Mr. Kimball laughed gently. "Your best bet is to go along with my suggestion. I married her in 1915, so I know her pretty good. Never had no children—I got over it. Nevermind."

Dave stared at him. He remembered Rocky's warning to April about the old people act. He conceded no indication of understanding.

After a moment he said, "Well. Mrs. Kimball may be old and have a temper, but she doesn't have rabies, and . . . " His voice was getting louder. ". . . and she's desecrating my wife's garden with her hoe and generally being a very unpleasant neighbor. I think she owes my wife an apology."

"Do not raise your voice to me, Mr. Nichols. Let me remind you that we know six former governors of the Commonwealth and several congressmen. We know all the lawyers around here, and the county judge and his daddy and his daddy's daddy. Now, pardon me, sir, but you bothered my wife in the garden yesterday. I have witnesses. We can pull strings, sir, get you hopping up and down like a lake toad." The gray eyebrows lifted like a pirate's, and he looked at Dave over the top of his gold-rims. "If you know what I mean." Mr. Kimball smiled, showing the tops of his inorganic gums again, adjusted his catheter and then, evidently, from the way his eyes went vacant for a moment, used it.

"Take the drawing and show your wife. And explain to her. A man, you know, has to explain this kind of thing, to a woman, in situations like we have. We don't want trouble, tell her that—just to have a garden before Mrs. Kimball passes on, God forbid."

"Then why don't you find a place for a garden where there's nobody around, so you don't have to be neighborly and make concessions and be regular like the rest of us?"

"I can see you feel strongly on this." Kimball leaned back, ready to get all philosophical. Then that kind look came over his face, and he said, "Women are the reason, you see. Women are why, generally speaking. Now take your wife the drawing. Tell her we might be gone next year or the year after that. We just want peace. I'm sure, in your selfish youthful somewhat blind and self-interested kind of way, you want peace, too. Excuse me, here's my dinner."

A cart was being rolled in behind Dave.

"'Peace,' tell her."

"Amen," Dave said, and he left, carrying the drawing.

He showed it to his wife. April was dumbstruck.

"You call this communicating?"

"April. We've got one half of one remaining tomato plant and about three hours left of this weekend. In the old days, a plant like this tomato, this far gone, would be taken out and shot."

"Oh, shut up, David—you're such a . . . "

Dave looked at his watch. "April. Let's cut down the darn tree."

"The garden's city property, honey. I don't think they'd like you logging their landscaping. Think, David. You're just such a . . . " She stopped, sighed, sat glaring at him. The only sound around was the coffee pot occasionally churning. The kids were abroad in the neighborhood. Elise was at Tamra's house, Dave imagined, trying on make-up. And Ryan was undoubtedly with his friend Peter punching goals on the soccer field at the park a few blocks away. The ballgame—it had been over for hours.

"Well," Dave said after a while.

"Well," April said. "We've got some more plants, did you notice? The whole neighborhood chipped in. Rocky planted them this morning while you were gone, and he hoed out a row of Mrs. Kimball's beans, to show her a thing or two. Here's the card." She set it on the table, next to the old man's shaky diagram of the garden area. The card was signed by many of the neighbors. It said simply, "We're behind you all the way, April. Love, the neighbors in the garden area." No mention of Dave.

"It's going to be a fight, Dave," April said. "You in?"

Dave stared at her. The afternoon was gone. It was evening. Monday was virtually upon them. The weekend was over, completely fried. Ready or not, he had to go back at it the next morning, back to work, the real trenches.

"It's an issue of respect" she said. "If you give in, you say 'they're just old people and they don't matter' and you have to treat them like pre-schoolers. Or you afford them respect, treat them like equals, and go at 'em like there's no tomorrow. Rocky said this is the way they did it last year, and we have to be consistent."

After work on Monday, despite having no buy-in from his wife, Dave drove downtown. He found the building Mr. Kimball had indicated. He went in, and went down a long narrow hall with a shiny brown linoleum floor, past a tiny office of a State Farm agent and a 24-hour crisis hotline switchboard which seemed to be in a closet. At the end of the hall was a door with a frosted glass window which had stenciled on it "D. Y. Kimball, Colonel, World War I."

A woman came out of the crisis office wearing a hat with fish-hooks in it and a "Say No to Drugs" pin on her dress and inquired what Dave was up to.

"I wanted to borrow Mr. Kimball's saw."

"Mr. Kimball is in the hospital. He had another wreck." The woman was pasty-faced and puffy, wore a jersey dress like a country girl. She had oily hair and was smoking. "Ran into a tree in his own yard."

"He said I could use his saw."

"I could unlock the door. I'd be treading on thin water. You sign for it?"

"For the saw?"

"No, for the door," she said, laughing. She went back in the crisis office.

"Of course I'll sign."

She got the key. She unlocked the door. Inside was a veritable museum of WWI, with rifles on the wall, and bayonets, and black and white pictures of D. Y. and Dwight Eisenhower, Smiley Burnett, Danny Kaye. One of the pictures was signed: "To a fellow old warhorse. Best, Ike." The crisis woman stood at the door and watched Dave as he looked around. On the wall was a long, rusty two-man lumberjack saw. He awkwardly lifted it off its mounting brackets, then turned to the woman and said, "Where do I sign?"

She laughed. "No where. It was a joke." She laughed, and locked the door behind him once he'd gotten the saw out of the office. All the way down the dim hall he could hear her laughing, and after he'd wrestled the saw outdoors, onto the downtown street, he could still hear her back there laughing.

Dave drove home with the saw sticking out the passenger window of his car. At the Olive Street stoplight, he looked in his rearview mirror and saw his neighbor, Rocky, in his pickup truck. Rocky leaned out the window and shouted, "Davey! Turn on your radio. Pendleton just hit one into the seats. Cards are up by three."

Dave could care about the ballgame.

"HEY! DAVE!" Rocky persisted.

Dave leaned out his window and looked back.

"Is that a saw, boy?" Rocky said.

"That's a serious saw," Dave said.

"They got 'em gas-powered these days. What're you up to? Antiques?"

Dave shouted back, "Nah, actually . . . for one thing . . . I'm gonna saw down a tree in guess who's yard." Dave took a glance around, making sure there were no other neighbors waiting at the stoplight. "I've had it with this mess, know what I mean?"

"C'mon!" Rocky said doubtfully. He turned down his radio, leaned back out to yell again. "C'mon, Dave—seriously."

"I AM serious."

"Let me help," Rocky said, a challenge in his voice. He turned his baseball cap around backwards, mischievous.

"Great. You can hold the old lady," Dave called back to him, and felt guilty about it despite how hard Rocky laughed in his rearview mirror.

Rocky followed Dave to his house, pulled up the driveway behind him.

Dave climbed out and stepped back to Rocky's truck.

"Seriously," Rocky said, "what're you up to with an old rusty saw like that?"

Dave looked at him. "I told you. I'm going to saw down some trees and settle this thing. Seriously."

"Uh, well, now Dave, I don't think you can do that. Really. It's an admirable sentiment, don't get me wrong, but . . . Think about it. Don't get in a bunch of trouble over this thing."

"Watch me." Dave was walking back to his car for the saw.

"C'mon!" Rocky said. He climbed out of his truck, slammed the door. He wanted to stop Dave from doing something rash. "Dave! If you . . . "

"Don't shout, Rock," Dave said quietly, indicating toward the house. He didn't want April charging out there with a bunch of opinions. He started wrestling the rusty saw out of his car. A heavy, rough machine, primitive but dead serious. Hell on vinyl seats. Made and operated by men who could handle it. No plastic here. "You know how to operate one of these things?"

"Davey, listen," Rocky whispered, grabbing at Dave's arm. "What're you doing? C'mon."

"C'mon yourself. I've had it with this stuff, get me? I need help. You in?" Dave indicated for him to take the other end.

"Jesus," Rocky said, lifting it. "Goddamn, we're jailbait this time."

"Yeah, well," Dave said, "sometimes a man's got to do what he's got to do."

In the Monday evening twilight and shadow, the two of them lugged the old saw across the neighbors' yards, the shortcut to Kimball's.

Vanishing Acts

Steven Gillis

"Man, man, man," Galile in the bedroom tells me to, "Shit or get off the pot."

I have the door open so I can watch dad in silk pajamas, his head propped up on three flat pillows, his cheeks caved and spiked with whiskers he would not have tolerated before. He thinks I can't see him but I do. "I know you're still there," I call from the toilet. Dad's skin is the color of parmesan cheese. His friend, Galile, is large and dark. He helps me whenever dad decides to hide beneath the bed. "Just pretend I'm not here," dad laughs as if to imply we won't be able to do it, but if we take too long to get him up, he'll slap at our feet with his fists and want to know, "What's the problem out there?"

I buckle my pants, wash my hands, come back into the bedroom where dad lights a cigarette though he hasn't smoked in years. Galile is gone, unable to wait anymore, he has walked outside and relieved himself on dad's roses, aiming his stream toward the wild vine of thorn. "MacLorne Park," dad says and points a bony finger. I answer, "The first time you tossed a frisbee with me."

"Red Diskcraft, 175g Ultrastar," dad knew his stuff, tells me to, "Go on."

I describe all I recall.

"Peddlemarks," he says.

"The restaurant you took me to the afternoon I left for college."

"John Garfield."

"Your favorite actor."

"September of '87."

"We drove down together for Barb's wedding."

"Got into it pretty good."

"You brought up Nixon."

"History will show," dad coughs.

The pills and water cover the nightstand beside his bed. Dad leans over and drops his cigarette on the floor. When I go around to crush it out, he crawls off the other side, shuffles as best he can to the closet and closes the door. "Pretend I'm not here," he says.

"I can't do that."

"Just try."

"Alright," I stand there and wait to see what will happen.

"Summer of '99," he says.

"I thought you wanted me to pretend."

"Can you?"

"No."

"Ha!"

I go to the closet and open the door. Dad has on one of mom's old hats. "Remember?" he asks.

"I didn't know you still had that."

"Did you think I gave it away?"

"I just didn't know."

"It's all here if you care to look."

I take a step closer, lift the hat carefully from dad's head and put it back on the shelf. "Let me help you," I say.

"If you don't mind," his head rolls on his neck, his frame as thin as pipe cleaner sticks. "Look both ways," he says.

"Do your homework."

"Alex Pierceal."

"You introduced us, got him to hire me."

"As an intern."

"All the same."

"You did the rest," Dad comes from the closet, lets me help him back to bed. "I should pee first," he says, and I take him to the bathroom. "One for the road," he chuckles softly and closes the door. "It doesn't hurt," he tells me. "Not in the way you think."

"I don't know what to think."

"Pretend I'm not here," he says again.

"Can you see the roses outside?" I want to distract us.

"I'm sitting," dad answers, "like a girl."

"Look out the window. Galile pissed all over them."

"It's ok," dad doesn't seem surprised. "You remember," he says, and I wait for him to continue. Several seconds elapse however. I call in, "Dad?" and he replies, "Well, do you?"

I open the door and he's standing naked in front of me. The idea of seeing him this way was unfathomable before, the situation unavoidable now. The shunt where the chemo went in is still in his chest, a porthole looking much like a hollow key to a strange wind instrument. "Did you have an accident?" I ask.

"St. Mercy's of the Valley."

"When I broke my wrist."

"Falling from your bike."

"You took me to the hospital in your barbecue apron."

"Lost my chef's hat in the wind," he slips slowly past me, the back of his legs, his arms and butt sagging like fleshy sacks of water halfway drained. He stands a moment at the side of the bed, feeling his feet on the floor and the force of gravity against him. "Alright then," he says, and lies down, pulling the sheet up to his waist. "Remember," he tells me, and slips one of the pillows from behind his head.

In my hands the weight is too much. "It's as it's supposed to be," dad says. Still, I feel if I let go the pillow will crash through the floor. I want to quit, but dad is smiling and telling me to, "Just pretend."

I think again of MacLorne Park, dad with the frisbee and how hard I tried to learn. My throws though were erratic, hooking every which way and often into the woods. "Thumb up. Hand straight. Your point of release is important," dad was patient with me. He did his best to make me laugh and waited as I chased all of my bad tosses down. Once I went deep into the woods and couldn't find the frisbee, and for a moment thought I was lost. I remember calling out, "Dad? Dad?" and how he answered, "I'm here," he said. "I'm here."

Regrets

James R. Cooley

I saw my friend David three weeks ago, just a few days before they executed him. I know, it surprised me, too: They never let guys on Death Row have non-family visitors. But my old sponsor Philip, sober three decades now, worked in and around the Kansas Department of Corrections and Osawatomie State Hospital for years before moving on to teach substance abuse counseling and criminology at a small college. A year ago he parlayed his assistant-professor-in-sociology gig into a fat job as an assistant managing warden at San Quentin. Not bad for a guy who threw newspapers for five years after he sobered up, eh? I was in the Bay area on business, and Philip was able to slip me onto East Block to see David. He told the security people I was David's counselor or confessor or something. Amazingly, they let me in. One more time: It's not what you know, but who.

I spent an hour with David there in his cell while the guards looked on. He was surprisingly upbeat. I don't know what his deal was. Maybe he was still far enough away that his denial system was more or less intact. We all secretly believe we're going to live forever, but it was still weird to see David so collected just—what was it?—four days before they cuffed him, shackled his ankles and put him on his leash for that last walk. You'd think that when the State of California makes up its dirty little mind to exterminate a guy, when that last appeal gets turned down, he'd see the writing on the wall. But I don't know. Maybe David had already worked through all that anger- grieving-acceptance-serenity bullshit the terminally ill are supposed to go through—although if he hadn't been hanging onto a little anger, I'll tell you this: He wouldn't have been David Oswald Edgerton.

We didn't avoid the matter, either. We've always been like that—outrageously honest with each other in a blunt, brutal sort of way. David's the guy who dubbed my last wife "the troll," described me one time as a "balding fat guy with two right eyes." Nailed every one of my insecurities in one unforgettable phrase. At least I've never forgotten it, although my therapist says I should. I'm telling you, the guy is a poet. Was a poet.

He only got a little weepy once, toward the end of our visit. I flatter myself to think it was because I was seeing him, alive anyway, for the last time. Dead, too, for that matter. David made me the executor of his will and "dispositioner" of his body. Can you believe it? That's actually what the California Department of Corrections calls it: the "dispositioner." Sounds like a word they lifted from Ebonics — and from the looks of David's peers on East block, the Ebonies got plenty of call for it. "Dispositioner." Jesus. Another ten years, we won't have a language left.

David dropped that little honor on me right when I walked in. He'd never mentioned it in his almost daily letters. After that we didn't talk about it—just slipped our minds, I guess. I disposed of him, all right. Had him burned. No point in mailing home the meat just to bury it, although among his meager effects I did find title to a gravesite on the edge of the family plot in Goodland. He never got along with them anyway. I sold it back to the cemetery—at a steep discount, of course. His mother's 86, senile, in a nursing home outside Topeka. I figured she could use the money.

The hour passed quickly. Time flies, you know. Just ask David. When a guard motioned it was time to leave, we were both surprised. David was telling me a story about his dad, which sounded like something out of his fifth step. I was afraid the guards were going to cut him off before I heard the punch line, but David was about done. Somehow these things just seem to work out.

"You know, Cool Jerk," he said—another of the pet names he has for me. I used to call him David the Psychotic Serial Killer, back before he got in trouble, then David O. Ed, The Walking Dead after his last appeal failed. "You know, Cool Jerk, I must have too much of my father's DNA in me."

I had no idea what he was talking about. His old man's been dead for 15 years. In fact, it was right after his father died that I met David, who had come back to Kansas from San Francisco to probate out the will and administer the estate. It was not long afterward he began to screw up with the law.

"Exactly half is the usual and customary amount," I suggested. He didn't laugh. "So why do you say that?"

"Well, we were out quail hunting one time, on those empty, windswept plains of Kansas"—no kidding, that's what he said, right there in the cell on Death Row, "those empty, windswept plains." I'm telling you, the guy was a poet. So anyway, he goes on—"and it was snowing, a steady, blowing, powder snow, just colder than hell. I was 12, maybe 13 at the time. We were having a great hunt. It was gray and windy, but the dog was pointing like every five minutes. We were walking right up on the birds. Sometimes we could just stand there looking at them before they flushed. Twice that day we caught a whole covey huddled together under a bush, you know how they do when they're really cold and won't flush at all. We'd just step back a few feet and get the dog clear, then blast the whole damn covey on the ground, or most of it.

"Anyway, I had just noticed the snow was letting up a bit, and somehow, I still don't know how I did it, I shot the old man in the back."

"No shit? From how far away?" I've been peppered myself a few times with birdshot. It can happen when you're shooting over an overgrown fence line and you don't see the other guy a couple of hundred yards away. No big deal. Number eight shot strings out and pitter-patters down like a light rain starting up, while sixes and fours splat down suddenly, a sharp, lead cloudburst. You holler, of course, so they don't shoot straight through the brush at you, but falling from the sky the shot's harmless enough. It happens less these days, but back when David and I were young no one wore flame orange while hunting quail.

"Oh, about 60 feet," David said. I was shocked. The son of a bitch really *had* shot his old man. "I don't know to this day how I did it. I must have gotten a faulty goddamn shell or something. Afterward, I took some bedsheets behind the house, hung them on the clothesline, drew a silhouette of my dad on one, and tried everything I could think of to duplicate the circumstances. But I couldn't. Shot up a whole box of field loads and ruined half our sheets trying. I'll be damned if I can tell you how it happened.

"So my dad, you know what he does? He doesn't say a word. He just picks himself up off the ground, motions me over with his finger, then slowly peels off his hunting jacket, his flannel shirt, his thermal underwear, glaring at me the whole time. When he turns around, he's got these pellet holes all across his back, plus a couple in his neck. Then he takes his hunting knife out of its sheath, hands it to me, and growls, 'You put 'em there, you dig 'em out.' That's all he says.

"So I spend the next half hour slicing little slits into my dad's back, noodling birdshot out of the fat underneath his skin, there in the freezing cold, as his bright, red blood drips onto the snow. Some of the pellets were in there pretty good, and he bled like a stuck pig. Never flinched, though. Never complained, or said a word. Oh, yeah, he did. Just once, he says, 'Goddamn, boy. I've had corpsmen dig bullets out of my butt that hurt less than that.'

"Two other hunters came along while we were doing this, hunting over a pair of Brittany spaniels. They were each packing a pint of peppermint schnapps. Both of them, a full pint—I mean, Christ, it was a cold son of a bitch that day. They passed their hooch around, we each got several good honks of the giant killer. The old man has me daub the schnapps on wads of toilet paper and dress his wounds with it. Good thing he always carried a roll in the field. 'My tickets to the outdoor outhouse,' he called it. The old man was big on creature comforts.

"Anyway, when I'd gotten most of the pellets out, all of them that I could see through the blood and the schnapps running down his back, he has me ease him back into his long johns, keeping as much of the toilet paper in place as we can, then I help him into his shirt, then his jacket. Then he thanks these guys for the schnapps and we go back to hunting. We hunted for the rest of the afternoon, three or four hours at least. He never says another word about it. We both got our limit that day, too. In fact, as I recall, one of us got a fair bit over the limit.

"He never mentioned it afterward. Later, mom told me he would grouse about it now and then, when a pellet I'd missed would work its way to the surface and he made her dig it out. But he never said jack shit about it again to me. It was like it had never happened, although of course we both knew it had.

"Hm," I said. "What a bummer." I closed my eyes, imagining young David out there in the snow, shotgun leaning against a fence post, his dad's knife in his hand. "So did you cry? I mean, were you crying at the time?"

"I plead the fifth, old buddy."

"Whatever." I looked around his cell. "Looks like taking the fifth hasn't proven to be such a hot strategy, David O." There wasn't much to look at. They don't let you keep a lot in those little cells. Not that he needed much where he was headed.

That's when the guard cleared his throat, pointed to his watch, and I had to go. David began to get tears in his eyes, just a bit. He rose, shook my hand, then gave me a big hug. The guards did *not* like that hug business, probably afraid I might try to slip David a weapon or something.

"Yeah, well. You know, I don't have many regrets in life, Cool Jerk, next to none. But that's definitely one of them."

"What is, David?"

"You know, there I was, out in the middle of nowhere, my father's blood all over my hands and clothes, crying, shaking, freezing my ass off in that snow. I'd already shot the bastard. I had two more shells in my gun and that big, razor-sharp Bowie in my hand. I could easily have blown his fucking head off, cut his throat, done *something*, right then and there. And I didn't do it."

"Oh, well. I wouldn't worry about it now, David. He died in his own sweet time, as do we all. So long, buddy."

"See you around, Cool Jerk."

The Rain Barrel

Jim Nichols

In the spring I always made my way down the stairway to the cellar of my father's empty house, and turned on the bulb above the workbench where his tools hung on the pegboard. The tools were dusty. It was very dim in the cellar even during the daytime, because there were no windows in the rock foundation of the old place, and I was as blind as my old man until the bulb blinked on.

On a small pallet at the end of the workbench lay his outboard, and I would lug it outside to the rain barrel beside the shed and crank it up. It was a special request he'd made his first spring in the nursing home, after he had his second stroke, the one that took his sight and speech. He had written the request in his new handwriting, that was all shaky and slanted, and which was half-and-half, now, English and French. Start up the le moteur, he wrote. Has to be commencez every spring or she won't be no good.

Anyway, I did it every year, because he'd always loved his boat and motor so much, and was thinking of them even now. I wrestled it out through the cellar doors across the lawn to the barrel, cleaned the plugs, filled it with fuel, and pulled the cord until it started. I adjusted the mix and left it running for a while; got it going no matter what the weather, so I could tell Papa everything was okay. For four years I did that.

The last year it started raining while I was driving over. It had been raining for a week, then stopped and looked as though it would clear, so I headed off. It was Saturday, and I drove into town and then through town: Papa's house, the house where I grew up, was on the other side of the river. The rain spattered my windshield before I was halfway there, and I thought about waiting for another day.

But I went on.

It had been a late spring. The hillsides beside the road were brown, the grass plastered flat. In the woods beyond the hills you could see bare, wet hardwood among the firs. My wipers squeaked across the glass, and the tires made a sticky noise on the pavement. I shut the wipers off to see how hard it was coming down, but the water blurred my windshield and I snapped them back on fast.

The rain was falling into the river, and I crossed the bridge and following the curve out of town I passed my sister Sylvie's road and thought about when she came to my place two days before. She had talked about Papa's house. Marie, my wife, had made an excuse and left the room: she didn't like Sylvie much. I had to listen, because she's my sister. She sat at the kitchen table, hair wet because she had run through the rain from her car.

Sylvie spoke to me every so often about the house. She knew it was hers in the will, and didn't want to wait until Papa passed on. Somebody might as well get something from the old place, she would say. It was ridiculous that that house had stayed empty for four years. It would keep better if somebody lived there.

"Why let it sit there empty?" she asked me. Her elbows were on the table and she moved one enough to lift the coffee cup. She stared at me, her eyes the same brown as our father's.

I shrugged.

She leaned forward. "In another four years that goddamn house will fall down. What good will it do anybody then?"

"How do you know it'll be four years?"

"He's still strong. You've talked to the doctors."

"You want him to cooperate, huh?"

"Don't give me that. You know how he feels, just like I do." She stared over the cup, knowing she was right. I knew it too. He didn't want to stick around, and would have gone right after out mother died, if it had been up to him. Maybe he tried, with the strokes. But he had tough old bones, with their own ideas about dying.

"You know we could use the money," Sylvie said.

That didn't make it right. It was Papa's house, he didn't want anybody else living there, and I wouldn't let her convince me different. When she left, she told me that if I was inheriting the house, I'd sell it for sure, but that wasn't the truth, not at all.

My wife came back into the room.

"I know she's your sister..."

"You don't have to say it."

Marie came over and sat down with me. "How was he today?"

I had been to visit. "Same as ever."

"Still not writing?"

"The pen and paper sit there on the table. He knows what you're saying, but won't lift a goddamn finger."

"Are you sure he knows?" she said.

"I'm sure."

"The poor man." Marie shook her head a little, pushed at her glasses. I was a late son, and then I got married a little late, so Papa was always old when Marie knew him, she never saw him in the little wooden boat, one hand on the outboard, le moteur, running down the river to the ocean, steering out the channel past Pound O' Tea island, squinting against the glare. He didn't like sunglasses, said they changed the color of things and he liked to see things the way they were. Even now, blind, he has the evidence: squint lines around his eyes.

"I wish you'd known him," I told Marie.

She made a sad smile, and I got up and looked out the window at the rain falling.

In ten minutes I took a left on Lambert Road. The house was a short distance away. It was still raining under a low gray sky. I parked in front of the shed and climbed the steps to the front door, went into the kitchen. Inside, I opened all the windows, and rain came in and speckled the dust on the sills. The house smelled damp, which reminded me of what Sylvie had said.

Upstairs in my old bedroom, I sat on the little bed and looked out the window, but couldn't see much of the yard because of the rain washing over the glass. On the shelf beside the bed were my old serial books: Tom Swift, The Rover Boys, The Army Boys. I remembered reading them in bed, late, with a flashlight, everything dark except me and my book. I took a book down and thumbed through it. Its pages were dry and the print seemed bigger than today's books.

Papa stopped printing his block-letter notes about six months before that. Until then, you could talk to him and he would print his answer. But he stopped. He had gotten grouchy and then he stopped writing. He got tired, I guess. The last thing he wrote was after I mentioned his blood count. I told him it was improved, and he wrote a note: BIG DEAL. He threw the felt-tip and pad on the floor, and hadn't written anything since. When I spoke to him, he pretended not to hear. All he did was lie in bed, he wouldn't talk to anybody. He'd wake up a little at mealtimes, though. He put on weight until it took two nurses to get him out of bed and into a wheelchair so they could push him to the dining room, and three to get him back into bed. I would help when I was there, and it was strange: he used to tuck me in when I was little, and now I was helping him.

I rolled out of my old bed, putting Tom Swift back on the shelf. I checked out the upstairs, then went down to the living room and sat on the couch. Everything was familiar: the braided rug my mother had made, the dark picture of an Indian sitting on a horse, sticking his arms into the air, that hung on the wall over the TV, the stack of National Geographics on the floor. Alone in the house I felt the past traveling away from me. I seemed too big for the small room. It made me nervous, and I got up and headed for the cellar door beside the stairway from my room.

The cellar was musty, like always. I felt around for the bulb, and saw the workbench and tools, the outboard on the pallet. I walked over, unlocked the cellar doors and shoved them open. The metal doors banged on the ground: there used to be a post for each of them, but they were gone.

Lifting the outboard made a twinge in my back, but it didn't seem serious, so I went ahead. But it seemed to gain weight every year. I staggered up the cement steps and through the rain to the barrel. There was scum on the water. I felt another twinge when I lifted the outboard into the barrel.

Back in the cellar, I cleaned the spark plug, brought it and the gas can outside to the barrel. By the time I had the motor running, my arm was dead tired from pulling the cord. It ran rough at first, as if it was cramped in the barrel, but after I set the mix the sound smoothed a little. I went inside to the kitchen and sat by a window watching the blue smoke rise through the rain, thinking that the outboard should have been on a boat in the water somewhere, instead of locked into the barrel.

Papa used to take me out in the boat. We'd run out to one of the islands, trolling on the way. If we caught something we'd eat it for lunch, cooking it in the frypan over one of those wire grills you stick in the ground. We'd burn driftwood and get a good fire going. I liked to watch the blue and green flames in the burning driftwood.

He didn't talk much even then, but he showed me things. Once we got caught in a shower and he built a lean-to with pine boughs and we sat underneath listening to the rain patter, watching the waves wash up on the dead seaweed at the high-water mark, and the rain, it didn't matter at all.

The wind shifted, and now the rain beat against the window. I couldn't see the outboard. Thirty minutes had passed; I went outside and cut the motor. It smelled smoky in the rain. The water stopped boiling, and I disconnected the fuel line from the can. When I lifted the outboard over the edge of the barrel, the twinge was sharper in my back, and I had to stop and hold my breath. Then it went away, and I was careful carrying it back to the cellar, easing it down onto the pallet. I went back for the gas can, then locked the cellar. Upstairs, after a last look around, I locked the windows shut, then the side door. Back in my car, I headed off through the downpour.

The next day it was still raining when we went to visit. We ran across the parking lot between cars. Papa wasn't in his room, so we walked through the big lobby to the dining room, and saw him in his wheelchair, feeling around on his plate and stuffing his food into his mouth. Sylvie sat beside him, guiding his fork hand, talking into his ear. I knew what she was saying: it was as plain on her face as the gravy on Papa's. When she saw us, she got a hard expression.

"Papa," I said loudly. "It's me and Marie."

He went on eating. I looked at Sylvie. "Any progress?"

"No," Sylvie said.

"He won't write, huh?"

She looked at the pad and pen on the table.

Papa was feeling around to see if he'd missed anything on his plate. A pretty nurse came over, said something in his ear and took his dishes away.

Papa sat back in the chair.

"Well, Daddy," Sylvie said, a hand on his shoulder. "I have to go. Robert's here. I'll see you tomorrow." She patted his shoulder; he didn't pay any attention. She said goodbye and left.

The nurse returned and cleaned him up with a washcloth.

"Would you like to go back to your room, Raymond?" she asked, pulling the chair back from the table. "We've tried the sitting room," she told me, "but he doesn't seem to want it."

Papa gave no sign he heard her. We walked beside them as she pushed the wheelchair through the corridor, chattering about what a sweetheart Dad was, how all the nurses loved him. "Aren't you a sweetheart, Raymond?" she cooed. Looking at me, she said, "The only thing we don't like is putting him back in bed." She laughed. "You've put on a little weight, haven't you dear?" Smiling brightly at me, she asked if I would help today.

"I'll help."

"Oh, good. Then we'll only need one more nurse." She stopped at the desk in the lobby, bringing another nurse along with us. We went into Papa's room, and she parked the chair next to the bed, locking the wheels. I moved the chair as the two nurses lifted him up by his arms, turned him and let his upper half down onto the mattress. I felt it in my back when I picked his legs up and swung them over. The back had been stiff all day, and I was careful when I straightened. The nurses rolled Papa over, tucked him in, and gave us a smile. Then they left.

I felt the small of my back with my fingertips.

Marie and I sat at the foot of the bed. Papa's head lay on the white pillow. I told him about my visit to the house, how I'd aired it, dusted the furniture, changed a couple of light bulbs. He just sat there until I mentioned the outboard. Then he did something with his head, a little movement, like he was cocking an ear.

Marie put a hand on my arm.

I described everything, from carrying it out of the cellar to putting the gas in, to the water boiling and the blue smoke rising. When I stopped, he held out his hands.

I smiled at Marie.

Papa struggled to sit up. He took the pad and pen from me and nodded his head. He wrote something and held the pad out. It said: BIG DEAL. I looked at Marie. Papa printed something else. He was pressing down hard on the paper. He turned it around, and I had to lean close. He had written: GIVE HER LA DAMN MAISON.

He ripped the paper off, crumpled it up and threw it away. He bounced the pad and pen off the wall, then lay back, real heavy. I couldn't look at him. I looked out the window. It was still raining, the glass was blurred. I listened to Papa breathing. Nobody said a word. We sat there until my back began to ache.

Gaarg. Gaarrgh. Gak.

Pamela Erens

I.

At the age of 27, Daniel Aker had reached that peak of physical robustness and appeal that is never sufficiently enjoyed at the time it is possessed. His bright blond hair was anchored to his well-shaped skull in tight corkscrews—a humorous feature that kept him from being placed in the very first rank by the female paralegals and ad reps that flirted with young lawyers and bankers in the beer bars of downtown Manhattan. There was a bit too much of the Little Prince in his looks: those curls, the bright blue eyes, the wide cheeks and small, childish chin. Still, his shoulders (two-eighty on the bench press at the O.K. Gym), his compact, V-shaped torso, his well-toned *gluteus maximus* and his sturdy, trunk-like legs gave him a certain status on the streets of Midtown, the Village and Hoboken. He knew that girls turned their heads to look at him, that elderly women despised him without quite knowing why, that middle-aged men silently measured their pecs and bellies against his, then sighed and pulled their paper-laden satchels in front of their groins. Daniel worked at the investment firm of Dolan, Fair and Schupack and was considered a competent and steady worker, loyal if not a star.

Daniel did not often take vacations out of the city—he kept no car and the dingy communal rentals of Fire Island and the Hamptons seemed less appealing than free concerts under the palms at the World Financial Center or a long solitary bike ride in the park. But this particular week in August his roommate had induced him to spend a long weekend at his parents' beach house in Southhampton. Daniel rented a car at the Hertz on East 48th Street. Before driving off he meticulously checked the lights, tires and brakes. He opened the hatch. The cover of the storage area was off of one of its hinges, and when he bent to adjust it he saw that it was altogether broken on that side. He signaled the supervisor, who walked over already mouthing a stream of justifications and challenges.

" . . . only one we got. I give you a five percent discount. The best I can do. Everybody's gone out of town this weekend. I can rent to someone else in five minutes. Take it, leave it."

For a moment Daniel cast his eyes in the direction of one of the few cars left in the lot, a green Lincoln Continental. It was much too showy for a drive into the country. Once again he felt the strangeness of having enough money to do almost anything he wanted and yet being prevented from doing it. Money was not freedom, exactly, as he'd once thought, but only an opportunity to wrestle with more and more obscure scruples for acting or not acting in any particular way.

He drove away in the car with the broken hatch, humming to himself from his large repertoire of Grateful Dead tunes. He had just gotten off of the expressway at Riverhead and was on the connector heading south when he noticed another car, a slate-blue compact with a rounded snout, disappearing and reappearing around the curves as it made its way toward him. Only when it was about to pass did it float slowly toward the median. Daniel wrenched the steering wheel to get out of the way, cursing; unbelievably, the other car followed, drifting calmly again into his path, then pushing its nose straight into the space between the two front seats.

Daniel was thrown through the shattered windshield twelve feet into the air and landed on the macadam next to his stalled, quivering car. In a moment, there were lights pulsing against his closed eyes, pinkish and white and yellow, and a grinding noise that built to an unbearable intensity and then faded to a prickly ongoing static. For a few moments he could not see or think. Then his vision cleared; in his mind's eye Daniel saw shoes. Pair after pair of brown, laced shoes: some pairs pointing east, others propped toe-up against a bare wall, others splayed; shoes in a pile, shoes filling his entire field of vision. Now he felt he was striding somewhere, the air pulsing against his ears and lifting the moist locks at his neck. Then he was being covered with many blankets, too many blankets—it was very hot—so that he tried to throw them off, but angry, persistent hands kept forcing them back into place. The heat against his chest became so great that it was as if he were being held too close to a flame, and he beat his hands in the air and tried to call for help, wondering why anyone would be so pointlessly cruel as to keep him smothered like this. Then he understood: he had been left alone in a field; there were in fact no hands or blankets; the sensation of the blankets was simply the startling pressure of grief on his heart. Every creature in the world had withdrawn and left him lying here among the cool grasses, passed over by the wind. He saw the blood seeping out of him—a circumstance that did not surprise him—flowing between his legs as in a great miscarriage. His groin and intestines cramped several times so strongly that his vision faded to a dirty brown. He was being emptied of something. Although he could not see his own chest he knew that it had split and was evacuating blood and that nobody was near to press the pieces shut again.

II.

In the hospital Daniel Aker, identified by a wallet found at the scene of the accident, was turned over to the care of a doctor named Lilia Probst. Under Dr. Probst there was a team of four specialists—a cardiologist, a neurologist, a kidney doctor, and an ear-nose-throat man—who in turn supervised numerous underlings, for there was much that needed to be repaired in Daniel Aker's broken body. For the time being, however, that body felt to Daniel simply like an enormously weighty carapace, a sarcophagus with his face painted in oranges and blues on the outside. From inside came the tiny, muffled cries of his internal organs, like the squeaks and skitters of small creatures—mice, spiders, caterpillars—doomed to suffocation. Daniel detected however that he seemed to be breathing on his own. He shifted his eyes from left to right and back again—he imagined that he heard a horrible scraping sound when he did so—and for the first time he realized the limits of his world: a blurred interval three inches to each side of him, a direct line down to where his belly button must once have been, and a cone-shaped space rising up to the water-stained ceiling, dematerialized by the fluorescent light hanging in a bright bar straight above him.

Then he remembered he had a family.

The doctor came in to speak with him. He made out that she was a slender woman, rather young, her hair pulled back in a stubby ponytail. She had large hands that seemed to be threatening to chop him up as they advanced toward him, moving rapidly up and down and from side to side.

"Can you hear me?" she asked.

Daniel nodded, but was aware that his head did not move. He blinked rapidly several times and attempted to stretch his mouth into a response. "Aaaah," he said. "Aaaah..... Gaaaaaa. Gaa." He felt immensely proud of the G.

"Good job!" The doctor sat down next to him on the bed and patted his chest—or the bed; he felt nothing—and her eyes, he thought, filled up with tears. This made Daniel wish to cry, too. He was instantly consumed by a desire to please this woman and to do whatever was needed to make her pain go away. He tried to shift to get a better look at her.

"Don't," she said, although again no motion had answered his intentions. "It will stress the organs. Don't even attempt to speak again." She looked down at her fleshy hands, now becalmed in her lap. "I'm bringing your parents and your sister in," she continued. "They've been waiting for you to regain consciousness. Don't try to speak to them. Just blink your eyes. They can see the life in your eyes."

Before he could say, Please, don't leave me, she was across the room and opening the door to a small collection of strangers.

His father, lumpish, with huge heaping shoulders—was this really his father? Had he always worn such dark, badly fitting suits, had he always looked so large? Had his jowls been so big, so loose, his face so dark and clotted? His mother—why did she hang back so shyly? His sister, her pretty blond hair tucked behind her ears—she was perhaps more familiar, but seemed older than he remembered. He attempted to fix her age in his mind. Eleven? No, older—at least sixteen. He scoured his mind for a recent image of her. The girl standing beside him, with his sister's face, looked to be in her early twenties.

They gazed down at him. His father spoke in low tones Daniel could not decipher. His mother wept. His sister held his mother and looked straight ahead, like someone forcing herself to watch a grotesque movie. The little doctor came in and, with words that sounded like sharp snips of a scissors, scattered them. They ran to the door like small routed animals.

Daniel slept.

III.

There was sunlight coming through the sectioned windows of the room when the doctor entered and told him he had slept through much of the past week. She sounded angry. She told him that he must make an effort to be alert for his parents.

"They have been living in a hotel for days on end. They need a scrap of hope, a sign that you care to come back to them." She flounced out the door, the back of her white jacket lifting like a sail.

In the moments of silence that followed Daniel had a little time to prepare himself. With great effort he brought his mind back to the trio that had stood by his bedside: the dark older man, the slim, self-effacing woman, and the girl with the mask-like face. He could not deny that they resembled his family, but he was again made uneasy by certain deformations he must have overlooked in the past. Why did his father scowl and slump so? Why did his mother hide her mouth behind her hand? Why didn't his sister greet him? He had always been good to her—teased her out of her blue moods, reassured her when a friend was cruel, given her the last piece of cake if she wanted it. Now he was in a bad spot and she ought at least to show the same kindness to him. He quickly reminded himself of the doctor: anything she wanted him to do must be correct, must be necessary. He would exert himself to perform for these hangers-on, to whom he supposed he owed some loyalty.

They walked in slowly, skirting the bed, as if making sure that he was not planning to spring at them with claws. When they saw that, as before, he did not move a muscle, they cautiously approached. His sister came nearest, standing close to where he supposed his chest to be.

His mother was bolder today. He saw that her grey hair was arranged in neat tight scallops, as if she had just been to the beauty parlor. She asked him how he was feeling. Gold hoops hung from her earlobes. They twitched and leaped as she bent down to speak to him.

"His eyes moved, Daddy," whispered his sister.

"Does he hear what we say?" his mother asked the doctor, who had reentered in another brisk gust.

"We're almost certain so. His scans show that his brain functioning in all four lobes is quite normal, considering. We haven't wanted to test his grosser physical or mental reponses yet, when he's still struggling to get his bearings."

"I understand," said his mother, as if she had been reprimanded. But then she burst out: "Does he realize his condition?"

"I've informed him."

Daniel tried to remember what he had been informed. All that came back to him was the doctor sitting by his side, the mild scent that rose from her neck and shoulders—he tried to recall its name: was it lemon? or was that a flower?—and how he had loved her and known that it was his job to protect her from that moment forward. He did not recall her speaking to him. It seemed to him that they had merely sat for a long time without words but in perfect recognition.

He saw that the woman with the gray hair—his mother—was making an effort; he felt her emotion rolling toward him in a series of dense, moist waves. He felt that there was something he was supposed to do to help. But he was very tired. He closed his eyes and wished everyone would leave.

"He's exhausted," said the doctor. "But he knew who you were this time, I'm sure of that. Did you see the way his eyes followed each of you? Amnesiacs, Alzheimer's patients—with them the gaze is different. Blank, frightened. Childlike. This was not that. He *sees* you."

His mother wept. His father cleared his throat uncomfortably. His sister, to his surprise, bent down and gave the back of his hand a tender kiss. First, he thought: my hand! He was delighted to remember that he had one, and to know where it was located. Second, he thought: "That is a grown-up kiss." He slit open his eyes. He saw his sister's smooth face, her high intelligent forehead, her neat blond hair. She wore hoop earrings like her mother, but these were doubled and much larger. The rings chimed pleasantly against each other. "She's a young woman," he thought, and then he remembered that she had been married last year, in a ceremony in which he had been the best man. There had been a flagpole, and little strawberry candies in crystal dishes. He could not remember the groom. His sister caught his hooded look, and grinned, but did not make a fuss or alert her parents, who were busy whispering to each other. The doctor put her hands gently on the parents' backs and pushed them toward the door.

He was left in silence. The sun seemed to have dropped in the sky, for the room was awash in a dim light, the tint that a movie screen takes on when the cameraman starts the fade to a new location. His sister's smile had excited him and filled him with a strange new energy. He felt as if he would like to join the circle of visitors who had hovered over his bed so solicitous and subdued: to crack jokes with them, link arms, swap old family tales. He wondered when they would next visit and imagined conversing amiably, intimately, around a Scrabble board in the living room, or in front of the TV. He attempted to sit taller so as to clear the phlegm from his throat and speak, but his body did not make the slightest response to his internal command. He then sought to raise his head to view his torso and hips, thinking that observation might give him some clue as to his impotence, but his neck, too, would not budge. He could feel the neck cords straining, his chin reaching forward; he felt a sensation that he would have called pain except that it was not accompanied by the sensory pressure he associated with that term. It was something worse than pain, a sentience far below the muscle stratum, within the tissues or perhaps deeper, an intuition of things ripping, pulling free of their attachments, of some sort of internal ransack and violation.

He attempted to remain perfectly still.

Slowly, the disturbance abated. His organs seemed to be anchored, sound. He breathed.

It was just then that the doctor returned. Again the sun seemed bright in the windows—perhaps it was still in fact morning, after the passing of some clouds. She was accompanied by another woman who looked even younger than herself, a woman who was dressed in sweatpants and a loose red long-sleeved T-shirt.

Before Daniel could finish inventorying the new visitor, the doctor had seized his left leg and begun tugging it toward her. He could not feel her hands on his skin—it was possible that he no longer had skin. He watched her attempt to rotate his knee to the left, then to the right, then left again. All of a sudden he felt it—a column of sheer hot pain. He opened his eyes wide. His mouth opened and said, "Aaaaaah."

The doctor did not look him in the eyes. She spoke rapidly to the other woman, but so deafened was Daniel by the sensations she was creating in him that he did not hear what she said. He was aware however that the other woman was writing in a notebook. She looked up from time to time to gaze sadly at some spot in the vicinity of his nose.

The doctor pushed and pulled at the leg a bit more and then circled the bed to grasp his opposite leg. There it was again—like someone driving a bolt of steel through the center of the limb, shattering the bone, each disk of his spine splitting open like a rotten plum. Yet his skin, to a depth of several layers, remained numb.

They moved on to his arms, neck and head.

The doctor spoke only to the woman taking notes. After a while a part of Daniel's mind was clear enough to make out parts of the conversation: "Mobility zero centimeters in the left elbow," said the doctor; or: "pain response right forearm: 8. No, make that 8 plus." When it was over the younger woman closed her notebook and stood next to Daniel, breathing rapidly, anxiously.

The doctor walked behind him and placed her hands on his head. "You were very good," she said. And then: "I can't shield you from the pain. The pain is good. It indicates a capacity for mobility." She appeared in front of him again and made a place for herself on the bed beside him, as she had on that first day when he had decided he loved her. Did he still? Then he had felt her gratitude, her relief, at his return to life. He had felt that she had suffered, waiting for him, and that by surviving he had alleviated her suffering. Now his survival seemed insufficient. He had thought she understood him—that she had accepted him for what he was: broken, immobile, helpless. But he had been wrong. She wanted more: cooperation, effort. Change.

Once more she patted the rigid shell that was him. "I will not baby you," she said. "We will work a little each day. This is Angela. From now on she will be in charge of your physical therapy sessions."

IV.

Daniel imagined that his body quivered to throw off the last reverberations of anguish, but he knew even that primitive reflex had been denied him. Though his mind was in riot, he was perfectly still. Nothing moved. Nothing moved. If the air passed across his face, he could not feel it, and no muscle trembled in response. He attempted to work his throat, his palate, to give a final "Aaaahhh . . . ," one that was for himself alone and not for them, his two lady inquisitors. But these organs must have become spent with their effort. He was a tomb.

He must have slept the night, because the next thing he was aware of was the thin light of early morning, and the arrival of his breakfast. He was learning to count from one day to the next by this meal, the only solid one he was given: cornflakes in warm milk, fed to him patiently by a nurse whose enormous bottom rested half on and half off the bed. "Soggy, yuck," the nurse commented as she slipped the plastic spoon between Daniel's slightly parted teeth. She kept up a running patter as she worked. "But they have to be soggy or you might choke on them, dear. Get better soon and we'll give you some nice, crisp cornflakes, that's a fact!"

When Angela returned, she was alone. Daniel was ready for her this time. He instructed his body to be heavy, motionless. He willed it to harden beyond the rigidity it already possessed in order to achieve infinitely less malleable levels of being, and finally a state where it was organically incapable of movement. His body would become zinc, quartz, diamond, would become part of the elemental, resistant core of the Earth.

He willed his body back in time as well, to the era before ferns and mosses, before algae, before bacteria itself—life—existed.

Angela was wearing a blue T-shirt this morning, identical to the red one she had worn the day before. She grunted as she grasped his left ankle; she did not possess the doctor's light grace. Daniel felt the iron shaft being driven through the marrow, deep into the bone's privacy, but the edge of the injury was infinitesimally dulled; he felt his resistance as a cushion, a balm placed on the site of outrage. After some time, the therapist seemed to hesitate. She stopped, shook out her arms. She looked fatigued. She studied his face, and he felt he was smiling, although he knew he could not smile—not yet. She sat in a chair across from the bed, watching him, and then wrote for a long time in her notebook.

The next day and the day after the same scene was repeated, except that Angela tired more quickly than before. Daniel lay with his eyes gazing upward, the ceiling spinning as his brain separated out the spotted strands of pain, and told himself that with a few more sessions like these his internal organs would simply mercifully give way. Angela put her head in her hands and breathed very slowly in and out, as if attempting to maintain her self-control. Then she left the room without writing in her notebook.

Very shortly the doctor was standing over him. She lectured him in long blocks of speech without pause.

"You don't seem to understand. I considered you an intelligent young man. I saw it in your eyes, the day you came back to consciousness; I thought you took in the truth. But you hesitate, you don't want to know. Must I spell it out for you?

"You are completely imprisoned by your body. Your essential organs are functioning—your liver, lungs, heart, kidneys—but hardly more than that. You are lucky to be alive, or perhaps you are unlucky. That is not for me to say. I am a doctor, not a philosopher. You are in my hands now and I am required to do the job that the state, your family and my professional affiliations demand of me. I must bring you back to life. Again, let me make the situation completely clear.

"You have no mobility in your head or neck. In your shoulders, arms, hands or fingers. In your torso, waist, hips or spine. In your legs, knees, feet or toes.

"Your eyes move. On the sheet of graph paper over there in the corner your brain spins out spirals and waves. Normal. That is how we know you are capable of regaining your motor functions. That and the pain. If you did not feel pain we would know that your nervous system had cut off these silent parts of your body. Exiled them. Declared them dead, no longer members of the corporate entity. Your body has not done that. Its yearning is still to remain intact. It will insist on its integrity.

"I know what you are trying to do. Angela is very young, but I have seen cases like this before. That is something our patients never realize: they are not unique. The most gruesome, bizarre, heaven-scarring cases: I have seen them. You want to be special, exempt from the process of healing. You are hiding from the mandates of your own body. Fool yourself then. Because while *you* cannot stir or speak or move your bowels, your body nevertheless acts. It crouches, waiting, gathers its forces. It plots to get well without you.

"Do you think your body concerns itself with your pain? It hungers for repair. It has a rage toward motion. Even if your brain was half dead, the manipulation Angela is practicing on you would result, gradually, in a softening of the tissues, a renewed yield and flexibility. After weeks of her treatment, there would begin to be some movement, very slight, in perhaps a toe or a finger: a reflex, perhaps, beyond your conscious control. Once this begins, you, the patient, begin to apply your own force to the locus of damage. We ask you to push, to pull, to bend, to point. Gradually, the body begins to respond to your directives. In its joy, it leaps farther than you request of it; it surprises you. You cannot possibly imagine the happiness you feel on that day, when you tell the body to move and it moves, it makes you master again, it dances to please you. It will surpass every agony you now feel and will feel. For several blissful moments, your terror is gone and you would pay again, with broken bones and crushed organs, to feel that sheer undiluted power.

"But you are rock. Angela has told me that you are more rigid today than on the first day we began work. That is only possible through will, perverse will.

"You want to die, do you? This hospital will not let you die. Not when you have a healthy heart and a healthy brain. You wish to be left in peace. We will not leave you in peace."

V.

In a book Daniel had once read—he no longer remembered which, or when—the writer had described how an Australian aborigine, condemned by his tribal court of some crime, would undergo a remarkable bodily crisis. As he lay in the exposed patch of desert to which he had exiled himself, his heartbeat would begin to slow, his body temperature to drop. Within eighteen to twenty hours he would begin to convulse; within twenty-four hours all vital signs would cease, his body willed to death by his own guilt and shame. Daniel believed that such a transformation was possible; in fact, the account had impressed him greatly. He had been awed at the power of the mind to reward, deform or punish the body, and had often thought about this passage at his health club, imagining the magnificence of, say, training himself to lift three times his weight, or to go without sleep for four days at a time. But turning it over in his mind now, as the hospital hushed and the lights snapped off in his room, he came to the conclusion that such power was possible only for believers. The generations before him—the scientists who had isolated sperm under a microscope and measured the relative properties of light and motion; his grandparents and great-grandparents who had first submitted to x-rays and bypass surgery—amounted to an inherited curse. His will would fail him. The aborigine had no doubt, while he, waiting for death, would constantly question: *Is it coming off?* His mind was too skeptical. And therefore, as the doctor said, his body had a will of its own. It would resist him even as he attempted to resist the dictates of those who insisted he recover.

He thought of how his family, if they understood, could spirit him out of this place, release him from his bondage with signatures on a few pieces of paper, bring him home and allow him the mercy of immobility, of stasis. He would regain his voice—he already was able to form a K sound in addition to G, and his throat and lips were the one part of his body that did not hurt when he roused them to exertion—and there would eventually be congenial talks from his place on the sofa. His sister and her husband, if she still had one, would drop by to chat and they would discuss books and baseball the way they'd used to. He would be the center of their little collective—it had badly needed a center, ever since he and his sister had gone off to school—and his upkeep would not be stressful for his mother, a mere matter of bathing and turning and changing him. They would even play Scrabble, if someone would sit out and place his tiles for him. His life might not be long, but it would be pleasant. And there was no reason, perhaps, that he might not live a long life after all.

He must find a way to signal his parents.

Rose, the nurse who served him his breakfast, entered his room promptly at 7 a.m. with her usual good cheer. "Blink your eyes, dearie, if you're happy to see me today." He blinked rapidly, content to play along. "Now blink twice if you don't got yourself the best-looking piece of ass in this here whole hospital." She laughed, a deep, vibrating bass, and waggled her massive bottom. Her breasts heaved up and down in her white nurse's jacket. "Oh, darling," she said. "It's going to be a long time till you got the manhood for the likes of me. But I'll wait for you, darling. Oh, you know I will."

VI.

The next time Angela appeared, both the doctor and his family were with her. His family seemed to have been brought along as a sort of cheering section. When the therapist grasped his left shoulder, heaving and wincing, he heard his cries in a new way. Listening with his parents' ears, he detected not just open-throated moans but gurgling sounds, gagging, high squeaks, rasps and snarls. For a few moments he was ashamed, but then the pain made him forget his observers almost altogether.

"Good going, go on, keep going," chanted the therapist.

"Help her. *Help* her!" demanded the doctor.

But Daniel could not help. From a distance he was aware of his mother's and his sister's eruptions of encouragement, their murmurs of concern and sympathy. Then his attention snapped back as he heard his father say: "Why doesn't he work harder? Can't you get him to cooperate?" His mother shushed him, but his father continued irritably, whether to the doctor or to Daniel it wasn't clear: "Come on, come on, come on." Daniel shifted his eyes in his father's direction and saw those terrible humping shoulders, whose origin he suddenly remembered. In his teenage years, before becoming an insurance salesman, his father had worked baling hay on a farm and had one day gotten his collarbone broken by a kick from an agitated horse. He had never healed quite straight, and the accident had made him less rather than more sympathetic to the injuries of others. His mother had once confided in Daniel: "Of course he married me. For him, well, there weren't that many choices."

Now his mother whispered loudly, as if on a stage where it is understood that the character being spoken about cannot hear: "Dr. Probst says we have to have patience. She says time will eventually bring him around."

Daniel waited for his sister to interrupt with some sort of sanity: a plea to end his torture, if only for a day; a point-by-point attack on the argument that restoring her brother's health was necessarily for the best. But he heard nothing. He knew then that things were terribly wrong, that he had horrendously misjudged his situation. The doctor—he saw now that he hated her—had enlisted his loved ones, his only possible saviors, in her project to reclaim him. To try to communicate with them, in whatever fashion he could manage, was pointless. Perhaps, if they would only watch and listen, they could learn the language of his eyes and moans, but the doctor had thrown them off the track, had assured them there was no message to be detected. They could not imagine his simple appeal: to be allowed to remain as he was. For the doctor had convinced them that he must not merely live: he must move, eat, act. He must be whole.

Daniel prayed that all the noise, grief, touch, importuning would disappear. He pictured his body as a broad column of white light under a white sheet: dematerialized, exempt.

Later, sometime, his sister leaned forward and said, "Don't resist so much. Give yourself up to the pain. Pretend you're riding in a big barrel down a waterfall—let the pain smash you down on the rocks."

He wanted to laugh—he wondered where his sister had picked up this glib therapeutic vocabulary. Yet he found himself examining her words—might they, after all, have any meaning? He had broken an arm once during soccer practice in college, and, earlier, had hurt himself while playing silly kids' games, once jumping from a stone wall and crushing two teeth. But had he ever "given himself up" to pain? Even in the broken-tooth incident, six years old, he'd clamped his bleeding mouth shut, held the howls and the panic in check. He had seen his body rise above the maiming, like an enormous blow-up clown, and had

had contempt for the small deflated cringing flesh below. He had been rewarded for being brave—"our tough little Danny," his mother said, using a nickname that even at that age he had detested. His uncle had called him a stoic, and when he'd asked what the word meant, his uncle, in his unhelpful way, had said, "The Stoic is the man who believes that indifference is the only reasonable attitude toward life."

As rods of flame splintered his body, he thought—not in words so much as in images, gleanings: Did giving oneself up to pain mean one felt it less—that in letting it saturate you completely it would somehow become diffused? Or was it rather that by this mental maneuver the body disappeared, annihilated by sensation, so that paradoxically one no longer had nerve endings and organs with which to feel? Did "giving up" release some obscure opiate in the brain, or clear the small white radiant space the gurus talked about, in which one could find peace amidst tortures? It seemed to Daniel rather that surrendering would only amplify the pain, give it license to increase, horribly, like a litter of wild dogs.

Before he fainted he had an image of a swami flinging himself on poison-tipped spears, then rolling, slowly and deliberately, on a bed of hot coals. The swami wore a calm, loving expression of complete satisfaction and Daniel wondered what made men bend themselves intentionally to suffering.

VII.

The room was empty. Within minutes after waking he could feel the change: a fluttering inside, a series of shy clicks and whisks, that signaled him his nerves were once again receiving signals from within, were renewing their delicate vibration. Random patches of his skin burned as if someone had put a match to them. Daniel wept without tears. His body was continuing its betrayal: seeking motion, indulging agitation. The motion would begin in the deepest tissues and spread upward and outward: to the organs, the blood canals, finally the skin. His caretakers had seduced his limbs, whispered pretty tales to the lymph and glands and cartilage. The life inside him was abnormally, deformedly stirring, like a stunted fetus pressing to emerge.

Rose entered with his first dinner. She was not so jaunty as usual. She looked tired, he noticed, her eyes smoky and raw. It occurred to him that she must of course have a husband or lover and he decided that this man was making her unhappy. He remembered that there was a world of human relationships outside this room—of people who caressed, beat, loved each other.

But when Rose drew near to the bed, her expression and her manner changed completely.

"Well, hello, soldier," she said, in her customary lively tone. "Meatloaf tonight. Yum, yum. They ground it up real good, so give it a try. Darling, I get a big rise out of sticking my fat fingers into that little mouth of yours but sooner or later you're going to have to do this yourself. I can't be your mammy forever. First they'll get you on this baby food, then you'll have solids, pretty soon they'll be making you cut it up yourself."

"Gaarg," said Daniel. "Gaarrgh. Gak."

Rose stopped mashing the meatloaf onto a fork and looked at him thoughtfully. "You, too, darling," she said, although Daniel had been telling her that he did not accept; that never, never would he be fed again except by other hands.

When he had finished taking his food Daniel held her eyes for a long moment. She did not look away as he had feared. "Poison me," he said with his eyes. "Find a way to put something in my meals. No one will know that it was you. Believe me, you'll be doing me a favor."

This time she seemed to understand. She folded the serving tray with a loud snap and raised her full bulk above his head. "You poor godforsaken thing," she said. "God save your soul."

Then he knew for certain that there would be no help, that he would be forced to return to the world not for his own sake but for the sake of others.

Rose lay the back of her hand against his forehead and he fought his terror at realizing that he could feel its dampness, the cool, oval fingernails.

A Face in Shadow

Joseph Freda

He had just picked up a bottle of wine for dinner, and there she was on the corner of 68th and Second, looking like 1970 all over again. Oh, not in the way she dressed or wore her hair. It was November, after all; she wore a black overcoat and a round woolen hat. No, it was more that the moment of recognition struck like a brisk wind and swept him back thirty-some years. He recognized her stance first, the way she stood tall and yet wavering among the other pedestrians on the far corner, the way she alone seemed to bend to the whoosh of the traffic. Then the way her Nordic features—nose and cheekbones, her polar eyes—reflected more light than the gray evening held. And then her stride. Or rather, her motion. She seemed to drift into the crosswalk, to be carried along with the uptown tide.

"Maggie?" he asked when she got to the curb.

She turned at his voice, a smile forming before comprehension, and then she recognized him and laughed out loud.

"Sam," she said. "Can it be?"

They hugged, kissed, stood at arms' length. She was leaner than he remembered, or maybe it was the effect of the long overcoat. Her face—always all angles and planes—was tighter, edgier under her black hat. But she still seemed to move without actually doing so, the way young willow trees do even when there is no wind. And she still had that way of looking him over and pulling him in, as if it were her arms and not her eyes that held him.

"Look at you," she said. "Just look. You've been in New York all these years?"

"Yeah, mostly. Susan and I've had a place upstate for a while. She's up there now. How about you?"

"California. I started having some health problems, so I came back," and she waved her hand as she always used to in his East Village loft, with the hot afternoon air pressing them against the sheets, and when something would intrude—a shout from the street, a fender scraping a meter, a garbage can slamming—she'd wave it away and then brush her hand across her forehead, her pale eyebrow, as if she were pushing away something soft and pliant, a spiderweb. She could push away anything with that motion: noise, headache, thoughts of her husband. So when she waved away her "health problems," he was back there for a moment, on a hot afternoon with taxi horns blaring and a cold Ballantine on the sill and her sweat mingling with his on the futon, but then he caught up with her words and latched onto "having some tests run at Sloan-Kettering," and he snapped to the present.

"Listen, you want to have a cup of coffee? A drink?"

She paused, smiled. Waved toward Third Avenue.

"Coffee would be good."

They were all sleeping with her back then. Or maybe it was the other way around, since she chose them: Mel Kaplov, Victor Sprague, Sam, Johnny Verona, others. They were all friends with Larry, her husband. They'd gone to art school together and some were painting now and others were acting like it. Some were hanging out taking classes, waiting for Vietnam to be over. Larry was the best painter in the bunch. He had some family money so he could go into his studio all day, all night if he wanted to, come out only to eat or to see Maggie, take the twins for a twirl around the loft or a piggy-back ride, throw some Chef Boy-R-Dee into a pan and eat it standing up, and then head back in for some more painting. He had had a show at Gorsky-Feinstadt while still in art school, and he had a solo show lined up for the fall. So he was painting like crazy that summer.

And Maggie was partying like crazy. There was a party nearly every night at somebody's place, and when there wasn't a party there was the ReBar. Sometimes she showed up by herself, but usually Larry came with her. She was vibrant and outgoing, like a concert-tuned guitar aching to be plucked. Larry was quiet and distracted. While she'd pass herself from this cluster to that huddle, he'd stay off to the side sipping wine. Usually one of the other painters would come over, and Larry would be soft-spoken and gracious, but they could always tell he was someplace else. To Sam, Larry always seemed to be a man standing in the shade.

Once Sam knew Maggie's pattern—after she had worked it on him—he began to notice how she would circulate through the room, chatting up everybody, slipping under this arm or that, easing away, catching someone's eye in the next group and moving on. Eventually she would lock onto one guy, plant herself before him with her shimmering hair and her bright-print miniskirt, and reflect all the light in the room into his face. She'd finish her wine and the guy'd get her another, smiling self-consciously and avoiding Larry's corner. By this time everybody knew what was going on, and the energy would shift, and all their attention kept sliding to

Maggie and the guy. The night he, Sam, was the guy, she'd shaken her head and the light glanced off her hair. She'd tucked a shoulder toward him and suggested a walk. They'd strolled to the foyer as if to get a breath of air, to look at an interesting painting. She'd held his arm as they walked, brushed against him, and when they were some blocks from the party she had pulled him into a doorway and kissed him so purposefully that neither of them had to say anything. He'd simply taken her arm and escorted her to his place.

Thus had commenced their fling, which lasted all of four weeks. By August, she had moved on. But while they were together, she had made him feel like he was hers alone. Afternoons in his loft were made of charmed time: Minutes turned liquid, and hours layered one upon the next without drying. When she came to him and unbuttoned his shirt, he was powerless to exert his will. And there was no need. She took charge and ran the show, from what they did then to what they talked about afterwards: her children, her mother's horses in New Jersey, her stepfather's beach house. Larry, of course. But she mentioned Larry as casually as if he were another piece of furniture in her life, and when she needed to rearrange him to make room for Sam or someone else, she did.

Sam was only too grateful and too overwhelmed to do anything but occupy the stage she cleared for him. He loved the feel of her legs alongside his, loved the line of her spine under his palm. When she was with him, time seemed to expand, to move forward without end. But that, he learned, was just love-addled folly. The end came in one single afternoon. She had stood at the window before dressing, gazing out, and then she finished her ale and said, "July's over." When she left, she was gone. He had resumed being one of the crowd that watched her work her tricks of light, and when she'd leave the party with another guy, everybody's attention would shift from the doorway, and that's when they'd notice that Larry was no longer in the room, either.

Nobody had seen him leave, and nobody knew where he went. Home, Sam figured at first, because she never took her lovers there. Maybe he went someplace else and picked up a girl. Or maybe he just walked over by the river until enough time had passed. Sam always wished Larry would take more of a stand, assert himself. Dig in and say no to Maggie, punch one of the guys, slap her. Sam had asked her once, as they lay tangled in his sheets, if she and Larry ever argued about "this," gesturing, and she said, "Not with words."

The café was busy with takeouts for dinner, but they found a table by the windows and ordered coffee. A delivery bicycle was chained outside. People streamed past—businessmen in buttoned-up topcoats, an Asian girl on a cell phone, a guy with his dry cleaning—and the street itself gave up a gunmetal blue sheen. Maggie settled into her chair and pulled at her gloves, slid her coat off her shoulders. She kept her hat on. She smiled easily at him and then she shrugged.

"Long time since we've done this," she said.

He set the bag with the bottle of wine by his feet.

"A long time," he agreed. "How are your girls?"

"Pretty good. Phoebe's a lawyer—corporate counsel for something to do with television. Divorced twice, no kids. Very glam in L.A. Robin's a stay-at-home mom. Married a good guy, has two adorable kids. Boy and a girl."

"So you're a grandmother."

"And proud as I can be."

"Grandma Maggie. Who would have imagined?"

"Life goes on," she said. "Life begets life. Look around."

She gestured to the street, to a nanny pushing a stroller shrouded in plastic, to a Spanish kid tottering his mountain bike between pedestrians. But Sam didn't want to look away from her face. Amazing, he thought, how a face could encounter all it does in thirty years and not show more signs of wear. Her skin was still taut on her cheeks, her eyes still animated. A little crinkling at the edges, a fold between the brows, but that was it. He, on the other hand, knew that his eyelids had pouched after years of work and stress, knew his chin drooped.

"Are you painting?" she asked.

"Not much," he said. "Not seriously. After I started doing agency work, there just wasn't much time left for painting. Susan still throws pots, though. She's got a nice kiln up in the country."

"Susan as beautiful as ever?"

"She's doing pretty well. Goes to the health club when we're in the city. Gardens and walks the property upstate."

"Never had any kids, Sam?"

"Never wanted any, never had any. We were careful about that."

She smiled a kind of teasing smile, and he wondered where this was headed.

"After Larry passed away, the girls meant so much to me. I mean, they were all I had, and they were so dependent. My own father left when I was young and I didn't want them to grow up like that, so I moved to California and married a sculptor."

Of course, a sculptor. A man good with his hands.

"That didn't last. But I thought they should have a father in their life. I guess I never forgave Larry for what he did. Until recently, maybe."

"So did you remarry?"

"Three times."

"So that's like—"

"Five husbands." She went *poof!* with her hands. "What can I tell you, Sam? I just wasn't a chained-at-the-altar kind of girl. Not like Susan, it sounds like."

"We've had our moments, as any couple has."

"Still, you've made it."

"That sounds pretty final."

"Hey, if you've made it thirty years, you've pretty well made it. Have you been a faithful husband?"

"That's none of your business."

"Ha. Always the proper one, Sam. Always the fastidious one. Tell me, do you still offer the towel to the lady first?"

He choked his coffee. In the Anne Taylor Loft across the street, halogen spotlights reflected off the fiberglass skulls of mannequins too chic for hair. How could she remember such details, all the guys she'd had? He imagined her mental catalog: Sam the fastidious one, Johnny the wild one, Mel the moaner. What was Larry?

"I know everybody felt sorry for Larry after what happened," she said, "but no one knew what it was like to live with him. It was like being in a room with too little air, because he was breathing it all up. He had to be the center of our life. He was the one who needed tending. Not the girls—certainly not me. It was *his* painting, *his* career, *his* life—we were just attachments, adornments, those last few drips of paint at the edge of the canvas that complete the picture."

"Ah, Maggie..." They were all so self-centered then. In your early twenties, it comes with the turf.

"If he'd just considered us. Me. If he'd just granted us some importance. Maybe things would have turned out differently."

Maybe. But he caught a vision of her flitting around a crowded apartment like a bright bird, of her standing naked by his window, already elsewhere. Maybe not.

For Labor Day weekend that year, the whole crew was to gather at Sam's uncle's farm in the Catskills. They had piled into various cars and made the run upstate. But Larry had to stay in the city a couple of days. His dealer was bringing a collector around for a studio visit, so Larry had asked Sam to take Maggie and the girls.

"Sure, Larry," Sam had said, surprised. "Of course."

He wanted to offer Larry some assurance, something to indicate that his friend's trust was justified. Something like, *They can have Uncle Walt's room while he's away,* but he knew it was his guilt talking and that Larry would hear it.

Larry had filled in the silence. "You'll take care of them, Sam. You're the only one who would."

And driving up Route 17 with Maggie riding shotgun and the girls sprawled asleep in the back seat, the hot summer air blasting through the windows and whipping Maggie's hair, Sam imagined that he was taking care of them; imagined that he had taken Larry's place. It felt good for a while, as Maggie punched radio buttons and sang along. It felt good when she touched his shoulder and thanked him for getting them out of the city. It felt less good when she went quiet and simply swayed to the music, and it felt positively weird when he looked into the rearview mirror and saw the twins leaned against each other in sleep, their curls matted to their sweaty foreheads. He was no father, nor could he work up the psych to act like one. The little girls intimidated him, made him feel as if he were being watched. He had imagined flirting with Maggie, imagined her sitting close to him on the bench seat. He had imagined the night at the farm as a resumption of the afternoons in his loft. But he hadn't factored in the girls.

After Maggie hadn't said anything in a few miles, he looked over and was surprised to see her crying.

"Hey Mags," he said. "What is it? What's wrong?"

She shook her head, wiped her cheeks. "Nothing. Nothing. Sometimes I just get weepy. Are the mountains always this blue?"

By the time they got to the farm she was nearly her old self, and she took the girls to Uncle Walt's room to clean them up. When she brought them downstairs and turned them loose on the crowd, she was bright again. She milled with everybody through the old house and around the grounds, discovering the barn and outbuildings, the grape arbor, the creek and the frog pond. And she helped with dinner and nursed a glass of wine, but she made no moves on Sam or any of the guys. When the party-hearty types started revving up for the evening, uncorking more wine and mixing margaritas, she begged off and said she was taking the girls to bed.

He intercepted her in the stair hall and asked if she was okay.

"I think all this—" She waved to the party spilling from the dining room onto the porch "—is starting to catch up with me. Everything does, Sam."

He touched her arm, wished her goodnight. It was okay. This new girl, Susan, had started paying attention to him, and she wanted to see the hayloft.

It was a spectacular suicide. When the state trooper called and said that the accident happened on the winding stretch of Route 97 called Hawk's Nest, Sam knew. Everybody took Route 17 to the country. It was faster. But the summer before, when Woodstock shut down 17 and the Thruway, Sam had shown Larry the back way through New Jersey and along the Delaware River. Larry had described with uncharacteristic awe the twisting curves and towering cliffs of Hawk's Nest, and after that his paintings showed a serpentine line coiling through the layers of paint, the kind of line that Brice Marden would later use to such languid effect. Sometimes, Larry told Sam, when he left the parties in the city, he'd drive out to Hawk's Nest just to take the curves at high speed and then to sit on the ledges and watch the light fade from the Delaware.

So on that Labor Day weekend he had driven his big-ass Chrysler New Yorker at eighty miles an hour through a break in the stone retaining wall of Hawk's Nest, and he had plummeted two hundred feet into the big maples and pines on the floor of the river valley. Several people saw the accident, and one driver described how Larry steered for the break in the wall and accelerated. "The car just took off," he said.

And a rock climber, scaling the cliffs below the highway, heard a screech and a rush and looked up to see the Chrysler's undercarriage. "Sparks were flying," he said, "and chunks of the wall started hitting me, so I tucked up against the cliff. But I saw the whole thing, the whole arc. The car stayed upright for a while, and the dude had his elbow out the window, like he was out for a Sunday drive."

Sam went straight to the hospital, but there wasn't much he could do. Larry was in intensive care and nobody could get inside, and they were going to chopper him to Westchester. But when the ICU door opened, Sam caught a glimpse of a swaddled figure, nurses and doctors hovering, and a snaking maze of tubes and hoses. By the time he got home, Maggie had split.

Larry was in Westchester for six weeks. Sam and Victor and Mel took turns driving out and sitting with him, reading the paper aloud, bringing news of his show, which opened to positive reviews. They talked to him through his bandages at first, and then later to his passive, sleeping face, about how many paintings had sold, and which ones, and who was doing what—Mel had given up smoking, Johnny had a new girlfriend—and how the Yankees were stuck in second place with no chance of catching the Orioles, how

Palestinian guerrillas had hijacked a Pan Am jet and blown it up. The doctor said this contact was important, that the coma state was mysterious: Sometimes comatose patients just woke up, and they could recall the television news or something a visiting relative had said. So Sam and the others came whenever they could. They'd arrange shifts. Not once during the hours and hours of sitting in the slick hospital chair did Sam see so much as a flicker of response from Larry. The man was deep inside himself. Sam hoped it was quiet and still in there, and that Larry was at peace.

During this time no one saw Maggie. She didn't answer the phone, she wasn't around the neighborhood. Finally, at the end of the sixth week, she walked into the hospital room. Sam was sitting by the window; Susan was reading to Larry from *Artforum*. Maggie had cut her hair short, like Mia Farrow in *Rosemary's Baby*. She held herself tightly, almost defiantly, and she asked if she could be alone with her husband, please.

They waited in the lounge at the end of the hall. Maggie was in the room a long time, and when she finally came out, she had been crying.

"He wanted to die," she said.

"What do you mean?" Sam asked.

"Larry wanted to die, for a long time. I'm surprised no one ever noticed."

She cried a little more and so did Susan, and then the three of them sank together onto the couch.

"I just gave him permission," Maggie said. "I held his hand and told him it was okay, that he could move on. The girls and I would be fine. I felt something then. He squeezed, and then he started to go. I stayed until he was gone."

Sam didn't see Maggie after the funeral, though he heard she'd left town. It felt all right. He was seeing Susan then, and the parties had stopped.

The sidewalk traffic began to thin; the streetlights had taken over. The waiter dimmed the lights and put out white tablecloths, dressed the café in its evening guise. He brought a candle to their table, asked if they wanted refills, and when Maggie said no, moved on.

"I don't think I ever properly thanked you for taking care of Larry," she said. The little candle flickered and her expression was hard to discern.

"Ah." He shook his head. "I don't know that I did much."

"You were there for him. I always appreciated it. I've always believed Larry did too."

He had never known. Larry had given no sign in the hospital room: no acknowledgement of the news of his show, nor of the paintings that sold. Not a muscle moved even when Sam, alone with Larry the day before Maggie showed up, confessed to the afternoons spent with her, unburdened his heart at the bedside, begged forgiveness for whatever portion of his hand had been on Larry's steering wheel, whatever weight of his foot had been on the gas.

"It was a long time ago, Maggie."

"Still, it's never too late to say thank you." She was smiling at him, her face framed by her soft black hat. His leg jittered and rocked the wine bottle in its bag. He reached down to steady the bottle.

"You haven't taken off your hat," he said. "Is your hair long or short these days?"

"Oh," she said and waved. "I haven't any."

He laughed. Surely she was joking. But she had moved her coffee cup between the candle and her face, and with the light so blocked, he couldn't read her at all.

Survival Traits

Nancy Ginzer

In the early days of their courtship, Martin took Nora canoeing in the Indian Arm fjord. The canoe was red-lacquered wood, built after the Second World War and passed down to Martin by his family. Martin's grandfather had been a fan of Charlie Chaplin and had christened it *The Little Tramp,* but Martin, with his typical irreverence, called it *The Tramp*.

In the canoe, Nora would lean back and close her eyes to the sun. Trailing her fingers in the water, she felt light and generous in the youthful expectation of happiness—and the hope of a ring. Whenever Martin kissed her, he'd push her to the canoe floor with such urgency she thought they would tip over and drown. The floor reeked of salmon and the back of her T-shirts got soggy and fishy-smelling with old seawater, but she never minded.

Martin was her first lover. They'd met at university in Vancouver where Nora was studying theatre costume design at UBC. At twenty-four, he was older than she was by four years, in his second year of law school.

There was a rumor circulating in Nora's dorm that Martin had dated a nursing student from the seventh floor and that he'd dropped her with no warning. Nora heard that the girl had taken it badly; she'd missed classes and had been seen puffy-eyed in the washroom of the Student Union. Sometimes, Nora saw her sitting in the cafeteria by herself. The girl had a delicate, angular face and a good figure—but cheapened herself, Nora thought, by wearing tight-fitting jeans and stretchy tube tops that revealed her belly button like a biker's girlfriend. Still, Nora worried if what she'd heard were true, and she wondered what the girl had done to deserve such treatment.

One afternoon in the canoe, Martin asked Nora to marry him. "There's only one girl for me," he said, looking into her eyes. "You're my guiding star."

In that moment, Nora forgot that her eyes were small and her jaw was heavy. She forgot the girl from the dorm and all the logical reasons why she should or shouldn't marry Martin—that he was brilliant but never on time, that he made her laugh and called her Norska but could never remember her middle name, that he drank too much Chianti on hot afternoons and would stand up, swaying in the canoe, singing "Cinnamon Girl" across the water in his off-key, gravelly voice. All of these things fell away when he told her she was his star. And for that brief, luminous moment, she was.

That night when they took *The Tramp* out of the water at Deep Cove and hoisted it onto the car rack, he took a small Swiss army knife from his khaki shorts pocket. Biting his lower lip, and with deadly serious concentration, he carved their initials under the edge of the canoe. Whenever they were paddling in the fjord, Nora would rub her fingers along the edge to make sure the letters were still there.

The day Martin said he wanted a divorce, a soft and humid winter wind had blown inland from the Georgia Strait. He'd come to pick up the skis he'd left behind when he'd moved out of the house three months earlier.

Before breakfast, Nora had put on a new sweater and felt almost cheerful, until it came to her with a sickening thud that she had nothing new to say to Martin, and that her old, deep, wellspring of love for him would never be—and never had been—enough.

To his credit, he was sheepish. "Sorry, Nor, so close to Christmas and everything." After he spoke, a crack came out of the sky like a sonic boom—ice sliding off the roof. For years afterwards, the sound of it—like the voice of God—would invade her dreams, and Nora would wake up in the dark, shaking and weeping, convinced the roof had caved in.

Under the glare of the garage light bulb, Martin looked ashen, older than his forty-three years. He gripped his skis with one hand and the canoe with the other, hoping, Nora could tell, that she wouldn't make things difficult for him, that she wouldn't cry or make some kind of awkward scene. Perhaps that was the problem all along, she thought—her lack of dramatic flare.

She shrugged and said quietly, "If that's what you want, Martin."

He nodded quickly then took his skis outside to the Jeep's rack, opening the tricky latches and clapping the snow from his leather gloves. She'd always liked the way he worked, with a sense of purpose and precision. That, at least, hadn't changed.

He'd met someone, the latest in a long line of conquests, although Nora had no proof of the others, only suspicions. This time it was different, a girl in her twenties, a department store buyer from San Antonio, Texas.

Martin's cousin, Anne, had delighted in telling Nora everything—that Martin and the girl had met while waiting for planes at La Guardia, and that Cara, that was the girl's name, was a "cute little blonde thing who dresses like one of those teen models in black knee-high boots and skirts cut way up to here." Anne had made a slicing motion across her crotch.

"What else?" Nora had asked. She'd wanted to hear it all, every microscopic detail. The pain was more intense that way, sharply clarified, like cut glass. Later, she would play it over in her mind, turning it this way and that.

The new studio apartment where he'd been living had little storage, so Nora had been keeping the rest of his things—what she thought of as the detritus of their marriage: his mother's antique bureau in the basement, an assortment of legal and personal files, ski equipment, *The Tramp.* Looking at them and at the dust they'd collected made her feel oddly detached, as if the fourteen years of their marriage were scenes from another couple's life.

Martin walked back to the garage with a step that was almost jaunty. "Feels right, doesn't it, Nor?" he said.

She feigned a smile.

He shifted a box on the floor with his foot. "How's your mother?"

"The same," Nora said. "Still can't speak."

"I'm sorry to hear that. Ten months is a long time."

A year, she silently corrected him.

He put his hand on her shoulder and she turned to the ping pong table behind her and picked up a trophy. It was a monstrous object she'd always hated, a prize he'd won during his law articling days for downhill racing. Chipped, with the plastic gold veneer peeling away to metal, the goggled little skier on top leaned forward in a racing position, grimly looking out to the future, ski poles in the air behind him. Martin used to show it off to friends, joking that it was a testament to his "championship bunged-up knees." Nora knew better. Like his colleagues, he was given to high ambition. And she knew there were other private, needy reasons for his keeping it, having to do with proving himself. But this was something she never brought up.

"Here," she said, smiling brightly and holding it out to him. "This might come in handy."

He looked at her, puzzled, took the trophy and carried it out to the Jeep.

The next week, Nora flew on a bumpy flight from Vancouver to Calgary to visit her parents. She spent the hour, nauseous, with her face pressed against the cold plastic window, huddled like a child in her coat with the collar pulled up around her throat. She would have taken him back, crawled to him across six lanes of traffic if it would have made a difference.

By mid-afternoon in Calgary, she and her father were on their way to visit her mother in the nursing home—what he called "the land of the living dead." The heater in the car was on high, yet Nora felt a cold heaviness in her limbs. Sadness did that to you, she thought, made your bones feel heavy as stone. The simplest acts—opening your eyes in the morning, greeting people at work—became Herculean tasks, demanding more than you're capable of giving the world.

Her father cleared his throat. "So, what will you do now?"

"I've got another year's contract."

"Where?'

"At the Playhouse, Dad. It's my ninth year."

He grunted. "Doesn't seem that long."

He was steering the car onto Elbow Drive, the long, tree-lined street where Nora used to ride her bicycle as a child and where Martin and she used to walk to the Dairy Queen whenever they visited Calgary in the summer. Now, the snow sat fat and rounded like loaves of white bread on the poplars, bending branches towards the road. She closed her eyes and had a vision of his teeth flashing in the sun. He'd be on the slopes of Whistler now with the new girlfriend. Anne had told her this, too.

Nora rolled down the window.

"Too warm?" her father said.

"I'm a little airsick. It was a rough flight. "

The radio was tuned to 1060, an Oldie station that played music from the wartime hit parade: big band by Les Brown, Guy Lombardo, Dick Haymes. Ella Fitzgerald was singing "Too Young for the Blues," a favorite of her mother's.

In the old days, Nora's father had been tone-deaf to jazz, tuning only to CBC: politics, sports, stock market reports. Nora guessed that the reason he was listening to it now had everything to do with Vivian, his new girlfriend.

He clenched the steering wheel, his mouth set against something or someone—undoubtedly her—Nora—for asking him to take her, for *forcing* him to put in an appearance. He looked different today. Sexier, she decided, with his new, frameless glasses and his blown-dried hair. Even the car was new: a small black Lincoln. This from a man who considered buying Nora's mother a new sofa or taking her on exotic vacations, sacrificial acts. You had to marvel at Vivian's powers of persuasion, Nora told herself. You really did.

He stopped the car in the circular driveway and waited for her to climb out. She squinted against the sun through the dirty windshield. Martin's girlfriend would be wearing one of those expensive metallic pink or silver ski suits with white fur around the hood. He'd be teaching her how to snow-plough, as he had Nora, once. The girl would be sporting a sunny, beauty pageant smile—Martin had always loved the young blondes who laughed with their mouths open, their big, white American teeth a tantalizing prelude to something more. The girl would tell Martin in her drawl that she just *lo-ved* the snow, so fluffy and white and *so* clean. What she wouldn't know, Nora thought, was that there was no such thing as clean snow. What she wouldn't know, because no one that young did, was that there were relics beneath that pristine blanket. Skeletons. Ancient stories, as old as the hills.

Nora put her hand on the door and waited. Her father cleaned wax out of his ear with his baby finger. "Go on, then, Norie" he said. "I'll be a minute."

In the lobby, a cluster of old men sat crumpled in their wheelchairs—the same scene as her last visit, three months earlier. Their bodies were as lifeless as soft, drooling puppets, only today they were dressed in brand new Christmas cardigans, robes, and slippers.

A silver-haired woman with her mother's high cheekbones came rolling in a wheelchair across the lobby towards her. Nora's heart froze, until she saw that the woman was in her late eighties, a good twenty years older.

Nora walked to the front station. "Excuse me. Which room is Evelyn Riley's?"

"Room 127," a nurse replied without looking up from her crossword puzzle. "Same as always."

Nora walked the long tiled corridor that was slick with freshly-mopped, lemony disinfectant. To her right, light fell across a card table in the games room where seniors were shuffling cards—a Norman Rockwell scene complete with gnarled hands, snowy hair, pastel cardigans. All ironically cheerful. Further down the hall, a woman's strangled voice cried out, "David." *David. A husband, or a son?* Nora glanced as she passed by the door and saw what looked to be no more than a heap of bird bones under a thin blanket, crowned with a tuft of white hair. She kept walking.

In room 127, Nora's mother was lying in bed, her head propped up on three pillows. The left side of her face was contorted as if pulled by gravity and her gaze was transfixed was on the ceiling, yet there was no disputing the family resemblance, the high forehead and the pale blue eyes. We're not a handsome lot, the Svensons, her mother used to say. But we have a saving grace, a Darwinian trait for survival: our Nordic stubbornness. Still, Nora wondered, wasn't it foolish gall to hang on—a childish refusal to allow death a foot in the door—like frozen goods past the expiration date?

She pulled a chair beside the bed and pushed a strand of hair away from her mother's forehead. A year earlier while frying eggs for breakfast, her mother had had a massive stroke, an aneurysm in the parietal lobe of her brain. She'd fallen to the floor clutching a spatula. To Nora, this gesture seemed an apt third act—a beautifully symbolic, unintentionally comic, *to-hell-with-you* fishwife's stance against her husband of forty-one years.

The doctors said her occasional stutter of baby vowels was only a reflex. Technically speaking, she was in a "dysphasic, vegetative state," which meant, said Nora's father, that she was alive enough to breathe and chew and swallow, but dead of mind. He called her a vegetable, a turnip. It wasn't meant to be cruel, simply the argot of his profession, crude shoptalk. A pathologist, now retired, he'd always called cadavers "stiffs, mummies, carcasses, dead Joes," and this to him was no different. After the stroke, he said it would have been easier for everyone if she'd died, that it was a shame she didn't need a feeding tube because if she had they could have legally put her out of her goddamned misery. "Only what nature intended." Nora had argued against him, albeit weakly.

In her darkest moments, she, too, had prayed for her mother to die, and that, more than anything else, shamed her.

Her father walked into the room, looked down at his wife, stonily, and pecked her forehead. He didn't take off his parka, a signal to Nora that they weren't to stay long. They were expected for dinner at Vivian's house—Vivian, the girlfriend of six months who he claimed he'd met on the golf course. Vivian used work as a nurse in the trauma centre at his hospital. *How could they not have known each other before the stroke?*

Nora didn't want to eat at Vivian's house. She didn't want to pretend she and Vivian could be friends, especially while her mother was still alive. She didn't want to make polite chit chat in a living room that reeked of smoke and cat pee and was cluttered with fake ferns and Royal Doulton figurines of shepherdesses in gauzy dresses.

So maybe Martin had a point. Maybe Nora was cold. It was the trait in her he said he could never understand, "that bloody wall of Scandinavian iciness" she'd inherited from her mother. Nora closed her eyes and silently railed. Shyness. Could he not see that?

She pulled her chair closer to the bed, stroked her mother's hand, willing her to show some sign of life, if only a murmur or a squeeze of the hand. *Prove Dad wrong*, she said under her breath. Her father cleared his throat and nodded to the lobby where he'd read the paper or chat up one of the pretty nurses. He had a knack for that. If Nora's mother hadn't been silenced, Nora thought, she could tell a host of stories.

Nora picked up a tube of lotion from the night table, squeezed out a creamy glob, and spread it on her mother's face in a thin film. She whispered, "Mom, I'm here."

One of the nurses said Nora's mother heard everything. Nora wasn't convinced, still, she stroked her mother's arm and talked about the masks she was constructing for "A Midsummer Night's Dream," the unreliable seamstress, the backstage intrigues and affairs, the sequins, the feathers, the ribbons, the gluey mess behind such exotic deceptions.

As she kissed her mother goodbye, Nora whispered in her ear, "Martin sends his love."

When she'd met Vivian months ago, Nora had expected an elegant, younger version of her mother. Fat chance, as Vivian would say. Vivian was a vivacious smoker with a raspy voice—a horse-faced, card-playing, sixty-ish divorcee with a hefty bust, dyed red hair, and Betty Grable legs, as Nora's mother would have called them—the type of person (did they really exist?) who was actually *proud* of the fact she hadn't picked up a book since college. Yet, Nora couldn't help but marvel at the raucous way Vivian laughed at her father's flat punch lines, the way she sat beside him and patted his thigh, or kissed his bald spot whenever she passed by.

On the way home Nora's father said, "I've been thinking, Norie. What you need is one of those pit-bull lawyers. A sharp Jew. Martin will have one, you can bet your bottom dollar on that. Or one of those slick Osgoode Hall partners of his." He clicked a denture. "Don't let him have the house under *any* circumstances. I put three hundred and eighty-five thousand into that house thirteen years ago, and it's prime Vancouver property, now. Prime." He stopped at a light and looked over at her. "*Jesus,* Nora. Are you listening? You'd think I was talking to the wind. I know you. You'll let him walk all over you. Just like your mother, sit there and won't say a goddamn thing, just brood, and then afterwards, piss and moan."

"Yes, Dad," she said, "the house."

The house. Since Martin had left, there wasn't anything left alive in it. A solitary plant in a Mexican pot sat on the kitchen windowsill, a baby basil that was now a withered, brown toothpick she'd killed from over watering or neglect. Silence greeted her at her door and silence shared her bed. There was no laughter in the house, only what one of her actress friends called "the humiliation of singlehood." To Nora, it was a sinister sounding word—a symbol of celibacy and self-denial—like the cowl of a monk.

"Speaking of houses," her father was saying, "I'm putting mine up for sale. Both the furnace and the roof are due for replacement and I'm tired of shoveling and mowing. Christ. I've had enough of that for a lifetime of Sundays." To hell with it, he was going to buy one of those condos on the golf course out in Heritage Pointe where they took care of all of that. He was thinking of buying a timeshare in Costa Rica or taking a cruise to St. Petersburg.

What you're thinking of, Nora wanted to say, is *Vivian.*

"Whatever makes you happy, Dad," she said, looking at the snow. They were driving along Sifton Boulevard now, past the monster-size houses backing along the river. All those wives, Nora thought, living their smug little lives under those snow-domed mansions. *Did they realize, any one of them, how easily a roof could cave in?*

She returned to Calgary after the papers for the sale of her father's house went through.

"And what about yours?" was all he asked.

"I'm keeping it. Martin didn't say a word."

He nodded, leaned back in his chair in the dining room and stretched his arms. "Speaking of belongings, if you want any of this, say so now or forever hold your peace. Other than the desk and my books, I'm taking nothing. No room.

Vivian's got everything all sewn up. She wants everything new in the new place. She's a lady who knows her mind."

Nora adjusted her placemat. This was the room where her parents used to bicker, her father's voice rising between her mother's low murmurs, while Nora lay on her bed upstairs, listening. And here he sat now, as cheerful as Santa.

She stood to clear the dishes, then walked through the house with a pencil grit between her teeth, scribbling the list of things she'd have sent to Vancouver: the Isfahan rug, the photograph albums, the Swedish silver, the English watercolors, the Methodist rectory table in the hallway, treasures her mother had chosen with such care. Nora wanted to take it all. But their—she couldn't stop thinking of it as Martin's and hers—house in Vancouver was a 1940's cottage, and her basement was already filled with costumes beyond shame.

As a child, she used to sneak into her father's study and look at the papers on his desk. His notes, full of cryptic numbers and formulas, were unfathomable and strange, and she was always sickened by the sweet smell of formaldehyde lifting from his cardigan on the back of the chair. Now the room was dusty and nearly empty, with the books packed away and pictures on the floor leaning against the wall.

Upstairs in her mother's bedroom, looking at all the things she could not take, Nora felt both guilty and light, unmoored. Maybe she was meant to float, aimlessly, she thought, like a leaf or an empty canoe, skimming the surface towards some precipice that lay ahead. Maybe she'd already passed the brink of catastrophe and was now on the downstream flow. Or, as the joke went, maybe she was already dead and no one had bothered to tell her.

She folded the list, walked downstairs, and put it in her father's hand. "I'd like to keep these."

He flattened the paper out on the arm of the chair. "I'm glad. Vivian was worried how you'd take this." He was watching a crime show where a pathologist was peeling scalp back from a skull, slicing into a cortex that looked like pale Swiss cheese. He shook his head. *They never got it right those shows. Nothing could describe the stench of the dead to someone who hadn't seen it up close.*

"It's a shame," Nora said, looking at the skull.

He lifted a hand. "Ah, what is furniture, really, but a bit of wood glued together? Like one of your flimsy balsam theatre sets. Poof and it's gone. Nothing lasts forever."

She put on her jacket and went out the front door, walking for blocks past her old high school haunts on Elbow Drive, past the grocery store where she and her girlfriends used to sneak smokes between classes, past the school parking lot, now littered with glass and bloated plastic bags, where the kids used to gather at noon hour.

"It's not you," was all Martin had said. She'd been pretty enough, once, that's what people had told her. But he'd liked her best rail thin, and in the last six years she'd gained thirty-five pounds. At five feet five inches, it showed.

She stopped at the front of the school. Martin hadn't wanted kids. Maybe she should have pushed harder. But there were his weekends away on businesss. Her late nights. A few meals not on the table in time, and once in a blue moon, his good white shirts hanging wrinkled in the laundry room when he needed a freshly ironed one. Trivial differences of opinion, mostly about other people's motives, or the slant to some political story on TV. No doubt she wasn't inventive enough in bed, or maybe she didn't laugh long and hard enough at his jokes. But nothing else was tangible. Nothing stuck. There was not a single thing she could point to, like a crack in the mirror, and say, *There. That's the reason he left you*—except her reserve. But maybe that was enough. And that her judgment was miles off when she chose him, or he chose *her*, however those things go.

She returned home to her father dozing in his chair with his hand across his chest. She felt she should kiss the top of his head and say something encouraging about his new life with Vivian, but even the livery spot on his bald head peeved her right now.

She perched on the arm of his chair. "Why aren't you taking any of Mom's things?" she said, "I'd like to know."

He slowly opened his eyes. "Did you know," he finally said, "I almost left her the year you started junior high? I couldn't take her passiveness any longer. Not another day, not one more day of such goddamn misery. Mine or hers."

"Why didn't you, then?"

He took off his glasses and rubbed his eyes.

"You."

On the weekend she returned to Vancouver, and Martin phoned to ask if he could pick up the rest of his belongings. He sounded as if he had a cold. She'd fallen for his gravelly voice the first time she heard him calling out to a friend across a skating rink one snowy night at university. How many more times would she hear it?

He told her he'd bought a house.

It wasn't news. Anne had already told her he'd purchased a four thousand square foot modern in the British Properties.

"Funny," Nora tried to make light of it, "he always said he liked his women and his houses doll-size."

After midnight, with the bedroom curtains billowing in the breeze, she couldn't sleep. She put on her glasses, took a file from the nightstand drawer and began to saw at the edges of her nails. She picked up a 19th century novel she'd always meant to read, but the first two pages struck her as quaintly archaic. She tossed the book on the bed.

She knotted the sash on her kimono and walked barefoot into the kitchen. She ran a glass of water and drank it, tapped the nail file against her hip, and looked at her reflection in the black window, at the deep hollows under her eyes. *Old old old.* Anne had told her something else, what Martin had said weeks ago, that he'd "never known what love was until now." Anne had twirled a finger at her temple, "Honey, he must be suffering from amnesia, that's all I can say."

Never known what love was. Nora walked down the hall, opened the garage door and turned on the light. The air in the garage was musty; the freezer hummed in the corner. *The Tramp* sat upside down on the table, gleaming under the light and looking as freshly painted as it did four years ago. It hadn't touched water all that time.

She ran her thumb along the canoe's smooth lip. Had he sanded off the letters? She closed her eyes and pushed her fingertip hard along the edge. *Ah, there.* Tiny bumps, as inscrutable as Braille.

She took her glasses from the top of her head, put them on and bent down to look closer at the faint impression: MH + NR carved in a crooked, squarish script, not much bigger than a thumb whorl. She closed her eyes and pictured him that night as he'd carved them—the muscles of his biceps, how he'd held the knife and grimaced like a child learning to use crayons. Her heart pulsing through silk, she took the file out of her kimono pocket and sanded off the raised paint around the letters, blew at the red dust and stood back to examine her work—the blotch of tiny ragged wood, left raw and blond, the indentations of the letters still filled with paint, only visible if she squinted.

They started in the basement. "*Jesus*," Martin said, lifting his end of his mother's bureau and bending his forehead to his sleeve to wipe the sweat, "the thing's a goddamn coffin."

They lumbered up the stairs with the chest when Nora tripped on the carpeted landing and dropped her end. They both laughed and picked up the chest again. After one of the drawers slid shut with a bang and caught her baby finger's knuckle, Nora went up to the kitchen and ran icy water over her hand. The finger was broken and was beginning to swell. Her face flushed with pain. She'd drive to the walk-in clinic after he left.

She went back downstairs. "Only bruised, I think," she said smiling, gamely lifting her end of the chest out of the house and into the back of the Jeep.

After the last suitcase was cleared from the basement, Martin paused in the hall to look around the living room, frowning as though something were missing.

"I'm thinking of moving myself one of these days," Nora said, smiling airily.

Was that a look of astonishment on Martin's face? Had he expected she would keep her life on hold for him, the way her father—rightly, she could see now—had not done for her mother? He should be relieved. He could go to his happiness now, guilt-free. Like the skier on the trophy, the race to the swift, eyes on the future and all of that.

They walked out to the garage. Lifting *The Tramp* pained her finger but she didn't wince.

At the Jeep, she insisted on buckling the strap on the side of the canoe with the letters.

"Okay, there?" he called from the other side.

"All done," she said. She came around to the driver's side and he picked up her hand, lightly rubbing the back of her finger.

"You should have someone look at that."

"I'll survive," she said. She spoke in the fake light brogue she used to use when she was happy. He made a dart-like move to kiss her goodbye and his lips nearly missed. They felt dry and weightless against her cheek, like the wings of a moth flitting past on a summer's evening.

"Call if you need anything."

She nodded.

"Promise."

She held up two fingers, wincing, "Scout's honor."

She walked back to the porch and sat on the steps with her shoulders hunched together, cupping her sore finger in her hand and blowing on it. She lifted a hand to wave and sat perfectly still, hand in the air until the tail of the Jeep turned the corner. The thought of being alone gripped her wholly then, but there was no single regret she could name, nothing to do but take comfort in her own body, put her arms around herself, close herself up like one of those spiders that rolls itself into a ball so that no one will disturb it.

He was a perfectionist of sorts. Some Saturday afternoon, she knew, this season or next, he'd see the letters, irritated that he'd have to make a trip to the hardware store to buy the small can of lacquer to paint over them. But he had a good sense of humor and would no doubt laugh.

No matter, she thought. Paint over the letters. Let the damned thing sink to the bottom of a lake. Let it burn. Some things endure, despite all attempts to the contrary.

My Father's Heart

David Abrams

True to form, my father maintained control even when his heart seized up like a jammed cogworks. He raised his hand and shook his head, refusing help from concerned friends slicing balls on the golf course near him. "It's just a little indigestion," he said. "I can handle it." Only when he started gulping air and the band of pain threatened to snap his ribs, only then did my father stow his golf clubs and allow himself to be driven to the emergency room. After so carefully building an ironclad reputation (Baptist pastor, Newspaper Columnist, Rotarian, All-Around Nice Guy) in his small Wyoming town, my father felt he had a lot to lose from something like a heart attack. It is, he would say, evidence of weakness.

The first thing I notice when I walk in the intensive care unit is the plastic tube disappearing down his throat like he's trying to swallow a corrugated snake. The second thing is how his body had gone gray and collapsed against the hospital sheets.

Even so—true to form—my father has triumphed over the heart attack and, according to his doctors, will emerge from the double-bypass with a textbook-perfect rebound. The Rev. Donald Dodge has many more sermons to preach from his pulpit at the First Baptist Church in Flint, Wyoming – throat-snake or no throat-snake.

That is months down the road, however. When I walk into that hospital room I'm entering a sliver of time when (*at last*) my father is as weak and powerless as he was fifty-six years earlier cradled in his own father's arms. I take pleasure in the fact that my father's heart has knocked him flat on his back like a newborn. I'm also delighted to see he's been rendered speechless.

This, after all, is why I responded so quickly to my mother's phone call. By that point, he'd already been airlifted from Flint to Salt Lake City, had his heart rerouted by the surgeons and started his recovery in a private room. My mother sounded serene, at peace with the whole situation. I knew it was only her dutiful, "it's-in-God's-hands" front. Inside, she really prayed God would give one hard squeeze with His hands and finish everything.

Before she got off the phone, my mother gave me a set of instructions all ICU visitors must follow: visiting hours, authorized gifts and cleansing procedures. "They don't want anything infectious coming in from the outside," she said.

So . . . here I stand at the sink with foot pedals for taps, my sleeves rolled to the elbows, water dripping from my raised wrists. The paper towel dispenser is empty. I wipe my hands on my pants, recycling my germs. The pneumatic doors part like a curtain and I enter the sterilized sanctuary of the ICU. Through half-open doors, I see other critically ill patients. The ones who have their eyes open stare blankly at the ceiling. At the nurse's station, I ask for my father's room and am pointed down the corridor. All around me, the rooms hiss and beep, sustaining even those who don't deserve to live.

It's been eighteen months since I last saw my father. Three days after my high school graduation, I'd gone away to the university in Laramie and stayed there, unwilling to come home on even the longest holidays. Eventually, the phone calls and letters from my parents dropped off to once a month. I told myself I could endure a monthly fifteen minutes of long-distance conversation.

I pierced my nose and wore a diamond stud; I changed my wardrobe, buying the blackest T-shirts and jeans K-Mart had to offer. I did this in defiance of what my father would call "good and proper behavior befitting a child of the Church." I also smoked marijuana and slept with a variety of girls. Maybe I went too far, a little too deep into this reactionary rebellion, but I couldn't help myself. I was addicted to hating my father.

That's why I strut into the ICU grinning, practically humming. I'm way beyond the Prodigal Son at this point.

Despite the collapsed gray, my father looks relatively the same—the receding crown of hair, the hooked nose, the original chin blanketed in the folds of the extra ones piled on by age and cholesterol. His mouth forms a tight "O" around the respirator tube; two thin wires—one red, one blue, like those on a detonation device—disappear into his chest. He has one leg outside of the bedsheet, no doubt trying to cool that half of his body. The sheet has fallen away a little and I see his nakedness. His pubic hair has flecks of gray; his penis is swollen and bloody from the catheter sunk down its center.

The room is crowded with machinery, tubes and the smell of a bedpan. A heart monitor hovers above the bed. On its tiny green screen, a line zig-zags like a horizontal lightning bolt.

My mother stands next to my father, at shoulder-level. She looks like she stumbled through a plate-glass door and kept right on walking. Two doctors bend their heads in her direction, murmuring long strings of words. It's hard to distinguish their voices from the machinery.

In the doorway, I shuffle my feet. My mother looks up. "Jonah," she says. "You made it."

The doctors stop talking, nod their hellos.

My mother can't even leave my father's side—that's how much control he has over her, even while lying semi-conscious and sedated. She touches his wrist just above the iodine stains and IV needles, but it's no different than if *he* were the one gripping *her* wrist. She looks down and says, "Jonah's here. Isn't that good news?" There is exhaustion and relief in her voice.

Because of the tube in his throat, my father can only communicate with his eyes. They roll in the sockets, bumping his shaggy eyebrows. (Down the road, he'll regain his voice, his strength, his character. He'll insist the nurses fold the blanket at the foot of his bed and that he be covered with only the sheet. The back of his hospital gown *must* be untied when he's lying down, tied the instant he sits up. My mother will have to wipe off her glossy lipstick before she kisses him. "It gives me a sore throat," he'll tell her. "You *know* that.")

I approach the bed. He smells like surgery—hot and medicinal and temporarily sterilized. Without touching him, I say, "Hello." This is not what I want to say. I want to greet him with, "Hello, Dimmesdale" (I'm in the third week of my Am Lit course at Laramie and this has been preying on my mind), but because my mother and the doctors are still in the room, I don't call him Dimmesdale. Still, it's enough to know I *can*.

My father takes one look at my diamond, gets one whiff of my stale cannabis breath, and rolls his eyes in wild circles. I know what he's saying; I've heard it all before.

I look over my mother's shoulder at the room's only window. I can see a fraction of the world outside. There are a few stripped trees trying to reach their branches as high as my father's window. Three people cross on the light at a street corner, two walking briskly toward the other who has his head down against the wind. In the distance, clouds lower across the Wasatch Mountains. The sky is dark gray, like the mood in my father's room.

When he does have full control of his body, my father uses his voice like a symphony, each word a perfect note. Much as I hate to admit it, there's poetry in my father's voice. When I was younger, it was the sound of his words, not the words themselves, that got me through each Sunday service. I'd look around at all the other people of Flint—the ranchers, the taxidermists, the Forest Service officials—and I saw they were just as spellbound.

After church, he'd be in his bedroom singing the hymns of the day as he changed his clothes. Thinking he was alone, he strained for the high notes on "How Great Thou Art," warbling like a songbird as he pulled up his socks. But when he emerged and caught me listening in the hallway, he blushed, cleared his throat and dropped to a low, restrained whistle.

There was another time when one of my father's favorite songs on the radio was something called "My Name's Not Lisa." I thought it was the stupidest song, probably because I never understood what the words meant. Now, I know it was about infidelity, this woman telling her philandering husband to quit calling her by his mistress' name. My father went around humming that song for nearly a year. It was his hymn to adultery.

We all knew about his woman. When I say "we," I mean me, my mother and my father. And when I say "woman," I mean it in the most generic sense of the word. My mother and I never learned her name, never knew what she looked like, never caught her scent or saw a loose strand of hair. Still, to us she was as real as the dining room furniture. And in my father's voice, under the whirling current of day-to-day chatter, something swam against the flow; something that was, when we later stopped to think about it, unmistakable passion; something like a prize trout that had eluded him for years and, by God, it was about time for him to hook it, bring it to the riverbank.

We discovered the woman the winter of my senior year in high school. When I say "we," I mean my mother and I reached the conclusion separately, never speaking about it, never admitting we each carried the truth that could kill my father's reputation in the town. But I knew she knew—it was in her eyes, her posture, the new tremble on the edge of her smile. I'll probably never know how my mother learned of the adultery—maybe it was like a freeway collision, a long chain of clues piling into each other, the endless crashing finally grinding to a halt. Maybe that's how it was for her. Maybe she saw the trout flipping on the shore, right there in the light of day.

For me, it was a scrap of paper. I sneaked into his church study one afternoon when he was at the county hospital praying for Chance Gooding's wife who was on her last leg of cancer. It was December, in fact it was the shortest day of the year and the sun was sinking behind the rim of Arrow Mountain. There was just enough light in the study for me to see what I was doing. I was playing a prank on my father, taking all the Bible commentaries off the bookshelf behind his desk, turning them upside down and then putting them back on the shelf in haphazard order. My father has this *thing* about alphabetizing.

The scrap of white paper, bright as neon in the dim, solstice room, fluttered to the floor out of the pages of *The Seminary Student's Guide to 2 Samuel.* I watched the note spiral down like a dead leaf, then bent to pick it up. There were only three words on the paper, written not in my father's hand, not in my mother's hand, but in another woman's hand. How could I be sure of its femininity? The blue ink was curved and flowery, softening the hard letters and, in some places, looked oddly like women's breasts. I knew even the most sensitive rancher in Flint couldn't form letters like those. I closed my eyes, imagining the hand: the fingers long, slender, tipped with red nails.

I didn't know who they belonged to. For weeks, I tried to guess her identity, choosing and rejecting dozens of names: Grace Black, the owner of Lilies of the Field Flower Shoppe and who handled all of the church's wedding, funeral and holiday arrangements; Shellie Monkle at the Wrangler Family Restaurant; Oona Packerby, lead alto in the church choir; Marilyn Withers, Edith Pond, Dot Bickley, Marion Ash, Wanda Holt, Desiree Fernandez—all lined up in my mind like beauty pageant contestants. But if it was any of them—or one of the other 1,400 women walking the snow-packed streets of Flint that winter—I'll never know.

I'll also never know what the rest of the note said, for the three words in my hand were part of a longer epistle (my father's word, "epistle;" he loves using it instead of "letter"). The scrap was bordered with descenders and ascenders: the hook of a "j," the mast of a "t." I had no doubt the trio of words were torn from a page of flowered stationery. I had no doubt it was my father's own fingers which had done the tearing and tucked the slip inside a commentary he could pull off the shelf at his convenience. I had no doubt he often stared at the blue ink, maybe even panting and throbbing in the hush of his study.

Before I left the room that solstice day, I rearranged the books on the shelves, putting them in proper order. Later, I burned the note—it went quickly under the match—but I've held onto the words ever since, waiting to use them.

Now my father lies in front of me—helpless, colorless, voiceless.

The doctors leave after once more consulting the charts. It is only two days since my father collapsed on the golf course and, though things are shaping up for a textbook recovery, they're still concerned. Before they go, they pull us aside and say, "His heart is not out of the woods yet. But that doesn't mean we're not hopeful."

My mother meets my eyes. We speak without speaking. We're both thinking of that purple-gray organ wandering lost among the tangle of underbrush and the tall, inward-pressing trees. At this point, I'll bet his heart would be happy for even the smallest patch of sunlight on the forest floor.

Neither of us are willing to provide that sunshine. All warmth has been pinched off my mother's face. She shows every one of her forty-eight years in her eyes and at the corners of her mouth. This is so unlike her usually bright, pastor's-wife cheer, I almost don't recognize her as my mother. Still, under the circumstances I think she's held up remarkably well.

We look down at my father. His eyes bounce between us.

My mother finally pulls her fingers from his wrist. She looks at me, then back down to my father. "Now that Jonah's here, I think I'll go grab something at the snack bar. I won't be long." She bends down, gives him a light kiss with her glossed lips then leaves the room. I watch her go. She only falters once—when she passes the nurses' station—but she has completely regained herself by the time she reaches the pneumatic doors.

Later that night, at the end of the hospital's visiting hours, she will drop her defenses again while waiting for the elevator. I'll come up beside her, hold her small shoulders under my arm and pull her against me. She'll say, "He drains me," and I'll see the hollows beneath her eyes moisten like groundwater seeping into a freshly plowed field.

I won't know how to say what I feel, so she'll say it for me in a whisper: "Sometimes I hate him so much." Her whisper will be like the first trickles of water hissing through the cracks of a dam.

I'll tighten my arm around her shoulders and for that moment we'll be something more than mother and son, something less than lovers. I'll feel a rush of passion for this woman beneath my arm. I won't think of all the girls back in Laramie, I won't think of mothers and sons on TV, I won't even think of Oedipus groping around his palace with the blood running from his empty sockets. No, by the time the elevator bongs and the doors open for us, I'll be thinking we're like two strangers who befriend each other in a jail cell.

But that's later that night. For now, my father and I are alone and I'm the only one who can speak. I have dreamed of this moment since childhood. I choose my words carefully, already knowing which three will pass from my lips. Since my mother's phone call, I've been standing in front of a mirror, practicing my delivery. In the History of Man, this moment is as important as when Jacob entered his father's tent to swindle the birthright.

I lean close, so close I can see the sweaty pores of his scalp. I brush my mouth against his ear and whisper the paper-scrap words: "I'm your Bathsheba."

Then, like an arson who has dropped the match, I turn to flee, only pausing once to look over my shoulder at the spreading damage. My father's eyes thrash in their sockets. His throat pushes against the tube. Above him, the heart monitors beep like smoke alarms. No matter what happens next, I have done the right thing.

The Well Head

Gabriel Welsch

The gardens stretched the length of the property, up against the road, a wall of tendrils and branch spans that left only a kidney of grass at the yard's center. Casey thought, really, it was one continuous expanse, weed-choked and dense with growth, a sprawl in need of a knowing hand. Emeline's gesture took in the entirety, one grand hand sweep as if from a throne. "Forty years of gardening," she said, "and five of neglect. How quickly it's all undone."

Her scooter engine whined as she drove along the gardens, and Casey followed, surprised that the woman who couldn't walk was actually going too fast for her to take it all in. But such was the bounty. Casey wanted to ask her to slow down but felt, for all of Emeline's rumored grit, that such a request would seem insensitive, perhaps cruel, given the task at hand.

"Do you recognize most of the plants?" Emeline said. It was the fourth time she'd asked. Casey had expected a demand for precision—the woman told her on the phone she was a retired botanical illustrator—but did not expect that the need would be so constantly restated.

"Yes, certainly, I recognize all of them," Casey said. She folded her arms. "I haven't yet seen a plant or weed I don't know." She tried to smile, sensed she might sound miffed. That wouldn't do. She needed this job, however lordly and demanding this woman was.

"You'll forgive the impertinence," Emeline said. "My last two gardeners said they knew everything, and they each lost plants, removed things I had gone to great effort to procure."

Casey imagined the scooter barreling through northern tundra, after an ice-shagged little moss growth or scrap of lichen. Emeline among the Aleutians. She rebuked herself, heard her mother's voice telling her to be nice. She made herself stop thinking about her mother. The beds here were beautiful, their erstwhile caretaker witty and direct, everything stable and well-built, and so for Casey, even thoughts of her mother had no place here. But she noticed the granular quality of the sunlight, how her mother might describe it as chunky, composed of many colors. Her mother would then hum arias as she painted, getting the notes wrong.

"When do you need me to start?" Casey asked. She controlled the want in her voice, the fatigue of three nights spent sleeping in a Corolla.

"As soon as you can move your things into the salt box," Emeline replied.

The salt box, an old shed basically, surprised Casey, both in how spacious it was and how cool it remained, in spite of Maine's thick summer and the lack of air conditioning. Positioned on a hill to the southeast of the house, the salt box caught air moving unabated across the sloping fields that swept up from their beginnings in Portsmouth. Her new home came pre-furnished, a gingham couch, two Adirondack chairs with worn but thick cushions on the seats, a distressed brass bed, a few iron lamps, and what must have been a very old chestnut drop-leaf table, its surface layered in dark knife cuts and mug rings. It appeared she was the first person to live in the salt box—it smelled of plaster, new paint, carpet glue. Later, Emeline told her the one man who had gardened

Granite Hill while her husband had been alive actually lived in the main house, but it became apparent to everyone that private living spaces were required, at the very least due to snoring, and at worst due to, and Emeline paused here, the proclivities of his private life.

Casey loved the way Emeline spoke. So refined, so—what was the word her mother used?—*patrician.* Emeline made Casey think of old Hollywood enduring some tragedy, old money slashed by some comeuppance. And her bearing, in spite of the scooters and wheelchairs and sling contraptions in her home, always had a dignity about it, as if the woman had an iron rod for a spine. Of course, Casey thought, she just *might* have a rod for a spine. Emeline had told Casey the various things that had gone wrong, health-wise, in the few years since Lloyd had passed, but it had been a blur to her. She didn't understand much about medicine or anatomy, and while she felt bad for Emeline, Casey knew her tasks would occupy most of her time, the garden would be interesting and challenging, the work would earn her the money she needed, and that would be it.

What she did know, revealed to her on one of her first days working in the gardens as Emeline kept her company on her scooter, is that a growth had been removed from near her spine in an attempt to relieve pressure on the spinal column itself. But, rather than remove the increasing difficulty Emeline experienced walking, it actually paralyzed her from the waist down. For this, Emeline was now embroiled in legal battles, the first of which she had won, and which provided her some of the resources, as she told Casey, "to employ medical brutishness for the management of my carcass, and talent for the management of my spiritual assets, the garden." It was, she said crisply, nice that her sons' efforts could be so enhanced.

"Sons?" Casey said. "I didn't realize you had sons. Are they in the area?" She waited for Emeline's answer, sketching out the bed they faced.

Emeline folded her hands in her lap and looked back at the house, then to Casey, as if she only had then remembered she were talking. "One lives in Arizona. He owns apartments and sells swimming pools. The other lives in Washington State where he is a tax attorney. He has a house bigger than a church."

Casey purchased tools and fertilizer, hired a refuse removal company, made sketches of the beds for a plant census, and immersed herself in the written records of the gardens' development. It was her first large scale job entirely on her own. There would be no landscape company, no architect involved, no other botanists, just her. The skills were there, she knew. For ten years, she had worked herself across the country from Alaska, taking jobs with big firms as well as guys working from the garages in their ranch homes, using their own pickup and magnetic signs. She had picked up a horticulture degree as she went, a semester here, one there, sustained on a mix of grants and jobs, taking six or nine credits at a time. Her mother and Maurice—her mother's second husband and, as he frequently reminded her, *not* her father—provided zero financial help after essentially announcing she was on her own after high school. As if apologizing for the pasty banker, her mother had said, "It's his money dear. I wish I could do better." *You could have,* Casey sometimes thought, *if you had spent less on trips for painting, loud clothes, and artist's retreats.*

By the time she was twenty-two, working for a firm outside Philadelphia, her pay was so good she put together four consecutive semesters at Delaware Valley. But the firm folded due to the owner's refusal to pay his taxes, and she decided to move again rather than seek another job in Philadelphia. Knowing she wanted to return to a coast, she moved to Portland. In her last semester at the University of Maine, when she felt the familiar pull of desperation, dissolution of funds, and an expiring lease, she saw the tidy flyer that demanded a "live-in, preferably female, with sufficient experience and tenacity to serve as personal gardener and virtual landscape architect for Granite Hill, the assets of a heretofore able botanical illustrator."

As Casey settled into the work at Granite Hill, Emeline was ever-present, nodding curtly. Emeline seemed pleased with Casey's efficiency and, for weeks, that calm understanding buoyed both women in the tasks they confronted. But Casey could also see in Emeline's face those few times when, had her legs worked, she would have pushed Casey out of the way and taken over. Emeline was particularly impatient with propagating divisions. She would inhale sharply if she heard a fan or tuber snap, or she would look away when Casey handled astilbe corms.

Even so, Emeline told Casey several times how pleased she was with her work. Casey wondered if Emeline was ever really pleased with anyone's contributions. When Emeline felt generous and invited Casey to the porch, to sit with her and talk about the day's successes, almost equal time was spent cordially on what had to improve. Casey knew she was doing a good job, if only from the sheer number of tasks Emeline would inventory. And as the weeks passed, Emeline became bolder with her scooter, and many mornings Casey would rise and see the scooter slightly akilter, wedged into a bed, with Emeline deadheading or bending to yank at weeds. Sometimes Casey would hear her softly cursing.

Casey spent much of her Tuesdays thinking about cribbage. She had discovered the game and attended on the exhortations of the pregnant cashier she met at Boonies, the moose antler-decorated general store at the town's edge. After a few games where she had decent luck, she was hooked. Every Tuesday evening, the town hall opened its doors for a brief public meeting, after which people would stay to play in a cribbage tournament for a nightly pot that, on occasion, reached four or five hundred dollars.

The games were always two-player, so your initial seat could determine your fate for the evening. Through the spring, Casey learned people arrived as early as they could, since latecomers always had to face one of The Three: Bertrand Fournier, Lorianne de Vieux, or Carl Miner. They sat in the middle of the room, Fournier always with his plump arms crossed and resting on his bulk, a porkpie hat flopped over his tangled hair and unusually fleshy ears, his jaws working to mash thoroughly an unlit cigar. Whenever Casey arrived, Fournier was always talking to Miner, his head slightly cocked over, his lips wet from chewing the stogie, his baritone audible but incomprehensible. Miner was his opposite, and not only physically—his game was as pointy as his frame, his tactics yellow as his teeth. Casey hated playing him. He was all business, all about the pot, no small talk. Not at all like Lorianne, the pleasant one, the matron right out of a Disney movie, shelf-bosomed and bow-mouthed, reading glasses on chains.

The Three had a greater significance as well, as Casey discovered. She was never able to get out the gardens early enough to avoid them, so she got to know the Three because she so often had to play against one of them. The Three had once been the Four; prior to her paralysis, Emeline had been the fourth. According to Lorianne, Emeline had been the only real competition with any charm. She had verve to her game, Lorianne went on, was not a bald capitalist. Casey thought she heard a break or small stutter in the baritone, but when she looked over, the conversation appeared still mired in its typical dragging momentum. She smelled them, heating oil, smoke, and sweat. Mostly heating oil, Fournier's primary business, the only real supplier in appreciable distance.

The first time she won anything, only a hundred dollars, she came home to see a Buick Park Avenue sitting near the salt box. It had a rental sticker on the bumper. In a town where only four-wheel drive vehicles meandered on the gravelly lake roads and everyone knew everyone else, the car was an even greater surprise. She looked to the salt box, saw no lights on. Only the living room was lit in the main house. She listened, not quite sure what to do. Emeline had said nothing about any visitors, and it was very unusual for the woman to still be awake at eleven or twelve, when Casey returned from cribbage nights. She stepped up to the house as quietly as she could. As she drew nearer, she began to wonder just what she *would* do if she looked in and discovered Emeline being robbed, or worse.

As she neared the front door, it swung open. A middle-aged man in a Titleist windbreaker, easily a head taller than her, seemed pressed into the door frame. The porch light came on then, and she held up a hand against her eyes. She could see even less of him.

"You're Casey," he said. His voice was deep, a smoker's voice.

She backed up a step as he came on to the porch. "Yes."

"I'm Phil," he said. He did not offer his hand. Instead he scowled, looking at his shoes, before he said, "Actually, my mother might have referred to me by my first name, as Napoleon, or Nap." He shoved his hands in the pocket of his windbreaker. "But I prefer Phil."

She had spoken about him. He was the one who lived in Arizona. Ironically, one of his buildings was an assisted living facility for seniors. Emeline pointed out that Nap pestered her to move out there, to let him take care of her, but, she said, he was completely unsympathetic to her "preference for my own gardens and the feel of sand." Beyond his expensive-looking hair, groomed eyebrows, and chunky Rolex, he also had an air of impatience. He fidgeted, enough for her to notice right away. He was supposedly the good one. The one who sent money, who visited frequently, who handled the estate, and whose name graced the checks she received every two weeks. She didn't know much about the other one. Louis.

"Okay, Phil," she said. She extended her hand, which he took with some surprise.

After shaking her hand, he nodded once and said, "Where were you?"

Not that it's any of your business, she thought, "I was at the cribbage game, in town."

He nodded twice, looked over at his car, then met her gaze.

"I know it's not in the contract, but I think it's kind of implied that you be around at night," he said.

She opened and closed her mouth before saying, "You're right, that wasn't in the agreement, nor was it ever, you know, *said* to me."

He put a hand to her elbow, and stepped off the porch. They took a few steps down the stone path until they got to the drive.

"I'm not a hard-ass. And I don't think I'm unreasonable," he said.

She held her tongue. She could feel the hundred dollars in her pocket as it pressed against her leg.

"It's just that my mother thinks she's still independent. She's not. If she fell out of that chair or if something caught fire or if any of a number of things happened, she'd be in a real fix." He looked at his feet again. "I know she told you she hired you to take care of the beds. That's true. But what I am paying for is someone to be here."

"That changes a few things," Casey said.

He exhaled heavily and pulled out his cigarettes. "I can pay you more."

"I don't know if that'd make the difference."

"Try me."

"You're really asking a lot."

"I care about my mother."

She hadn't spoken to her own mother for a month. Casey thought she might still be up near the Bering Strait, painting in her now grossly renovated home, letting Maurice pay for everything as if she really were a delicate genius. As if. And she wasn't going to let this slum lord push her into signing her life over.

"It'd have to be, like, double."

"Done."

"What?"

"Done. If you'll do it, if you'll be here, if you'll carry a cell phone, if you will make sure that someone is there for her, I'll do it. I will pay you double what you currently make. My mother really likes you, and she's hard to please, so I am willing to do this."

"You're not kidding."

"No. I'm not."

"Why don't you just hire a nurse, or some other health care person to stop here at nights?"

Phil pulled a pack of cigarettes from his pocket. He pulled one out, glanced back at the house, and then lit it.

"I'm not ready to do that to her yet," he said. "She can do everything on her own. She can move in and out of the chair, she can get around her house, she is sharp and can manage her medications. She doesn't need that. But I would really like it if someone were around for just in case."

She went over objections but, as she tried to focus on specific ones, they blurred, and she thought of the money, of paying off her car, of paying off her loans, of the freedom a year might buy, of all of it. She looked at him, how he looked like some crabby banker, like a Scrooge, like a younger version of Maurice. He struck her as every asshole business major she'd ever met. By the time he started the Buick, she could not remember much of the remaining conversation, other than that she was making more money than she ever had in her life, and she was not sure she would be able to keep her end of the bargain.

When Emeline sat in the yard and watched Casey work, she seldom kept her gaze completely focused on her, instead looking out to the fuzzy line of faded blue, miles away where the ocean sat, or across the other side of the yard to where distant hills began their ascent toward the White Mountains. For several weeks, as Casey worked on the thickest and most expansive plantings of the middle beds, Emeline perched at the end of the flagstone walk, her fingers worrying at the seams of her pants, her shirts puffing cavernous around her thin frame.

The work was physically demanding, but not otherwise hard. After the first week's effort to remove the bindweed, briars, and thistle from the beds and rediscovering the plants installed there, the work was healing and inspiring. Emeline had been dutiful in ways most gardeners are not—each clump of plants had a brass or copper tag, stamped with the plants' genera and species, as well as the date of the planting. The variety was amazing, and Casey was surprised at what she was actually learning.

One day, Casey found a long-plugged well-head at the back of a bed. Emeline grinned tightly when Casey asked about it. Her former husband had put a cover on it once the scooter and wheelchairs became Emeline's only way of getting around. He was worried Emeline would tip a chair and fall in. "Not only did he think I was feeble," she said, "he thought I was a moron without the wherewithal to avoid a gaping hole in the ground." At first, he had put a board and bricks over it, but she had simply removed them each day to lower a hose, kick on the pump, and water the garden. When he discovered her set-up, he hired a mason to seal it correctly. Emeline's jaw stiffened as she said, "I withheld myself from him for a month afterward." Casey wanted to joke, say *Only a month?*, but she sensed the rift had been longer, and that it was not her place to joke.

Two days after Phil's visit, Casey looked up from cutting back a straggly Obedient Plant to see a UPS delivery woman striding across the yard. From her chaired perch, Emeline watched her as if prepared to yell at her for stepping on a rare thyme or dianthus. The woman brought Casey a large box, from Phil. Casey looked to Emeline, who looked away, watching the UPS truck ramble back down the drive.

Casey took off her gloves and walked the package down to the salt box. It contained a cell phone, instructions and the new number, and all the charging accessories. It also included a note from Phil, telling her he had purchased the phone in town, and had paid to have it sent. He wrote that he had it charged, and that he would call her that evening, at 7, to confirm that it worked. Bills would go to him, but she should not feel at all limited in her use of the phone.

It was a good plan, thousands of minutes, and she should feel welcome to call family and friends and so on, perhaps thinking of it as a "perk." She shook her head as she turned on the phone.

Before going to cribbage, she wrote and mailed a postcard to her mother, telling her she had a new job as a caretaker. She provided her address and included the cell phone number. She told her the gardens were beautiful, and wrote nothing else.

Fournier was well into a rant about the conspiracy of property taxes when Casey nosed in the front door of the hall. He stopped when she sat down. The three looked at her.

"What's the pot look like tonight?" Casey asked Fournier.

He waggled his hand. So-so.

Miner fidgeted his hands in his lap. Casey looked at him for a moment, wondered what else she might ask of any of them, then looked away. She put her hand over the phone in her pocket. Her plan was to feel the ring, demurely leave, walk outside, and then answer, so Phil could not be certain of where she was. Of course, he could call Emeline and check, but Casey had left lights on at the salt box in hopes she would simply glance out the window and assume she was there.

Miner and Lorianne started their deals, and as she peeked at her cards and worked two of the pegs in her fingers, Casey considered Lorianne's hands, their redness, their obvious familiarity with work. She wondered if Lorianne gardened. Or perhaps cooked.

Lorianne's first move put her well into the board. Casey only moved two pegs.

"How's the garden?" Lorianne asked her. She didn't look at Casey, glanced back and forth between the cards in her hand

and the board. Casey told her about the beds, how they were coming, and asked Lorianne if she gardened. Lorianne pursed her lips. Casey couldn't tell if it was a grimace or a tight smile.

Miner cut in. "Everything she plants dies. Her yard is mostly sand."

Casey looked at him. He slumped in his seat. One could hardly tell he was in a conversation.

"He's right," Lorianne said. "I've got a black thumb."

"Emeline's soil is no better," Miner said. "Only she was a miracle worker. You've got your work cut out for you."

Casey worked her way through another crappy hand. "What does that mean?"

Miner shrugged, kept his eyes on the board. Fournier made little sighing, almost deflating noises. Casey heard someone win a few tables away.

"No offense, but Emeline was a master gardener, or was," Miner says. "She knows her way around flowers."

Casey felt the phone vibrate. The sensation was like a shock buzzer.

"How do you know I don't?" Casey said.

Miner looked at the board, grinned.

"Seriously, how do you know I'm not?" she asked.

The phone buzzed again. Casey glowered at Miner, who pretended not to notice. When she said "fuck you," it rang a little louder than she thought it would, and while many heads turned, Miner's did not. She turned and shuffled out among the tables as a low chuckle passed through the room. Outside, she caught her breath, and on the fifth buzz, she answered.

"Did you hear it?" Phil asked. Each syllable crackled; he spoke too close to the receiver.

"Did I answer too slowly for you?" Her tone surprised her, and it occurred to her she'd once again gotten let a conversation with Phil seem more like an argument.

"I didn't say that. I just wanted to make sure you had it working okay, volume loud enough, all that."

As he rattled on about the phone's features, again, this time in more zealous detail, she moved off the step and jogged along the side of the building, away from the lot and near to where the pines started their ascent up the small rise backing town.

He suddenly stopped talking, then said, "Where are you?"

Her face tingled. "Right here, home, you know—the salt box?"

"Mmm," he said. "Okay. Thought I heard something. Must have been here."

She heard him start chewing then, and was not surprised to learn he was the kind of man who ate while on the phone. She also knew, then, he was a man who checks up, and she thought about heading home. The next thing he might have done was to call his mother, ask her to look out the window and tell him what she saw. She was disappointed in herself; she had been ready to tear into Miner for a minor slight, but when it came to standing up for herself, and for completely reasonable job expectations, she skulked around it.

The next morning, Emeline called. Casey hadn't had coffee yet, had barely managed to flip through the three channels she had on the ancient black and white.

"We need to access the well," Emeline announced.

"I thought you told me it was sealed."

"That's the point. We need to unseal it."

"Why? You have water from the town, don't you?"

"It's not for the house. It's for the garden."

Casey looked out the window toward the well head and noted, as she had in the log in recent weeks, the burnt gold of the grass, the curled and ticking leaves in the beds.

"Is there even going to be any water? How long has it been unused?"

"We won't know the answer to any of it until we open it."

She almost asked what Phil would say, but then imagined Emeline's response to needing Phil's permission would be more violent than her own.

"Emeline, I have no idea how to go about unsealing such a thing," she said. "I have no masonry experience, I can't do plumbing—"

"That is why God gave us contractors and the ability to discern talent in others," Emeline said.

Casey laughed. It hurt her head. She had polished off a bottle of Merlot after the cribbage game, and it was now reminding her of her lapse. "We do need to check it out, first, so we know what we're getting into."

Emeline let a pause hang in the air before saying, "I have thought about that well for a long time. I know what is down there, how it was sealed. I watched it. We can go forward with this."

Casey gulped down a piece of toast and a Diet Coke, pulled on her jeans and a t-shirt, and strode through the beds toward the well head. Emeline already sat, perched on her scooter, near the well, and she balanced a clipboard on her lap while sketching the contraption in broad, almost violent strokes. She informed Casey that the sketch would be necessary for explaining to a contractor what services they required. Casey said the contractor would likely just come look at it. Emeline laid her pencil down on the clipboard. She turned slowly to look at Casey. "I just want it done. I want it open. There is a drought. Can we get someone here today?"

"Do you know anyone, have anyone particular in mind?"

"No, unless you do."

Casey snorted, then wished she could take the action back. "Well, I've only been here for two months. I don't really know anyone."

Emeline looked at her as if she were four and had lied about taking a cookie. "You know Lorianne de Vieux, and she knows everyone else."

"I don't know her that well. We play cribbage. I see her in town."

Emeline crossed her hands on top of the clipboard. "She thinks well of you, and since her opinion is seldom given on such subjects, I suspect you know her better than you let on."

Casey frowned, hoping Emeline would read the discomfort and knock it off. She wondered what Emeline really knew of the arrangement between herself and Phil. Bending to look closer at the well head, she stopped looking at Emeline and concentrated on the head. It was welded to rebar stakes in several places, and the stakes, from the look of it, were rooted in a concrete and stone wall surrounding the well. It would be hard work, but it would certainly be feasible for someone with the right tools.

"It might be," Emeline began languorously, "that she likes you all the more for the way you play the game, hold your own with her and the other two."

"Why don't you call her if you know everyone and everything so well?"

Emeline frowned, straightened in her chair.

"You're the groundskeeper, you hire the contractors," Emeline said. She looked at her lap and paused before adding, "And besides, you probably know them now better than I do, since you see them all the time."

Casey stood, put a hand to her forehead and, with eyes closed against the sun, said, "Emeline, do you have a problem with my going to the games?"

Emeline was quiet, and when Casey opened her eyes, she saw the woman was holding tight to the arms of her chair. "Have I not been direct with you on every occasion?"

"Up until now."

"I am being direct now," she said, her voice hardening slightly. "I want this well open. You know the person who could best recommend a contractor. I do not know why you are downplaying how you know her."

Casey put her hands on her hips, and as she did, felt the top of the cell phone in her pocket. She pulled it out.

"See this? Your son gave me this, so he could check up on me and so that you would have a way to call me. He also told me, in so many words, that I was not to leave the farm for very long, at any time."

Emeline looked at the horizon and squinted before she turned back to Casey. "You do what you want. Don't listen to him. If he had his way, I'd be in the ground so he would know exactly where to find me and how to deal with me."

Casey sat in the parking lot outside the town hall for a long time before going in. She hadn't seen any of them, even around town, since the incident with Miner. She told herself it was not a big deal, that they would have forgotten it, that it was only a huge slight to her, but she also knew that the minute she asked Miner to come look at the well, they'd all remember it. Looking at the cell phone laying in the ashtray, she thought about calling her mother, just to see if the woman remembered where she was.

As she flipped open the phone, Miner rapped on her window, then stepped back so she could open the door. He wore a Big Peckers t-shirt and frayed Dickies. His hair was wet down, though he hadn't shaved in a few days. When she got out of the car, he attempted a grin. It was teeth and exuberance, not a grin.

"Just wondered if you were going in, seeing you out sitting in your car," he said.

She cracked her window, locked the doors, closed up. The only thing she could think to say was to ask him why he was talking to her, but that would come off badly, so she tried to maintain a neutral expression.

"Uh, okay, look," he began, "I just want to apologize for last week. I didn't mean to upset you so much. I was"—he ran a hand through his hair—"insensitive."

Lorianne had put him up to this. He would never use a word like *insensitive.*

He ran a hand over his hair, looked at her shoes. "So, you're coming in to play tonight?"

She nodded. She put the cell phone in her pocket. "It wasn't a big deal. I was just in a bad mood, a bit touchy. I'm sorry I said what I did."

He tried not to look too pleased. Clearly Lorianne had not prepared him for a reciprocal apology.

"Let's go in," she said.

In the hall, Fournier looked at them both, stopped chomping on his cigar for a few beats, then returned his attention to his cards. Lorianne's seat was empty. Fournier said he was glad that conversation finally arrived, smiling at Casey. Miner sat, sour-faced.

After she was settled, Casey turned to Miner and said, "Do you know anyone who does welding work, or masonry—particularly, well, undoing of that stuff?"

Miner said, "Demolition? We do demolition."

Casey twisted her lips. "Not quite demolition. I need the thing mostly left intact. Just something removed."

"Well, what is it?" Fournier said. "I do masonry. But if you give me specifics, I can recommend someone."

She nodded. "Sure, right. Okay, Emeline has a well with the top sealed. I need to remove the top."

Both men started to chuckle.

"What?"

Fournier leaned back and drew a hand along his chest. "I put that cover on years back, before her husband passed. She glared at me the entire time from that contraption of hers. I felt bad, but in my estimation he was right about it being unsafe."

"I cut the steel piece for it, or had it cut, I guess," Miner said. "It was heavy. He wanted it heavy. As if she'd head down there and pop the welds. Can you see it? Sitting on the chair, pry bar wedged in under there, her tiny arms heaving?"

Casey laughed, against her will, picturing Emeline doing that. But then she really thought about it, and her husband's worry was right on. Had it been a light piece, she would have dragged a pry bar down and popped the top off. If he had left it so she could run a hose to the water, or had even rigged a pump, it would have put her out in the garden, out in her chair, teetering, with no one there for her. In trying to keep her safe, he had taken away one of the most important parts of her life. But that wasn't the sad part. It was picturing Emeline, in her chair, cursing or weeping, wanting simply to be able to get water to take care of her plants, and being stuck, no one to help her, no one to even hear her or share in her frustration. It was imagining that overwhelming hopelessness and the urge to throw yourself up against it that surprised Casey with its force. And then, she thought of Emeline's sons, as far away from her as they could reasonably get, and she wondered what Emeline had been like as a mother, because there Casey was herself, as far from her mother as she could be, geographically, psychically, financially, and absolutely staunch about never going back, never conceding anything. She wondered, then, if there would be someone years from now, in some nursing home or working for an agency, who would feel this way for her own mother, who would want to hold her at moments, would want to soothe the frustrations borne by her mother's years of focusing solely on herself.

She couldn't help any of it. There was only one thing she could do that felt at all right. She drummed her fingers, looked up to see Fournier already waiting for her, and she said, "I want you to come by the house tomorrow. And I want you to look at the well head. I'd like it off before next week's game."

Later, toward the end of the game, the phone buzzed. Casey didn't look to see who it was. It could only have been Phil, Emeline, or her mother. She didn't want to talk to any of them. She stared hard at the filigree around the head of the Jack of Spades, considered the weave of the card she held, inhaled the sharp dusty scent of the hall. The noises blended into one hum in her ears. The light weighed like a blanket, a web of shadow and dust. She tried to ignore it. In Lorianne's chair sat a different woman, one who owned a motel near the lake, and she played as though Casey's presence was an affront. The phone buzzed again. Casey didn't move until it stopped.

As she prepared to head out into the yard the next morning, the phone buzzed at her from her nightstand. She pushed her hair back, rubbed her cheeks, as if she would actually see Phil, and then answered the phone.

"Where were you last night?" Phil said.

"Everything is fine here."

"That's not what I asked," Phil sputtered. "I want to know where you were."

"I had my phone with me."

"You went to the cribbage game," he said.

"So what? So I went to the game? Why are we even talking about this?"

He exhaled loudly. “I am paying you to be there, you don’t answer your phone, so I start wondering what I’m paying for.”

“I was in touch. I had the phone.”

“So, you just saw it was me and didn’t answer?”

“You are making too big a deal out of this,” she said, loathing the way her voice thinned as she spoke to him. “Emeline is a grown woman, and she has the number, too.”

“My mother is not the best judge of her abilities,” he said. She heard a car door slam on his end. “But, wait, you know what? I don’t need to explain this to you. I am paying you a shitload of money. You need to either hold up your end or tell me so I can get somebody else.”

“You’re asking something ridiculous,” she said.

“Well, those are the terms. My mother, my money, my terms.”

She forced down the knot in her throat. “I’m beginning to think I can’t do this,” she said.

“I don’t want to hear this.”

“I can’t help it. It’s just that, with all due respect, I think you’re being unreasonable about what you can expect from the gardener.”

“I have to go,” he said. She heard other voices around him. “But I don’t want to leave this unresolved. We need to reach agreement here, or come up with some other plan.”

Her eyes started to sting. She did not want him to hear any catch in her voice. “Then I need to move on, find something else. I will try to be gone by the end of the week.”

“No, dammit, that’s not—that’s not good. We can reach some resolution here,” he said. “I will call you tonight. Answer the phone, please, when I call.”

“I’ve made up my mind,” she said. Her voice tremored once, and then she said, “I need to go.”

When she pushed the END button, she cocked back her arm to throw the phone, then pressed it against her forehead. She leaned into the doorjamb and let two harsh sobs out, and then pushed her fingers into her forehead to make herself stop.

When she looked out the door, she saw Miner and Fournier, silhouetted against the hills and the morning light, like Laurel and Hardy strolling across the field in a dream. They stopped at the well. Fournier knew exactly where it was. She heard his laughter, Miner mumbling something. And then she heard the sound of Emeline's chair, a faint buzz, as she made her way across the field. As they noticed her, the chair became the only sound. Casey watched them regard one another, and her chest fluttered as she waited for someone to speak. She backed into the door, hoping no one had seen her. She wanted Emeline to let one of them talk first. She wanted them to fall into their familiar ways. She wanted them to realize how lucky they were to have history, the place, understanding, even the awkwardness at seeing one another frail and broken. She wanted them to thank something, God or whatever, that they were still here.

A metallic boom shuddered out of the field. They all laughed afterward. The boom came again, and Casey realized Fournier was banging at the well head with a digging bar.

By lunchtime, the well was open, and later in the day, Miner brought a pump and set up a spigot. Granite Hill was to have irrigation. But it would not long have a gardener.

Phil tried to call once more. She had considered heading into Wells Beach to watch the fireworks, but the evening was cool, the flies down, a light breeze pushing through the salt box, and she could not overcome the inertia that kept her at the table. She watched the phone buzz, hop around on the table, as if containing an angry, hopping Phil. Later, long after she had let the cell phone buzz and wobble a few more times, after the light winked out on the hill, after she stopped listening to the racket of the loons to distract her from Phil, she calculated the time difference for calling her mother.

Alaska was five hours behind, it would be just after dinner, they would be cleaning up, or Maurice would be cleaning up, long since having learned that worship of her was critical to a happy life with her. She might light a cigarette and consider the curve of the horizon. Casey thought for a moment that she would look west, away from her, without knowing why. Were Casey to call, she would answer, her voice a chirp, and she would ask about Maine, about the food. She would tell her daughter to describe the light. And if she did, Casey thought, I would say for the first time ever, you have me all wrong, You always have. I have never seen the light. I don't give a damn about the light. And it would be a lie that felt good, because she has always seen light in its variety, the one gift that miserly woman ever gave to her. But she would not let her know. She would deny ever seeing it, even though that light, reflected in the things that she loved to make grow around her, that light was often reward enough of its own.

She put the phone down. What would she have told her—she needed money, she needed to come home? Neither would do it. Those concerns weren't even close to worth putting up with her again. Or with Maurice's miserly bullshit. She shook the change in her pocket. She knew she had a few hundred in the bank. She almost said it aloud, *there are only so many times I can start again.* She slept fitfully through the night.

When she saw Emeline's chair on its side by the well, she dropped her coffee cup. Hot coffee splashed back up her leg, stinging her as she charged out the door. She shouted Emeline's name twice, and then saw her hand wave out above the low grasses and nodding daisies, from near the well head. Casey leaped across the bed, landing next to the chair, and she barked, "Are you okay? What were you *doing*?"

Emeline stuck her hand out, and her voice pinched into a wince.

"Casey," she said, "can you help me to sit up?"

"What happened?"

When she bent to pull the woman upright, she felt her chest bloom, then she fell next to Emeline. While Emeline sat next to her, Casey sobbed until she was curled in a ball next to Emeline, while the older woman, serene and bewildered at once, ran a hand up and down her arm. When Casey was able to ask Emeline how long she had tried to yell, Emeline shook her head. Casey sat up, held Emeline's wrist, and asked again. Not long, she said.

"Long enough," Casey replied. She wiped her face, felt she had smeared dirt under her eye.

She saw a crusted spot of blood just above Emeline's temple. Casey asked if she hit her head, and Emeline said it was nothing, Casey knew she meant it, but did not, herself, believe it.

"If I hadn't been here, how long would you have lain by the well?"

Emeline waved her hand at Casey, but Emeline's eye had twitched, something in her throat jumped. Casey grasped her hand. She was surprised to realize she would stay.

The Kiss-Me-Quick

Rochelle Distelheim

I visited my friend and we talked about shoes instead of about dying. I wanted to talk about dying, but she's the one who's dying and she wanted to talk about shoes. We looked at the three shoe boxes lined up on the carpet next to the couch where she was. The boxes were open and I saw the tips of three new pairs of shoes.

There was that faintly sour smell new shoes have that reminds me of going with my mother into a shoe store, with her holding my hand and telling me, all right, all right, you can have a new pair of Buster Browns.

I wanted to tell my friend anything that would sound to her the way *Buster Brown* used to sound to me. But we're grown women with grown children and mothers who are dead. I can't take her hand and say, "Listen, don't walk out on me, not yet."

I used my excited voice. "Who brought these?" I asked, and I picked up a shoe box. My friend hadn't left her house in two months. I knew she hadn't gone to the shoe store, but it was a way to get into the conversation without saying, "Why do you need so many new pairs of shoes?"

"I called Marshall Field's, told the woman what I wanted, and asked her to send them. I said I had parties to go to, a wedding, I was too busy to shop." She shrugged.

"You *are* too busy," I said.

She looked pretty. Her dark blond hair was fluffy and long and flattering bangs fell like a soft curtain across her forehead. But it wasn't her hair. I couldn't say, "I like your hair," so I said, "Then you're going out. That's great."

I took out a pair of black patent leather shoes. They had narrow grosgrain bows across the toes, and low heels. They looked like a little girl's party shoes. Once they walked out of the house and into the world, wonderful things would happen.

"This isn't your kind of shoe," I said. "Your shoes have heels like skyscrapers."

I outlined two high, narrow shapes against the empty air, as though I had to show my friend what kind of shoes she wears.

"Not anymore. High heels are bad for my health, like wine when I take my pills." She was smiling; her mouth was, her eyes were sad.

"Well..." I held one shoe up and squinted at it like a jeweler checking a gem. "What's so wonderful, anyway, about walking around on stilts? I hate them."

"So who says you're the perfect woman?"

"I do," I said, and brushed my hand against her cheek. "You've got some of your lunch on your face. How about a cup of tea?"

"Everybody who comes here," she said, "wants to boil water."

I lifted a pair of beige silk pumps from another box. They were perfectly plain with square heels. I wore this kind of shoe in college. "My god," I said, "remember these? Remember how we wore white gloves and had to sign in by twelve-thirty?"

"Ten-thirty," my friend said.

"I mean on Saturday nights."

I put a hand in each shoe and walked them across my lap. "Can you believe how green we were?"

"What did we know?" She leaned her head against the back of the couch and closed her eyes.

"Kiss me quick!" I said.

My friend sat up and stared at me.

"That was the name of that little foyer inside the front door of our dorm, don't you remember, the kiss-me-quick, because that was all the time we had for necking after a date? Remember how the damned bell always went off, and the housemother came down the stairs hollering, 'Time, girls!' just when we were warming up?"

We both laughed; laughed so hard, we began to cry and had to wipe our eyes on our sleeves. Then she made a face and I knew her ribs hurt.

"Try this on." I pulled her house slippers off and tried to slip her foot into one of the beige shoes. It didn't fit. The shoe was too small or her foot was swollen, or I was trying too hard.

"It's no good," she said, "we can't make it work."

"My god, oh my god," I said, "nothing the hell works anymore!"

"What's the difference?" my friend asked. "It was a crazy idea, I don't need new shoes."

"Just push," I said, forcing her foot downward and the show upward, gripping her ankle so hard my fingers left red marks on her skin.

One Moment: 1330 South McLeod
Kaytie M. Lee

Steven sat in the back seat of a police cruiser, the first time he'd ever seen the view from behind scratched Plexiglas. He wasn't paying much attention to it except to notice that Midge's blood had dripped onto the dingy, white vinyl seat, a bright smear dribbling onto the plastic floor mat. He held Midge's head in his lap, his shaking hands cupping her jaw. One brown eye gazed intently on him, pupils fully dilated, rims of white where the eyelids pulled back in shock. He massaged her velvet jowls with his thumbs. Her pink tongue lolled from her gaping mouth; blood flecked her canines.

For whatever reason—denial, possibly, or simple medical ignorance—the fact that his dapple-brown greyhound's blood oozed from a gash in her side and onto the police car's upholstery bothered him more than the caved-in appearance of her ribs and the peculiar angle her pelvis jutted out. Not because the blood made a mess. Surely the back seat of this police car had seen nastier fluids—cruisers were made to be hosed out. No, it bothered him because blood was supposed to stay inside the body. It didn't matter how broken the bones were, provided Midge's insides stayed inside.

"You're all right," he whispered.

Midge whined, tried to swallow. Steven held her steady. She kept trying to sit up. Her retired racing legs splayed forward, paws brushing the panel that had been installed to divide the felons from the officers.

"Almost there," the officer said.

To the officer's credit, he'd been dismayed when he got out of the cruiser and saw that he had hit Steven's dog. He had held the dog steady as Steven ran the half-block that separated them. He'd offered to take Steven and Midge to the Emergency Animal Hospital, had even, Steven gratefully noted, turned on the sirens and the swirling police lights, though loud wailing did doing nothing for Midge's panic at finding herself in pain, incapacitated, unable to run away. But Steven would never forgive the man for asking, in an incredulous voice, "Why isn't that dog on a leash?"

What reasonable answer could Steven have had?

He'd said, "It was an accident." But in fact, it was just chaos. Riding in the backseat of the cruiser, Steven felt as out of control as he had that morning, the moment when he and his wife, Rebecca, discovered something had gone wrong in their neighborhood.

Coffee had been percolating, scrambled eggs frying in real butter. Rebecca stood at the kitchen island with the newspaper. She opened a section and sent random inserts fluttering to the floor. She flapped the pages until they took shape, upright and stiff, ends curling in to cover the news.

"That journalist is still missing in Pakistan."

He didn't know whom she was talking about. He concentrated on scrambling the eggs, poking at them with a white plastic spatula.

"Daniel Pearl," she said, rather sharply. "It's been a week."

"That's not good," he agreed.

Too much was happening around the world for Steven to keep up with current events. He worked hard as a technology strategist covering all of South America. He knew more about Brazil than the Middle East, and had several projects to wind up before all of his South American counterparts disappeared for Carnival.

"The kidnappers sent an email to Fox News claiming they've killed him."

"Until it's on CNN, I'm not believing it," Steven declared.

He wondered if he should put off his April trip to Brazil, but that seemed paranoid. He wasn't a journalist, after all.

The sizzle of frying eggs wholly satisfied Steven. Eggs would have almost (but not quite) made up for having to wake up early on the weekend to work in the backyard.

Outside his kitchen window, suburban serenity—tiny brown birds hopped in the dirt that would someday be a landscaped garden and patio. His wife, his coffee, his eggs. Then the atmosphere had gone from serenity to sirens. A minor shift in consonants made all the difference.

Usually, emergency vehicles screamed past their house, traveling up Parkway, the busy thoroughfare, on their way to unknown emergencies. Steven had paused over his eggs, waiting for the wave of noise to crest and fade.

Hearing sirens in his kitchen was nothing compared to the constant blare he suffered now, in the backseat of the police cruiser.

The car turned, then turned again, and Steven braced himself to hold Midge's broken body in place. Then the officer cut the siren, cut his engines, and slammed the door on his way into the hospital to find help. Midge relaxed in the quiet. Still, her breath came in tight hitches as though her diaphragm caught itself on some sharp shard before it could fully inflate her lungs.

"You're okay, you're okay," Steven crooned. Curling his spine, he hunched over and kissed Midge on the smooth bridge of her nose. She whimpered and tried to lick back.

His right arm supported most of her weight and it had started to cramp.

Steven shifted so that his back rested partially on the door. Awkward, but doing so allowed Midge more room. And it was a police door. Locked from the outside. He couldn't get out until someone opened it for him.

People dressed in periwinkle or salmon scrubs passed by the windows that framed torsos and lower chins. Doors opened, someone placed a strong hand on Steven's shoulder to help him balance. The vets, with professional caution, spent agonizing seconds analyzing the best way to transfer Midge from his lap and into a canvas bag with two straps, each held by a technician. A pet gurney, because a struggling animal would fall off a flat surface. A man with a full, bushy beard and blue eyes under salt and pepper eyebrows, took charge.

"Support its head through the car. I'm going to draw the dog towards me and into the holster."

Steven complied. Midge let out a gargling yip that cut into Steven deeper than if the pain had been his own. Secured in the bag, she was rushed into the hospital. Steven was left in the parking lot.

"You'll be okay?" the officer asked.

No, he would not be okay, not ever. Running through the neighborhood in search of his lost dog, stumbling around the corner to see Midge crumpled in front of a bumper . . . he would not be okay. But Steven nodded and the officer took off. Hustled into the cruiser and drove away. There were other emergencies that needed his attention, Steven knew that. A little girl from the neighborhood, missing out of her own bedroom.

Pushing through the glass door to the waiting room, Steven was met with the required paperwork of emergency care. He called home, first.

"Becca." Steven swallowed, coughed to clear his throat. "We're at the Emergency Animal Hospital."

"I'll be right—" but she cut herself off in her haste to hang up the phone.

He took a seat, clipboard in hand, a pen tied to a string, in turn taped to the board. Relentless air-conditioning from multiple vents in the ceiling meant there was no warm place to sit. Shivering, he rested the board on his knee. He noticed bloodstains on his jeans and tee-shirt, blood wedged under his fingernails. Bloody prints on the plastic pen.

He put the point of the pen on the page to write his name on the first line. Steven Golde. Phone number, address. Pet: greyhound. Allergies to medication: none. Reason for visit: procrastination of seemingly inconsequential but ultimately critical home repair. Steven had neglected to install the new deadbolt.

Still in its packaging, the distressed bronze, single cylinder deadbolt gathered dust on a workshop table in his garage. Solid brass, a keyhole for the outside and a knob for the inside, bought on sale for $49.99 down from sixty. Rebecca had been on him for weeks to install it, because of the ingenuity of their fat orange cat.

Miss Deeds stands on her hind legs and paws at the current lock's knob until it turns. She then grabs hold of the modern lever that is the door handle, and with her seventeen pound weight, forces the catch. The door swings open and she sits on the mat, all smugness and pride, before sauntering into the shrubs to stalk hummingbirds. Very clever, except for Midge and Steele, jittery rescue greyhounds that bolt through any egress.

Steven hadn't installed the lock because he resented the need for one in the first place. It embodied all of the shoddy craftsmanship he'd had to fix after buying the brand-new house. If the front door had been professionally fitted into the doorway and sealed with the proper rubber material when the house had been constructed, there would be no give. Miss Deeds, whose only desire was to be outside, could rattle it as much as she wanted but wouldn't open the door.

"She did it again," Rebecca said when he had come down for breakfast that morning, before sirens and searches. "You must install that lock today."

"First thing after breakfast."

Breakfast he hadn't had the chance to eat. His scrambled eggs had probably congealed in the pan, attracting flies and ants. His stomach chortled audibly, though the thought of food made him sick. Horrible, Steven thought, the way your body continues to impose life on you when everything else seems to have stopped.

Steven filled out the last section of the form and returned to the counter.

"Just leave it," the receptionist said in that harried but controlled way emergency technicians have.

"Sorry, I got blood on it," he said, showing her where. She glanced at it and nodded, then turned back to the prescription she was filling. Steven had been dismissed.

A television in the corner played a kiddy movie, though there were no children in the waiting room to watch it. A younger couple with a cardboard carrier placed on the seat between them pretended they weren't watching him.

Steven sat in the same chair, reached over and grabbed a magazine with his cleaner hand. *Cat Fancy.* Pamper Your Persian, Satisfy Your Siamese. Kittens, kittens, kittens. The warped pages had been mauled by grubbier hands than his, hands anointed with oil and dander from the skin of nervous pets.

A bell announced an entrance, then Rebecca was standing over him in dark sunglasses and her red track suit, the one that made her look like her mother.

"Where is she?"

Steven jutted his chin in the direction of the battered white swinging doors. Midge was somewhere beyond them, in the small-scale labyrinth of exam rooms and labs And a morgue, he thought before he could stop himself.

As Rebecca sat next to him, Steven could see her jaw set in the line it took when she was upset. Her anger radiated in all directions but was focused, he could tell, at himself. Even though it was her half-feral cat who'd opened the door, even though she could have leashed up the dogs and taken them down the block when she had disappeared, so that they would think they were getting their customary walk instead of the ruin their morning had become. She always did this, always disappeared during unpleasant jobs to appear later with criticism.

When the sirens had shown no signs of fading, Rebecca had dropped the newspaper and ran to the picture window to investigate, hands clapped over her ears, Midge howling at her heels. The cat disappeared in a terrorized supernova of fur. Steel, who couldn't handle a car alarm six blocks away, lost bladder control. Urine splashed to the floor, splattering the island and the carpet that began where the linoleum ended.

"There...they're turning onto our street!" Rebecca called from the living room over Midge's yodeling.

Steven grabbed Steel's collar to herd him towards the sliding glass doors that led out back but the dog's legs were rigid from fright. Smoke—his eggs were burning. He shoved the pan to the back burner and turned off the gas element. "Shit!"

"God, there are five—no, six cop cars and two fire trucks!"

"A little help here," he called, masking his annoyance with urgency. Any emergency outside could wait until their emergency inside was cleaned up. He pushed Steel aside and retrieved a new roll of paper towels from the top of the fridge. Rebecca maintained her post at the window, oblivious to his plea.

The sirens cut off, one lingering a second longer than the others. Steven's stomach twisted with vertigo as though the sudden ceasing of sound had knocked him off balance. The way his ears rang, it probably had. His nose burned at the acrid smell of Steel's yellow puddle mixed with the ammonia-based cleanser. Midge stopped barking, her dappled back arched, her whip-like tail wagging to one side in confusion.

"I can't tell which house they're for. They parked all up and down the block and the officers are walking to the playground."

"Could you maybe help?"

But he had mostly finished soaking up the stain by the time Rebecca returned to the kitchen. She coddled Steel while Steven pitched soiled and soaked wads into the trash bin.

"I'm going to take a shower," he said. "Finish the carpet when you can."

For all the good the shower had done him, Steven might as well have skipped it. He did not feel April fresh, sitting next to his wife in the Emergency Veterinary Hospital's waiting room. His jeans were stiff where blood had begun to dry. Ammonia lingered in his nostrils and there was the gore under his fingernails.

"I'm going to go wash my hands," he said. Rebecca rolled her shoulders back once, as though relieving herself of the tension he had caused her. He walked away; her unspoken accusation pulled between them like taffy.

The unisex bathroom was dark when he entered. Flipping the switch started a buzz that was supposedly a fan and revealed white tiled floor and walls, scuffed but scrubbed clean. The toilet seat was up. At the sink, Steven turned the hot and cold handles and waited for the water to warm. His awful appearance met him in the mirror. When had he gotten that smear of blood across his cheek? He knew the bags under his eyes had been there.

It had been a tough week. Tough couple of months, actually, with everyone's nerves scraped raw by Afghanistan, layoffs, and the continued tanking of 401k accounts. Not to mention the National Guard at airports and the smoldering ruins of the World Trade Center, and every evening the half-smiling face of Osama bin Laden reminding the world that he remained at large in Pakistani mountains Steven had never heard of. A girl missing on his own street. And now Midge.

He put his hands in the stream of water. Warm. He hadn't realized his hands had gotten so cold in the waiting room. Pushing the lever on the soap dispenser, pink granules poured into his palm. The soap scoured like sand but it was exactly what he needed to get the coppery blood out of the cracks of his skin. When his hands were clean he lathered up his forearms, then splashed water on his face. He reached for coarse brown paper to dry off with.

After his shower, he had been rubbing his hair dry with an expensive terrycloth towel when the doorbell rang. Naked, he moved from the master bath to the bedroom to listen for Rebecca's steps. Nothing until the doorbell rang again. He called for his wife but she didn't answer, so Steven threw on underwear, jeans and button-down shirt. He took the stairs faster than he should have, nearly pitching into the greyhounds that hovered at the door. Opened it a crack while keeping the dogs to one side with his leg. Steven faced a young officer, so blond he had no eyebrows, his face set to neutral. He had a fierce-looking German Shepherd on a short tether.

"My name is Officer Jenkins and I would like permission to search your backyard." He held out a badge, as though the uniform and perfectly behaved canine weren't proof enough of his authority.

"Sure," Steven said, peering over Jenkins' head for Rebecca. He spotted her down the block, her arms crossed, conversing with the neighbors who milled about the playground. The street had been taken over by emergency vehicles—police cruisers blocked driveways and two fire trucks took up the road. "The gate's locked. Hang on while I get shoes."

Steven closed the door, retrieved flip-flops from the closet, rebuked Midge who excitedly leapt on him thinking she was going for her walk, then rejoined the officer on the porch. He knew he had no reason to be nervous but his palms had begun to sweat. "So, what's going on?" he asked as he shoved his left foot into its corresponding flop.

"A girl is missing. Pauline Carrico."

Steven couldn't picture her. He didn't know any of the children on the street, barely knew their parents from the homeowners' association meetings. He'd probably recognizer her if he saw her—the greyhounds attracted kids like the ice-cream man.

"That's terrible," Steven said. He hoped his sincerity didn't ring false. It was terrible, frightening, in fact. But then again, kids disappear all the time, only to be discovered after a few panicked hours at a friend's house or playing in a schoolyard. Probably no big deal. All those fire trucks and cruisers—must be a slow crime day.

Officer Jenkins led the way around the house, or rather, the German shepherd led the officer. At the gate,

Steven fumbled with the lock as he tried to remember the combination. They'd put the lock on after catching teenagers cutting through the backyard at night. When the lock clicked free, he opened the gate and stepped aside.

"Got your work cut out for you," Officer Jenkins observed, scanning the dirt where a lawn should be. The dog started sniffing, its industrial nose pulling air in and parsing the particles for minute traces of missing girl.

"Sorry," Steven said. Then it occurred to him that he didn't need to apologize to Officer Jenkins for the state of his yard. Flustered, he felt as if he was failing an interview. He decided to shut up and let the cop do his job.

"Have the neighborhood kids ever been back here?"

"Some teenagers, before we put the locks on the gates. Other than that, not that I'm aware of."

The greyhounds peered at them through the vertical blinds across the sliding glass doors, shifting their muzzles when the blinds bumped their sensitive noses. They begged with their sad little eyes to be let out to play with the police dog. Steven ignored them.

"Sandy ground here, isn't it?" Officer Jenkins noted, scuffing his shoe in the dirt.

"This area used to be a riverbed, like twenty-thousand years ago," Steven replied, pointing to a rock pile in the back corner of the yard. "We'll have to remove another ton of those if we want a decent garden."

Officer Jenkins directed his dog to the corner. With belated horror, Steven realized that a pile of rocks would be an obvious place to hide a body in a hurry. The dog sniffed the stones, poked his nose in crannies. The last thing Steven needed was a police dog to get bit by the black widow spiders he knew skulked along the fence. But the dog moved on, unharmed.

Officer Jenkins hadn't found any bodies buried in his backyard, of course. They'd found no trace of the missing girl, either. And when Steven emerged from the unisex bathroom, his arms pink from the hot water, he returned to the waiting room to find no sign of Rebecca, either. She'd disappeared behind the swinging doors, no thought of waiting for him. When he questioned the receptionist she seemed much warmer to him now. What did she know that he didn't? She directed him to room two, through the swinging doors and down the left corridor.

Becca sat in the only chair next to a stainless steel table. The walls had been papered with Escher-esque Scotties, alternating white and black, all with red scarves. The resulting herringbone hurt his eyes.

"They're doing X-rays," she whispered. So he hadn't missed anything.

"What a day," Steven said. He immediately regretted it. Such trite bullshit. He glanced at Rebecca, fearing she'd pounce on the opening he'd made, but she was crying silent tears. He wanted to hold her against his stomach as he stood over her, but at the last moment remembered his bloodied tee-shirt. He touched her arm but she twisted away from him.

The bearded vet entered, his facial hair covering a stern expression. "I'm Dr. Richards," he said. Steven shook the man's hand, noticed that it was as clean as his own.

There was no good way for the vet to deliver his news so Dr. Richards went right into it, hanging X-rays on a light board fixed to the wall. White bone structure as faint as wisps of back-lit cigarette smoke sprung from the black film.

"When Midge was hit she sustained several broken vertebrae near her tail." Dr. Richards pointed at a section of spine. When they were pointed out, Steven could distinguish fine cracks in the white. "At least seven vertebras were affected, possibly as many as twelve."

Rebecca wiped her cheeks with the back of her hand, raking her skin with her diamond and leaving a welt. "What's your recommendation?"

"Midge won't walk again. I'm not sure it's in her best interest to keep a dog in her condition alive."

How could a doctor come in and deliver news like that? It was cold, it was unfeeling. It reeked of judgement. He probably blamed Steven for the accident without knowing the details, the self-righteous prick.

"What about those chariot dogs?" Steven asked, inspired by his desire to prove the doctor wrong. He'd seen them on television, little dogs who had lost the use of their hind legs and moved around in custom wheelchairs. "Can't we get Midge one of those?"

"She suffered more than broken bones. There's internal damage, hemorrhaging around her liver. I can't know more without exploratory surgery." Dr. Richards looked back and forth between Steven and Rebecca as an uncomfortable moment grew unbearable. Retreating from the room, he said, "I'll give you some time."

Steven leaned against the table—he wanted to lie down, or sit. He felt off-kilter, like a man in a life-raft floating on unceasing waves. "What do you want to do?"

Rebecca didn't answer. She cried inconsolably, keeping sounds in but unable to communicate. She reached for him. Steven held her then, forgetting bloodstains. She pulled at the back of his shirt. The door behind them opened but closed again when the unseen intruder hastily shut it on their grief.

Steven stroked his wife's hair. Their shared hurt burned red hot between them with the shame of their failed responsibility for another living creature. Rebecca's hair was silky, smooth and soft like a child's hair, and all at once Steven pictured Pauline Carrico. She was the little girl with hair like spun sugar, so fine her pony tails were mere tendrils. Remembering how she had once shyly approached Steel, her fingers sticky with melted cherry Popsicle, and Steel had rewarded her with an enthusiastic lick that sent her giggling away.

"How did this happen?" Rebecca's muted cry, her face pressed to his stomach.

Where was the answer? Was it good enough? Through a chink in the armor, a crack in the dike. In a crowded café among dozens of people, through an open bedroom window in a safe neighborhood. It had happened in the time it took Steven to walk from the backyard to the driveway with Officer Jenkins and his German shepherd. In that moment when his attention was on something else. It happened then.

"Your front door is open," Officer Jenkins had said on his way to the next house.

Steven had swiveled in place to see the partial opening. His eye caught a flick of the cat's tail as she skulked into her favorite shrubbery. Steel quivered on the front porch, alone. Midge was nowhere. Steven sprinted up the lawn and pushed Steel back inside. Rebecca still hadn't come home. Fuck.

From the sidewalk, he had no way of knowing where Midge had run, and the problem with tracking greyhounds is their top speed, forty-five miles an hour. Worst case, Midge had run to Parkway, the main thoroughfare that local drivers treated like a freeway, himself included. That's where he ran, as best he could in flip-flops.

Cars speeding by, big trucks barreling down. Steven coughed on exhaust, squinting in the sunlight to catch a glimpse of Midge. He was afraid to call her name in case she'd made it across the street—he didn't want her sprinting into traffic. Sweating, his head pounding from the exertion of running through the neighborhood, he noticed how uncomfortably hot it was. Strange for February, even in San Diego.

Rebecca was waiting for him on the porch, dismayed that he was alone.

"What now?" Panic had pitched her voice higher. Steven didn't know what to do; the dogs had never run away before. He stood there, panting to catch his breath. Before he could answer he heard it, a siren. The sound that had frozen them in the kitchen less than an hour before. The siren, a horn, and then the long squeal of brakes.

The Dead Woman From the Newspaper

Patry Francis

When Johnny Sheehan fell in love for the last time, it was an ordinary Tuesday. His wife Alice was beside him on the bus, heading for an appointment with his opthamologist. Taking the bus to various medical appointments had become their morning routine as Johnny's body found new and interesting ways to betray him almost daily. It wasn't Alice's choice. She had once loved to drive, had, in fact, done her best thinking behind the wheel of their old Volkswagen beetle. But eighteen years earlier, after finishing a biography of Gandhi, Johnny decided that private transportation was immoral and sold the thing. Alice had held a grudge against the Mahatma for years.

But despite its inconvenient schedule, the long waits in winter cold and summer heat, despite the awkwardness of maneuvering her nearly blind husband and whatever packages the days errands had produced on and off the bus, Alice had eventually come to enjoy this mode of transportation. She particularly liked the morning commute when it was filled with the regulars. Johnny's infirmities had transformed a bus load of strangers into something of an a.m. discussion group. Because of his glaucoma, Alice read the newspaper to him on the bus, and to accommodate his hearing loss, she read it loudly. In equal volume, Johnny contemplated the day's affairs.

Once a popular professor of Romantic Poetry, Johnny addressed the bus as he had once lectured to a roomful of rapt undergraduates, with his own particular vigor and intimacy. But now the passion of the poets had been replaced by the mundane varieties that were found in the daily newspaper. Criminal events, particularly murders, were of special interest. At first, his fellow commuters had done their best to ignore Johnny's impassioned diatribes; but eventually, they, like even his most reticent students, had been seduced.

One morning Johnny had asked Alice to reread a story about a woman's body that had been found stuffed in the trunk of a car three months after her demise. "Doesn't it say anything about the *odor?*" Johnny bellowed after the second reading. "For god's sake, that corpse must have stunk to kingdom come!"

Well, that had done it. A heavy set man in a uniform that suggested a hotel bellman, had groaned aloud. "Listen man, if you want to talk about rotting corpses, do it somewhere else. I just had breakfast."

But a middle aged woman who always sat with her hands folded neatly on her lap, (obviously a lifelong victim of the good girl syndrome) spoke up in Johnny's defense. "As if we all aren't interested in that stuff. Murder. Mutilation. The stench of death. It fascinates us. Why else would Hollywood make so many movies about it?" Later Alice would learn that her name was Isabel and she worked the cosmetic counter at a local department store.

But on the day Johnny fell in love for the last time, the bus was particularly hushed. Alice had been reading about the disappearance of Lina Maguire, a painter in her forties for over a week. And as she read the daily articles, lingering on the comments of Lina's friends, passing around the paper so all the commuters could examine her photograph, everyone on the bus had begun to root for the attractive, smiling blond. None, of course, more ardently than Johnny Sheehan, whose subject, as previously mentioned, was passion. On this day, however, the headlines announced that Lina's body had been discovered in the woods, and the passengers' hope and fascination, had given way to grief.

"Probably raped, too, " the bellman said, interrupting Alice's reading. "Was she found naked?"

"Nothing like a naked female to arouse a man's interest. Dead or alive," Isabel put in. "Why do you think Hollywood makes so many movies about them?" As they'd gotten to know her better, Johnny and Alice had learned that Hollywood was to Isabel what passion was to Johnny: her subject.

But this time, Johnny wasn't listening, even though Isabel spoke in a raised voice for his benefit. "Go on, Alice," he said sorrowfully, tapping the paper with his index finger. "Please go on."

When she had finished reading and the bus had fallen into a grinding, lonely silence, she noticed Johnny staring through his magnifiers at the grainy photograph of Lina. Uncharitably, Alice said, "That picture must have been taken at least twenty years ago." But Johnny didn't seem to hear her. Anyway, it didn't really matter what the picture showed. With Johnny's poor eyesight, Lina Maguire was a flash of pure blond hair, a shimmery smile, and whatever he imagined her to be. Though no one on the bus would have seen it, or would have understood how a dead woman can be a threat even if they had, Alice saw. Alice knew.

Lina Maguire was hardly the first woman Johnny had fallen in love with in the course of their long marriage. The only difference was that Lina could not fall in love back. Nor could she disillusion him as the others invariably had. In that way, she was even more dangerous than the colleagues and wives of colleagues, the graduate students, and visiting poets with whom Johnny had become infatuated over the years.

The worst part of it was that Alice had always known. Sometimes she could predict who Johnny would fall in love with even before he actually tumbled. All through the years she spent washing his clothes, typing the eager notes he made for his classes in romantic poetry, or listening to his excited rants about some astonishing new writer he'd discovered, she'd waited for the one woman who would outshine all the others. The one who wouldn't disappoint him with her mundane humanity in the end. The woman who was as capricious and interesting and as endlessly childish as Johnny Sheehan himself. Even in more recent years when she read aloud to him, administered his endless glaucoma drops, make sure he got his high blood pressure medication, and massaged his poor ruined body so he could sleep at night, Alice could look into his astonishing blue eyes and see it was still there. The passion. The foolishness. The quest.

At the doctor's office, the opthamologist once more tried to persuade Johnny that he needed surgery. And as he did on all the previous visits, Johnny refused. Perhaps fired up by his grief over Lina, he refused even more adamantly. Johnny claimed he saw the loss of his sight as an opportunity to develop other faculties. He left the office in a spirit of triumph, gleeful that he had thoroughly exasperated what he called "another narrow minded physician."

At home, over tea, Johnny took out the newspaper again and held it in his hand, pondering the words Alice had read earlier. "Not a single photograph of her paintings in all this drivel," he said. "All that about where she lived and what she taught, and that she had a twenty-whatever year old daughter when it's obvious the only thing that really mattered to the woman was the *work.*" Johnny pounded the table so hard that he upset his teacup and the liquid seeped into Alice's favorite table cloth.

Alice got up to get a rag. "Well, I hope the daughter mattered ," she said quietly. "At least a little." The fact that she herself had never had children was a sore point with Alice, and her voice quavered slightly as she spoke.

"Well, not to me," Johnny bellowed, not noticing—*never* noticing Alice's private grief over their lack of children. He squinched up his eyes to get a better look at the dead woman's fading face. "What I need to see here is the work." He looked up briefly. "Alice, could you be a love and get me my magnifier?"

Johnny sat there with his thick magnifier, his white head bent over the image of a dead stranger while Alice moved around the kitchen cleaning up. For a few moments, she lost herself in her own under appreciated art form: efficiency. But then she looked up and saw the expression on his face, saw that what she suspected on the bus had happened for sure: the poor jowly, blinding fool had fallen in love right before her eyes. Sometimes she positively hated the man.

As it turned out, Lina Maguire's murder was a crime that was easily solved. A neighbor's gardener who she'd met several times on her own street and later encountered in a bar was arrested. The physical evidence, combined with the man's troubled history suggested an easy conviction.

After Alice read the story aloud on the bus, Isabel grasped for the newspaper. "Look at his eyes! It's obvious the man is unbalanced. Why in the world would a woman—a teacher—for goodness sake, leave a bar with a man like that?" she asked.

"I can't imagine," Johnny said, staring straight ahead, seeing nothing but the image of his sainted blond.

At this point, Alice was tempted to speak up and say something uncharitable: *Because she was a floozy, that's why Johnny. Your angel with the pure white hair was nothing but a common tart.* But she couldn't bring herself to utter the words—partially because she could see that Johnny's grief for the dead woman was genuine. And partially because of an ethic instilled in childhood that prohibited speaking ill of the dead.

"She just did something foolish, that's all. Like we all do," Alice sighed. But the truth was that foolishness was reserved for people like Lina Maguire and Johnny. She, Alice Wexley Sheehan, would never have climbed into that gardener's truck. Not on her loneliest, most desperate day. And that was precisely why Johnny could never love her the way he loved the dead woman from the newspaper.

At Lina's wake, Alice found an inconspicuous chair in the back while Johnny dove into the crowd with the boldness that had always ignited his wife's admiration. Not only was he unchastened by the fact that he hadn't known the deceased; he didn't seem to notice that he was lame, half-blind, and in danger of stumbling into some unfamiliar lap at any moment. At first, Lina's friends mistook him for a former professor from her art school days. But even after they realized that Johnny had merely fallen in love with an elusive essence he drew from the dead woman's story, they welcomed him. Perhaps even more warmly than they had when they thought he actually had a right to be there. Alice folded her hands and tried not to listen as Johnny rhapsodized over Lina's special qualities. He finally settled his attentions on a lanky redhead who claimed to have been the dead woman's closest friend.

"The paper sensationalized the whole thing," the redhead was saying angrily. "They made it sound as if she picked up this total *stranger* in that bar. But Lina had seen this guy around for months..." She ferreted in an oversized bag for a Kleenex before Johnny came up with the handkerchief Alice had pressed and folded that morning.

"It was Lina's nature to trust," Johnny said authoritatively, his blue eyes growing brighter as he added flesh to the woman of his imagination. "That was part of her beauty."

"You know, Lina searched for someone who understood her like you do all her life," the redhead said, absently stuffing Johnny's neatly ironed handkerchief into her bag.

"That was what she was looking for it the night she died," Johnny said, his arm around the redhead's shoulder. "Not some sordid sexual encounter, the way they made it sound."

Alice was about to get up and remind him it was time for the glaucoma drops with the purple cap when she was distracted by the sound of nearby sniffling. She'd been so absorbed in her husband's nauseating show of empathy, she hadn't noticed girl beside her. The girl was unnaturally pale under cap of monotone hair so black it was almost purple; she dressed in layers of clothing that vaguely recalled the sixties.

Alice knew the polite thing to do once their eyes met was to ask the girl about her relationship with the dead woman. But instead, she blurted out, "Goodness dear, aren't you hot in all those clothes?" As if to relieve the girl, Alice unfastened the top button of her own princess collar.

The girl with the harshly dyed hair shrugged. "Clothes are my armor. At least, that's what my shrink says."

"Were you very close?" Alice asked. "I mean, to the unfortunate woman?" She nodded in the direction of the coffin, unable to utter her dead rival's name.

"Uh-uh." The girl shook her head and looked down at her long skirt. "At least, I never thought we were. But when I heard she was dead, I just fell apart."

As the sniffling gave way to sobs, Alice inched closer in her chair, and lay an arm over the girl's shoulder. Beneath the layers of clothing, it felt bony. "My husband had students who felt that way about him, too. Though of course, he hasn't died. Not yet anyway." As Johnny leaned closer to the redhead, undoubtedly to offer another insight into Lina's character, Alice pictured him in the coffin instead of the blond.

"She wasn't my teacher." The girl wiped her eyes with the sleeves if her outer layer, softening the forbidding black eye make-up into a pathetic smudge. "She was my mother."

Alice drew back to get a better look at the girl who seemed to bear no resemblance to Lina. "You're the twenty-two year old daughter from Seattle? You're *Zoe?"* she asked incredulously. "What on earth are you doing back here?"

"Where should I be?" the girl asked, chewing her already bitten down nails. Alice noticed that she'd painted alternate nails black and white like piano keys.

"Well, *there*, of course," Alice said, gesturing vaguely at the place beside the casket where Johnny stood as if he were the chief mourner. "Where people can offer you their condolences." As if to demonstrate, a young woman in dark green stepped forward and shook Johnny's hand.

But Zoe only shrugged. "I don't know any of these people anyway. I left home at seventeen and since then, I haven't been back much..."

"But your family..." Alice began. Then suddenly feeling the need for armor herself, she stopped and rebuttoned her princess collar.

By then Zoe was already shaking her head. "No family," she said. "At least none that had any use for Lina. And none of her friends knew me. So, well, here I am."

Alice looked at the girl more closely. She noticed that Zoe's pale face was extraordinarily pretty, though she was clearly doing her best to disguise it. Feeling angry at Lina—an obviously incompetent mother—Alice suddenly felt that this was the child she should have had. She, Alice Wexley Sheehan, would have known exactly what Zoe needed to prosper. And the girl wouldn't have grown up hiding beneath layers of clothes and harshly dyed hair.

"I'm sorry," Zoe said, looking deeply at Alice for the first time. "I didn't even ask how you knew my mother."

"Oh I didn't," Alice said, deflecting the question with a dismissive flick of the wrist. Then, when a look of puzzlement crossed Zoe's face, she pointed at Johnny who was mooning over the photograph that had been set up beside the coffin. "She was a friend of my husband's," Alice explained. And finally, unable to quell her natural candor, she added, "Actually, he's in love with her."

Alice immediately wanted to apologize for her strange admission, but Zoe's face brightened with interest. "He'll get over it once he knows her better," she said, speaking of Lina as if she were still able to act and be acted upon. "They all do."

Alice was about to ask her what she meant when Johnny abruptly moved to her side. "Alice dear," he said, taking her by the hand. "It's getting a bit warm in here, don't you think? We should go."

But now it was Alice who wanted to stay. She was about to introduce Johnny to his beloved's only child when something in her husband's eyes stopped her. Something that resembled panic. Alice gathered up her things, again offered her condolences to Lina's daughter, and took Johnny's arm. Then, impulsively, she pulled an old receipt from her purse and scrawled her name and number on the back. "Call me," she said, handing the crumpled slip to Zoe. "We'll have tea." She could think of no reason the girl would want to call an aging stranger in a princess collar and sensible shoes, but somehow Alice knew that she would.

In the parking lot, Johnny stopped and steadied himself on Alice's arm. "All of a sudden, I felt dizzy in there; I'm not sure why," he said. His eyes were bright with curiosity, as if the failures of his own body were merely another fascinating subject of study.

"Must have been that blond. She's too much for a man your age," Alice said. But as she dabbed spittle from the corner of his mouth, she, too, felt a tinge of alarm.

When Johnny laughed, however, the anxiety quickly passed. "Ah, my Alice. How on God's earth do you put up with me?" Johnny Sheehan said. For a moment, Alice thought that his own foolishness had actually caused him to blush.

But as it turned out, it was more than the dead blond from the newspaper that had made Johnny dizzy at the wake. The next morning Alice found him on the floor. The alert blue of his eyes only served to emphasize his immobility. He held her still with those eyes for a long moment before allowing her to pick up the phone and set the future in motion, a future Alice would eventually name The End of Everything. Everything, it turned out, but the startling life that continued to burn in Johnny Sheehan's azure, nearly sightless eyes. And there, without movement or speech to soften it, it burned brighter than ever.

But at long last, Alice was the only one to see it, the only one to possess it. In her long visits to the nursing home, she carried on deep conversations with those mobile, expressive eyes. She argued with them, consoled them, listened to them, and above all, she cajoled them onward. Looking in those bright irises when she arrived each morning promptly at nine, she saw that she had finally become what Johnny had always been to her: center, focal point, source.

According to the doctors, another stroke would surely finish him off. Thus, Alice sat by the bed, from eight to six fifteen when the last bus left, keeping vigil on his excitable nature.

But it soon became apparent that Johnny was beginning to play children's games with death. Hide and Seek. Tag. Red light, Green Light. Just as he had denied the opthamologist's urgings toward surgery, he resisted the efforts of the speech therapist to help him regain language. And when the earnest young woman, approached his wife, baffled at his failure to try, how could Alice answer for a man she never truly understand herself? How could she explain that he had probably decided to forego speech and see what happened? Or that he was hoping to develop other faculties in its wake? No, there was no explaining Johnny Sheehan. Not even to herself.

At first, there had been many visitors. Old friends. Former students. Even Justine Gossett, a faculty wife Johnny had once loved. Alice was pleased to note that Justine had grown creased and brittle, and even more pleased that her presence elicited barely a flicker in Johnny's once hungry eyes. Most came only once. Without the delicious talk that had always eddied around him, it hardly seemed that Johnny was there at all. Only Alice knew that inside that still and silent body, Johnny Sheehan was as fascinating a man as he'd always been. More so. He was a man involved in intensive study of one of the world's greatest subject: death. And if only he could speak, he would have described his travels to its periphery with great excitement.

But eventually, Alice Sheehan discovered that the End of Everything was also a strange beginning. At first, she had continued to live as she always had, riding the bus, listening to Mahler and Coltrane, the difficult music that Johnny loved. She spent the evenings as they always had.

In Johnny's empty study, she read aloud to his vacant chair, then imagined him pacing, tugging at his white hair, carrying on impassioned arguments with distant authors he would never meet. She even ate the foods that agreed with Johnny's delicate stomach. But as the weeks wore on, Alice realized for the first time that Mahler's music was too stormy for her blood, and that if she never heard "A Love Supreme" again, it would be fine with her.

When she could no longer bear to read Johnny's books into the silence, she packed them into crates and took them to the swap shop at the dump, tossing Johnny's favorite CDs into the box in one impulsive gesture. Enjoying the spaciousness they left behind, Alice developed a passion for sorting and clearing out. She threw away all the notes Johnny had made for his manuscripts, mostly out of print treatises on the romantic poets, the address books filled with the names of students and former lovers. She also tossed his own failed efforts at verse, gifts from four decades of admiring students, and the nearly unreadable notebooks Johnny had kept for as many years, rambling personal observations that ultimately formed the abstruse philosophy he lived by.

Among Johnny's things, there were also mementos from the affairs or flirtations that Johnny had conducted with his women (Alice had never taken the trouble to find out how far these things had gone. And in the end, when he could be sent reeling by a dead woman from the newspaper, how much did it really matter?) There were many photographs, including an attractive snapshot of the now crinkled Justine with a scarf twined glamourously around her neck and head like Lana Turner . These Alice preserved in a strong box, though she wasn't exactly sure why. When she came across an old photograph of herself at around the time she first met Johnny, looking almost pretty and very unafraid, she studied it for a long time, wondering who that girl had been, and what she had seen when she looked into the camera with such clearsighted optimism. Above all, she wondered why Johnny had married her. She knew it was a question that others, seeing the charismatic professor and his dutiful, dowdy wife, had often entertained. But it was the first time Alice had allowed herself to contemplate it. And now the answer was obvious. She, the anchored and anchoring Alice had made Johnny's flights of brilliance and folly possible. And being, after all, a brilliant man, Johnny had known it. Feeling discomfited by this uncharacteristic introspection, Alice tossed her former self into the strong box with the others.

Once she had succeeded in getting rid of everything that Johnny would not use again, his writing and his music, his loves and his books, it seemed that the only thing left in the house was the image of him lying on the floor. That and silence. That morning Alice took the bus down town to the music store Johnny sometimes frequented hoping to banish the image and the silence with something of her own. But once inside, she realized she had no idea what kind of music she, Alice Wexley Sheehan, enjoyed. She wandered through aisles labeled Rap, World, Gospel and Alternative as if she were in a foreign country. When a clerk asked her (somewhat suspiciously) if she needed help, she fled the store, feeling vaguely dizzy the way Johnny had at Lina Maguire's wake. Outside, if she could have, she would have broken into a run, would have galloped from the life she no longer knew how to inhabit.

But in the middle of the night, the words to a song she had once loved seemed to spin in her head, jarring her from sleep. "Begin the Beguine," she said, sitting up in bed. She stared at her husband's empty spot. "That's the kind of music I like, Johnny," she told him forcefully. "Gershwin! Ella! Sinatra! That's what *I* like."

The next day at the nursing home, Johnny blinked at her with his sea blue eyes as she told him that she had thrown out his entire music collection and was planning to stop and buy some Gershwin on the way home. For the first time, he struggled for speech, but all that came out was something that sounded like *Nah Zah. Nah Zah!* he repeated until he collapsed in frustrated exhaustion. And for the first time since she found him, Alice understood that he was no longer studying his own misfortunes. They had overcome him at last. The brilliant Johnny Sheehan who had once held armies of students rapt with his passionate diatribes and overheated opinions could no longer speak one intelligible word.

When she entered her house, the phone was ringing. Alice almost expected it to be Johnny. The old Johnny, calling to castigate her for her failures as a wife. As she picked up the receiver, Alice felt herself bristling. But on the other end of the line an unfamiliar small voice spoke up tentatively, "Alice? You might not,uh, remember me, but you told me I could call..."

Immediately, Alice pictured the pale girl with her tatterdemalion clothes and piano key fingernails who she'd met at Lina's wake. "Of course, I remember you, Zoe dear. How are you doing?"

At that, Zoe burst into tears. "I know I'm practically a total stranger, but I have no one out here. No one but my Mom's friends and they're driving me crazy."

Thinking of some of the annoying academics Johnny had brought home over the years, Alice cooed sympathetically.

"And there's so much to do," Zoe continued in her tiny voice. "You wouldn't believe all the stuff my mom accumulated over the years. I don't even have a truck to get her paintings to the dump."

"Her *paintings?* But aren't they worth something? The paper said..."

"My mother was a respectable dilettante if you know what I mean," Zoe interrupted.

"I'm not quite sure I do," Alice said, wishing Johnny were there to explain.

"Her paintings aren't worth shit," Zoe said with surprising vigor. "Her friends took a few of them for sentimental reasons, I guess. The rest I'm getting rid of."

After her recent binge of cleaning away Johnny, Alice suddenly understood. "Is there any way I could help?"

"Well, you mentioned tea?" Zoe said, her voice once again shrinking. "I just really need someone to talk to, and you seemed so, so, I don't know...I just felt a connection."

"Of course, dear. When would you like to come?" Alice said, her new life taking shape as she spoke.

Within weeks of her first tea with Zoe, Alice went out and bought herself the two things that Johnny railed most loudly against: a television set and a car. And not just ordinary ones either. The TV was one of those big screen varieties that even Johnny could have seen clearly if he had allowed himself the mundane enjoyment of watching one. And the car was neither used, as theirs had been before Johnny turned against the automobile altogether, nor an economy model. It was one of those ridiculous tank like vehicles they call a Sports Utility. Though Alice had no idea what sports they were intended for, and found it difficult to climb into, she liked the sense of power she felt in the high driver's seat, commanding the sheer weight of the thing. It would also be very useful in helping Zoe to sweep away her mother's life. Just thinking how much Johnny would detest it was enough to convince Alice she had to have it.

She told herself that the car would allow her to be free of the restrictions of the bus schedule, and thus spend more time with Johnny. But once she had the vehicle, her hours in the nursing home diminished even more. When she wasn't using the car to help Zoe clean out her mother's apartment, she took long aimless rides, enjoying the sense that she was driving away from her old life with Johnny. And then there was her TV schedule. Alice soon formed attachments to an alarming number of Zoe's "reality shows", as well as several medical and legal dramas.

On every show Alice watched, men fell in love with women like Lina Maguire, women with swirling long hair and exciting professions. She could hardly blame Johnny, Alice thought, furrowing her brow during one such episode. That night she fell asleep with the remote in her hand, still wearing her sensible shoes. Frozen in a position of watching, she dreamed of Johnny making love to a string of attractive lawyers and women detectives she'd seen on TV.

She no longer spent much time with her husband, but she hadn't left him entirely alone. She brought in the strong box full of pictures which she hung around the room so that when he was lonely, he could look out upon the various women he had loved over the course of their marriage. As he squinted at the gallery of women through his weakened eyes, Johnny looked more saddened than exalted by their presence. But Alice left them up anyway.

When the cold weather came, Lina Maguire's murderer went on trial. Alice accompanied the pale Zoe to the courtroom each day, holding her hand throughout the hours of unnerving and sometimes sordid testimony. Afterwards, the two of them would go out for something to eat at Zoe's favorite Indian restaurant. There they talked about anything but the two erratic people who dominated their thoughts and their lives.

On weekends, when Alice visited Johnny, she had so much to tell him that his lack of response was hardly noticeable. She read him every newspaper account of the trial, filling in the gaps with her own recollections of the dramatic testimony. When he turned away in disinterest, she produced an enlarged photograph of the dead woman hoping to reengage him. Her lovely white blond hair tumbling around her shoulders, Lina Maguire smiled provocatively at Johnny, beckoning him from eternity. Shortly after Alice had hung it, a male aide, who'd come in to deliver Johnny's supper paused before the photograph, saying, "Hey, isn't that the broad that was killed over in out on Route 9?"

Alice admitted it was, then went on to elaborate that Johnny had been in love with the victim.

"Well, you old goat," the aide said to Johnny with obvious admiration. "You like the young stuff, huh?" Then remembering Alice, he quickly apologized. "Uh sorry, Mrs.. Sheehan..."

"Yes, and so am I," Alice said. But she found she was addressing her comments to Johnny, not to the aide. "So very sorry." While her husband watched her helplessly from the bed, Alice made a quick survey of the images of former beauty that surrounded him. She nodded first to the aide, then to the picture of Lina Maguire, and finally to the great Johnny Sheehan himself. "Have a good week now," she said blithely. "All of you." Then she put on her coat, gathered up her bag, and left.

From the hallway, she could hear Johnny calling out from his bed. *Nah Zah! Nah Zah!* But she kept moving. Firing up the SUV outside, Alice stared straight into the eye of a bright blue day, and wondered if she would ever return.

After the trial was over, and the murderer had walked out of Alice and Zoe's lives and into a new existence in prison, after all the paintings Lina had struggled to make had been turned to ash at the dump, Zoe Maguire went back to Seattle, looking smaller than ever in her overlapping clothes. In the airport, Alice wondered if she would ever see the girl again. They were, after, all, strangers. Or should have been.

But then Zoe spoke up in her tentative way, "You'll keep in touch, won't you, Alice?" Alice quickly hugged her bony frame and assured her that *of course, she would.* That gave Zoe the courage to say, "I was thinking this year, well, the holidays might be kind of tough. Do you think—"

"They'll be tough for both of us," Alice said, smiling. "And yes, I *do* think...it would be wonderful if you came home." She wasn't sure where the word *home* had come from, but neither of them corrected it.

Driving away, Alice thought of how young and unsure Zoe looked boarding the plane, and she herself felt equally vulnerable. But it wasn't until one morning when she was sitting in her SUV, wondering where on earth she might want to go, that she suddenly felt the weight of her loneliness. Zoe still called frequently, but it had been months since Alice had seen her and even longer since she'd crossed the threshold of the nursing home. She missed the crow haired girl hidden beneath her layers of clothes. And she missed Johnny. She missed the people from the bus. She even missed Lina Maguire. The poor foolish woman she had lived with all these fateful months since she first read her story to Johnny on the way to the opthamologist's office. She wasn't sure why, but somehow it seemed like it was all Lina's fault that the beautiful ordinariness of that day, that bus ride, had been shattered forever. Impulsively, she directed her car toward the cemetery where Lina was buried, determined to give the dead woman from the newspaper a piece of her mind.

But once she found the grave that was simply marked LINA MAGUIRE, no dates, no beloveds, no possessive husband or parent claiming her in death, Alice was no longer angry. And even if she were, she wouldn't have been able to shout at the dead. Such folly was strictly Johnny's domain. She thought she should kneel, but it was raining lightly, the ground was damp, and besides, Alice was not quite sure to whom or to what she would be kneeling. Instead, she closed her eyes, and thought of Lina and her good but not good enough paintings, Lina and her neglected daughter, Lina and the desperate loneliness that had caused her to get in the truck with the rough looking character Alice had seen in court.

As she had several times during the trial, she tried to imagine Lina's face when she first realized her fatal mistake. But all she could see was Johnny and his blinding blue eyes. Her poor foolish Johnny. Suddenly, she was wild to see him. *Nah Zah* he called to her through his wounded body, through the nursing home walls, across the busy city, the quiet field of the dead that separated them. *Nah Zah!*

She didn't even realize she was sobbing until a woman approached her from behind, and put an arm on her shoulder. "I'm sorry to intrude, but are you all right?" the woman said gently.

Rummaging through her handbag for a handkerchief, the embarrassed Alice only nodded.

"She must have been someone very close to you," the stranger said, staring down at the carved letters that summed up Lina Maguire's tumultuous life.

"Oh, she was, she *was,*" Alice sobbed, surprising herself with the passion in her voice. "Closer than I ever knew."

If You Should Die Before I Wake (an excerpt)

Lauren Baratz-Logsted

I remember what the Kid said about Aristotle in the antique bookshop in Luxembourg. I remember about drama, the reversal of expectation, and things bein' surprising and inevitable all at the same time.

I think particularly about the reversal of expectation part and start wonderin' how, with her dyin' and all, maybe she won't have to die after all, that her expectations'll be reversed and we can all call it great drama and go on with our lives.

But then I remember about the inevitable part and somehow I don't think so. I remember *Anna: The Musical*, and I wonder if at any given time, even with the fake duel the Kid threw into it, it was ever possible that Anna's story could have ended in any other way than the way in which it did—could she ever have *not* thrown herself under the train?—and I know that it's impossible, that it could end no other way.

Still, if there are any surprises left out there, I'd sure like to see them.

"As long as you can still hear the other person's words in your head, they're never dead," she says to me from the hospital bed. "It's just like a friend who's moved to another country. If you know the person really well, then you know and can hear exactly what they would say to you in any given situation."

"Oh yeah? If you're so smart, what do you imagine me sayin' to you right now?"

She looks at me closely. "You'd say that my new glasses remind you of something that someone's grandmother would wear." She laughs. "You'd ask me if I'm planning on losing more weight, that I look like I had lunch again at the concentration camp."

I feel myself coloring and try to look away, but she catches me under the chin with one finger, guiding my gaze back towards hers.

"And you'd say that you love me more than anything else that ever walked on the face of this planet," she finishes fiercely, defying me to say her wrong.

What could I say?

With my whole hand I hold onto that finger that had been under my chin as if it's some kind of cord, like it's somehow the only thing connecting me to the world.

"Huh," I say. "It must be nice to know all the answers to everything all the time."

A little while later, she says, "That's the only thing that ever bothers me about all of this; I'm never going to finish the List, Ma."

It must be weighin' on her mind, 'cause in the middle of the night, I'm sleepin' there in the chair by her bed, when I hear her screamin', "I'm only on F! What the fuck am I gonna do now?"

"Sh, sh," I say to her, tryin' not to disrupt any of the wires and sittin' down on the bed with my back against the backboard, takin' her head into my lap and smoothin' her hair like I used to do the few times she had nightmares when she was a little girl.

In the morning she's calm again.

"Could you read to me for a while?" she asks with a smile.

"Sure," I say, thinkin' of where she is on the List. "What do you want to hear? F. Scott Fitzgerald? E.M. Forster?"

"No," she says. "I want to hear Trixie Belden."

I grab my coat and say, "That might take a little bit of work. Can you wait here til I come back?" and she looks at me and smiles weakly and says, "Sure. I can wait. Of course I'll be here when you get back. Where else am I going to go?" and I see how weak she is, how goddamned small, and I think, You might not be here when I get back, and I realize that I'd better hurry.

The hunt for Trixie Belden is nowhere near as easy as I thought it was gonna be.

I go into the first bookstore I see and ask the clerk at the counter, the one with the pierced bellybutton and the jeans hangin' off her hips so low that they look like they're about to puddle down around her ankles, where the Trixie Belden mysteries are kept.

The clerk looks at me like I'm from Mars. "The what?" she asks me.

"The Trixie Belden mysteries. They're for my daughter. I've gotta have 'em."

"Are they something new?" she asks, starting to punch keys on her computer.

"No," I say, lookin' at her now like she's the one from Mars. "They're from the sixties."

"Oh," she says, and stops punching the keys. "Then we don't have them. The only old series we have are the Hardy Boys and Nancy Drew. I have plenty of Nancy Drew," she smiles, perky. "Would you like one of those?"

"No, it has to be Trixie Belden. Do you know some other store where I could find them?"

"No," she says. "All I know is what we have."

"This is an emergency," I say. "Is there anyone else here who might know?"

"Jill!" she shouts, and in a few minutes a middle-aged woman, looking much more like what I expect a clerk in a bookstore to look like, appears from a back room.

"Can I help you?"

I explain my predicament.

"Trixie Belden!" she laughs. "My word, I haven't seen one of those in years. They're out of print, you know."

No, I don't know, and I don't know exactly what out of print means either although I'm sure it's no good. "So another bookstore wouldn't have it?" I say.

"Not unless you have a lot of time to spend looking."

"Time is one thing I don't have. Not anymore."

"Well, then, you might want to try the public library. They have plenty of out-of-print books there. You might get lucky."

Yeah, I think, some luck would be good right now.

I do no better at the public library.

Same thing. First I talk to a young person who hasn't got a clue, then I talk to an older person who practically laughs in my face. This one's got glasses hangin' on a beaded chain around her neck. When she starts to laugh, I want to take one of the arms of those glasses and ram it down her giggling throat.

Instead, I say, "Do you have any suggestions?"

"You might try a used bookstore, or check out tag sales, maybe pay someone to do a book search for you. Of course, a book search can sometimes take weeks or months, but if you're really desperate . . . "

"Thanks a lot," I say.

I'm on my way back to the hospital, wonderin' how I'm gonna explain to the Kid that I'm not gonna be able to get her the thing she wants so badly, that the thing she wants so badly seems to be somethin' that no one else wants, when I remember the crowded attic back home and I turn the car around, drivin' like Speed Racer or somethin'.

I pull up in front of the curb, go tearin' into the house and up the stairs as fast as my legs'll take me, pull down the trapdoor to the attic, take my time goin' up the rickety stairs 'cause this is no time to kill myself, and pull the string on the overhead light. I'm huffin' and puffin', but in the corner I see somethin' that makes me smile for maybe the first time all day: a cedar chest.

When I open the chest, I know what I'll find: a copy of the Kid's birth certificate, her christening dress, her first shoe, her silver rattle, all of her report cards and every note any teacher ever wrote home about her includin' the bad ones from Miss Winter, the presents that she made for me and her father in arts-and-crafts classes when she was small, and Volume 1 from the Trixie Belden mystery series. I didn't keep the whole collection of nineteen that she had, but I did keep the very first one because I remembered how much she loved the series.

"Look," I say, walkin' into the hospital room. "Look what I found in the attic. It's *The Secret of the Mansion*."

"Great," she smiles, and she looks even weaker than when I left just a few hours ago.

"Do you want I should start?"

"Sure," she says, and closes her eyes, still smilin'. "Read me a story."

"Chapter 1, The Haunted House. ' "Oh, Moms," ' Trixie moaned, running her hands through her short, sandy curls. "I'll just die if I don't have a horse." ' "

And so I read to my daughter about Trixie Belden, with the tight blond curls and the house in Sleepyside on the Hudson that they call Crabapple Farm, and the adventures that she has with her new best friend Honey Wheeler, who just moved in next door, and Trixie's pain-in-the-neck and much younger brother Bobby who gets himself bit by a snake, and the troubled runaway orphan Jim Frayne who gets himself adopted by Honey's incredibly wealthy family before the book ends and who becomes Trixie's squeaky clean boy to flirt with throughout the series, and as I'm reading, I begin to realize, Oh no, this isn't any good, the first one in the series doesn't have Trixie's two older brothers, Mart and Brian, in it yet 'cause they're still workin' at summer camp and plus the Lynch girl, the one with the pretty violet eyes, isn't even in the series at all yet, so it's not complete, and for the first time, I begin to cry in front of her.

But then I look over at the Kid and I can see that she's still smilin' and I realize that this is enough, that this has to be enough, and it's okay.

She reaches out to pat at my hand and she says to me again, "Ma, don't go turning this into some kind of tragedy or something." She makes me promise her, "Ma, whatever you do, don't waste your life."

Well, what could I say? Your kid's hooked up to an IV, she weighs less than she did when she was ten years old, that monitor thing's beepin' slower and slower all the time. What else *could* I say?

Oh, well.

So, now what'm I gonna do?

When she was born, she was just about the cutest thing you ever saw in your life. She was so small, that I thought she could practically fit in the palm of my hand if only I wasn't so scared to death of not givin' her neck enough support.

I can still see her in my mind when we brought her home, the picture a little jerky like from out of one of those projection cameras we all used to have, a long, long time ago. I see her father and I, catchin' each other whenever the other one sneaks into her bedroom at night, watchin' her little chest rise and fall to make sure she's still breathin'. I see her father liftin' her up high in the air and she's laughin'. People always said that it was just gas, that babies don't smile when they're that young, but I know she was smilin' and laughin'. She was always the happiest baby.

A little bit later on, I see her father pushin' her on the swing in the backyard and she's laughin', laughin', pumpin' her little legs and then lyin' almost flat out with her ankles crossed as he pushes her higher and higher into the red-gold sunset sky.

Not Waving but Drowning
Ron Rash

Across the room a woman cups her front teeth in the palm of her left hand. She stares at them as if they were a bad throw of the dice. The man who brought her through the emergency room door leans his cheek against her swollen face. "You *know* I love you," he whispers. Her hand tightens around the teeth. A red drool is all she can get out before clamping her mouth shut, leaning her head back against the wall. The man yanks a soiled handkerchief from his back pocket. He wets the cloth with his spit and wipes blood from her mouth and chin.

I turn to see if Mary is watching, but her eyes are closed, her lips moving. For a moment I think she is praying, but she is doing what we learned at our Lamaze classes, counting to ten, then exhaling, slow and steady, like a tire leaking air. Her hand presses her belly, as if the spread fingers might somehow hold inside what's been there four months. I place my hand over hers, wanting to believe the weight of another hand might make a difference to the baby, to Mary. She takes away my hand.

I remember what she said as we sped here, the road coiling around the black silence of Lake Jocassee where this night began one afternoon four months ago.

"It's our baby, not just yours," I had said when she wouldn't answer my questions.

"Not yet," Mary had said. "Not until it's born. Then it's ours."

A big man dressed in jeans and a black, long-sleeved dress shirt shoulders through the door. His right hand is swollen like a snakebite, the knuckles scraped raw. The receptionist, a gray-haired woman in a white nursing uniform, has disappeared. When she comes back she shoves a clipboard through a hole in the bottom of the glass that separates her from a circle of metal folding-back chairs filled with varying degrees of catastrophe. The man raises the damaged hand by clutching his wrist.

"Can't, ma'am. It's broken."

The gray-haired woman pulls the clipboard back to her side, places her pencil on the first line.

"Name" she says, not even looking at him.

I don't hear his name. I'm thinking eleven months back to another night, July, not June, but a night like this, muggy, loud with tree frogs and crickets. I'm thinking about how I'd waked in the dark and Mary was crying. A nightmare, I thought, and pulled her to me and felt what was too sticky to be sweat staining her skin, I touched a damp finger to my tongue. A taste hard as copper filled my mouth.

"What's happened?" I asked.

"The baby," she said.

So we dressed and came here and sat in maybe these same two chairs and waited to be told what we already knew. The doctor said Mary should stay overnight, and they gave her a blue pill and when the pill had done its work I drove home and pulled the sheets off the bed only to find the blood had soaked onto the mattress pad. So I pulled if off too and saw on the mattress a black spot like a waterstain. Maybe it was lack of sleep, but for a moment I was convinced it had gone through the mattress and would cover the whole room if I didn't contain it. I jerked the mattress off. Through the boxsprings I saw there was no blood on the floor.

I bundled up the sheets and mattress pad and carried them into the backyard. I dragged the mattress out there too, then soaked everything with lighter fluid and listened to the crackle of the fire, the tree frogs and crickets and a far-off owl. I was back at the hospital by first light.

Mary didn't speak on the drive home. I let her wrap herself in silence. I pulled around to the back so she wouldn't have but a few steps. She saw the charred mattress, the wisps of smoke that rose toward a sky that promised a day without rain.

"You think it's that simple, don't you?" she had asked.

The man with the broken hand sits down next to the entrance. I look at my watch—seventeen minutes since we came in. I step up to the window, bend to speak through the hole in the glass, but the woman is gone. The door at the back of her office is half open. I see that it leads to the other emergency room, the one where they carry you in on a stretcher. The receptionist finally comes back, leaves the door cracked behind her.

"We have to see the doctor now," I tell her. "My wife may be having a miscarriage. Please," I say.

"Just a few minutes more and the doctor will be free," she says. "There's two boys next door." The woman nods toward the room she has just come from. "They've been in a car wreck. Those boys are in bad shape."

"My wife's in bad shape too," I say. "The baby is."

"I understand," she says.

I sit back down.

"Just a few more minutes," I tell Mary. "It won't be long. O.K.?"

Mary looks at me but says nothing.

"She's a cold bitch, ain't she?" the man next to the door says to me.

"What?" I say, hoping I heard wrong, because if I didn't I know how this conversation will end. I'm not a big guy, and I haven't been in a fight since the seventh grade, but it's a sorry part of our history here that these kinds of things are settled with fists at best, knives and guns at worst.

He nods toward the receptionist's glassed-in cubicle.

"I say she's a cold one."

I look up to see if the receptionist has heard, but she's gone. The phone rings.

"They give them enough breaks around here," the man next to the door says. "Damn if I don't think I'll put me in a application here. Where I work they won't let you go to the bathroom but once a shift."

"Where you work?" asks the man who's with the woman holding the teeth.

"Hamrick Mill."

The man nods at the woman beside him.

"Her brother worked there a few months. He said they'd treat you like a dog if you'd let them. He wouldn't put up with that so they fired him."

"What's his name?"

"Billy Goins."

"Don't remember him."

"Like I said, he wasn't there but a couple of months."

The woman stares at the teeth in her hand.

"Is that your wife?"

"Yes."

The woman doesn't look up. It's like she's deaf. Maybe she is. Maybe she's like the Cambodian women I've read about, the ones who witnessed so many atrocities that they have willed themselves blind. Maybe that's what you have to do sometimes to survive. You kill off a part of yourself, your hearing or eyesight, your capacity for hope.

"What happened to her?" The moment he speaks the man with the hurt hand seems to realize the answer.

"I mean she's going to be O.K., isn't she?'

"Accident," the husband answers. He places his arm around his wife's hunched shoulders. "She's going to be fine."

The door that leads into the hospital opens halfway. An intern, probably not even thirty, grips the door's edge with both hands and leans his head in as if afraid to come among us. He looks at the couple across the room and then at Mary and me.

"Mrs. Triplett?" he asks, looking at Mary.

Mary keeps her hand on her belly as I ease her to her feet. I walk her to where the doctor holds the door open.

"You stay here," she says. "I don't want you with men. Not until I know."

I start to speak.

"No," Mary says, her voice rising, more emphatic with each word. "You stay here."

So I do. The others have been listening. When I sit back down, the man by the door picks up a tattered *Sports Afield* with his good hand and stares at the cover. The man with the woman takes a jackknife from his pocket and pares his nails. His wife is the only one who looks at me. Her jaw is darkening into a bruise, and I realize the bastard hit her more than once.

I lean my head back against the wall and close my eyes, think about the day four months back that brought us to this place, one of those late-February days you get around here, a kind of miracle when the sky opens up deep and blue and the temperature rises into the seventies. It's more than weather a couple of weeks ahead of schedule. There's no wind like there is in March or early April. It's like you've leapfrogged two months. All that's missing are the dogwood blossoms.

Mary had said we should fix a picnic lunch and go to Lake Jocassee, take the boat out and eat our lunch on the far shore where the Horsepasture River enters the lake. I was glad she wanted to leave the house, gladder still she wanted to do something with me. Since the second miscarriage she hadn't wanted to do much of anything but sit at home on weekends and watch T.V. or read. We'd been more like roommates than husband and wife.

I hadn't taken the boat out since September, so I checked it good before I hitched the boat trailer onto the car. Mary stayed inside and made our lunch.

We were on the water by ten. Since there was no wind, I cut the motor halfway across and we drifted. We looked down into mountain water so clear it was like looking through a window. After a few minutes we saw what we were looking for. Eighty feet down were farmhouses Duke Power hadn't bothered to raze when they'd built the dam. And it wasn't just the houses but also barns, woodsheds, even mailboxes. Everything was there but the people.

"It's like if you watched long enough somebody would walk out of one of those houses and look up and wave at us the same way we'd look up and wave at a low-flying plane," Mary said, and her saying that spooked me, because I'd been thinking the same thing, not the part about the plane but that there were still people down there, people who didn't know they were buried under eighty feet of water.

I'd moored the boat in the cove where the Horsepasture slowed and lost itself in the lake. We walked a quarter mile through woods that still had patches of snow and spread a quilt in a meadow we'd found years back right after we'd gotten married. It had been cool on the water and in the woods, but here the noon sun poured down on us. The surrounding oaks and poplars seemed to wedge all the sun's heat into the meadow. A few wildflowers opened their petals. I took off my sweatshirt.

Mary unpacked cheese, apples, a loaf of bread and a bottle of wine from the picnic basket. I'd been expecting turkey sandwiches and Cokes. Neither one of us had ever been much of a wine drinker, and I almost said something about getting above our raising, acting like we'd been born in California instead of western Carolina. But I didn't. Mary seemed happy, and she hadn't been happy for a long time.

"Here," she said, handing me the wine, paper cups and corkscrew, "make yourself useful."

In the distance I could hear the last waterfall before the river entered the lake, but I heard nothing else. No boat motors, no squirrels or birds. You could have almost believed there was no world beyond the meadow's tree line. I handed her a cup of wine.

"To the future," she said and tapped her cup against mine. She took a sip, then placed the cup on the grass and did not drink from it again.

Our appetites were keen. We ate all the bread and cheese and halved an apple. When we finished we put everything back in the basket and lay down on the quilt, drowsy from the food and warmth. I was almost asleep when Mary sat up and unlaced her hiking boots. She took off her sweatshirt. There was nothing, not even a bra, underneath. Mary lay down beside me and took off her jeans and then unbuttoned my shirt. I was surprised because I knew that it was the time of month she was most fertile. Since the second miscarriage she hadn't let me touch her during this time, even with her diaphragm in. I felt the goosebumps on her arms, so I folded the quilt over us.

"What about your diaphragm?" I asked.

"I want us to try again," she said and pulled me to her.

We slept afterward. I woke before Mary and listened to her breath merge with the sound of the waterfall. I lay there knowing our future together would come down to this last gamble, for our marriage had barely survived the last miscarriage. If it had survived. I wasn't sure.

Something happens to a couple after a miscarriage, or at least it had happened to us. You cry together, you talk to the counselor and preacher, you hear the same stupid and callous remarks from friends and kin who should know better, but there's still a part of the pain you can't share, even with the person who went through it with you. You carry that pain inside like a tumor, and though it may shrink with time, it never disappears, and it's malignant.

Shadows had covered us by the time Mary waked. She'd pressed against me and we'd made love again, then walked back into the woods, leaving behind the last rays of sunshine filtering through the trees, wildflowers that would die in a few days when the frost returned.

I open my eyes, try to believe Mary's going to come through the door, smile and say everything is O.K. The woman across the room is still looking at me. She opens her mouth, slow like a rusty hinge. Her forehead creases. She speaks, a mumble of blood and words that I can't understand.

"No, darling," her husband says, placing his arm around her. "Don't try to talk."

Up the highway toward Westminster I hear an ambulance, the wail increasing as it nears, then silenced as it turns into the emergency entrance, red light drenching all of us as the ambulance passes the glass door Mary and I hurried through an hour ago.

The phone at the reception desk rings.

"Mr. Triplett." The receptionist motions for me.

I walk over to the window.

"Doctor Walton needs to talk with you. He's down the corridor, second room on the right."

Her voice is muffled by the glass between us, and I cannot shake the feeling that she is speaking to a man underwater. She points at the door as if we are in a place where we can communicate only in gestures.

I look back at the woman with the battered face. Her brown eyes hold mine for a moment. She nods as if to reassure me that our lives might somehow turn out better than we can believe at this moment. I walk through the door that says "Do Not Enter" and down the corridor. I walk slow as the dead might walk across the cold and silent floor of Lake Jocassee.

Taughannock Falls

Bill Roorbach

To fly anywhere at a moment's notice is my job, very nearly. At Merrymount Hospice, the morning after the afternoon of Japonica's call ("Stephen has been asking for you"), I have to fill out a form explaining my relationship to the patient. I write, *Friends from birth*. This relationship occasions no questions, and I'm given a wristband. *Visitor*. Red letters. In the plane I've whipped my hurt and resentment into a froth, but here on the quiet walkways of this elegant factory of mental health I'm calm again, if worried: apparently Stephen has neither spoken nor otherwise communicated for two full weeks, not a peep since June 1, not until yesterday, when he began repeating my name. Which is simple: Bob Smith.

Japonica hates Bob Smith. This true fact once amused me, brought jokes to my lips, and while the jokes still fight to come, I guess I know more about me now, more of jealousy, and more what a loud and lousy influence I may have been on Stephen, and maybe just the faintest little bit about which of my qualities would have made Stephen so willing to abandon me. He hasn't spoken to anyone at all these two weeks, but he hasn't spoken to me for twenty years.

Japonica (once Janet—but I'll repress the satire): Japonica worked against me with Stephen, worked hard since the very day of the big party in Santa Barbara that saw my glorious best friend wed, but which she (and so he) wouldn't call a wedding. And I was best man, but not called best man, that phrase never used. But I accompanied the male-human-about-to-get-lawfully-attached through the days and events and pressures preceding the ceremony, and stood beside him while he made his promises in front of a room full of people seated on two sides of an aisle. A person who was not a religious figure—a ship's captain, I believe—said the twenty legal words of the rite, and the two of them, Stephen and Japonica, exchanged golden rings and read their invented vows. And we who had watched ate fish under white tents, then showered the frowning results of the day's work with birdseed, showered them and laughed and screamed till they were safe in a long, white, California limousine, just a car, really, just a tremendously long car that one wondered what movie star must have sat in, and what ex-president.

In Stephen's "pod" at Merrymount, I find the "pod station," and the "pod nurse" is lovely and gentle and not too young and smiles at me gently, with a quick eye to my red visitor's bracelet. "You're an old friend of Mr. Massuau's."

"The oldest."

"He's in the Santa Cruz space, just there."

And she glides around the desk on a cushion of air and glides beside me past the many potted plants and couches and low marble tables with magazines and through the perfect silence into Stephen's "space" (she can't say room, or even podlet), which is costing MacDonell-Douglas

Aerospace plenty, at a guess. It's a hotel room, this "space," not even a heart monitor in sight, chromium and leather furnishings, million-dollar view through high glass out to the Pacific, only the hospital bed to give it away. Stephen is still as the air in there, seated (good posture) in an expensive modular chair not quite facing the window.

"Stephen," I say gently. I'm washed in emotion; it's all I can do to stand upright and breathe.

The pod nurse floats away.

"Long time," I say, trying a couple of steps around him to look in his blank face. He looks just fine, to my untrained eye, fit and tanned and only a little gray at the temples, nicely shaven, brave and trim, athletic as ever, ready to spring, hale and handsome, all fine except brown eyes aimed a little high and just to the right of the window. He doesn't move, not a blink or twitch or breath, and he doesn't gain any expression at all, just sits pleasant and expectant, a little remote, like someone waiting for good news.

"Twenty years," I say.

He just keeps waiting.

"Stephen, twenty years."

And waits.

So I give him, or what passes for him, a speech, as follows, quoting as many of our old jokes as possible, hearing their misfirings even as I speak, using our old high-goof diction, seeing myself as Japonica must have all these years, that is: negatively, inescapably negative, all my organs sinking in the cavity of my chest, pressing on my guts. And through this speech, anger rises.

I say, "I missed you, brother. You move out to the land where plastic plants grow wild, and never again do I hear from you. Oh, I know you must have wanted to stay in touch. I know this, and I know that it's Janet to blame—Japonica, I mean, sorry, sorry—but twenty years, Stephen. You deserve some of the blame, too, rocket boy. I hear about your kids from Billy O'Rourke, I hear about your big promotions from the fucking *Wall Street Journal*. I send congrats. I send stuffed toys. I send checks for sweet sixteen to Miranda, a pretty name, your daughter, Stephen, a pretty young woman, no doubt. I send birth announcements for my kids you've never met and never a note back from you, Stephen. And I know what it is. It's her. What'd I ever do to her? At worst what? Maybe put her down to you and occasionally made fun of her to you, and okay: impugn her, indict her, malign her, denounce her, spoof her? Twenty years back, though. I was just jealous, I was, I understand that now, I see that about myself now. I was jealous and felt abandoned, I suppose the therapists would say. In fact, I had a therapist and that's what she said, exactly. And I talked about you pretty much the whole three sessions. Yes, only three because it was all just talk (also, I had a dream wherein the word therapist was broken in two: *the rapist*). And the talk did make me realize what a hole you left. Oh, Stephen. You look great. You look just great to me sitting here. You look like the last time I clapped eyes on you. Not a day older. But Stephen, come on, no note, nothing when Linda passed away? Nothing when my wife you never met died? I didn't send you a *note*, was that it? I know my father did send you a note, a quiet tasteful note, and not a word from you. But all that's forgiven. All that. Twenty years. Was my contempt at the surface of those letters I wrote? Did I brag too much, trying to impress you? Was I nothing to you? Did you ever even think of me?"

Long pause. He's impassive. The stillness invites calm. I settle down, change gears, give him news: "My girls have a car each now. Can you imagine our folks buying us cars at that age? Not a chance. And Sarah is gay, she thinks.

Can you imagine a parent copping to that when we were kids? She has a partner who's big as me, and tougher and I let them sleep in her room together. What the hell, right? It's their lives, and I like having smart women around. I told them your joke from college: *What's the difference between a whale and an Ithaca lesbian*? Fifty pounds and a flannel shirt. Is the punch line. Now they want to go to Cornell. And with her grades and her girlfriend's connections they'll get in."

Where the newlycommitteds went after the ceremony, I can't quite remember—never heard details. Because that was it, that hug between Stephen and me just before the clunky ceremony in the little side room at the mansion Japonica's chilly folks rented for the nuptials (I believe is a fair word). That hug lasted so long that the synthesizer player had to come back and ask us to come on out and join the party, unless we weren't invited, ho ho. She was a funny one, that little synthesizer player, and played the Wedding March despite being instructed, even commanded, not to by Stephen's new legal life partner.

Not a movement from my old friend. Not a blink of the eye, not a nod of the head, not a tear on the cheek, not a tap of the foot, not a twitch of the lip. He looks *tremendous*—healthy and wise, clean and brave, courteous and kind. The room is sparkling, pinks and ivories; the curtains billow with sweet Pacific wind. I keep talking. His presence is so human and electrical somehow that I start to believe he is listening. I go on and on, interrogating the past, trying to build something firm, a temple of friendship in which we might meet.

I fire questions: "Did we hike in the forests, you and I? Did we drink in the bars? Did we study till morning, side by side? Did we eat LSD and stare at snow banks? Did we sleep with brilliant women, sometimes the same one? Did we wrestle and grapple and fistfight and hug? Did we eat methamphetamines on long drives and talk nonstop and confess our beautiful Platonic love for one another? Did people not refer to us as Steve and Bob? Or Bob and Steve? Were we not closer than twin suns bound by gravity eternally (or at least till super nova did us part)?

"Did we not finish college and finish well despite all? Did I not move to California with you when the time came for graduate school? Did you not make fun of me for taking yoga classes? Did I chastise you for seeking and finding high-end work in the Military Industrial Complex? Did we handle this, too, and all things? Was it not I who introduced you to Janet from Yoga class? Yoga class, Stevie! We used to shout with laughter, you making fun of me for yoga. But I found you a girl, I did"

Not a twitch.

"You are my friend," I say. "Twenty years cannot change that." I get up and look out the window. This is too painful. Far below us the ocean is rough and roiling, one surfer out there paddling around, no wave to catch. But the breeze is strong, rattles the stout jade plants outside the podlet window. I live in Virginia, for lovers. I work in Washington, D.C., for lawyers. There is no ocean upon which to gaze in those precincts. I'm a lobbyist for anyone who will hire me, except Tobacco, War, Gross Polluter, Fundamentalist. Which leaves almost nothing.

"You little fuck," Stephen says distinctly.

But I'm staring out the window at the ocean. When I look back Stephen's as still as before. I'm not hearing things,

I know; I never hear things, I know a voice when I hear it, and I know Stevie's fond voice, too, the voice of old.

"Stephen?"

His face is composed and fresh and just the same as when I first walked in, but for a stronger smile.

"I see you grinning," I say.

And the grin grows and the eyes flash with fire and he rocks in his chair all youthful energy and says "Get me out of here!" And he's giggling, tittering, trying to hold it back, snorting, spitting. He manages a stage whisper: "Jesus, Bobbo, what happened to me?"

I sputter. It's all a joke: "You were, uh, catatonic for a few weeks there." And we just roar like little boys, like when together we went to his synagogue and he couldn't control himself at the sight of goyim me in a *yarmulke*: junior high school.

"Sounds *great*," he says. And he's up on his feet—no stopping him, looking at his clothes, looking at me. And looking at me, he's taken aback. Our laughter just dies. "How long've I been *out*?" he says. "You look *fifty years old*, you fucker!"

"I'm forty-five," I say soberly.

"Rip Van fucking Winkle," he says, examining me closely, as if to understand my disguise. "Political satire. A critique of the new vulgar America." He's quoting something wryly verbatim from our sophomore English class, something a middle-aged engineer ought to have forgotten. Then, "Two minutes ago you're passing me a bong of red Leb, turn around and you're *fat* and you're *gray*. He is making fun of me in his oldest style, but at the same time he's shocked by my appearance, trying unsuccessfully to hide dismay with laughter. He's one of these never-let-'em-see-you-sweat guys, and he's always been damn good at it: *Your friends are suddenly middle aged? No problem.*

"I'm not so goddamn fat," I tell him.

He leaps to his feet, limps around the room clowning to hide any panic, gets in front of the mirror, examines himself, clutches his thighs in real pain, slumps to the floor, loose as a college kid. "Okay," he says seriously. "What happened?"

"Well, you seem to be missing a few years, Stephen. Probably it'll all come back to you. Japonica and your daughter and MacDonell-Douglas Aerospace, the works."

"Accident?"

"You just went blank, apparently."

"Japonica?"

"You know: *Janet*?"

Nothing.

She is your wife."

He takes this news calmly, looks at me a long time. He's going to make do with what he's got. He says, "Last I remember is you at Taughannock. Oh! That fucking shale! You had my wrist, right? Oh, shit, oh my god, that fucking shale! I fucking *fell*!" He's terrified, suddenly, feels his head where the brutal split was twenty-five years back, but there's no split there now. He fell, all right, fell in a shower of shale ledge that no one smart would have climbed ever, not to 200 feet. But we did, having argued its safety, me on the side of climbing, I regret to say. Bounced all the way down to the creek, he did. Split his scalp, cracked the skull, bathed himself in blood, head to foot. Broke both *thighs*, his two femurs, the heaviest bones in the human body. To hear the cries that preceded the silence! To climb down in the growing dusk! To have to leave him to climb back out and sprint for help!

"I'll get a nurse," I say.

"No way," he says. "Get a wheelchair. No one'll think twice. We're *out of here*."

Word for word and tone for tone, this is precisely what he said in the neurological unit at Tompkins County Hospital when we were twenty. I mean exactly, and with the exact look in his eye, and the same hand on his head, only now there is no shaved skull, no bandage. At that age and all those years ago I was game, baby, and I wheeled him out to my disintegrating station wagon and off to the Falls to show him where he fell, and to spend the night with him in the woods there by a big fire with two girls, one named Chrissy Miles, one forgotten. Next day the doctors didn't think it was funny, but they released him. His folks, they never forgave me.

"Well, we better not do that," I say. "I'll go get that pod nurse."

"Is she *sexy*?" Stephen says. He's twenty. He says, "God, I haven't gotten laid in *weeks*."

"She's sexy," I say. I haven't gotten laid in longer than weeks, is what I'm thinking, till death do you part notwithstanding.

"Get me out of here," Stephen says, and we can't help it, we laugh and laugh and laugh and laugh. And laugh.

Japonica is civil with me, and I'm careful not to call her Janet. She doesn't invite me over to their canyon home, nothing like that, but the two of us meet in the Main Pod Lobby of Merrypod, which is very comfortable, like a hotel bar without the bar, leather club chairs and many plants, sun from the skylights high above.

She's still good looking, still with the slight cast in her eye, but now she's behind giant designer eyeglasses. She's tall as ever, but thinner than I recall, which was too thin always. Her lips are puffed unnaturally and her mouth, really, it's gorgeous, oh my, still gorgeous. I can picture her in a bikini and also topless on Muir Beach all those years ago and also naked in my bed (baby talk) and in hers, two weeks of good fun. I can remember her laughing with me after Yoga class, cruel laugh. I can remember introducing her to Steve at the beach party I brought her to. And I remember the mechanism by which my hot and hopeful fling became Steve's girlfriend over the next several days: *We're just not right together*. Stevie missing at night for weeks, nothing said till my old girl Jill turned up for an extended stay, then love in the open, Stevie and Janet, a thin wall away.

My jealousy, my god, it was like horses inside me, horses reined to the very posts of my heart, their snorting breath escaping my mouth snidely, restrained fury writing my joky, mean script, my lips smiling, always smiling, never saying the central thing. Jill said I'd changed, and then she left me, too.

"Remember that little miniscule Yogi?" I bark.

"Can a person be both little and miniscule at once?" Japonica answers, not kidding.

"I used to sit behind you in that class to smell your perfume," I say.

"I cannot handle any more of these tests they're putting him through," she says. But her gaze has flickered: she loved me briefly.

"And that's how you and Steve met," I say.

"Oh, Bobby, one minute he was fine, the next minute he was sitting stock still out by the pool with the phone still in his hand. And poor Miranda thought, Well, he's joking! And she's out there laughing at him! Giving him tickles! Poor child. She's devastated. Blames herself, irrationally."

"It's that little smile. That makes it seem like he's kidding."

"He asked for you," she says for the tenth time in ten conversations, in a tone as if to say I should agree that this request of his was preposterous and a sure sign of worse affliction than any of us want to imagine.

"He thinks he's back in Ithaca," I say for the tenth time in ten conversations. Then add fresh material: "He wants to escape the hospital like we did back then. He wants a bong hit. You know, that kind of thing."

"You two were such thorough reprobates."

"We were very close, Japonica."

"Doctor Smolkins doesn't buy your theory."

Which is that Stephen's old injury has come back, is all, and somehow the brain damage from back then has suddenly decided to erase everything that happened since. Smolkins says it's a stroke, which he calls an episode—but he hasn't actually denounced my theory, not at all. That's an exaggeration. He's only cautious about it.

Japonica sighs mightily, looks at me accusingly. "Stephen doesn't remember me at all," she says.

"That must hurt," I tell her softly.

Dr. Smolkins is not sure at all what to do with Stephen, who is awake now, and very polite with everyone who comes to visit, but doesn't remember them, not a glimmer. I come every afternoon, just after five, so as to briefly see Japonica, who must fetch their daughter up from field hockey practice daily.

Stephen says, "I can't believe I married that chick. She's like my mother. She's a *bitch*. She's awful. And she hates you. What did you do to her, fucker?"

"She was a great beauty," I say.

"No one is that great a beauty."

"I brought a little something," I say. And present the pink shopping bag from the Sunshine Daydream store in the Escondito Mall. Ceremoniously, I pull out the bong. There's no weed to go with it, of course, though Doctor Smolkins says there's no defect that would prevent our man from living a normal life. He might possibly go home as soon as Tuesday, if the last test comes out as the good doctor predicts. But home is where the heart is, and Stevie's heart is with me for the moment. Or me at age twenty, at any rate.

"And my daughter, shit, my *daughter*, Bob. She is—*hot*! My god. She must have friends, right? I mean, I can't touch her, right? Even though I don't know her?"

His daughter is pretty, all right, pierced belly button and tall heels. I've only glimpsed her, older high-school girl. We must forgive him. Stephen is to re-learn not only his life, but years of gained maturity. That's the plan. He's to go in there and play the role till he grows back into it. Twenty-five years he'll have to age. Aeronautical engineering he'll have to re-study, though Smolkins says it may all come back at any time. And he'll have to walk a little better, too. His legs are weak for no reason Smolkins can figure, but I know what it is: twin fractured femurs. Our boy Stevie hobbled around for months after, limped for years. I recognize the hobble, I tell Smolkins, but Smolkins has got his cues from Janet, and just closes his ears to me, shakes his head.

Japonica's call was a sudden rip in the healing fabric of my life. Not a word from her in twenty years, not a word from Stephen for seventeen (and that word a Christmas card picturing their new daughter). I stayed big as I could, called a lot and wrote and later faxed and later still e-mailed, and even in mourning begged a little: just a word, just a nod. I even told them as I grew older and more able to confess my feelings that I was hurt. And further, apologized for anything I might have done. But nothing.

In fact, this tough and wily Washington lobbyist, myself, began to weep the second Japonica said her name. I wept and moaned and carried on, all my losses mounting.

She said, "Stephen is asking for you."

Stevie-boy rolls the bong in his hands critically, a budding engineer, not even a BA left in his head: "This is drilled all wrong, the carburetor invection is reversed." And inspects it some more, suddenly agitated. He looks at me in undisguised undergraduate panic: "Bobbo, you got to get me out of here. These people are fucked. That woman? I don't want to live with her!"

That's it. I go down to the nurse's pod and greet Marylou, who is sexy indeed and moreover seems to like me. "A wheelchair?" I ask, casually. "Stephen wants a little walk."

"Oh! Wonderful!" says Marylou. My god, she's cheerful.

She goes to the storage podlet and locates us a fine little chariot. I decline her help and roll the thing down to the space named Santa Cruz. Stephen giggles when he sees me, hobbles across the room despite healthy legs, falls into the chair in a way I recall exactly, accepts the blanket across his lap, and we are off, brothers in crime. I wheel him clear to the back of the property, where there's a redwood fence of some quality. I simply and would like to say deftly kick a few boards out and crawl through and I'm in the parking lot I've been towed from twice now. Steve crawls through, too, with difficulty, as if his perfectly good, middle-aged legs are broken, then I fold the chair and pull it through. I set the fence boards more or less back in place, no one to see us, and then I wheel my best and oldest friend down the hill to my red rental car, an upgrade, still small.

And we're off, laughing and singing, trading insults, rock and roll radio, waving at girls too young by miles, stopping off for beer. My I.D. is fine, I tell Stephen, it's just fucking fine. And we laugh and laugh and laugh and laugh until the old man comes out of the store to see what's funny, and we're laughing so jollily, he laughs, too. We speed down to Muir Beach, an old haunt that Stevie cannot remember, and wheel that deluxe pod chair out on the sand and sit there in the sun drinking beers and laughing more, and harder. He's twenty and I'm twenty and he's just defied the gods and lived through the worst climbing accident his doctors have ever seen or heard of. We're good students at a great American university, and we're alive, alive, alive. And the world, weirdly, has changed little at all. Stevie punches my shoulder and I punch his and we swim naked as seals and he hobbles up onto the beach as if his legs are fresh out of casts and hot girls walking by check us out because we are twenty and we are full of the universe and roaring with fun and we are beautiful, full of possibility.

When the massive cerebral hemorrhage kills him he has just punched my shoulder again, and called me Bobbo, and the waves are rolling in, and Japonica may forgive me yet, as Smolkins does, based on that last test he did: Stevie's brain was a time bomb, it was. And I, well, I just count myself lucky to have been back in his heart when the big bang came, and to know there are more hearts to win.

Wanderlust

Michael Milliken

Once on the highway, a small hour separates me from the sight of my father as I've never seen him. Just forty miles, an exit, follow the signs through an unfamiliar landscape. In that short time, I'll see my father, confined, stationary, and William, my four-year-old son, will meet him.

My mother called some hours ago. He's in the state, in Augusta at the Veterans' Hospital. Hasn't taken care of himself and his feet are real bad. She'll visit in a few days. Sooner if needed. After her call, I spent the next few hours procrastinating. I read to William, played card games, all while watching the long arm of the regulator clock drop, then rise, and knowing that Sheila would come tomorrow morning and take our son away for her week. We had to drive up today.

William sits in his car seat in the back, turns the wide pages of a book and slides his little hand over the bright illustrations. Soon, I know, he'll close the book, concede its colors to the thinning light, the sun already distant, dusk-drawn, closing in on time. But he'll remain quiet for awhile, already taken with stories though he can't read, with his sense of their offerings, of spectacle and flight. My father, though, had his own stories for me.

Those years of William's age, those years beyond, I knew my father as a figure who came unannounced and unexpected into our home, who came for a short string of days like on vacation, just time to fish or hike, time to put forth his stories. My father told of redwood trees like steeples, turquoise seas, rainbows of fishes, of lightning bugs in blue grass and how to squeeze water, in desperate times, from the flesh of a barrel cactus. At the end of each story, he'd look in my eyes and tell me the story was true, not one word stretched or altered, all true because he knew it, because he had lived it, and that was important.

I read my stories to William. But I am with him.

"Tell me about the man."

I hear William's soft voice, the sound of his book close.

"He is your grandfather," I say. "And he is sick."

I see William in the rearview mirror, his face turned away, eyes intent and fixed out the window on the fields and forest we pass. I've asked him why he spends so much time looking out windows, and he tells me he just doesn't know.

"Tell me a story about him," he says.

"Your grandfather wasn't around much."

"You must have one story."

"I do."

"Then tell me that story. If it's true. I only want to hear it if it's true."

"One Christmas. I was a few years older than you. Your grandfather came running in that evening, after the presents had been unwrapped, after your aunt had left. We hadn't seen him since the previous summer. Well, he came in through the front door and surprised us."

"Just checking on the progress." It was a thing he said.

He saw me and Mom slumped on the couch watching a movie, some cartoon Christmas story, and walked toward us, stood in front of the TV.

"You're blocking our view," my mother said, her only greeting. After I was born, it seems, their marriage lay down and dried out. Still, he was my father.

I looked up to him and an enormous grin spread over his face. I didn't know why. He had a few dark holes where teeth should be. Plenty of stubble and matted down cowlicks on his head. He looked like one of the men who slept on the benches in the city park. And Mom had told me they were all lost souls.

My father stepped aside from the TV, towards me, then reached into his black overcoat and took out a crumbled paper bag.

"Merry Christmas," he said and held the bag out.

Mom snorted. I looked at her and she threw out her arm, like shooing a fly, so I took the bag, felt that it was heavy, and started to open it.

"Oh, no," he said, reached down and took back the paper bag. "Can't open that in here. You gotta get your coat and your snow pants and bring it outside."

I looked at Mom and again she swatted at the invisible fly. So I ran to the mudroom and got dressed for the outside.

My father led me to the backyard, then jumped into the air with the paper bag, laughed and landed in the snow on his back.

"You next," he said.

I jumped into the air and landed beside him, lay there in the cold watching my white breath before me.

"What are we doing?" I asked.

"I've been down in Key West, Florida." He set the bag at his side. "And you wouldn't believe what kind of place Key West is. Ocean everywhere. And it's not ocean like up here. It's ocean like the sky. Bright blue along the beaches, like at noontime, then dark toward the horizon, like the sky when the first stars come out. You know that blue?"

"Yep," I said. A white puff of air popped up from my mouth.

"Well, they got water like the hours of sky down there. And it's warm, like a nice bath water. You know what I mean?"

"Yep."

"Well, I want you to pretend with me that we're down at Key West. We're not lying on snow in the backyard, but floating in the sky water of Key West, in the warm water down there looking up at the same stars like we are now. And with our ears in the water, we can hear the whales singing. They sing, you know, swim down from the cold north and when they get to Key West they're home and they sing. Do you hear them?"

"Not yet," I said.

"Well, open that bag."

I removed a mitten from one hand, unfurled the crumpled top of the bag and pushed my fingers inside. A tape recorder.

"Play the tape," he said.

I pressed the play button and set the tape recorder on the empty bag between us, then put on the mitten. And the whales sang. Deep notes, some short, some stretched out long. Bass sounds, but beautiful, these cries from the heart inside each giant creature. We lay there afloat on the warm sky snow, our eyes in the stars and our ears and our bodies lost to the murmurs and moans of whales.

"Is that a true story?" William asks, his doubtful voice soft in the darkness behind me.

"It is."

"Why didn't you go to Key West?"

"That's just how it was. Your grandfather went all over this country, like a gypsy all over America. He said he collected experiences and brought them home."

"I'd like to do that," William says.

"It makes lives difficult. But in some ways," I say, "I think we all would."

We arrive at the hospital at the edge of night, under a navy sky speckled with new stars. I park the car, remove William from his seat and the two of us walk hand-in-hand into the hospital. At the front desk, I tell the young woman that I'm looking for Wesley Wendell and she directs us to his room in the east wing.

My father lies under a blue blanket on a hospital bed, staring at the ceiling. The other bed is empty. He is thin, much thinner than I remember, the skin of his cheeks falling over his jaw, the eyes sunken, dark. He turns his head toward us and grins.

"I hoped you'd come," he says.

William wiggles his hand out from my grip, runs to the bed and holds on to the railing.

"Mr. William," he says. "I'm glad you came here, too."

I sit down in the chair next to the bed and take William onto my lap.

"Have you been up here all along?" I ask.

"No. I came up here for autumn. Nothing nicer than autumn in Maine." He chuckles. "And it seems I'm getting tired."

"You haven't been taking care of yourself."

He laughs again.

"Oh, I've been taking care of myself for a long time. It's just this diabetes has caught up with me. Far enough along that it's slowing down my heart."

William slides down from my lap, runs over to the window at the end of the room and looks behind the drawn shade.

"That's a curious boy you got. Wants to see the world."

"Let's hope he doesn't."

"You don't mean that."

"Like hell," I snap.

I stare at my father and he turns his head, sets his eyes back toward the ceiling.

"I suppose you have every right."

I exhale, pinch my nose. He takes his hands out from under the blanket, hard, worn hands of endless barter jobs, interlaces his fingers and holds them over his chest.

"I didn't come here to fight," I say.

"I know that. And I'm happy you did come. I'm happy to see William."

I have a few responses stored up for that, but I've already offered my olive branch.

"On the way up, he asked me to tell a story about you."

"And what'd you say?" His eyes turn back to me.

"I told him about the singing whales."

He nods, smiles.

"I'm glad you remember that one. It's important that you remember."

"It's just one of some hundred little stories you told me."

"It's important."

"What's so important?" I look to William who's still looking behind the window shade. "You're not dying right now. Are you?"

"No." He waves the question away, then looks to William, the boy's head still hidden, then down the length of his bed. He lifts the bed blanket.

His feet are bad. Dry and swollen, toes missing. Each foot has an open sore like a deep cigar burn. His feet are so bad I want to look away.

"The doctor said I'll lose both feet," he says. "I can't lose my feet."

"How did you get up here? How far was it?"

"I was in Georgia. Hot, hot air. I knew my feet were bad when the sores set in." He covers his feet with the blanket.

"You didn't go to the hospital there?"

"No," he says. "I wanted to be back here, on home soil. I guess I've seen it all out there. And there's not much anyone can do but take my feet."

"You should have done something."

"They're not taking my feet." He's almost shouting. He shakes his head, quiets. "It wouldn't matter. These sores don't heal. Not enough circulation."

I look down and see that William stands beside me. I pull him onto my lap.

"You should have been taking care of yourself, not hitching and tramping all over the country."

"What could I do?" he asks. "It's in the blood."

Before I can respond, I hear a knock behind me and turn my head. A nurse stands in the doorway.

"I'm sorry to disturb you," she says. "But we're closing down for the night." She looks at her watch. "Actually, ten minutes ago."

"We'll be out soon," I say, wait until she turns around and walks down the hallway.

"What do you mean?" I ask.

"It's in our blood. Something we're born with. And I want you to know that it skips a generation, that it starts real early. Teenage years. My grandfather was the same way."

I wrap my arms around William and he looks up to me.

"What is he talking about?" William asks.

"Nothing." I circle my hand over his hair again and again.

"Do I get to collect experiences?"

I hear another knock and turn to see the nurse.

"I'm really sorry," she says.

William slides off my lap and I stand. I reach down and pick him up, hold him against my chest.

"I guess I need to leave."

"Your turn," he says. "I can keep myself company."

I walk out into the hallway and hear my father start to sing, the strong bass tone of his voice. I hear him until we walk out into the parking lot, under the stars spread across a dark sky. Cold air, the nip of winter has settled down and I see my breath out before me. I hold William in my arms, squeeze him against my chest harder than I've ever held my son, hard like already he's slipping away and I wonder if he is.

Visiting Hours

Roberta Israeloff

"Ready?" Rose asked, Wednesday morning ticking away. Her husband Max was standing, as he always did before he went anywhere by car, even down to Chinatown, which on a good day took only about twenty minutes, in front of his ever-growing CD collection that dominated an entire living room wall. Head cocked, he walked his fingers over the spines of the plastic boxes, clicking them from right to left, trying to anticipate what would best complement the unfolding courses of the day, selecting music as deliberately as others did wine.

Jill, his sister, sat on the couch, her feet cradling her huge leather backpack. For all the years she'd flown home from abroad—she'd left nearly twenty years ago, the year her father remarried, the year before Jed was born—that worn, cordovan leather backpack constituted her only luggage. Softened and darkened with her sweat, it seemed an extra part of her body, a hump, a child who never outgrew its papoose. Ineffectively, she fanned herself with the scrap of paper on which she'd written the hospital patient information number, looking at her watch and the door, her watch, the door.

"Jill wants to be there when Sidney gets out of surgery, before visiting hours end," Rose said to Max, trying to slide the comment around the corner so it wouldn't meet him head on.

"Visiting hours for fathers never end," he said. Then he sighed, squared his slender shoulders, his only remaining boyish feature, and said that he was ready. His hands were empty.

By noon, the July day was hot but cloudless and dry. "I'll drive," Rose said, before realizing that Max was already heading for the passenger door. Usually he took the first shift, navigating them through the city and halfway up the Taconic, through those narrow, poorly-banked lanes demarcated by toothpick-thin guard rails, past the section mistakenly lined with the type of concrete that actually gets more slippery when it's wet.

"It's really a shame to move the car," Rose sighed. Last night returning to Manhattan from Queens where they'd spent the day nosing around Sidney's apartment, they'd found the perfect parking space, right across the street from their building, under a shady tree and the watchful eye of the neighborhood fire house.

"Americans," Jill said, under her breath. Max snorted. Jill worked for the UN, tending to babies with AIDS, flying to any country with an airstrip dispensing medicine. After so many years abroad, her feeling for her country had gradually expired, patriotism a kind of vaccine doomed to lose its blanketing effectiveness over time. She'd also learned to accommodate discomfort in a way Americans don't. Rose saw it in the way she'd settled her tall frame and long limbs in the cramped back seat. It could always be worse, was what Jill's every movement said. That's how people met the day in the other corners of the world, voicing not disappointment when things turned out badly but quiet relief that they worked at all.

"Sorry, I know it's awfully tight back there," Rose said, wondering how Jill could have gained so much weight in Japan, with only those tiny seaweed cones and knuckle-sized pieces of raw fish to eat. Maybe she'd gained the weight years earlier, when she'd lived in India, only the saris she'd worn had hidden it. But now that she was back in Western clothes, Rose noticed, in the rear view mirror, as she put the car in reverse and began inching out of the space she'd been shoehorned into, the soft swell of Jill's stomach and her beefy arms.

"Call the hospital," Jill said, as Rose drove west toward the Hudson. Still jetlagged, she massaged her face trying to rouse stodgy muscles.

"Look," Max said, sounding as if he'd spent most of his life trying to find the right tone with which to address his sister who was not only six years older but also almost as tall, "you more than anyone knows the procedure is not complicated. They're inserting a feeding tube. He'll be out in a half hour. Stop worrying."

"Easy for you to say," Jill said, "since you've already seen him. I haven't. In case you forgot."

You're the one who left the country, Rose said to herself.

"Just call the operating room nurse and get an update," Jill insisted.

"After I hear the traffic report," he said, switching on the AM radio.

What difference will it make, Rose was on the verge of asking. But she'd learned over the course of a quarter century of marriage the corrosive effect of beginning a dialogue in which you could predict every word. Now she specialized in knowing what not to say and when not to say it.

"Get in the far left lane," Max said.

"Leave her alone," Jill said. "She knows how to drive."

Rose put on her left signal.

"Is he dead?" Jill had asked, when Max and Rose met her flight early Monday evening at Kennedy. Though Max had called her on Friday, the day Sidney suffered his stroke, she was living in such a remote and swampy island of Japan that it took her two days to get to Tokyo and a flight home.

"Not yet," Max said. "Actually, he's stable. But hooked up to every possible machine, in and out of consciousness, and not talking. No speech at all."

"He never said that much anyway," Jill said. "Look, all I need is to grab a bite to eat, you know airline food, and then we can get going . . . "

"We're not going upstate today," Rose said. "We'll go the day after tomorrow."

Max exhaled noisily. "I think we should go up tonight," he said. "Tomorrow at the latest."

"Jill needs to rest," Rose said. "And anyway, we need to get some papers from Sidney's apartment . . . "

"The famous strongbox, open only in case of emergency, right?" Jill said to Max. He managed a grin. Rose saw Jill sizing up her brother, as they began walking toward the exit, looking for signs of age. His brown hair was graying, the lines around his eyes deepening. But he hadn't put on too much weight and his gaze was as intent as ever.

"Have you told Jed?" Jill asked.

"He's staying in Rome this summer," Rose said, unsure if Jill even remembered that her nephew spent his junior year in Italy. "We spoke to him. He wanted to know if he should come home but we told him not yet. We'd keep him updated . . . " Rose felt her chest clench remembering how the news about his grandfather had left her son speechless, near tears, a reaction so unexpected that Rose nearly asked him if something else was wrong.

"Let's go," Max said. "We're going to hit rush hour traffic as it is." He tried to reach for Jill's backpack but she hoisted it herself.

"For years I've been asking Sidney to send me copies of his important papers, the will and things like that," Jill said. "'I'm not going anywhere,' is what he always said."

"He was slowing down this past year," Max said mostly to himself, as they traversed the parking lot. "He kept forgetting things, not having energy. I should have noticed."

"Well," Jill went on, "it's not like he's cut down in the prime of life. He's seventy-eight, for God's sake."

"Seventy-six," Max said.

"I like your new hair color," Jill said to Rose when they reached the car and Max fumbled in his pockets for the keys. "Red becomes you." What she was really saying, Rose knew, was, You haven't aged as much as I feared you would. It was also a peace offering.

"You're supposed to just say your hair looks good," Max said, beeping the car doors open.

"It's all right," Rose said. "I know I dye my hair. It's not a secret."

"You could be more polite, that's all," Max said. "How could you spend six years in Japan and come back so impolite?"

"What's this, a BMW?" Jill asked, sliding ungracefully into the back seat, shrugging off her backpack onto the seat next to her. "Sidney know you bought a German car?"

"Leave me alone," Max had said, turning on the headlights.

Though still squinting in the brilliant midday sun, Rose relaxed as soon as they slipped out of Manhattan and into Riverdale. Max marked their progress north by switching on WQXR. One of Mozart's late string quintets filled the car.

"Why is there all this traffic?" Jill asked, almost panicky, as if driving habits in the developed world no longer made sense to her.

"It's the funniest thing," Rose said. "There used to be a tollbooth here years ago. They'd collect a dime or a quarter, something like that. And then one day they got rid of it, and everybody still slows down." She smiled to remember *The Phantom Tollbooth*, one of Jed's favorite childhood books

"Give me the phone," Jill said. "I'm calling. "No procedure's simply when you're five days post CVA."

Max dialed the phone. "I'm calling to determine the condition of my father, Sidney Bergson, who is in surgery," he said. Hearing the fatigue in his voice—he'd been up late listening to music after they'd returned from Queens—Rose glanced at him just in time to see him blanch, the color leaving his forehead, cheeks, neck; he nearly started to shiver.

"Something happened," he said. "He had some kind of seizure, it may be another stroke, there's pressure on the brain . . . "

Jill reached over the seat and took the phone from Max' hand. "I'm Sidney Bergson's daughter," she said. "I'm a doctor. What is going on?"

"They said it was touch and go," Max whispered to Rose.

Jill listened more than spoke. When she hung up, she began massaging her face and neck. Oh my God, Rose thought, suddenly as aware of what Jill was thinking as if she'd had tapped her on the shoulder and told her—that Sidney would die before they arrived and it would all be Rose's fault, that she'd never get to say goodbye to her father and would blame Rose forever.

"What did they say?" Max asked.

"To get there as quickly as we could."

"See that guy in the green convertible?" Max said. "He's trouble. Lose him."

"I think Rose knows how to drive," Jill said.

"I drive over twenty thousand miles a year," he said

to his sister. "She walks to her office and drives one day a week if at all. She appreciates my help."

Coming up was the spot she most hated, the treacherous interchange careening to the left where two other parkways joined the Taconic. Usually she switched into the right lane and kept her foot hovering over the break. This time she stayed where she was, in the fast lane, and her foot didn't leave the accelerator.

When they were on the straightaway, crossing the bridge over the reservoir that fed them the water they drank in the city, Max leaned forward to turn up the music.

"Turn it off, will you?" Jill asked.

Sidney's house, which they'd visited just yesterday, was dotted by densely paned but tiny windows hooded with ratty striped awnings. Narrow as a tenement, it was separated from identical houses on either side by a thin concrete strip about as wide as three garbage pails. When the Bergsons first moved to 58th Avenue in the late forties, soon after Sidney returned from Normandy—he'd taken some of the first photos of the D-Day invasion—Fresh Meadows was a green swath of farmland, with goats bleating and chickens pecking in not a few backyards. The Long Island Expressway, running perpendicular to the avenue down a steep slope, wasn't even built. Now, midday, the block was deserted, the two-story brick houses looked worn, the curbside trees had become so overgrown that their roots buckled the sidewalks, contorting the concrete at impossible angles, and the traffic on the road below never ceased. "I've got a mule and her name is Sal," Sidney used to sing to him, Max had told Rose, when earthmovers appeared on their block that day years ago to gouge out a path for the heralded expressway, a canal for cars. After it was completed, Max said, he'd fallen asleep, night after night, lulled by the current of traffic, imagining he lived on the banks of a huge waterway.

When Max and Jill were growing up, they'd lived in the main part of the house and Ruth, their mother, used the downstairs apartment as her office. Tall and imposing, she was a pediatrician who was known and loved throughout the neighborhood.

But Max and Jill were devoted to their father, and Rose knew why. While Ruth slogged through medical school and residency, and then devoted years to establishing her practice, seeing sick babies and hysterical parents all hours of the day and night, through school vacations and long summers, Sidney was the one who cared for them. A photographer who made his own hours and worked from his basement office, he scheduled his appointments so that he could get them ready for school, prepare their sandwiches, take their temperature when they were sick.

After Ruth died, the virulent breast cancer barely announcing itself before killing her the year Max left for college and Jill began graduate school, Sidney rented the house to a Korean family, sold most of her medical equipment—the examining tables, the scales—and moved a few essentials downstairs, burrowing into his wife's former office like a mole.

His children fretted about him, wanted him to leave the darkroom his apartment had become, to spend summers in the Berkshires, in a cabin on the Housatonic River that had been in Ruth's family for generations. But Sidney had never liked being there, even when Ruth was alive. It reminded him of his father-in-law, a self-made businessman who translated the small fortune he'd amassed selling plumbing supplies into real estate. He never approved of the young photographer. Even Sidney's distinguished service in the war didn't dissuade him. "Taking pictures, that's a profession?" Sidney had heard the old man say to his daughter, "Who takes pictures for a living? You take pictures on vacation."

About two years after Ruth's death, on Memorial Day weekend, Jill convinced her father to drive up with her. "We got up there after dinner on Friday in time for the sunset over the river," Jill recounted many times. "Sidney found a lawn chair, put it on the deck, and basically sat still for the entire weekend." After years in the darkroom, he discovered that he loved the outdoors. He began gardening. Over the next decade he gradually moved there, fixing up and adding onto the original house as needed.

And that's where he met blowsy, blond Linette, now his wife. She was the cashier at Sidney's favorite nursery, the employee he approached for advice on how to care for a particular type of rose bush. "I don't actually garden," she told him, "I just like being around flowers." Jill was furious to learn of her father's engagement; within weeks, she applied for and took the UN job, leaving for her first posting to Botswana. But Max and Rose happily attended Sidney's wedding, relieved that he wouldn't be alone, and that at least Linette wasn't someone he knew when Ruth was alive. It seemed cleaner that she was a stranger, and that the serendipity of a rose bush brought them together.

It was Linette who'd called Friday morning, before seven in the morning, when the news can't be good. "Maxwell?" she'd begun. She always called him by his formal name, God knows why. "Maxwell, your father's had a stroke. A bad one. Devastating, that's the word the doctor used." She was shouting as if communicating this news from the river's opposite bank without a megaphone. "I'm at the hospital . . . "

"We're leaving now," Max said. He drove. The trip, which usually took four hours, took less time than the hospital elevator ride to the fourth floor. Ascending, Rose felt a column of panic gathering within her, the way iron filings rush to a magnet. Max, who had never seemed so resolute, paused outside Room 409—there were two patients in the room, each hooked up to innumerable tubes. "Dad?" Max said, stepping up to the first bed.

"Over here," someone said, and only then did Rose see Linette sitting in a chair by the window, close to the second bed, with her red hair tied back in a pony tail, staring out the window overlooking the parking lot. She'd probably seen them drive up. Sidney had a tube taped to his nose, and thin plastic lines disappearing into his mottled flesh. All that looked familiar was his deeply freckled, tanned left arm and hand, the one he always cocked out the car window when he drove. "Dad," Max said, his voice breaking. "It's Max."

Sidney gave his wanest smile and blinked.

Linette stood up. "He was out early, before breakfast, to string up the gladiolas so their stems wouldn't snap," she said. "'Sid,' I said, 'I'm making coffee now, you having?'" When he didn't answer, and I was standing right there by the window, so I knew he heard me, I looked outside, and he was staggering, sort of, the spade still in his hand. 'I think, I think,' he said over and over. 'What do you think?' I said. But he couldn't answer. He just stood there, staring at me. The next second he started to swoon, so I ran outside and just about caught him. I had to leave him there on the ground to run inside and call 911 . . . " She was softly crying, recalling her abandonment.

Rose approached the bed, tasting panic, feeling lightheaded. It was as if the room had no gravity, as if nothing had an edge or a boundary. Sidney seemed to lift the second finger on his left hand, as if he were positioning her where to stand. "It's Rose," she said, praying she wouldn't faint. "Remember?" He was too tall for the bed, his feet dangling off the mattress. He'd been a handsome man, taller and more classically good-looking than Max, with angular features and a shock of gray hair he'd never lost. He coughed, smiled.

"I think he knows me," Rose said.

Linette looked at her a long time, as if she'd never seen her before. "Sid honey," she finally said, "who am I, Minnie Mouse?"

Sidney smiled and nodded. Linette looked at Max. "I think you better call that globe-trotting sister of yours," she said.

"Touch and go," Max said softly, as they passed the Pudding Street exit. Jed loved the name; it never failed to crack him up as they'd pass it on their summer trips to the cabin when he was little. Rose glanced at the clock. The Pudding Street Diner served breakfast all day. She thought of telling Max that she wanted to stop for a cup of coffee. But he was sitting with his shoulders slumped, his hands planted on his knees, peering ahead as if the car were running on his intensity alone. He'd been up very late—Beethoven had followed Mozart, and then Schubert; always Schubert in the dead of night—and was fighting sleep. Rose knew that he retreated when he was agitated, that he intuitively conserved his energy, stilled his metabolism. That's the way to stay alive forever, Rose had recently read, to put yourself on a near-starvation diet, to stop oxidation, to make yourself as inert as possible.

"Touch and go," Max said again, as Ruth drove passed the mountainside where the artist lived, who'd planted statues of huge, primitive heads in his field like a grove of trees. "What do you think that means? Where does it come from? Touch what and go where?"

"I don't think Sidney's been here for at least five years," Max had said yesterday, opening the door to the downstairs apartment. They all recoiled from the dark, fetid air.

"This was the waiting room," Jill said, as if recounting a fairy tale. An old-fashioned oak secretary, with rows of cubby holes and compartments but miniaturized, almost a piece of child's furniture, stood against one wall. Across the room was a leather swivel chair; Jill sat down in it and said, "Miss Reginald. God, Max, remember her? She was my mother's nurse"—this was directed at Rose. "She was terribly thin, only then thin wasn't fashionable, and she had this long hair she always wore coiled up in a thin little band, like a snake. But she was meticulous and my mother relied on her totally. She told Miss Reginald, 'Never say I can't see someone,'" Jill remembered, as if that were the most admirable doctorly act her mother had performed, the one that propelled Jill into medical school.

Max was inspecting the small, dusty bedrooms, once examination rooms, into which Sidney had moved a single bed and dresser and the detritus of his profession—old cameras, cartons of negatives and small black and white photos, the kind with the crinkled edges, and a metal file box full of contracts. An old typewriter stood in a corner facing the wall as if it had misbehaved.

Max picked up one of the old Polaroid cameras and held it to his eye. "He was always after us to pose, remember?"

Jill shuddered. "Max," she said, "You have to look for the box." She was sitting at the desk, peering into every cubby hole and drawer.

"I know where it is," he said, opening the bottom drawer of the dresser to reveal the metal box, the one Sidney had showed him after Ruth passed away. "I hate this," he said, hesitating before lifting the clasp, as if the contents were radioactive, or would dissolve with the inrush of air. Rose knew he was as close to tears as he ever got. She wasn't sure where to put herself; feeling like a trespasser, she headed for the minuscule kitchen and had just turned on the faucet which was groaning back to life, the first drops of water rusty red and almost viscous, when she heard Max whisper, "Jesus Christ." She knew he wanted her.

Entering the small bedroom, she saw Max holding a clutch of papers in one hand, raking his hair with the other. "Is that his will?" she asked.

"No," Max said, seething. "I have no fucking idea where his will is. Or his insurance policies. Or the cemetery deeds or the title to his car. Nothing's here. Just this, this stuff." Rose sat down and leafed through the papers Max handed her. Sidney's father's passport from Russia. An application to open a shoe store. A tax bill from 1943 for $51.36.

And a single small photograph, an old one, with an erose white border, of a young woman with a blanket of dark hair falling over her shoulders and naked breasts. Rose looked up at Max, and silently asked, Miss Reginald? He closed his eyes, barely nodding his head; then tilted it toward the room where his sister stood and shook his head no. Don't tell her. Rose tried to hand the photo back to Max but shook his head again. "The bastard," he said, under his breath. He was done talking. Rose could do what she wanted with the photo; for him, it had ceased to exist the moment it left his hands. She slipped it into her purse. "Where the hell is everything?" Max said again, this time for Jill's benefit.

"Maybe he moved everything up to the country," Jill said. She sounded as tentative as Rose had ever heard her.

"He told me everything was here," Max said. "He told me not to ask Linette about things, that she didn't know anything. And now he can't talk. So what happens now?"

The cell phone rang. Jill pounced on it, speaking quietly so Rose and Max couldn't really hear. "He went into arrest," she said, "but they revived him. He's still in the OR."

"Step on it," Max said. "The car won't explode."

"I'm pushing eighty-five," Rose said—thirty miles above the posted speed limit on a twisty road for which a speed limit was anything but frivolous. She pictured police cars lying in wait behind bushes in the median strip only to materialize in her rear-view mirror like a bad dream, Gestapo sirens wailing. "Do you know how fast you were going?" the steely-faced cop would ask her, his eyes obscured behind mirrored sunglasses. Yes, Rose knew; she could feel tiny, telltale vibrations in the steering wheel.

Speed makes everything worse, Rose had told Jed when she was teaching him to drive. She taught him, as her father had taught her, the art of deliberate deceleration, he aim of which was to avoid using the brake altogether. Jed never really took to driving; he passed his road test but never drove. The wrecked cars strategically positioned on high school lawns to scare kids out of drinking and driving scared no one but Jed. Not that he drank. But he knew others would. He couldn't control that.

The Hortontown Road exit, Rose said to herself. It had always reminded Jed of his favorite Dr. Seuss story, *Horton Hears a Who*. Speeding past, Rose remembered how Jed would squirm on the bed, pressing into her as if he wanted to crawl back inside, until he somehow landed on her lap, his scalp positioned directly under her nose so she could inhale his the strong aroma emanating from his head as she read to him.

He was a fearful child, and he'd become a fearful young man. That he agreed to spend a semester abroad shocked both his parents. He was traveling with friends, by train. It was the first summer he hadn't come home.

"Max," Rose said suddenly, "is this the exit?" She never remembered if they got out at the roadside diner or kept going. But after fighting sleep the entire ride Max had finally drifted off, his head lolling forward deeper and deeper into his chest. For an instant she could see through him, as if all his younger selves were nested inside like one of those Russian dolls, to the boy who fell asleep each night to the current of traffic outside his bedroom window.

Rose glanced in the rear view mirror: Jill had dozed off too. She slammed on the brakes. The car bucked but held the road. As she careened around the clover leaf, Max jolted awake. "Oh my God," he said, stretching so violently that his head nearly went through the roof of the car, "what happened?

"You feel asleep is all," Rose said. "We're here."

"Try the hospital," Max said to his sister.

Jill groped around on the seat for the cell phone and pushed some buttons. "No reception," she said.

"For God's sake," Max roared, pounding the window with his fist. "I just want to know if the man is alive or dead."

"You know Max, if this were a hundred years ago, or even seventy, or in many of the places I've worked, he'd be dead by now," Jill said. "Dead and buried."

"Thanks for that," Max said. He exhaled noisily and then turned to Rose. "Maintain your speed," he said, as Rose negotiated the two-lane road. She was going about seventy. People walking to their cars in the gravel parking lots of the antique stores and diners lining the route glared at her for kicking up dust, shattering the peace of the late afternoon. But Rose kept her foot on the gas. The closer their destination, the faster she had to drive. It would be too ironic, she thought, to have Sidney die when they were so close, after four long hours in the car.

A bright red Taurus leaving the post office turned onto the road in front of her. Rose slammed on her brakes. The car was going about thirty. She waited. The Taurus didn't speed up. "You're going to have to pass her," Max said.

"I can't yet," Rose said, praying that the double yellow line would continue for miles and miles. But she saw up ahead that the line was broken. "Start accelerating," Max said. "Get into fourth to build up speed." This was the most animated he had sounded all day.

"Don't make her do this," Jill said.

"Faster," he said.

"It's near the red line," Rose said.

"Fuck that. Don't worry about that. The car can take it, Jesus Christ, it can go a hundred and twenty. Just gun it."

"I can't believe you," Jill said. "You're going to kill us."

"I know what I'm doing," Max said. Rose sped up and nosed out of her lane. The car in front of them seemed to speed up, too. A pick-up truck appeared coming toward them. The double line was beginning again. Rose started panting.

"GO!" Max said. Rose accelerated past the Taurus and eased back into the lane. She hardly noticed the pick-up truck as it went by.

"You're such an asshole to make her do that," Jill said.

"You know," Max said, turning around to face his sister for the first time since they'd left the city "you have some damn nerve. How many years have you not been here?" He wanted to say more; Rose saw his throat working.

"Listen," Jill began to say, breathing heavily. Rose wanted to intervene, to say something ameliatory. But she found she couldn't speak. It wasn't that she knew what to say and held back, as she had earlier with Max. If anything, she felt too happy to speak—giddy, nearly elated, as if by passing the Taurus she'd forded a river of speed she'd always avoided, had never even known about. She'd felt her wheels leave the road, felt the absence of friction, the absence of anything except unimpeded forward motion. Glancing back, she could hardly see the Taurus behind her. She'd broken through. She could feel fear draining from her as if it were nothing more than a bodily fluid.

No one spoke for the next fifteen minutes as Rose gently slowed down, guiding the car from one two-lane road to the next, arriving eventually on the outskirts of Pittsfield, taking the bypass through the abandoned underside of town, past dilapidated corner groceries, St. Stanislav, the Polish church built squat like a fire hydrant of burnt-red brick. Expertly, she turned into circular driveway of the hospital's main entrance heading for the multi-leveled parking garage they'd used just a few days earlier.

Jill got out of the car immediately and began striding to the entrance. "Jesus, wait up," Rose said, stiff from driving. She waited for Max, who was also moving slowly, as if he didn't trust his bones to hold him.

The nursing shift was changing. A flock of women in white clogs and cheerful, brightly-colored smocks filed out of the automated doors Jill was trying to enter, walking so slowly they seemed to be standing still, talking raucously among themselves, finally free from having to stoop, lift, or clean up for anyone else. They looked like exotic birds, Rose thought, trying to negotiate her way between them, to catch up with Jill.

The hospital was deserted, the smell of canned vegetables and gummy gravy filling the lobby. A young girl at the desk tapped computer keys with fingernails as long as straight pins, adorned with tiny rainbows at the moons. "Mr. Bergson was just moved to cardiac ICU," she said. "Take the third bank of elevators to the third floor."

"Oh thank God," Jill said. She turned away for a moment, and looked down at the floor, her fingers at the corners of each eye.

"Visiting hours are, like, technically over," the girl said. "They begin again at 7." For a few moments no one spoke. The clock on the wall behind her, which read four fifteen, ticked. "But go ahead up. Maybe they'll let you in."

"Mr. Bergson's critical," the nurse at the ICU desk told them. "Only one of you can go in now since the wife is there."

"What about visiting hours?" Rose asked.

"We don't really worry about that up here," the nurse said.

"You go," Rose said to Jill.

"You go, Max," she said. "I need a minute."

Max looked like he needed a minute, too. Tentatively, slowly, he began walking toward the double doors, looking back to his wife and sister as if confused, as if he forgot for a moment why they were here.

Rose and Jill sat down on adjoining chairs. A family—parents and three young kids—clustered near the blaring TV in the corner; two ceiling fans ineffectively whirred. The walls were painted a dirty beige, like the interior of their car. "I feel like I'm still driving," Rose said.

"You did great," Jill said. Dumping her backpack on the floor between her legs, she slumped down in the chair. Suddenly her face showed its age; she looked as though she'd walked here. "You know, it really didn't matter how fast we got here. One waiting room's the same as another. You can sit anywhere and wait for the future to catch up to you, to figure out how to fit it into the present."

Rose nodded, but realized that she didn't agree. A waiting room isn't really about time. It's about displacement. It's about a boat waiting in the lock of a canal for the water level to rise or fall so you can keep going.

Rose glanced at Jill's backpack; in the room's grainy light it looked almost liverish. Shuddering, Rose reached over and took Jill's hand, a gesture of affection she'd never before ventured. They sat without speaking for nearly five minutes; Rose studied the clock's imperceptible movement. "It's like the neutron bomb went off in this hospital," Jill said. "You should see the places I work, teeming with people." She paused, rooting around in her pack. "I have to find a bathroom. I'll be right back." Before she left, she slipped something into Rose's hand. A photograph. With a curly edge.

Max came out walking quickly. "Where's Jill?"

"Bathroom," Rose said, slipping the photo into her purse. "How is he?"

Max sat down in the seat Jill had vacated. He took Rose's hand, interlacing their fingers. "Scared. Too scared to die just yet," he said, rubbing his hand over his face; he hadn't shaved in days. "It was ridiculous, but I kept wanting to ask him about his papers, where they were. You'd think I'd ask him something important, like how he was. *Where* he was. What it was like. If I'd been a good son. If he was as frightened as he looked. But all I can think about is those papers, existing somewhere, and I don't know where."

"I'd want to ask him about Ms. Reginald," Rose said.

Max shrugged. "Honestly, I don't think I want to know."

A doctor in scrubs, still wearing his mask, entered the waiting room and approached the family clustered near the TV. As if hypnotized, they rose and followed him out. Jill returned the second Linette walked in. "There you are," Linette said, "Hi Rosie," she said, blowing a kiss. "Hi, Jill. Max I already saw." She sat down with a loud sigh. Her eye makeup sat heavy on her lids. "Now don't be afraid to go in there, honey," she said to Jill, who was still standing. Jill looked at Linette, for perhaps the first time in her life. Then she walked to her, took her arm, and together they entered the ICU.

Max turned to look at the TV. Glancing down, Rose caught sight of Jill's blood-red pack on the floor, looking half alive. It reminded her of the afterbirth that slithered out of her with no effort at all after the incalculable effort of giving birth to Jed, how it puddled to the floor, the thing that had kept her son alive now a piece of organic garbage. In some cultures, people ate it, she remembered hearing, and she suddenly understood why. She remembered how stunned Max had looked in the delivery room, holding the squalling newborn, looking from mother to son, trying to understand the new calculus of their suddenly expanded family.

"What's wrong?" Max asked her, rousing her from her memory of that other hospital.

"How do you know something's wrong?"

"You kind of shuddered."

Twenty-six years of marriage. Was there anything he didn't know about her? "Nothing," Rose said. "I'm fine."

"I should have brought the Walkman and some CDs," Max said. "It's going to be a long night. Why didn't I? What was I thinking?"

"You weren't," Rose said. "None of us were."

"I'm sorry I was such a bully in the car," he said. "You did a great job getting us here. I'm not entirely sure, but I think at one point you were going over a hundred."

"Passing that Taurus," Rose said, smiling, thinking of what Jill had said, about waiting for the future to catch up to the present. "Why don't you go be with your sister?" she said. Max squeezed her hand, sighed, nodded, and rose.

Alone in the waiting room, Rose reached into her purse, retrieving the photo Jill had given her. She knew exactly what she'd see—another compromising photo of Miss Reginald, which Jill needed to keep secret from her brother. Were there more? Had it been an extended affair or just a terrible mistake on a summer afternoon as sultry as this one? Could Max be nursing a secret as his father had? Is that why he didn't want to ask? Not that his father could answer. His father who was already gone, whether or not he survived, whose stroke turned the tide: first the family swells, then it contracts. A contraction almost as painful as birth.

"Excuse me, Mrs. Bergson? Are you all right?" The nurse from the desk was standing in front of her with a concerned look. Rose realized she'd been slumped over, her head in her hands.

"I'm fine, thank you," Rose said, straightening up. She glanced at the clock—it was nearly five. The television was still on. Slowly Rose got up and lowered the volume. She made a circuit of the small room, noticing the chairs and tables, the countless magazines, the white sign with black stenciled letters that read, "Visiting hours strictly observed."

A welcome sight, welcome as a speed limit, as a lock on a canal.

"You know, honestly, you can go in any time," the nurse said, straightening up some magazines, pushing a chair against the wall. "We're not really picky about the hours. That sign's just there."

"I know," Rose answered. She tucked both photos behind the flap in her wallet where the kept her largest bills. "I think I'll wait."

Contributors' Notes

David Abrams earned his BA in English from the University of Oregon and his MFA in Creative Writing from the University of Alaska. His stories and essays have appeared in *Esquire, Glimmer Train Stories, The Greensboro Review, The Missouri Review, The North Dakota Review* and other literary quarterlies. He regularly contributes book reviews to *The Barnes and Noble Review, The San Francisco Chronicle* and *January Magazine.*

By the end of 2008, **Lauren Baratz-Logsted** will have had 12 books published since 2003 in a variety of genres. For adults: *Vertigo* (Random House); *The Thin Pink Line, Crossing the Line, A Little Change of Face, How Nancy Drew Saved My Life*, and *Baby Needs a New Pair of Shoes* (all from RDI). For teens: *Angel's Choice* and *Secrets of My Suburban Life* (both from Simon & Schuster). For tweens: *Me, In Between* (S&S). For young readers: the first two volumes in *The Sisters Eight* series, co-written with her husband Greg Logsted and their eight-year-old daughter Jackie, both of which books will be twin lead titles from Houghton Mifflin in December. Lauren is also the editor and a contributor to the anthology *This*

Is Chick-Lit (BenBella) and has had several stories and essays published. Her books have been published in 11 countries and you can read more about her life and work at www.laurenbaratzlogsted.com.

Beth Ann Bauman is the author of the short story collection *Beautiful Girls* (MacAdam/Cage) and a young-adult novel *Rosie and Skate*, forthcoming from Random House in fall '09. Her work has been published in literary journals and anthologies, including *The Barcelona Review* and *Many Lights in Many Windows*. She has received grants from the Jerome Foundation and the New York Foundation for the Arts. She teaches fiction writing at the Writer's Voice of the West Side YMCA in New York City and online at UCLA Extension.

Jim Cooley, a fifty-something native Missourian, received his Bachelor of Arts with General Honors from the University of Chicago in 1977, where he remained to pursue graduate work in philosophy, public policy studies, and chronic alcoholism. This last course of study led by 1984 to a secure position on Skid Row in Kansas City, Missouri. Clean and sober now for almost a quarter of a century, he was awarded a Master's degree in Professional Writing with a concentration in Poetry and Fiction by the University of Missouri at Kansas City in 2001. Jim enjoys writing short stories based on his lavishly misspent youth or the recovery therefrom, publishing in a number of small journals. A director of the Missouri Speleological Survey and member of the national Cave Research Foundation, Jim also writes feature articles about his other passion: Discovering, exploring, surveying and photodocumenting unknown caves in southern Missouri, focussing on Federally designated wilderness areas. Teams he's led have discovered 15 new caves in the last year. Jim will retire from the phone company in 661 days.

Quinn Dalton is the author of a novel, *High Strung*, and two story collections, *Bulletproof Girl* and *Stories from the Afterlife*. Stories have appeared in publications such as *Glimmer Train, One Story,* and *Verb* and in anthologies such as *New Stories from the South: The Year's Best.*

Philip F. Deaver is the 13th winner of the Flannery O'Connor Award. He has held fellowships from the National Endowment of the Arts and Bread Loaf. Known best as a writer of short fiction, his work has appeared in *Prize Stories: The O. Henry Awards* and, in addition, has been recognized in *Best American Short Stories* and *The Pushcart Prize*. His poems are collected in *How Men Pray*, Anhinga Press. In recent years, he has also published memoir and creative nonfiction in the literary magazines and recently edited a book of creative nonfiction essays on baseball, entitled *Scoring from Second: Writers on Baseball* (University of Nebraska Press). He is a professor of English and permanent Writer in Residence at Rollins College, Winter Park, FL and teaches on the fiction faculty in the Spalding University brief residency MFA program in Louisville, KY.

Rochelle Distelheim has taught creative writing at Mundelein College, Chicago. Her work has been published in a number of literary journals, including, *The North American Review, Confrontation, Story Quarterly, Nimrod, Other Voices,* and *Whetstone*, and has been awarded the Katharine Anne Prize in Fiction, Illinois Arts Council Fellowships and Literary Awards, several Pushcart Press nominations, as well as Fellowships to Ragdale Colony and the Sewanee Writer's Conference. Her novel *Jerusalem as a Second Language*, is presently being circulated.

Pamela Erens's novel *The Understory* (Ironweed Press, 2007) was the winner of the Ironweed Press Fiction Prize as well as a finalist for the Los Angeles Times Book Prize and the William Saroyan International Prize for Writing. Pamela's short fiction has appeared in magazines including *Chicago Review*, *Boston Review*, *The Literary Review*, and *Redivider*. She is the recipient of two New Jersey State Council on the Arts fellowships in fiction. Pamela has also published poetry, literary and personal essays, articles, and book reviews in a wide variety of newspapers and journals. Her website is www.pamela-erens.com.

Patry Francis's novel *The Liar's Diary* was published by Dutton in February, 2007. It has been or soon will be translated into Dutch, French, German, Spanish, and Polish. She's published stories and/or poems in *The Ontario Review, Tampa Review, Antioch Review, Colorado Review, The American Poetry Review, Massachusetts Review*, and elsewhere. She is a three time nominee for the Pushcart Prize and has been the recipient of a grant from the Massachusetts Cultural Council twice, once for poetry and once for fiction. Her website is www.patryfrancis.com and blogs at www.simplywait.blogspot.com.

Joseph Freda is the author of two novels, *The Patience of Rivers* and *Suburban Guerrillas*, both published by W.W. Norton. He has published short fiction in *The Kenyon Review, StoryQuarterly, Five Points, LIT* and other literary magazines. Freda lives in New York 's Catskills with his wife Elise, a painter. www.joefreda.com.

Steven Gillis is the author of the novels *Walter Falls* and *The Weight of Nothing*, both finalists for the Independent

Publishers Book of the Year and *ForeWord* Magazine Book of the Year 2003 and 2005, as well as *Temporary People*, published by Black Lawrence Press in 2008. Steve's stories, articles and book reviews have appeared in over three dozen journals. A 6 time Pushcart nominee and 4 time Best Of... Notable Stories, a collection of Steve's stories - titled *Giraffes* - was published in February, 2007. A second collection of Steve's stories - titled *The Principles of Landscape*- will be published by BLP in 2009. A member of the Ann Arbor Book Festival Board of Directors, and a finalist for the 2007 Ann Arbor News Citizen of the Year, Steve teaches writing at Eastern Michigan University and is the founder of 826 Michigan and the co-founder of Dzanc Books. All proceeds from Steve's writing go to Dzanc.

Nancy Ginzer holds a Doctorate in Music from The University of Colorado at Boulder and a Master of Fine Arts (creative writing) from The Ohio State University. Formerly a teacher in Africa and radio arts producer with the CBC, she now lives in Alberta, Canada. This is her first published story.

Roberta Israeloff has written four books of personal non-fiction, most recently *Kindling the Flame: Reflections on Ritual, Faith and Family* (Simon & Schuster). Her short stories, essays and articles have been published and anthologized in a host of journals, magazines and newspapers including *The North American Review*, *The New York Times*, and *Lilith*. She attended the Johns Hopkins University Writing Seminars, and lives on Long Island, NY where she is also director of The Squire Family Foundation which advocates for pre-college instruction in philosophy.

Kaytie M. Lee is a graduate of the University of Southern California's Master of Professional Writing program where she was a recipient of a Freida Fox Fellowship and a 2005 Phi Kappa Phi Honors Award for *Missing: A Novel in Stories*. "One Moment" is the first story of that work and its inclusion in this anthology marks her first publication. She is a regular contributor to a blog collective known as thenervousbreakdown.com and can be contacted there or at her website, www.kaytie.net.

T.M. McNally is the author of six works of fiction, including the novels *Until Your Heart Stops*, a *New York Times* Notable Book; *Almost Home*, a *St. Louis Post-Dispatch* Best Book of the Year; and *The Goat Bridge*, a *Booklist* Editors' Choice. He is also the author of the short story collections *Low Flying Aircraft* and *Quick*. The recipient of fellowships from the Howard Foundation at Brown University and the National Endowment for the Arts, he teaches at Arizona State University. His most recent book, finalist for the Pen/Faulkner Award, is a collection of stories — *The Gateway.*

Michael Milliken lives, writes, reads and works near and within Portland, Maine. He is a graduate of Yale University and the Fiction Writing Program at the University of New Hampshire. His work has appeared in *Better Fiction*, *Cellar Door*, and multiple anthologies.

Kyle Minor's short story collection, *In the Devil's Territory* will be published by Dzanc Books in November 2008. His work has appeared widely in magazines and anthologies, among them *Best American Mystery Stories 2008, The Southern Review, The Gettysburg Review, Surreal South, and*

Twentysomething Essays by Twentysomething Writers: The Best New Voices of 2006. His work has been twice nominated for the Pushcart Prize.

Kyle is also co-editor, with Okla Elliott, of *The Other Chekhov* (New American Press, 2008). His writing has been lauded by *The Atlantic Monthly, The Columbus Dispatch*, and Random House. Originally from Florida, he now lives in Ohio, where he is Visiting Writer at the University of Toledo. www.kyleminor.com.

Jim Nichols lives on a little river in Maine with his wife Anne. He has published stories in numerous magazines, including *Esquire, Zoetrope ASE, Night Train, paris transcontinental, Portland Monthly, The Clackamas Review, American Fiction* and *River City*. He won the Willamette Prize in 2000. His collection *Slow Monkeys and Other Stories* was published by Carnegie Mellon Press.

Benjamin Percy is the author of two books of short stories, *Refresh, Refresh* (Graywolf, 2007) and *The Language of Elk* (Carnegie Mellon University Press, 2006), and will see his debut novel, *The Wilding* published by Graywolf next year. His fiction appears in *Esquire, The Paris Review, Best American Short Stories, The Chicago Tribune, Glimmer Train*, and many other publications. His honors include the Plimpton Prize and the Pushcart Prize. He teaches writing at Iowa State University. www.benjaminpercy.com.

Ron Rash's debut novel, *One Foot in Eden* (2002), won the Novello Literary Award, the Appalachian Book of the Year Award, and *Forward* magazine's Gold Medal for Literary Novel of the Year, was shortlisted for the William Saroyan International Prize for Writing, and went on to become an

SIBA bestseller. His second novel, *Saints at the River* (2004), was also an SIBA bestseller and won the Southern Book Award (presented by the Southern Book Critics Circle), the SIBA Book of the Year Award, and the Weatherford Award. Author also of several collections of poetry and short stories, he is the recipient of an O. Henry Prize, the James Still Award from the Fellowship of Southern Writers, and two NEA grants. His third novel, *The World Made Straight*, won the 2006 Sir Walter Raleigh Award for Fiction and the 2007 ALA Alex Award and is now available in paperback from Picador (April 2007). Picador published a collection of his short stories, titled *Chemistry.* His most recent novel, *Serena* from Ecco was published In October 2008. Ron Rash holds the John Parris Chair in Appalachian Studies at Western Carolina University.

Bill Roorbach's newest book is *Temple Stream: A Rural Odyssey*, which won the Maine Literary Award in Nonfction in 2006. Other nonfiction includes *Into Woods, Summers with Juliet, A Place on Water* (with Wes McNair and Bob Kimberr), and *Writing Life Stories* (instruction). He's the editor of the *Oxford anthology Creative Nonfiction: The Art of Truth.* He writes fiction, too, including a novel, *The Smallest Color*, and a collection of short fiction, *Big Bend*, which won the Flannery O'Connor Award. His short work has appeared in *Harper's, the Atlantic, The New York Times Magazine*, and has been featured on the NPR program Selected Shorts, and has won an O. Henry Award. Bill Holds the William H.P. Jenks Chair in Contemporary American Letters at the College of the Holy Cross in Worcester, Mass. He lives in Maine. www.billroorbach.com.

Max Ruback has completed a collection of short fiction, titled, *The Kindest Light*, which seeks representation. He has published stories in magazines ranging from *Quick Fiction* to *Adbusters* to *New Orleans Review* to *The Frostproof Review*, elsewhere. He teaches high school English and Reading, as well as coach basketball. He was born in 1970.

Gabriel Welsch is the author of the poetry collection *Dirt and All Its Dense Labor,* as well as stories that have appeared widely, in journals including *Mid-American Review, New Letters, Georgia Review, Other Voices, Iron Horse Literary Review, Chautauqua Literary Journal, Cream City Review, Inkwell,* and *Pank.* He lives in central Pennsylvania, with his wife and daughters, and works at Juniata College.